The Old Army Game

the Old Army Game

A Novel and Stories by

George Garrett

Introduction by

George Core

Southern Methodist University Press
Dallas

The novel and stories in this book are works of fiction. Names, characters, places, and incidents are either the product of the author's imagination or are used fictitiously.

Copyright © 1994 by George Garrett
Introduction © 1994 by Southern Methodist University Press

FIRST EDITION, 1994

Requests for permission to reproduce material from this work should be sent to:
   Rights and Permissions
   Southern Methodist University Press
   Box 415
   Dallas, Texas 75275

Library of Congress Cataloging-in-Publication Data

Garrett, George P., 1929-
    The old Army game : a novel and stories / by George
    Garrett : introduction by George Core. — 1st. ed.
        p.   cm.
    ISBN 0-87074-380-5 (cloth) — ISBN 0-87074-381-3
    (paper)
    1. United States—Armed Forces—Military life—Fiction.
    2. Americans—Europe—Fiction. 3. Soldiers—Europe—
    Fiction.
    I. Title.
    PS3557.A72043   1994
    813'.54—dc20   94-27048

Design by Barbara Whitehead

Cover photograph: Sergeant First Class George Garrett (front row, far right) with other members of the cadre at Camp Chaffee, Arkansas, 1953.

Printed in the United States of America on acid-free paper
10 9 8 7 6 5 4 3 2 1

For Susan

CONTENTS

INTRODUCTION

WHEN GEORGE GARRETT published his second novel, *Which Ones Are the Enemy?*, in 1961, he was just over thirty years of age; but he already had six books behind him, including a collection of short fiction, *King of the Mountain* (1959), that contains related stories—"Don't Take No for an Answer," "How the Last War Ended," "What's the Purpose of the Bayonet?" and "The Blood of Strangers." Afterward he would write other military stories that are related in time, place, and theme and that appear in *Cold Ground Was My Bed Last Night* (1964)—"The Old Army Game," "The Wounded Soldier," "Unmapped Country," and "Texarkana Was a Crazy Town"; and still later he would return to this same subject in "Crowfoot" and "Heroes," which demonstrate his exact knowledge of army life.

"Garrett's army fiction," Richard Dillard has shrewdly observed, "takes place within the context of the 'invisible world' of suffering, and the army—with its system of rigorously controlled order which exists only because of a larger disorder—offers a powerful metaphoric structure with which to deal with the fallen world of lies at its worst." "Each of these works," he continues, "opens a window on that 'invisible world,' with its rules and regulations of the army as a system of artificially imposed coordinates by which the reader is able to comprehend fully the chaos of that terrible reality." The centerpiece and anchor of this impressive body of fiction is *Which Ones Are the Enemy?*, on which I naturally and properly will focus my attention.

Whistling in the Dark (1992), a collection of memoirs and personal reports, starkly reveals how the military life, especially war, has occupied a central place in George Garrett's imagination from the moment his career got under way some forty years ago. (See the title essay, "Uncles and Others," "The Tanks," and "Under Two Flags.") Not only does he know this subject in the blood through his family's experience and its collective memory, but he knows it thoroughly as a student of history and literature. He has written regularly about the American civil war and both world wars in essays and reviews as well as using the military life as principal action and as backdrop for much of his fiction, including his great trilogy of novels on the Elizabethan world. So much for the windup: here is the pitch.

Which Ones Are the Enemy? is one of a handful of American novels in which the military life at once is described accurately and dramatized memorably. Of course we begin with Stephen Crane's *Red Badge of Courage,* and we linger, as we must, on such novels as *A Farewell to Arms* and *From Here to Eternity.* The latter, as Garrett points out, has enabled writers like himself to write about life in the military service without qualm or queasiness, to look at that experience anew and to seize its distinctive qualities as the stuff of fiction. James Jones, as our author tells us, opened up this territory for art. In so doing, he showed others how to write about military life, not merely about war. War is a great subject, needless to say; but it tends to overwhelm fiction and the fiction writer: even so great an artist as Leo Tolstoy cannot always keep the upper hand when it comes to war. On the one hand think of the philosophical passages in *War and Peace,* which tend to bore the reader as nearly witless as the cetology passages in *Moby-Dick.* We do not yearn for the lucubrations of

Count Tolstoy on the theory of war: for that we can read Jomini or Clausewitz. Instead we crave the panoramic drama of the battle of Borodino or the piercing sadness of the scene in which Prince Andrei lies dying under the cold blue sky. On the other hand the very fact of war, its historicity, can stop the fiction writer dead in his tracks: a battle or a campaign is not easy to recapture and limn and re-create as human action.

Military life entails many aspects aside from war: indeed the preparation for war and the waiting, even when war itself has irrupted, is more nearly the essential subject of military fiction than combat. If *From Here to Eternity* pictures life in the old army before World War II, *Which Ones Are the Enemy?* involves postwar Europe during the Korean war, a special period that we now see, with painful clarity, was the most dangerous and intense time during the Cold War. It would have been relatively simple for the Russian armored divisions to move through Western Europe with almost the ease of Hitler's legions in 1940. In the late forties and early fifties NATO troops were badly outnumbered and outgunned.

Against this background the action of *Which Ones Are the Enemy?* unfolds in Trieste and, more especially, in a *caserma* in the mountains north of the city near the border of Yugoslavia. The troops in the Nth Field Artillery are chiefly misfits, has-beens, ne'er-do-wells, madmen of one kind and another, and, make no mistake about it, criminals. They have one saving grace that is stressed in varying ways throughout the action: they are, for the most part, good mechanics and gunners and, if need be, actual soldiers. They are even good at playacting as spit-and-polish military types. In fact they relish bending and breaking every rule and regulation, every tradition and custom. But, were they to be engaged in combat, against Tito's troops or Chinese communist volunteers or the Russians themselves, they would be a formidable opponent because they know their jobs as artillerymen and, in a crisis, would pull together instinctively and persistently and ruthlessly against a common enemy.

Of course no one who reads *Which Ones Are the Enemy?* with even a modicum of attention can ever forget the corrosive irony of the title. The enemy is everywhere: first and foremost it is the numbing military bureaucracy that our hero fights hammer and tong, tooth and nail, with every fiber of his being. John Riche despises the beadledom of the army as much as he hates phoniness in general, as the struggle between him and the executive officer shows. He hates Lt. Costello because Costello represents everything that is mechanical and corrupting about army bureaucracy. In combat Costello would probably be among the first to cut and run or to freeze.

As the author and his putative hero also reveal to us, the enemy can and does include the dark side or alter ego of the fretful individual soldier. "They ought to have a ribbon and a medal for guys like me," Riche sardonically remarks, "a Congressional Medal for Losers." Riche cannot stand prosperity, as he tells us time and again, and so a winning streak in poker leads him to make a dare to a woman whom he wishes to possess and then, to make that dare good and to win her, he returns to crime. Next he fools himself into thinking that he can withdraw from this criminal enterprise before it engulfs him and he is again exposed and thrown into a military stockade, but a concatenation of events that inexorably proceeds with unpredictable quickness and violence leads speedily to his downfall. Were Riche a different kind of figure, closer to Othello than to Iago, we might be tempted to call this moving novel a tragedy. Instead, we realize, it is a powerful version of picaresque.

No one could mistake John Riche for a tragic hero, even in our befuddled time when the word *tragic* signifies little. Our man Riche, as both actor and observer, is a psychopath, a man who is unmoved by moral considerations and who is fixated hopelessly and finally upon himself and what promotes his self-interest. At the same time, in many respects, he is a representative man among types often no better and sometimes worse than he. Certainly that is true of Corporal

Stitch and of Lt. Costello. Riche, intimately knowing the system, can use it to his own advantage almost at will, as the opening scene shows in a small but decisive way. One of the novel's greatest ironies is that his downfall results when he opens himself to commitment and love.

Which Ones Are the Enemy? is a sustained tour de force in which John Riche, the savvy protagonist and narrator, tells us time and again, in a wholly unvarnished and unsentimental fashion, how he has come to grief in the U.S. Army and how he will continue to come to grief. As the novel begins, he has just been released from prison; at its end he is serving an indefinite term. Even so we are not prepared for the searing conclusion when a scene unfolds that is so extraordinary and chilling and outrageous that even the sardonic and hard-hearted Riche cannot contain his tears. Nor can we.

This novel, like any good work of art, can be viewed from more than one perspective, with John Riche as the picaro enduring the vicissitudes of Dame Fortune, making and unmaking, inventing and reinventing, himself on the road of life as it unfolds before him in the postwar (and yet wartime) army. *Which Ones Are the Enemy?* is also a chronicle of military life in which we learn about the tedium of the army and the little details such as shining boots or cleaning a machine gun or maintaining an artillery piece that add up to quotidian life in the service, the life of the GI. And, from yet another perspective, it is an allegory of postwar Europe with Riche as the heartless representative GI—the GI as Everyman—who is taking advantage of the chaos that the Wehrmacht and its conquerors left in their wake. In the same manner Angela (the fallen angel), his mistress and lover, represents the ravaged and ravished Europe that war has left devastated and rudderless. The love affair that slowly blooms between Johnny and Angela stands as the most moving and important part of the novel, its slowly developing middle, a sequence that reverses our expectations and gradually and steadily complicates and intensifies the action.

Which Ones Are the Enemy? is also a novel that is a near-perfect instance of how to use and maintain the first-person post of observation, the viewpoint of the sophisticated and ironic observer who is also the protagonist. As a master of the first-person narrative George Garrett stands in the company of Mark Twain, Henry James, Joseph Conrad, F. M. Ford, and such contemporary writers as the author of *The Remains of the Day*—Kazuo Ishaguro.

That this brilliant novel is now being reissued is cause for celebration. *Which Ones Are the Enemy?*, while not neglected, did not upon its original publication receive the full plaudits it had earned by virtue of its author's astute and original craftsmanship. The literary community, as is often the case, was nodding at the switch, diverted by other matters. Now another generation of readers is available; now the Cold War has ended; now the author himself has long since become a distinguished man of letters; now we have no reason not to give this remarkable work of fiction our undivided attention.

—George Core

PREFACE

I WROTE *Which Ones Are the Enemy?* at the kitchen table of a large and shabby old rented house on High Street in Middletown, Connecticut. I was teaching at Wesleyan University, a couple of blocks down the street. We had two young children and a brand-new baby; and everybody except the baby and me, including my wife, had the mumps. I would run and teach my classes, then run home and feed and change the baby and look after the others. Somehow or other, in the midst of everything else, I would find some time every day and late at night to work on what began as a brisk novella and grew into a novel. I worked hard and fast for a few dazed weeks and finished the draft of it even as everybody was up and around again and life fell into familiar patterns.

By the time it came out, we were living in Houston, Texas, and I was working at the Alley Theater.

The Army, the military life, had long been a serious part of my experience, directly during the time I served and indirectly (though, I think, no less deeply) as a part of family history, the lives of close friends and kinfolk. It says nothing, is purely and simply a fact, that people in my family have fought in all the wars this country ever had and, indeed, even before that while we were still colonies. Only a very few were professional military men. Most were citizen soldiers who did their duty and, if they survived, returned home to pick up their lives again. But this was our memory, reinforced by odds and ends—pieces of old equipment, motheaten uniforms in attic trunks, a rusty sword, faded campaign ribbons, a painting or two and some photographs. It was a matter-of-fact memory, untested and unquestioned, really, until the Vietnam War when some of our kin went to serve and to bleed and others emphatically did not.

My direct experience had been as a sergeant first class in the Field Artillery during the Korean War. I had already been to military school as a boy and had logged some time in the Reserves. I was called up to active duty during Korea; then sent not to Korea but to Trieste, the Free Territory of Trieste. Our unit, the 12th Field, was stationed in an Italian *caserma*, from Mussolini days, up above the city and close to the Yugoslav border where there was always a certain amount of serious friction, posturing and bluffing going on. Later our unit was sent up to Austria, to Linz on the Danube, forming part of the most advanced units of the American forces in Europe except for the MPs and ceremonial units in Vienna.

I wanted to write something good and true about those times, those places, and above all, the lives of soldiers within the ancient institution of the Army. The great American military novel for and of our age, *From Here to Eternity*, had already been written and was still new at the time I served. Everybody in our outfit (and probably the whole U.S. Army) had already read it and referred to it, alluded to it with an easy familiarity. It was as real and solid to us as the landscape and the weather. It could not be improved upon—who would want to?—or even much modified. But even as James Jones had wonderfully captured the subject, he had opened doors and windows for the rest of us who came after him. That is the way of great writers. They do not exhaust the resources of their subjects. They discover and define the shapes and forms. They open up the territory. It becomes not a matter of competition but, instead, of contagious and shared creativity, a challenge which calls not for arrogance but a kind of humility in response.

Which may be a way of saying that the achievement of James Jones did not discourage me or turn me away from the wish to make sense, and, from that sense, to make fiction out of my own experience.

There were other things worth thinking about. *From Here to Eternity* was a chronicle of the old Regular Army at the tag end of the Great Depression and just as World War II was about to change everything for Americans. A decade later the cadre of our Armed Services was composed of regulars, but the overwhelming number of servicemen was made up of draftees, volunteers, reservists, that is civilian soldiers in the original and honorable American model. And there were more than ten million veterans of World War II now returned to civilian life, to Real Life, they would have said.

So in a sense, a decade after World War II, by the time *From Here to Eternity* was published and at once became a part of our experience, we, the people in the Army, though young as always, were a little more experienced than we might have been.

In many ways the Army was a fair representation of our nation in those days. We had all kinds, even, thanks to Harry Truman and his determined policy of integration, Black soldiers among us, no longer kept apart in their segregated (and demoralized) units. Whoever you were, whatever your hopes and plans might be, when they called your name and number you had to go. The way they ran things during the Vietnam War, allowing all kinds of deferments for those who could afford them and knew the rules and angles of the game, even creating a climate of opinion which allowed many to avoid service without shame then or later, was entirely different. Unthinkable and unimaginable to us in more innocent times. We had, after all, been brought up to disapprove, if not to scorn, the wellborn and privileged of the North who, during the Civil War, could actually buy out of service. For political reasons and fears, the Congress and the Vietnam presidents—Kennedy, Johnson, Nixon—allowed the lucky and the privileged to avoid their duty and, some would say, their honor and country, too. Those leaders also, foolishly I believe, allowed the Reserves and the National Guard, full of veterans who had freely elected to serve in that capacity for the sake of money and benefits and with full knowledge of the risks involved, that they might be called up someday, any day they were needed, allowed the Reserves and National Guard to escape from their obligation.

Service was already the destiny of the poor even before, again out of pure political fear, the American Army was returned to its earlier status as Regular. But before all that, from the days of World War II through much of the time of the Cold War, the service, the Army, even with all its elaborate hierarchy and rank and privileges, was the great democratic equalizer. In all our unselfconscious diversity we wore the same uniform, lived together and learned to know and respect each other enough to love and hate each other. This was some of the news of my novel and the stories written before then and ever since, from time to time. Some of it would have been news to James Jones and other veterans of his generation—not the bitching and petty rebellion, the code of conduct, the underworld forms of honor. These are as old as soldiering itself. The new thing (already old now in my lifetime) was the sending forth of waves of American citizen soldiers all over the world where, quite aside from their duties, just by being there they came to know foreign people and languages and cultures, in bits and pieces, true, but more closely than even they could have imagined. We had been strictly local and were now bound to be global.

What was a kind of news is now a form of memory. What was reportage is historical.

Out of that history comes this novel, then. It had a short

and not unhappy life (history) of its own in hardcover and paperback. And now it is being resurrected, together with some new and old stories about the same general subject. And I am glad and grateful for that.

The world changes and I have changed, and chances are I would not write this novel today or, if I did, would not write it in the same way.

But when I wrote it at that kitchen table in Middletown, when I was young and my family was young and even the world was younger than now, I made it as real and true and solid as I knew how and was able to. And that is all we can ask of anyone, even of ourselves.

—*George Garrett*
1994

Which Ones Are the Enemy?

A Novel

Is it any pleasure to the Almighty, that thou art righteous? or is it gain to him, that thou makest thy ways perfect?
—Job 22:3

Tenderly, be not impatient
(Strong is your hold O mortal flesh.
Strong is your hold O love.)
—Walt Whitman:
"The Last Invocation"

FOR SAM GELFMAN
"It's all good time"

Author's Note

THIS STORY is set in Trieste during the occupation of that city by American and British troops. That occupation began when the 88th Division moved in and the war against the Germans was still going on. It ended in the fall of 1954. The time of the story is during the '50s while the Korean War was winding up across the world. At that time, Trieste and the territory around it made up the Free Territory of Trieste. The American troops, members of the 351st Regimental Combat Team and supporting forces, were in the command TRUST—Trieste United States Troops.

The place and the time are as real as I can remember and make them. The people and events are fictional. Any resemblance to actual people and events is coincidental.

—G. G.
1961

PART ONE

New Man

1 DON'T ASK ME why. Never ask me why. I mean if I knew *all* the answers I wouldn't be where I am now—down again, one more time, but not out. I've been whipped down to my knees before, on all fours like a dog or a drunk, and I'll be back. I'm going to keep on standing up and asking for more (more *what?* well, trouble maybe) until I'm *really* out, horizontal, heels up, white-eyed. They ought to call me Johnny Jack-in-the-box. I won't quit. And if I move around with a permanent stockade shuffle, why at least it's nobody else's fault but my own. They ought to have a ribbon and a medal for guys like me—a Congressional Medal for Losers. You could wear a ribbon around your neck, and instead of saluting you people could give you a high sign with the middle finger.

Once I almost fooled myself that I was breaking the mold, getting out from under. What a laugh! What a dirty, grubby laugh! Well, it's easy enough to fool yourself. That was in Trieste, and I came close to kidding myself right out of the habit of losing.

7

Like I said, don't ask me why. I just knew the minute the truck slowed down and stopped that the lazy bastard wasn't going to get out of the cab and come back. He was just going to sit up there in the cab, high as a turkey buzzard in a nest, and let me go out and leave me. So I sat there in the truck and waited. He and the driver both started hollering at me from the cab, but I didn't pay any attention. They might just as well have been yelling in Chinese. I can be hard of hearing when I feel like it. So I just waited and after some more yelling and a little while they shut the engine off and I heard the door squeak open and slam to and then the sound of a pair of boots crunching on the gravel, getting louder and coming slowly back to me. I sat still and stiff on the bench and held on to my duffel bag.

"Okay," he said. "We're here. Pick up your bag and get off."

He was a tall, heavy, big-bellied master sergeant with one game leg. He used to be in the Infantry in World War II. He was wearing the Combat Infantryman's Badge and a double row of ribbons over his pocket. If that proves anything, which it doesn't. Oh, he might have been one hell of a soldier once upon a time for all I know. Or care. But right now anyway he was working in Classification and Assignment, sitting around and getting himself a duckpin spread behind some desk and probably choking and coughing himself to death from the dust on a lot of papers. Guys like that can get pretty tired of it all just assigning other people to jobs and outfits. The only kind of routine fun they get out of life is assigning a clarinet player to drive a truck and finding a place in the band for some truck driver. So when somebody like me comes along, comes in the office with his orders and his records in his hand, a *special* case, why it's cause for jubilation. He didn't even have to leave his desk. He could have sent any four-eyed private in the office or he could have sent me alone with the driver. No risk. Where was I going? Where in the hell would I run to? But he wanted to handle it all by himself.

8

I bring that kind of thing out in people sometimes.

The color in his face and the little map of wrinkles around his eyes, the swell and the veins on the nose, came from too much cheap whisky, not from wind and sun and open weather. I guess it was tough luck to have to ride into retirement on a swivel chair, nursing a game leg. But that was his worry and not mine. Let's face it, if a man tried to give sympathy and pity to everybody who's asking for it, all the ones who think they really *need* it, pretty soon he'd be as buck naked and hard up as old Job himself. And that wouldn't be enough either. They'd keep right on asking *Gimme, gimme, gimme.*

"I said pick up that duffel bag and get off the truck," he said. "Now *move!*"

He stood there with his head tilted back and his hands on his hips studying me. I didn't blame him a bit for being suspicious. I would have been, too, in his shoes. He didn't have the least clue what I might do next. I probably could have given him a really rough time and had some fun myself, but I didn't want to make a big thing out of nothing.

"Unhook the safety strap and let down the tailgate," I said. "Then I'll get off."

That stopped him cold. That surprised him so much he didn't know what to do. And all he could do was laugh. He grabbed the tailgate with both hands, to hold on to himself more than anything else, while he was laughing and looking at me.

"That's pretty funny," he said finally, when he was able to swallow his laugh whole. "You're a clown. Maybe you ought to be a comedian. But I'll clue you in on one little thing—you ain't no kind of a sergeant. Not anymore. Get your ass off of that truck."

I nodded like I agreed with him and then slid down the bench toward him close enough so he could reach me with his hands if he wanted to. What I wanted to see was if he was going to try.

"I may be a buckass private, a yardbird," I said, grinning, "but let me tell *you* one little thing. I know what it says in the book. What it says is the man in the truck is supposed to wait for the driver to come back and unhook the safety strap and let down the tailgate. *It's the responsibility of the driver.*"

The old sergeant flushed red as a new brick, wrinkled his face and looked puzzled.

"I ain't the driver," he said.

"Well, if you don't want to wait around here all day long, you'd just as well tell him to come on back and do it himself."

He whistled through his gritted teeth and started to cuss me. Up one side and down the other. I didn't pay any attention. I leaned back, shut my eyes and folded my hands over the strap of the duffel bag. Finally he kind of got the idea I wasn't going anyplace and he had to make the driver climb out of the cab and come on back and do the job. The driver was a fat, easy-going motor pool character, but he didn't mind. Judging by his silly grin and the wink he gave me, I guess he thought it was funny enough to be worth the trouble. He did the job, then I stood up and got off.

I dropped off on the gravel road, took a deep whiff of the dry new air and a look around. Rocks, that's the first thing I saw, the shine and sparkle of sunlight on rocks. Rocks everywhere, more rocks than I had ever seen before in one place except in a quarry or a graveyard. There were small cleared fields for farming, with high walls of picked-up rocks around them. And there were a few stunted pine trees, all twisted and gnarled from fighting for life and juice among the rocks, and it looked like they had suffered plenty from wind too, a big wind that must have blown in regular from the north and the east. Just try and imagine farming land like that! That's exactly what the people in the little villages in that part did for a living. If you care to call it living. It would break your back and pull your kidneys out of place just bending over and trying to pick up all the rocks. It would wring the last ounce of sweat out of you in one lifetime, and you would probably end up sitting with your face in the sun, nothing but a dry, rattling husk, like a cured gourd of skin and bones.

I could tell at first sight that the country and I deserved each other. Talk about the right place and the right time! If God Himself had wanted to find the right spot to assign me to, He couldn't have done any better.

I found out later on from somebody who ought to know that it was supposed to be the end of an ancient glacier up there in those hills. And that's something to think about: half the world covered up with slick ice. Well, the old glacier had finally melted and left this bounty of rocks behind it to remind people that it had been there once and might even be back again. Like a huge slag heap.

I had already had a look at the city of Trieste. Trieste looked all right, framed in the oval of the overhead canvas, a fine bright city and a good place to be. But I only got a peek. We had turned away from the city—and the city smells and sights and the whine and snarl of Vespas and Fiats—and climbed and climbed. Now we were way out in the country and up near the border of the Free Territory and Yugoslavia. The sun glared and danced off of the rocks and the crushed gravel of the road.

I stood there next to my duffel bag, blinking against the light like somebody who has just climbed out of a deep cellar or a cave, looking.

"Kind of scenic, huh?" the sergeant said sarcastically. "Just like a goddamn picture postcard."

I cleared my throat of dust and spat on the gravel in front of my boots.

"I've seen worse."

"I reckon so. I just bet you have."

He was pretty relaxed and loose now that he had me safely off his truck. It seemed like it was a great big joke on me I guess. I'd have to grant him that much. No doubt about it, no matter how you cared to look at it, he *did* have the last laugh now that he was rid of me.

"And you're just liable to see a whole lot worse before you're done," he added.

"Give me odds?"

But he had turned his back on me and missed that. He waddled back to the cab and took my records jacket off the seat and brought it to me.

"What am I supposed to do with this?"

"Give it to the battery clerk, that's what you're supposed to do," he said. "Tell you the truth, though, boy, I don't give a tinker's damn what you do with it. If I had a record like yours, if I was you, I'd burn the freaking thing."

"That's one thing you'll never be."

"Thank God for that among other blessings," he said.

He turned again and started to get back in the cab, without so much as a good luck or a grin. Just then, while looking at his wide back, I heard a wild, crazy, beautiful, mournful sound coming from a clump of those little dwarf trees.

"Hey, Sarge!" I yelled. "What's that? What's that noise?"

The driver already had the engine running. The sergeant was sitting up there, high, leaning all his weight on one big arm in the window. That arm looked like a big stuffed sausage, tightly cased in his tailored khaki shirt sleeve.

"*That?* Oh, that's the cuckoo bird, boy."

Well, what do you know? First the rocks, then a cuckoo bird to greet me. Welcome stranger, welcome home.

"I never heard one before. Except in a clock."

"You will here. You'll even get used to it up here," he said. "It gets old fast, just like everything else."

He laid his head on his arm and closed his eyes out of the purest boredom in the world. The driver was in a hurry to get on back to town. He doodle-bugged the big truck around and drove away, leaving me standing in the cloud of dust and shower of gravel behind. I watched the truck bounce along the road, roar around a curve with a little puff of dust chasing just behind it, hell-for-leather.

When I turned back I saw I was standing right near to the gate of the *caserma* of the Nth Field Artillery. There was a gate guard there, standing in front of a little sentry box, and he was a sight to behold, all dressed up with white gloves on and white shoelaces and a black, brass-studded pistol belt. He looked like some kind of a hotel bellhop. He was a jivy little gook of some kind or another. (I found out later he was from Guam.) And he looked like he wouldn't give you the time of day if you asked him. Well, I was wrong about that. I asked him which way to the orderly room and his face broke into a big, simple, good-natured grin and he pointed me the way to go.

2 I WALKED INTO the orderly room and handed my orders and my records jacket to the clerk. He was a young corporal. He looked like he might be a nice kid, a college boy probably—wore glasses, had a shy grin, was soft-spoken and had good manners. He asked me would I please take a seat and wait for the first sergeant. He ought to be back any minute now.

That's a good sign, when the clerk of an outfit doesn't give you a bad time right off to start with or try and get wise with you. It can give you the tone of the whole outfit. It probably means that somebody, whoever it is that sets the style for the rest, has got an even temper and some good sense. That's as hard to find in the Army as anywhere else. Most of the time they give the job of clerk to some clown or no-good punk. One time *I* was even the clerk of one freaked-up outfit, and that one, believe me, was the worst outfit I was ever with. Run into one of those, a clown or a smart-aleck sitting behind the clerk's desk, and you can bet your last dollar bill it's a lousy, fouled-up outfit. You won't lose either.

Looking at him I figured I could even bum a smoke off of him without having to work at it too hard. I just asked him and he gave me one, my first one in a long time, I mean a *long* time for a smoker. Then I sat back in my chair and took it easy, leaned back against the wall and blew smoke rings, wheels within wheels, while he was looking at my orders and my service record. I closed my eyes like I wasn't paying him any attention, then opened them up quick and naturally caught him staring at me.

"What's the matter?" I said. "You never seen a stranger before?"

He smiled and made a kind of whistle between his teeth.

"I've seen all kinds come and go in this outfit," he said. "But this beats all. I mean you've got yourself a real record."

"It's not as bad as all that. It just *looks* bad when they type it up and make a list. Everybody says I'm a real nice guy when they get to know me."

I don't know just how far I would have let myself go that time. I was starting to warm myself up to it. I felt so relieved to be in an orderly room again, taking it all in, free and sitting down, just taking it easy and smoking my first cigarette and not thinking about anything, just letting it happen. I felt so good—it probably *was* that cigarette—so lightheaded and lighthearted that it was making me act edgy and empty. Whenever that happens to me, when that mood gets a grip on me, which isn't very often, I get myself going on a talking jag. And I never know where I'm going to end up. Most of the time in a fight. I could feel that mood beginning in me and I knew I couldn't help myself.

About that time the first sergeant came busting into the room. He passed on, nodding at me and the clerk without a word or a change of expression (I don't think he would have cracked and changed the look on his face if a kangaroo had been sitting in the chair instead of me), picked up a copy of my orders, ignoring the records jacket and the rest of the stuff, and went straight on into the Old Man's office without bothering to knock.

I took that for a sign too, probably a good one. It either meant the first sergeant was the real bossman or, more likely, that he and the Old Man got along like a pair of Siamese twins.

I liked his looks right away. M/SGT RYDER, the brass nameplate on his empty desk said. Sergeant Ryder was neat enough without overdoing it, enough to get by and do his job. Nothing fancy or phony. Like some first sergeants splurge and buy themselves tailored gabardines instead of khaki and expensive shoes instead of issue low quarters. Ryder wasn't bucking for anything. That may not seem to mean much; it's just common sense. But common sense is as hard to find in the Army as anywhere, maybe harder. I have known of high-ranking officers, men who had it made as long as they didn't really foul up, who would spend hours of their spare time getting a classy spit shine on their boots and getting their uniforms just so. That's as good a way to kill time as any if you like it, I guess, but it can get you down thinking of a man with the rank of, say, a colonel, getting a good salary and with *my* freaking life on his hands, spending his time shining shoes and trying to be sharper than other people. I'd have more faith in a man who just got drunk every night or chased after cheap whores. Bucking gets to be a kind of disease, especially in a spit-and-polish command like Trieste. My first guess was that Sergeant Ryder would have looked exactly the same and acted exactly the same in Panama or Alaska. He wasn't wearing any ribbons at all on his shirt, which probably meant he had his share, too many to bother with every time he changed his shirt. He had his trousers bloused over the tops of his boots in a funny way, all sort of loose and floppy at first sight, but still, as you looked again, creased and hanging over in four corners. I looked and I couldn't place that style for a minute, then it came to me. That style was around way before the airborne was anything

16

but a bug in some old general's bonnet. It was the careful, careless-looking style of the mulepack artillery. Sergeant Ryder must have been a mulepack soldier once upon a time. In my book, short as it is, they are the very best—randy, raunchy men, easy-going, not scared or shook by anything, tough enough to spit in the devil's eye. He would probably chew tobacco once in a while. Sergeant Ryder had a long, large, bare, sad, weather-beaten face, like it was smoked and cured, but you could see in a minute that he knew how to laugh if he had a mind to.

After a little while he opened the door to the battery commander's office. He looked at me, jerked his head at me, and I got up and followed him inside. He shut the door and stood behind me with his back to it. I stepped up close to the desk, clicked my heels like a Kraut, standing tall, and tossed the Old Man my best highball.

"All right, Riche," he said. "That's the right way to say it, isn't it?"

He tried to pronounce it the French way. Like *Reesh*.

"No sir, it's just plain Riche, like in son-of-a-bitch."

He grinned at that. He was short and fat, but strong-looking, a hogshead barrel-shaped bear of a man, balding, jowly, red-eyed. He could never win a beauty contest. In a bathing suit he would look like a cave man. He was all rumpled and wrinkled like maybe he had been sleeping on the ground in his uniform for the last few nights (and here it was only the middle of the morning). Sweat stained his shirt around the collar and spread under his armpits. He looked much too old to be only a captain, but it would have been hard to guess exactly how old he was. Maybe his skin had just been pretty well lived in over a short time. Another loser in the old Army game, I guessed. Two real good genuine losers face-to-face. Well, he had a good face and a good grin. I liked him at first sight and figured right then I wouldn't ever want to cross him, to lie to him or try and fox him. Worn down on the grindstone, tired out, bored silly and slap-happy, it was true. But not the kind of a man to spend a whole lot of his time kidding himself or anybody else, and fair enough and sure enough of himself because of it, even if being sure just meant he only knew pretty well some of the many things he was *not* and never would be. That's one hell of a lot more than most people ever get to know. Believe me.

"When I first came in the Army there was a guy in my outfit name of Buzzard, B–U–Z–Z–A–R–D," he said. "First roll call I ever stood, the first sergeant called his name and pronounced it Buzz*ard*. That old country boy corrected him. Said 'Here, Sergeant, but that ain't the way you say it.' Sergeant thought he had something good going, maybe a big laugh. Put his hands on his hips and grinned like an undertaker. 'How *do* you say it?' 'Buzzard, just like the bird.' That old boy had it made from that day on."

While he was talking a fat cigar was quietly burning in his tin butt can. When he finished, laughed to himself, he sniffed the smoke, remembered it, picked it up and stared at the thick, gray, growing ash. From the expression on his face it looked like about half the cigars he had ever smoked had been loaded. When he decided it wasn't going to blow up he pleasured himself with a deep puff.

His desk was a complete mess of strewn and stacked and crumpled papers. It looked like he had been trying to build paper houses or something. Or maybe somebody had opened a window and let in a gale wind. Most officers' desks that I've seen are pretty bare. It makes it look like they're up-to-date, like they've got all their work done. Anybody who's been in the Army more than an hour or so couldn't be fooled by a thing like that. There are so goddamn many papers you could *never* get done with them. All those papers laying around on the Old Man's desk proved he was *trying* anyway, playing the part.

"So they nailed you to the cross in Germany, huh, Riche?"

"I got myself caught, if that's what you mean, sir."

18

"Well, I don't care what they done to you or what you done to them. That's your problem. You got yourself a clean slate here. I mean that all the way. But I don't want you to get the idea you can go around looking for *sympathy* either. Being a jailbird won't hurt you. But it damn sure isn't going to help you. Not in this outfit. We've got our share. I've even seen the inside of a couple of good stockades myself once upon a time. And I'm not running for President of the United States."

He stopped long enough to catch his breath, like he wasn't used to a big burst of talk like that, and to have another puff on his cigar and look me up and down from sole to crown. He held his cigar at arm's length from his face when he wasn't puffing on it, like maybe he thought it still might blow up on him. Delayed-action type. Time fuse. Force of habit I guess.

"What do you know?"

"Sir?"

"What *good* are you?"

"Sir, I don't get you . . ."

"What kind of work can you do in this outfit?"

"Oh, I know everything there is to the Field Artillery."

Sergeant Ryder, standing behind me, coughed, trying to hide a laugh. Even the Old Man grinned. If you push a little, make a smart-aleck wisecrack just every once in a while, it's all right. The thing to do is to keep a straight face and look innocent. Maybe you didn't say it at all.

"Don't that make it nice?" the captain said. "That's good. In fact that's wonderful."

"We need a good man," Sergeant Ryder growled.

"We sure do," the captain said. "We can use a freaking expert like you. Just what we need."

He looked past me.

"Just where do you think Private Riche will fit into the outfit?" he said to Sergeant Ryder. "What do we *really* need?"

19

"Warm bodies for the gun sections."

That gag was coming from the minute I led with my chin. It was coming anyway. I had just set it up and made it easy for them. Nobody *wants* to be on a gun section. All that lifting and digging and cleaning. Everybody tries to con his way into one of the clean, soft jobs.

"It was worth a try, Cap'n," I said. "You guys might have been saving a chair behind some desk for me."

"Not freaking likely," the captain said. "We may look dumb, me and Sergeant Ryder, but we ain't blind. The minute you walked in I knew the place for you. Trouble with you, Riche, is you just *look* like a cannoneer."

"Don't he, though," Sergeant Ryder said.

"That suits me fine, sir. I never did like to have to think too much. Especially on the job."

"You'll work all right," he said. "And don't go and get the wrong idea. This is a pretty good outfit. I'll admit we got more than our share of eightballs. In fact that's just about *all* we've got. Sometimes I used to think we had them all. See? I was wrong again. Story of my life! Here you come out of the blue, all the way from Germany to prove I'm a liar. I've been kidding myself. Well, keep your ass clean and if you've got to loaf, loaf gracefully. That's my motto. And that's all, soldier."

I saluted him and spun around in a smart about-face.

Back in the orderly room Sergeant Ryder told me to pick up my duffel bag and follow him. He said he was going to show me where my bunk was. First-class service. So we went down a hall and up one flight of stairs. It looked to be a fairly modern building, concrete walls and tile floors, with bars on all the windows and lots of small rooms. I found out later on that it had been built for a boys' reformatory just before the war. I don't know if it was ever used for that before we moved in. Maybe we were the first inmates. Anyhow, it turned out to be good, clean, comfortable living. With so many rooms in the place we lived two to a room, three at the most. It was sure a far cry from the typical long frame stateside barracks.

Halfway up the stairs he stopped long enough to tell me not to pay any mind to the guy who would be in the room with me. It was an old master sergeant, a twenty-year man, who had cracked up a while back and was going to be shipped home to a psycho hospital soon. He was only waiting around for orders and a boat. His name was Jethroe and he was crazy as a coot. But not dangerous. He was completely harmless.

Sergeant Ryder showed me to the door of my room and told me where to find the supply room in the basement where I could draw my bedding and equipment.

"Just one more thing," he said. "Don't you go and screw up and get yourself thrown in jail *here*. They got a tough one. You won't like it. What happens to you I can stand if you can. But the one thing I *can't* stand is the extra trouble it gives me filling out the morning report when I got a man in jail. I hate that."

"Don't sweat, Sergeant. I'm not going back to jail right away. I like to smoke too much."

"Yeah? Well, that's one reason."

"By the way, you wouldn't just happen to have an extra smoke on you, would you?"

"That's another thing I hate—guys who all the time bum smokes."

"I'll keep that in mind."

He squinted his eyes and stared at me. You could tell he had a good, man-size temper and you better not try it. You better walk right and not rub him the wrong way. But he wasn't mad at anything yet. He reached in his shirt pocket and gave me a cigarette. I held it in my hand and smiled at him.

"Well, what are you waiting for?"

"A light."

He held his lighter for me.

"I sure hope you enjoy it," he said. "Because this is the last time you'll ever bum a smoke and a light off of me."

He meant it too. I liked him fine.

3 AS SOON AS I got settled in I didn't mind it at all.

As soon as I got settled in . . .

That took some real doing in a command like Trieste. It was a display window, a showplace like Berlin. They had *us,* the poor old freaking Nth Field, away up there in the country, as far out of it as possible, guarding the Jug border, but the general idea downtown of the whole command was contagious. To start with, every single item of the uniform had to be tailored to a perfect fit. Even our fatigues were tailored and we wore them starched and creased and often changed them once a day. We were only allowed to wear jump boots, not the regular QM issue. That caused headaches and cost a lot of money out of your own pocket. Running around on all those rocks a man could wear a pair of the best boots to flapping shreds in two months or six weeks. Then all your patches, stripes and chevrons (if you *had* any) had to be specially cross-stitched with white thread. That little notion kept a couple of Italian girls busy most of the time at the *caserma,* just sewing. We had two full issues of almost every item of equipment. One was for parades and inspections and all that. The other was for real. For show we had nickel-plated mess gear and chrome-plated bayonets that looked good and keen in the light and wouldn't cut soft butter. We had black web equipment all studded with brass. We had white gloves and white shoelaces for our boots, and we wore white chinstraps and Simonized helmets. Instead of a necktie we wore a special dark blue scarf. Class! Like the whole command was just one big honor guard.

I think they had a reason for all that. There's almost always a reason for everything they do even if you have to be a private eye to find out what it is. They were trying to impress the Guineas. The Krauts had been there before us and one thing about those mothers, they're sharp. As the world knows the U.S. Army is famous for being sloppy. So I guess we were really trying to prove something even if it was phony as hell and cost the taxpayers twice as much as it ought to. I hate phony things and I have to admit I like the way the Limeys soldiered better. Nothing special. They just soldiered the same as they would anywhere else. I don't think they gave a shit who had been there before or about trying to make an impression on anybody. Especially the *Guineas!* Maybe you don't win popularity contests that way, but who cares? Who needs to win a popularity contest?

Naturally in an outfit like the Nth Field they figured out all the ways to beat the system. I mean, if you didn't come up with the shortcuts you would have spent half your time polishing and shining and all that. For example, everybody in the Nth Field had two footlockers. We fixed one of them up, a GI one, perfectly; and then we never even opened it except for inspections. All you had to do was blow the dust off. The other one was made by a carpenter in the village of Padriciano. We *lived* out of that one. Just before any big inspection we loaded all the real ones on a truck and they were hidden until after it was over. Take a couple of more examples. We could make a pair of jumpboots look almost spit-shined in about ten minutes just by smearing a big thick gob of polish all over the boot, sprinkling shaving lotion all over that, then wiping it off with a nylon stocking. When you wiped it off you had yourself a shine that looked, to anybody except an expert in shoeshining, like you had spent an hour or two on it. Or take brass. Trieste was a command with a lot of brass to take care of. Well, we polished the brass real good once, then put clear nail polish on it and after that all you'd have to do for a month is dust it off with a clean handkerchief.

What with nylons and clear nail polish the boys in the Nth Field did a pretty good business in things made for women at the PX. I saw one thing I had never seen in the Army before in the old Nth Field. (I guess it was because there were so many old-timers in the outfit and the old-timers are always *thinking,* thinking of ways to make their work—whatever it is—easier and more comfortable. Old-timers are the guys who always seem to have dry socks and cigarettes even in a rainstorm.) One of the things that used to turn up on the training schedule of the Nth Field was a road march, a long hot hike in the country with rifles and full field gear. On the mornings that we had a road march scheduled you'd see everybody in the outfit put on ladies' panties for underwear. The regular GI undershorts get all wrinkled and crawly—"Indian drawers," the old-timers called them—when you sweat a lot. Not so for some reason with panties. It certainly was a sight in the latrine on a morning like that when everybody was shaving and getting ready for reveille, a whole lot of hairy, potbellied, knob-kneed old sergeants running around in pink panties.

Why do I bother with all this about clothes? I don't know for sure myself, but maybe it's important. Sitting around here and there I've had some time to think it over. Look at it this way. Clothes begin by being phony. They are the beginning of phoniness. Underneath them we are all pretty much the same, just naked and hairy and worried as hell. We already know about nakedness. That's no mystery. So maybe it's true that everything we really know is about clothes. Not just about people, but about things too. A man might think that in a place like the Army, or even in jail, where everybody has to wear the same thing all the time, *clothes* wouldn't make any difference at all. You'd be just sloppy or neat, dirty or clean. When you are green as new grass and first go in the Army, you figure maybe you can hide yourself in a long rank of men in uniform and nobody will ever notice you. It doesn't take long to find out that every man has a kind of a style, whether he knows it or not, about the way he wears a uniform. And if you can train your eye, you soon get where you can tell almost everything you need to know about one single man or even a whole command by little things. At least that's the way I figure it. And I've staked my hide and hair, some big chunks of my lifetime, on it a number of times. I'd be lying if I didn't admit I've been dead wrong some of the times too.

The Infantry outfits were either downtown in Trieste or in the nearby town of Opicina. They had it pretty well made. They trained only in the morning. Training was usually a practice assault on Dragass Hill. Dragass Hill was a hell of a big, rocky, bare mountainside. It would wear you down just to walk up it. They would *charge* up the whole way, firing and yelling. It used to impress the visiting brass; they had never seen Infantry so eager or in better shape. It impressed me too the first time I saw it until I found out every last one of them was on Benny. With a jolt of that stuff inside them they could have done it two or three times in one day. They trained only in the mornings and a whole lot of them could get off on pass every afternoon. (I think there was probably a reason for that too. More popularity contest stuff. If you can't win friends, you can always *buy* some.) The Artillery, Armored, Recon, Engineers and such were scattered all over the territory. And the Nth Field, we were the farthest out, the most remote of all. I guess you might say our outfit was like the phony footlockers that we hid for inspection. Down at Headquarters they could fool themselves and pretend most of the time that we didn't even exist. We didn't get down to town much to remind them.

That wasn't so bad for me. On a private's salary I didn't have enough money to do much, anyway. And the way I looked at it was that if I was to spend a whole lot of time in Trieste and get a good look at what you can do with some money in this world, I would start to get nervous and restless all over again. Money does that to some people, especially me, just the idea of it and what all you can do with it. It makes me shiver and sweat. I got myself into enough trouble trying to make out on a sergeant's pay in Germany. The thing is, the truth is, if I ever saw all the different things I was missing out on, I'd get as anxious as a woman with labor pains. Next thing you know I'd get to scheming about all the different ways I could get ahold of a chunk of money quick. And sooner or later I'd wind up right back where I started. I'd be jailhouse bound.

Buddy, if I had've known where I really was headed, I'd have saved myself and Them a lot of trouble by just going straight to the jail and reserving myself a room. If They had've known, They never would have let me out in Germany in the first place.

Now, there are jails and jails. Even if I plan to stay clean and straight, tiptoe on the old straight and narrow path, that's the first thing I've got to find out about a new place. What kind of a jail do they have? Just in case I may end up there I have to know.

The one in Trieste was phony like everything else. It wasn't really a jail at all, it was a disciplinary barracks. The way I look at it, that is by far the worst kind to get thrown into. I'll have to admit it sounds all right, the name and all. And even the idea. The idea is supposed to be that it's a kind of a "school" where you can always shape up and soldier your way out and cut some time off your sentence. One time in Fort Campbell, Kentucky, I got myself out from under a six months' sentence in just a little over thirty days. Well, I was younger and stronger and fresher then. And dumber. God, I was stupid to start with! Oh, you can do it all right. It can be done. And when you can fox them good and do it and get out, you're pretty proud of yourself. I look out for old number one, you think, and old number one is a winner. Then one day later on you wise up and figure out that what really happened is They foxed you. When you know that, it gets where it isn't worth the trouble any more. What are you proving? Who are you trying to prove it to? Yourself or Them? Six months' time in a regular stockade would be a whole lot better.

I know there are a lot of guys around who claim they'd rather get sent to a disciplinary barracks than a stockade. They always give the same old reason, about being able to cut down on the time. But I think the real reason is they don't like the humiliation of being a plain old prisoner. Disciplinary barracks *sounds* better. I pity poor fools like that. As long as They can humiliate you or as long as you are afraid of being humiliated, then They have got a grip on you. They've got you by the balls.

In a regular stockade the life may be grim and gray. But you are just a prisoner being punished, passing time, nothing more and nothing less. You wear cruddy, crummy old fatigues and you have to put in a day's work doing whatever They can think of, from breaking big rocks into little ones to going around with a pointed stick and a bag and picking up wastepaper. You do your time and then They open the gate and let you out. They may be hard on you. They may ride herd on you, if They don't like your face or your attitude or the way you spell your name. But the thing is, nobody is interested in trying to make a *better man* out of you. In a disciplinary barracks They are always busy trying to rehabilitate you. God save me from rehabilitation! I got troubles and sorrows and faults enough without having to start over.

Rehabilitation . . . What that really means is that They are trying to break you down, to sweat you down to the original jelly. They are going to make a new soldier out of you the hard way. They usually put some pretty smart men to work on the idea. (Most of the brains in the world are busy working on new ways to hurt people. That's where the brains are all right. It takes a stupid bastard or a poor simple-minded slob to want to do you well.) Usually, in a DB, They make you have your bed all made up and laid out with all your gear for a full field inspection at 5 A.M. That's the way the day begins. What that means is, if you're lucky or experienced or just good at it you can laze around in bed until maybe 4:30. Most poor suckers sleep on the floor. The trouble is They keep you on the dead sweaty run training and drilling all day long and up until about 11 P.M. and after. You can't even sit down during that time. You eat standing up. When They finally give up on you and get around to letting you go to bed, then you proceed to try and get everything ready for the next day. You have to clean your rifle. (It doesn't have a firing pin, so you couldn't even shoot Them or yourself if you wanted to.) You clean up all your other gear, which is naturally filthy dirty; then you wash out your fatigues in a washbasin and iron them dry. All this in the pitch-dark. There will be maybe one iron to a whole barracks. So you just have to wait your turn and be ready to fight for it when you've got it. You've got to be ready to fight all the time, or go under. If you can do all that and be pretty near *perfect* in everything, without blowing your top and getting thrown in a solitary cell, for thirty or sixty days in a row, then maybe you will get out early.

When you are just a prisoner, it's all so simple. It's Us against Them. When you are driving yourself to soldier your way out of a DB, it's You against Everybody.

• • •

I'm not looking for sympathy. I'm not sorry for me or any-body else. I'd be kidding myself if I claimed that was the case. The first time I got slapped in a jail I used to feel sorry for all prisoners everywhere in the world. It didn't take too many lumps or too much time, though, for me to figure out how cheap and phony *that* kind of feeling was. All I really was, was sorry for myself. I've even run into some guards who felt sorry for prisoners. Not permanent, full-time guards. Just the temporary ones, the amateurs. They could put them-selves in your shoes and it pinched their toes and hurt. I fig-ured out that kind of pity was just fear. Nobody can really wear my shoes for me, ever. And I damn sure don't want them to, either. For better or worse my shoes are mine and fit *me*. I'm used to them. To tell the truth, it makes me fighting mad when somebody tries to put himself in my place. It's so phony. My place is mine; and if somebody thinks he can guess just what it's like and know all about it, then he is trying to knock me down to nothing. When a man feels sorry for somebody else in that phony way, he's just knocking the wind out of the other guy, breaking him down to nothing but the pile of dust he came from in the first place. I may hate a lot of people and a lot of things. I may have too much hate in me at times for my own good. But I've seen people put up with most everything terrible you can think of and still keep the breath of life in them and still never get broken the whole way down to dust. So one thought can do what all the force and power and muscle in the world can't do. The way I feel is, if a man has to think about how other people are suffering every minute of every day—and he'd better think about it once in a while if he doesn't want to spend his whole life in cloudland—then the thing to do is not to settle for cheap feelings. Ask for some-thing better than that. Salute every bastard in the world who can take it, and be sorry and ashamed that some of them couldn't.

• • •

It wasn't long before I found out what I wanted to know about the jail in Trieste. They called it Trust College. (I better explain right now about TRUST. That was the initials for the Trieste command—Trieste United States Troops. They liked that. You could do a lot with the word. I remember there was a sign in the Officers' Club in Opicina—I got inside there one time unloading cases of whisky. The sign said IN GOD WE TRUST. IN TRUST WE'RE GOD. A joke. In our Army all these initials have to add up and spell something these days. Which is one more thing I happen to like about the Limeys. I never saw one of theirs that spelled anything. Too much trouble. Or maybe it was too corny for them. The initials of their Trieste forces was BETFOR. If that spells a word, even to a Limey, I'll salute it.) Trust College was an old gray-walled Italian Army *caserma* downtown in the section called San Giovanni, right near to the public lunatic asylum. (That was probably the right place to have it, but it must have been rough on the people who were trying to live in the neighborhood, what with howls coming night and day from both places and mixing together.) From what I could gather, the College sounded like a rough one. When I got to the Nth Field there were two guys in the outfit who were fresh out of there. One looked to be all right. That was my buddy, Angus Singletree. He looked like he could take on anything that was coming to him. (I was wrong about that. Later on, much later, I heard he blew way up and went off in a lot of little pieces like a skyrocket. But that's another sad tale of woe, not this one.) Singletree could talk and joke about it easy enough. Still, it didn't take a mastermind to figure out he would do a lot of backing and filling to keep from having to go down there and pull time again. The other guy—they called him "Bang Bang" because he used to be nuts on the subject of weapons—was a complete wreck. He kept strictly to himself and wouldn't talk to anybody about anything. The only thing left in the whole world that he really seemed to care about was his harmonica. The only thing they could find to do with him anymore was to put him on odd jobs around the *caserma* like painting butt cans red and sweeping and mopping or wandering around picking up trash and paper. He was on the main line to the psycho ward.

Both of them had lost about twenty pounds apiece down there, in the short time they took the course. (I figured I didn't have any more weight to lose. They already had worked me down to skin and bones, sackcloth and ashes. I didn't have a thing left to give Them.)

I admit even if I wasn't scared of the College I was bound and determined to walk the chalk line and keep out of there if I could.

The work in the outfit wasn't too bad, and the time passed easy. We trained fairly hard in the mornings, pulled maintenance on the howitzers and vehicles and other gear in the afternoons, and took turns pulling border guard at the checkpoints along the Jug border. It was specially fine in the early morning when the air was warm and fresh. It was springtime. Sometimes we would start off the morning with a road march along the back roads—just to prove that the Artillery still knows how to walk, I guess. Or we might mount up on the trucks and go out in the country and run a field problem. I remember that time laying half asleep in the clean grass—I always volunteered for perimeter duty if I could get it—with a .30 caliber machine gun or a rocket launcher nestled next to me, half asleep, feeling the easy breeze flow and bathe over me, looking up into the heart of the blue windy sky, smelling the warm earth, feeling the heat off of the rocks and often hearing a cuckoo in the trees nearby somewhere. It was the season for that shy, crazy bird. And like the C & A Sergeant had warned me, I did get used to it. In fact I really started to like it soon, the sound of it. They had found the right name for it. I would be laying there dozing, half dreaming and happy, and I'd think that if I ever had to be a bird at all, I'd want to be a cuckoo. People tell you different things about the cuckoo when you ask them. They say it's a dirty bird and a thief and all. I couldn't have cared less. What he does with himself is his business. It was his cry or his song or whatever it was that seemed like it was my language. And you never saw one. At least I never did. You could only hear him, here, there, and then gone again like a ghost. The cuckoo bird suited me fine in those days.

The good thing about working in the Nth Field was nobody ever screwed up when it really mattered. That made the hard work go easier for everybody. Many an outfit looks good, seems good on paper or on parade or at inspection, but turns out to be just a nest of mean snakes fighting each other. And that's just the kind of outfit that can crack up and bug out on you in combat. If it turns out that you have to die heels up with your boots on, why you might just as well do it along with some buddies you can count on. Not with some sad bunch of phonies. I had been in and among phonies before, and I guess the only thing besides luck that kept me going and alive was to prove that none of those bastards was going to live to step over my corpse.

When it's plain ordinary garrison work, then it's a matter of knowing when to goof off and when not to. There are times when you goof off and everybody else is hurting. Like the Old Man promised, they stuck me on a gun section. But it wasn't long before I was the gunner even without any stripes. I don't know much, but I can do anything there is to do with a howitzer blindfolded. That may not be much of a claim, but it's the truth and worth something anyway. On maintenance of the howitzers and vehicles—which as everybody knows is the real pain in the ass of the Field Artillery—all the guys worked well together and worked fast. Nobody had to stand around and tell anybody else what to do next. They just did it. That's the way to do things because that's the way to get done. Sometimes it takes a good soldier years to learn a simple thing like that the hard way.

Some guys never learn.

• • •

It was a hell of a big change for me. I had just come burrowing out from the dark underground like an old groundhog or a blind mole. I was lousy, a lousy bum. I had spent too much of my time in lousy outfits and lousy jails. Now all of a sudden it started to look like maybe I had accidentally stumbled into the right place and the right home. When people say like a dream come true I finally know what they mean. Not a phony dream. At night when I was in the stockade for the first time I used to lay on my bunk and close my eyes and picture a paradise. Me on a desert island, a little tiny one like the magazine cartoons about people stranded on a desert island, me with one big lush blonde about as huge as a statue in a park and as ripe and curvy as a watermelon to pass the time with. Later on, as the real time got longer and longer, I couldn't—even in a dream—be satisfied with just one. I had to have myself a whole harem, all sizes and shapes and colors just like so many beads on a string. My private rosary. And all the time all kinds of rare flowers like orchids were blooming and coconuts fell off of a palm tree whenever I got hungry or thirsty.

Well, this Nth Field was no kind of a paradise like that. No palm trees or orchids or lush girls with or without grass skirts. That's the kind of nonsense a man bothers himself with most of the time when he plays like he's God and tries to make the world over the way it ought to be. But in its own way the outfit was a kind of peaceable island for me. I was beginning to be about as pleased with myself as I ever had been or could be.

PART TWO

The Men

4

SPARE TIME. Real life.

That's a complicated story. We all went our own ways. Some guys bugged out for the city of Trieste every time they had the chance, spent every dime they had and tried to live it up. A few of the younger ones would go down to the Main PX and the Service Club on the bay and try to pick up one of the girls they called Hamburger Bandits that hung around there. Most of them usually hung around a little hole-in-the-wall nicknamed the Poker Bar, and they didn't let anybody but the Artillery in. And the whores. The cheaper ones. *Mille lire* for a quickie, standing up in a dark alley probably. Those old whores may have been cheap but they had skill and imagination. There was one who made a good living taking on the sentries at the main ammo dump. *Through* the cyclone fence. I got a good mind for picturing that kind of thing and I still don't know how she did it, but she did. The guys in the Nth Field knew every cheap whore in the Territory by her right name. When they went down to town they played hide-and-seek with the MPs, the plainclothes vice squad and the VG

policemen all over town. (Those Venezia Giulia cops were
the local police force. They wore London bobby hats and
carried American M–2 carbines, fully automatic. Some of
them had horses. They were good cops and tough.) Some
good nights the MPs would bring in a whole truckload of our
guys at one time. We had a terrible reputation downtown.
There was always the chance of getting yourself picked up by
the MPs just on general principle, just because you happened
to be wearing the red braid of the Artillery on your cap.

I went down to the city a few times in spite of myself, just
to take a look around. It was a beautiful city all right, but it
put you in mind of a great big head on the body of a dwarf
or a midget. There was a fine blue deep-water harbor and a
wide boulevard running right along the edge of the harbor.
The bay was like a big round half-bowl with the hills and low
mountains all around. There were a lot of bank buildings and
offices and such, big heavy ones that looked a little like parts
of Germany. But that was just a front. Back of them the town
scrambled and staggered up the hills Italian-style with bright-
colored stucco walls and slate roofs. It looked to be a good
place. And it had probably been a real good place once.

The people were handsome, all mixed up with Italian,
Yugoslav, Austrian and the old, original Triestine strains.
The men were tall and good-looking. A lot of them were
sailors when they could find work. The women were a special breed. They had all that good Italian ripeness and round-
ness and color, but they also had sort of Jug angles and bones,
with high cheekbones and a Jug look around the eyes. I saw
some of the best-looking women I've ever seen anywhere
there.

Some of the guys in the outfit were strictly loners. They
either went their own ways or else they were shacked up in
one of the villages out our way. The rest of them just naturally fell in loose groups and bunches. Some hung around the
caserma all the time. I guess it wasn't so bad for them. Even if
we were isolated, there were some things to do. For one

thing we had our own movie projector. Sergeant Loller, the mess sergeant, was a wheeler and dealer, a first-class operator when it came to getting things done. If we had waited for Special Services of the Army to furnish the movies we would have still been seeing Shirley Temple and Buck Jones. So he would trade off, illegally, some of our fresh rations to the Navy for some good new movies whenever one of their ships was tied up in the port. And there was stuff like volleyball and basketball for the jocks. Thank God there weren't many of *those* around. (There's nothing like having a lot of athletes to screw up an outfit.) And on top of that we had our own little club where you could buy good strong Kraut beer cheap.

The bunch I spent most of my time with wanted a little bit of quiet mischief without a whole lot of pain and strain. It was easy. There were a couple of dirty little villages within fair walking distance of the *caserma* where you could sit around and drink *grappa* and *vino* and cognac, and the MPs would never think to come and look for you. The only reason most of those crummy places weren't off limits was that even if they had ever heard of them or could find where they were—and I doubt it—they would never have dreamed that any of their good, clean-cut American GIs would go in a place like that. How wrong can you get?

Old Sergeant Ryder went his own way. They only thing he liked to drink in those days was *slivovitz*. You had to go across the border into Yugoslavia to get that. And he went almost every night. He would walk right past the Jug border guards. They would usually point their burp guns and holler at him in Jug to stop. He'd always just wave them away like gnats or mosquitos and go straight on without even slowing down or speeding up to the first village and the nearest little grubby Jug bar. Ryder had a little black mongrel dog named Pat that he took with him on those nighttime expeditions. Pat was his only real close friend in the whole world. Whenever he went, Pat went with him. Crossing the border was a big thing. A lot of GIs had been shot for even looking like they might be getting ready to in the early days of the Occupation. But for some reason they didn't seem to want to tangle with Ryder. I guess maybe it's because when you strip back to the naked truth all armies are about the same. Ryder would have been a topkick, a first sergeant, in anybody's army. And they wouldn't any more have thought of shooting him than they would their own fathers.

Ryder would find the bar and go sit down at a table and quietly get drunk as a lord. Along about midnight, if he hadn't already passed out, he would get up and start to stagger and weave home to the outfit. If he had passed out or was too weak in the knees to make it standing up on his own somebody would help him get to the border. Then the Jug guards would try to find one of our guards or somebody on our side of the line who would bring him in. Ryder never missed a reveille formation. He was always there, neat in a clean uniform and blowing the whistle for us to fall in. People said the border used to be pretty tense before all that. I like to think Sergeant Ryder and his dog Pat did more to help the whole situation than all the treaties and loans and threats and conferences put together.

The pack I ran with had a favorite bar in the village of Padriciano. It was at the dead end of a dark, twisty alley that was just about wide enough for a skinny goat to walk up. It didn't have a sign or an outside light or anything. You had to know where it was. We named it the "Hidden Bar." The story was that it was for sure the one bar in the Territory entirely and absolutely unknown to the MPs, the Vice Squad, CID, VGs and anybody else who was hell-bent to keep you out of trouble even if it meant cracking your skull and breaking your heart to do it. A man who was AWOL could probably have lived there to a ripe old age without getting himself caught. It was about the safest place around for some heavy drinking and a little rowdy noise.

We got along pretty good with the people of Padriciano.

They didn't bother us even that one time when all the villages were worked up against the American GIs. (There had been a rape. Some GI from one of the Infantry outfits raped a village girl. Then some innocent GIs came along and got in a hell of a fight with the local characters. A couple of them got pronged with pitchforks. There was a rough time for a while. Feelings ran pretty high on both sides. But the red braid of the Nth Field was like a safe-conduct pass.)

The usual routine was that all of us kept civilian clothes there in a back room of the Hidden Bar hanging on nails and pegs. It was against regulations to wear civilian clothes in TRUST. I guess that's why we always changed out of our uniforms as quick as we got there. It helped us to feel like we were having a good time. It put us in the mood for it. The reason we were supposed to be doing it was just in case any of the MPs ever did discover the place and come in to take a look around. Lots of characters and operators tried to run around Trieste in civvies, to get in places like the big cat houses that were off limits and so forth or maybe just for the pure hell of it. They nearly always got caught. They were so stupid they went out and got themselves good Guinea clothes. They would get the whole works. Except most of them didn't change their shoes. They didn't like the Guinea shoes with the high heels and the pointed toes, so they wouldn't wear them. You can spot a pair of American-made shoes in a crowd over there a country mile. The ones who got caught that way deserved to.

All our bunch that hung around the Hidden Bar got raggedy old clothes from the farmers around the *caserma*. The ones I bought came off of a scarecrow. Any of us all dressed up in the castoff clothes of some poor farmer or his scarecrow were safe as could be. None of us would ever be stopped by an MP.

Angus Singletree, who was nutty as an old squirrel anyway, walked all over downtown Trieste one day in his Hidden Bar clothes just to prove it and win a bet. He even went right up to an MP lieutenant and asked him for a light in phony broken English.

Well, he could get away with it. Since I've had so much time to think about it—oh, I've had plenty of time on my hands to think it all over—I figure there may be a moral to that too. Nobody else will ever figure you want to look and be taken for being worse off than you really are. Only a fool would act that way and who's ready and willing to admit he's a fool? But the hell with it. Never mind the moral. We just did it. And we liked it that way.

5 THE MEN of the outfit? Like I said, they suited me fine. They were crazy and up to no good, but all right. The Old Man had really been telling the truth when he told me I would be nobody special in his outfit. There were some guys around who had spent more time in various stockades than I had in the Army. We had pretty near everything you can find, all shapes and sizes, colors and dispositions. You better believe we must have been one funny-looking, raunchy crew all lined up for inspection or something. The Old Man always used to shake his head in sheer amazement or frustration every time he had to look at the Battery in formation. He would salute the first sergeant and start in on us with some wise remark like "What hath God wrought?" or "I thought the Zoo was closed on Tuesdays," or "What did I do to deserve a thing like this?"

How did a thing like this happen? Well, the Nth Field had been formed up overseas instead of in the States. It was supposed to be made up of men from the Regimental Infantry companies who had an Artillery MOS. So they sent a letter down to all the company commanders, telling them about the brand-new outfit and asking them if they had any good men to spare who happened to have an Artillery MOS. The company commander would study the letter awhile until he got the idea, then a great big mischievous grin would light up his face and he'd holler for his first sergeant and his company clerk. It was an amazing coincidence how all the losers, misfits, deadbeats, bums, eightballs, VD cases, alcoholics and walleyed, knock-kneed, slew-footed, mangy-headed stockade bait all of a sudden turned out to be well-trained artillerymen. Then they flew the Old Man over from the States to take charge of the pirate crew. They—the officers down at the Officers' Club—probably bit their tongues in two trying to keep from laughing in his face and giving the whole thing away before he actually *saw* what he had gotten out of the grab bag. He was the man about to sit down on the old Whoopee Cushion. He was the guy who was being sent out to bring in a left-handed monkey wrench and one bucket of polka-dot paint. He was a poor slob scheduled to be nailed to the cross with tramps and thieves for company.

Lucky for him, he was one of us, a kind of a bum himself.

There were several guys still around who had been there the first day he saw the outfit lined up. They never forgot it or what he said to them, his pep talk.

"I'll be a son-of-a-bitch!" Those were his first words to his troops. The rest of the speech was short and to the point. "You freaking guys!" he said. "You are without a doubt the crummiest collection of decayed humankind I ever laid eyes on, so help me God. We deserve each other. If you want to be soldiers, try it. See if I care. First Sergeant, take charge of this so-called battery. I'm going to get drunk."

The whole battery cheered him. They threw their helmet liners in the air. And even later on, by the time I was with the Nth Field, everybody still felt like cheering for the Old Man.

Besides having so many professional losers all under one roof, we had some other kinds of real variety. We had men from all over the States and from some of the possessions too—like Guam, Puerto Rico and the Virgin Islands. We had white and black and yellow and mixed. We even had a couple of full-blooded American Indians. We were Protestants and Catholics and Jews of all types and descriptions. There was even one jivy little colored guy down at the motor pool, one of those real double-clutching drivers, who claimed he was some kind of Moslem. We stuck pretty well together on the job because we had to. When everybody is so different and has to go his own way, you tend to get along better. That might seem like it couldn't be true. Well, if you're clinging to a life raft, say, every man is on his own because you, yourself, can only drown once. Nobody else can do it for you. With this in mind maybe everybody works together and keeps the other guy in mind. We didn't have many serious fights among ourselves or much friction. Except for the clerk, the armorer, and the fire direction center (where you got to have more than just brains, you got to have some training and education too) we were almost all Regular Army, longtime veterans.

This particular pack I fell in with was all kinds too.

There was Mooney, big old Mooney, a colored guy and the chief of Firing Battery. Mooney was the best all-around artilleryman I've ever known. And I've known some good ones. He was dedicated to those howitzers, he worshipped them. He was always thinking of ways to save time and make it easier to get into position and poop out the rounds faster. He was a kind of a genius at field expedients. In the Artillery where the terrain is almost always different, the book isn't a whole lot of help. You have to know it cold, then throw it away because every problem you run into, every snag is different. Mooney thrived on new problems. Let a howitzer skid off a muddy road, jackknife the truck and block the road up so nobody behind could move—and naturally we are in a hell of a hurry and there's no special equipment to lift a six-ton howitzer out of the muddy ditch—old Mooney would come arunning, grinning and rubbing his big hands together like he thought maybe he could strike a spark or a flame just rubbing them together. He would rig up some intricate, crazy-looking network of winches and ropes, and in five minutes the howitzer would be out of the ditch and the Battery would be rolling again. That was Mooney, a real field soldier.

I had heard of Mooney before and I saw him one time in Korea when I was attached to his battalion for a while doing forward observing. He remembered me. The first time I went down to the gun park to work he came over to our gun section and he stood there watching me work for a while.

"Hey," he said finally. "Don't I know you from somewhere?"

I told him the time and the place.

"That's right," he said. "I know you now. You wasn't a bad soldier either, but you sure were in one freaked-up outfit."

I guess he expected me to stand there and argue with him and maybe stick up for the crummy yellow phonies I had been with. Well, I wasn't about to argue in their behalf.

"You can say that again," I said. "They weren't worth a country fart."

"This here is a pretty good little outfit," he said. "Don't you go freaking around here."

"Don't sweat over me, Sergeant Mooney. I can tell when a shoe is a good fit."

"Yeah? Well, we'll see about that in due time."

I could tell he liked me right away. But he was too good a man to take a chance on me. He studied me out for a while and when he saw I knew the right way to treat a howitzer and had the right attitude we got to be pretty good friends. If Mooney was your friend—and he was anybody's friend who could soldier in a gun section—he'd stick right with you all the way to any kind of bitter end you can think of. If he was your enemy, God help you. Nobody else could.

Mooney was naturally pissed off about being born black. Who could blame him? It's like a great big Joke, a Joke with a capital J, one of God's Jokes, the way people come all different. (I got that idea of the Joke one time when I went to an aquarium and saw all the different kinds of fish there. Some of them were just *made* helpless. And some of them were so crazy-looking you didn't know whether to bust out laughing or crying. I've noticed the same thing in the zoo. Animals probably have it worse than people, when you think about it.) Anyway Mooney was too good a man to let it ruin him like some people do. He was a man first and a black man second. And first and last he was a soldier. On duty he was all eyes and ears and a brain like a well-oiled machine. Off duty he could drink enough *grappa* to float a barge.

"Man, I like this *grappa*," he'd say. "When I get going and get high on *grappa* I'm nothing but big and bad-assed and mean and, buddy, you better look out. You better make way for me."

That may be the way he saw himself. I would say he was the mildest, quietest kind of drunk. A perfect gentleman.

Next to Mooney there was Angus Singletree. Singletree had served under Mooney in Korea and he was his best friend. That was a kind of funny thing because Singletree was from the Deep South where a "nigger" is dirt. But that's the way it goes. This Angus was a strange character. He was a hell of a good soldier, because Mooney had taught him. He had been in and out of some colleges and a state bughouse and then Korea. He had a twin brother named T.J. he used to show us pictures of. He claimed the plan was for him and his twin brother to split up the time in the Army and then split the pension after twenty years. He was a medium-size, good-looking guy and most of the time as easygoing and soft-spoken as anybody could ask. But you knew the first time you saw him and looked at the funny light in his eyes that he was as crazy as hell. He looked like he would kill without even working up a sweat about it if he had to. Mooney said he was the coolest man under fire he had ever seen.

I believe it. I think he was the only man I ever knew who really *liked* combat. I saw him one time in Korea, one day. It was when the chickenshit lieutenant and I were attached to Mooney's outfit to help out with the observing. They were short on officers and Singletree was holding down one hot Observation Post all by himself, just a soldier and a telephone and a radio. We went to relieve him. We had to crawl on our bellies about half a mile to get there and not be spotted by the gooks. We crawled into the dugout, sweating like pigs and breathing hard, and there was Singletree sitting on a packing box with his head cocked to hold the field phone, and he was reading a skin magazine. He didn't even say hello he was glad to see us. And he had double bags under his eyes from lack of sleep.

"Look here," he said, pointing to a picture of a naked girl. "Did you ever see anything like that? It says here her name is Honey Bear and she works as a receptionist for some psychiatrist. Do you believe that?"

We just lay there on the dirt still catching our breath so he went on.

"Now I'll tell you all something. I'm just a wee bit crazy and that gives me an edge. I can get in and see that psychiatrist. On business, so to speak. If I get out of here, balls and all, I tell you that's just what I'm going to do. I'm going to go straight to that psychiatrist and tell him the only thing that can cure me is a course with Honey Bear."

The lieutenant looked at me. I could tell he figured Singletree was scared out of his mind. I don't know what I thought, but I didn't figure he was scared. I guessed maybe he was just trying to initiate us to his war.

48

"Look at that. Did you ever see such a fine ass? Not all the smooth surface of the Elgin marbles could equal . . ."

"Soldier!" The lieutenant had got his breath and courage back. "Are there any gooks out there?"

"Sure," he said. "The whole hill is crawling with them at night. They try and sneak up here and you've got to kill them. But it's pretty quiet in the daytime. They're still out there all right, but they don't do much."

"What do you mean *they're still out there?*" The lieutenant didn't like that idea much. He crawled up beside Singletree where he could see. "I don't see anything."

"Let me show you," Singletree said.

And with that he jumped out of the dugout and ran around yelling and waving his arms. All hell broke loose. Gooks opened up with small arms from all over the hill and he came diving back in the dugout laughing his guts out. We lay flat on the dirt and listened to the lead smack against the earth above and behind us. After a while it stopped. Singletree threw a grenade down the hill just for the hell of it. Then he took his rifle and started crawling out the way he had come.

"Good luck," he said. "If they come in too close on you, you can always call a mission in right on this spot and that will chase 'em back down the hill."

I found out later that's exactly how he had held the post for three nights running. We didn't have to. Before dark some Infantry came up to support us. But it was a long day, and the only thing good about it was that my lieutenant wet his pants when Singletree drew all that fire.

When I met him again in the Nth Field, it was a joke between us.

"Draw fire, Singletree," I'd yell.

And he would jump up and do something crazy and make everybody laugh.

There was Clayton, called Cool Breeze. We kept him around for laughs. He didn't mind. Clayton was as dumb as a mule and just as stubborn. He would be in the Army until they threw him out for old age. But the only thing he ever talked about was what he was going to do on the outside as soon as this hitch was up. He wasn't really a soldier, he claimed, he was just passing the time and preparing himself to be a great big Success in Real Life. With this in mind he took all kinds of extension and correspondence courses. The legitimate ones he flunked flat. He had passed one that qualified him as an "Expert Masseur." (How you do that by extension I don't know.) And one that he passed all right was some kind of a course in "How to Be a Private Detective." They mailed him a big tin badge and a booklet and an "All-Purpose Detective Kit" when he passed.

Clayton like to have driven everybody nuts talking about being a detective until one time when somebody stole about ten gallons of OD paint from the motor pool. The Old Man himself called Clayton in and told him to investigate the theft.

"Goddamn you, Cool Breeze," he said, "all I ever hear around here is what a bigshot private detective you are. All right, I'm going to give you three days, three full days, to find out who swiped that paint. If you do, I'll promote you to Pfc. If you *don't,* I don't want to ever have to hear about that detective stuff again. If you fail, you got to turn in your badge to me. For keeps."

Cool Breeze told the Old Man he figured three days was more than enough time to solve a simple case like that.

He spent the next three days running around fingerprinting everybody who would stand still for him long enough, dusting everything in sight with his special fingerprint powder and looking at the world through a magnifying glass.

"What's that, itching powder?" guys hollered when he dusted for prints.

"Do you get a pipe with that kit?"

But Cool Breeze shrugged them off.

"There's always wise guys that don't know no better," he said. "I don't pay them any mind."

At the end of the three days the Old Man called a special formation and lined us all up.

"All right, Cool Breeze," he said. "Which one stole the freaking paint?"

"I conducted me a very thorough investigation," Cool Breeze started, still at attention in his place in ranks.

"Never mind the story of your life. Who's guilty?"

"Well, sir, I just don't . . ."

"Know? Don't you *know?*"

Then we had one of those long, itching, sweaty, painful silences.

"No, sir."

"You come up here. Front and center."

Cool Breeze stepped out of ranks and marched up, cutting square corners, until he stood directly in front of the Old Man and saluted him.

"Give me that freaking badge."

Cool Breeze had been allowed to wear his badge all during those three days of the investigation. Now he unpinned it and handed it over to the Old Man. When the Old Man took it, I swear, Cool Breeze busted out crying like a little kid in front of the whole Battery. The Old Man put his arm around him.

"Don't feel bad," he told him. "Being a detective is too dangerous anyway."

Then: "You know one time I used to want to be a goddamn tap dancer like Fred Astaire. Sometimes I still do. But the truth is I have enough trouble keeping in step, let alone dancing. There's worse things than being a soldier. Battery, dismissed!"

About a week later the Old Man went chickenhearted and actually gave him back the badge. That was a hell of a big mistake, killing with kindness. Once he got his badge back Cool Breeze was worse than ever. He said he was going to crack that case if it killed him. It would have, too. If some-body hadn't found the paint where it had been mislaid under a tarp in back of the motor pool, some of the guys would've killed old Clayton for sure. Out of self-defense.

6 ANOTHER ONE, one of the boys, was
Zwicker, the Tattooed Wonder of the Western
World, and up there in the running for the title
of the ugliest man alive. Whoever his competition was and *where*ver it was, Alaska to Afghanistan, it was
bound to be a dead heat with a photo finish. Who would
look at the photo if Zwicker was in it, though?

I pause for him. And I would like to linger longer as long
as I'm thumbing through the family album of the wharf rats,
termites, peckerheads, the pigeon-toed, cross-eyed, freakish,
bald-headed, humpbacked, peanut-brained, snaggletoothed
Prides of the Nation I found myself at home with in the old
Nth Field.

Well then, Zwicker. There are lots of things you could tell
about Zwicker. For one thing I could begin by saying, and
it probably is the truth, that he was not just the best gunner
in the Nth Field, he may have been the best gunner in the
Army or the world. That's hard for me to say because I think
I'm a pretty good one myself. It was really a pleasure to
see Zwicker working around a gun. It was joy to see him

perched up on the left trail of the howitzer, peering into the eyepiece of the panoramic telescope, with both hands at once whirling the handwheels for elevation and deflection without making any mistake as the commands came down from the battery exec. He was fast, sure and steady. He was a great driver, too, for the Artillery. He could handle a deuce-and-a-half or a big 6-by where most guys would be afraid to take a tank. And, put him on the driver's seat holding on to the twin sticks of a high-speed tractor, he was a devil with a machine.

"If they call for a gun position in outer space," he used to say, "I'll get you there some way. I'll drop you down right in the middle of the winking stars all set, pointed in the direction of fire, ready to go."

He was a freaking perfectionist on a gun. He had a big voice like a dark thundercloud, and he could ride herd on any gun section made up of lead-footed, cotton-brained, mitten-handed, typical hairy-eared cannoneers. That's Zwicker's *technical* side, so to speak.

Or you could start in on his appearance. Zwicker was a great hulking brute of a man, rolling-gaited like a sailor on dry land, about the shape and beauty and grace of a grizzly bear, and a clumsy one at that, on his hind legs. He was a regular package of contradictions. For one thing he was a liar even when he didn't have to be. He just couldn't help it. He used to lie all the time about the different things he had done in civilian life. Zwicker had really done a lot of things. He had honestly been a truck driver, a nightclub bouncer, a merchant sailor, a lumberjack, a heavy-construction worker, a part-time carpenter, a farmhand, an oil field roughneck and a carnival barker. All that was true; I checked on his records. But he never mentioned any of that. Instead he claimed to have been a professional wrestler, a bellhop in a Hollywood hotel, a locomotive engineer, a masseur in Miami Beach, a jailbird, a rodeo cowboy, a deep-sea diver, a steeplejack, and in the Coast Guard. I guess the plain truth wasn't good enough for him.

Same way with soldiering. I know for a fact he had been through hell in Korea. His whole outfit had been overrun and he lay in a ditch wounded for two or three days before somebody finally found him and heaved him in an ambulance and sort of patched him up. If you listened to Zwicker you'd never hear one word about Korea. Instead he was all full of long-winded stories about the duty he had pulled in Alaska ("The *snow,* man, you ain't never seen snow like they got up there. Them polar bears and Eskimo women!"), Panama ("Hot, man, and the jungle was full of monkeys and all different-colored birds. I remember I got lost out on patrol one time . . ."), and Puerto Rico ("They don't drink nothing but rum down there, even for breakfast, because the water is so bad. And they got beautiful women! You can go and buy yourself one of those broads for five bucks, just like a slave. The only trouble is they won't speak nothing but Puerto Rican. It's some kind of a foreign language. I can speak it, but it even took *me* a long time to learn . . ."), and other places on the globe he had never been to. Nobody ever believed him for a minute, but nobody cared. Sometimes we would listen to him. Sometimes not.

Zwicker was going to be a private or, if he was lucky, maybe a corporal to the end of his Army days. Not because he ever got himself in any real deep trouble. But just because he had the habit—he was a steady, long-term, installment-plan loser. The Old Man kept telling him that if he would just keep clean and neat and try to look a little bit like a soldier he would promote him. (After all a gunner on the T/O & E was supposed to be a sergeant.) It wasn't that Zwicker didn't want to look sharp. You would have to admit that Zwicker really tried. He went down to the Quartermaster Supply Store and bought himself about a jillion extra fatigue uniforms. Every morning at reveille formation he would fall out with spit-shined jumpboots, his brass belt buckle gleaming like a little sun, his fatigues heavily starched and ironed. At that moment you could have crammed him into two dimensions and stuffed him right into the recruiting poster in front of your local PO. I mean he was spic-and-span, like he just stepped out of a bandbox. Trouble is, there never were any officers at reveille formation to see him. They usually didn't show up until eight o'clock Work Call. That left about two hours for Zwicker to get himself thoroughly freaked-up. And he would. The trouble was that Zwicker was our Mister Fixit. He claimed that he was a Jack-of-all-trades and could fix anything. It wasn't that people imposed on him: he really liked to fool around and try and fix things. In an outfit like ours there always seemed to be something that needed fixing first thing in the morning—a stove in the mess hall, a machine gun in the arms room that needed attention, a howitzer in the gun park or a vehicle in the motor pool that had to have a quick, dirty job done on it. Zwicker would volunteer or be drafted; and in an hour—half an hour—he'd look like he had just dropped off a passing freight train or maybe he had just been rolled. By Work Call he would have it, whatever it was, fixed up, but he would be a total wreck and he wouldn't have time to repair the damage on himself. Of course the Old Man always showed up at Work Call to look at his menagerie. And there he'd see Zwicker for the first time that day.

I'll never forget one time he came late, running from the motor pool, still trying to button up his fatigue jacket and tuck it in. His pants were torn, he was covered with grease and oil, shining with sweat, and he had lost his field cap somewhere. He fell into his place in ranks and stood there waiting to take it.

"Zwicker!" the Old Man yelled.

"Sir?"

"What the hell are you supposed to be?"

"*Sir?*"

"What are you today—a circus clown?"

(This was hitting pretty close to home. Zwicker was a natural all right, a clown without a circus tent or a false nose. I mean his big red nose was *real*.)

"No, sir."

"Well, let me guess. You wouldn't be trying to pretend you're a soldier, would you?"

"I ain't pretending nothing, sir."

"Who issued you that uniform, Zwicker, the Salvation Army?"

By now all the guys were half choked to death to keep from laughing. Zwicker was slowly shrinking like he was made out of wax and melting. He must have wished he could be a magician and could say a magic spell and just vanish.

"I woke up this morning with a smile on my face. I was thinking maybe one of these days we could make a corporal out of you. I mean, you being the oldest living Pfc. in the world, I figured I'd fox you and make you just another corporal. How would you like that?"

"I'd like that fine, sir."

"Let me tell you, Zwicker, I wouldn't dream of spoiling your record. You can stay a Pfc. forever. No, on second thought, if I was you I'd nail that one stripe on my arm or get it tattooed there. That's the only way you'll be able to keep it."

"Yes, sir."

Poor old ugly Zwicker.

But it was the tattoos I started to tell about. Zwicker used to be married, in fact he still was, legally. One fine day, or night as the case may be, his wife Clarissa ran off with a saxophone player from a big-name band that was passing through his home town. That was after Zwicker had paid four-fifty apiece the night before so that they, Zwicker and Clarissa, could dance half the night to the big-name band's music. That was mighty hard to take. Zwicker didn't even like to dance. Once you'd seen him try, you knew why. Like a donkey in Dutch wooden shoes. So, Zwicker got good and drunk for ten days and woke up in the Army. Sure, he could have gotten a divorce, but he wanted her back. While he was overseas she and some smart lawyer she got next to got together and worked out a separation. He got separated from her and she got his car, the house he had saved and almost paid for, and everything else including his civilian clothes. It isn't an unusual story, but it gives an idea about Zwicker and how and why he found a home in the U.S. Army.

Zwicker figured TRUST was going to mean trouble for him from the start. He took it for an ill omen when he accidentally dropped his duffel bag over the side of the troopship just as it was docking with a shiny honor guard lined up along the dock and a band playing "The Stars and Stripes Forever." That bulging duffel bag, with all his worldly goods stuffed into it, took a long slow lazy fall, end over end, hit between the ship and the pier with a big *splat,* floated a minute, then sank.

"My dumbbells!" they say Zwicker hollered. "If I hadn't of put them dumbbells in my bag it would've floated."

He got the idea of what kind of a command TRUST was going to be when not a man in the honor guard twitched, not a single musician skipped or missed a beat of the music when Zwicker's bag sailed over and hit the water. They didn't know, it could just as well have been a man.

"The hell with this place," Zwicker told Mullins, who came on the same ship with him. They were leaning over the rail watching the bubbles his sinking bag made. "I want to go home."

"Where would you go, Zwicker? You ain't got a home."

"Just anywhere," he said. "Anywhere but here."

So that's how he started off in TRUST, owning nothing but the ODs on his back. Of course he had to go out and buy all new uniforms with his own money. Which meant Zwicker didn't have enough left to buy a postage stamp with for the first few months.

"Don't bitch," everybody told him. "Who would you write to, anyway? Who do you know that can read?"

Next it was the teeth. They had a wild hair about teeth in
TRUST. They liked to yank them out right away if anything
was wrong with them. That wouldn't have been so bad by itself. Every command has got a wild hair about something,
and, like they say, you got to take the bitter with the sweet.
Trouble was, they couldn't *replace* them with false ones,
there. They had to send all the way to Germany for false
teeth. This usually took time, a couple of months, or more.
And some guys never got them. There was this spit-and-
polish command where show was everything, where all the
troops were slicked up like Miami bellhops or tin soldiers in
a box, with the most snaggledy, raggedy, gap-toothed bunch
of mouths in the world. Like I said, Zwicker was never a
thing of beauty, but with all his front teeth looking like
somebody had clipped him on the choppers with a rifle butt,
he was wild-looking, to say the nicest. Besides even Zwicker,
like everybody else in God's green creation, was a vain man.
He had the nerve to be proud of his appearance (though
you'd have to be Zwicker to even guess why), and it hurt his
feelings.

The tattoos. Almost every inch of Zwicker was covered
with tattoos. There were all kinds—anchors, hula dancers,
hearts and flowers, initials, a great big screaming eagle (that
looked more like a constipated rooster than the National
Bird) all the way across his chest, wing tips from nipple to
nipple. Each one of them stood for a broken romance. (Oh,
he was a *lover,* that boy.) He could get a girl all right, pro-
vided it was right after payday. She would take him for every
cent he had and he would go out and prove his undying de-
votion by getting a tattoo in her honor. He thought those
tattoos were kind of like the notches on a gunfighter's .44.
Each one of them was really a kind of a tombstone. I'll always
remember the shock of seeing Zwicker in the shower, dancing around in a cloud of steaming water, soaping himself and
singing like a crow with a sore throat. I remember one tattoo
on his leg that said "Laura Loves Zwicky Forever."

"Why do you do it?" I asked him one time. "Do you really like tattoos?"

"Hell no," he said. "Believe me, I really hate them. They're ugly to look at and it hurts to get one put on."

"It don't make any sense then."

"What do you mean saying something like that to me?" Zwicker angry was a sight to behold. "It makes plenty of sense. If I hate it so much, then it *proves* how much in love I am."

"Do any of them like tattoos?"

"No."

"Has it ever worked for you?"

"No," he said. "But it's always worth a try."

He got his last one just about the time that I joined the outfit. He still had this patch of smooth naked flesh on his left upper arm and everybody was betting on how soon it would get tattooed. One evening Zwicker showed up at the Poker Bar with a chick named Nivis. Now Nivis was a doll, officer's stuff, real Pure Food and Drug Act material. Nobody could figure out how he had done it. And she was all over him, smiling, laughing, even *listening* to him.

Next thing you know Zwicker put in for a thirty-day furlough and was off for Rome, Italy.

He was back in three days, drunk, dirty and broke. It seems like he had reenlisted for six more years and took all the bonus money (more than a thousand bucks in all) and Nivis off to Rome with him. They hadn't been in Rome twelve hours before she skipped out on him with all the loot. Well, all he could do was to roar like a backwoods preacher and stagger around the barracks. The guys decided they better put him into the shower to sober him up. They got him in the shower and then they saw it, the last available inch of Zwicker with a brand-new tattoo on it: *Io te amo, Nivis, con tutto il mio cuore.*

Zwicker cried like a baby.

"She was going to *marry* me."

"But you're already married, Zwicker."

"Never mind, she was going to," he said. "The thing that really hurts is she run out on me the very first time I turned my back on her. She run out *while I was having the tattoo put on*."

Somebody felt sorry for him and figured maybe he had salvaged something.

"Did you get any? Was it as good as it looks?"

Zwicker just shook his head, wet-eyed like an old cow.

"She was going to marry me, see?"

There were others in the pack. There was Mullins, who used to be a welterweight prizefighter and had been beaten up and knocked silly by some of the best fighters in the business. He looked more like a heavyweight now. He had about as much shape to him as a sack of Christmas mail. But better not mess with him. He could stand on a handkerchief and let you swing at him all day and you'd never touch him with anything but breeze. He could still hit too. I saw him crump three big kids from the Infantry one time in Opicina. He hired a fruit wagon and had the guy to wheel them all over the streets until the MPs picked them up.

There was Longman, the full-blooded Cherokee Indian who used to get in trouble because whenever he got good and drunk he liked to go around naked. And there was Fishbein, the clerk. How Fishbein ever fell in with a crew like us I'll never know. There were *some* nice kids in the outfit he could have buddied with. But whenever we went to the Hidden Bar or just sat around and played blackjack or poker he was always there, bug-eyed, amazed and staring, but one of the boys all the way, drink for drink. You might say he was completing his education. There is a lot they don't cover in college nowadays.

There was one woman that used to come to the Hidden Bar sometimes and end up drinking with us. That was Mrs. Higgins, called the Snake. She was a local girl from the village who had married a Private Higgins of the First Battalion. And they were still married, even if he was long gone years ago back to the States and she was still here. He made sure she got her allotment check every month, but he damn sure was never going to send for her. I don't blame him a damn bit. In the first place Mrs. Higgins was a kind of a nympho. She got her name, the Snake, because she not only had horizontal and vertical motions, but she had a shivery, all over, snakelike one too. Simultaneously. She was just a little too much for any one man to handle. I think something like a little less than three minutes was said to be the absolute world's record with the Snake. People hardly ever went out with her more than one time. It was too much for a man's pride and self-confidence. Once in a while if some new guy showed up, a stud who had the habit of bragging about how great he was, he would get sent down to the Snake for the Cure. Like a lamb to the slaughterhouse. She was always ready and willing, and probably hoping too that someday somebody would come along who could tame her. He would always come reeling back to reveille, all white in the face and around the eyes, trembly at the knees and fingertips. And he probably wouldn't mention the subject of sex for a month.

The funny thing about the Snake was, even if she wasn't what you'd call a raving beauty, she looked pretty and clean and sweet and innocent enough to take home to meet Mama. Which only goes to prove one more time that you can't tell what's in a package by the wrapping paper.

When we went to the Hidden Bar we went to drink. It's only the kids who can afford to mix their pleasures and vices all the time. None of us ever bothered her. Oh, we'd joke with her and so forth, but nobody tried to put the old make on her. She used to mock us and call us "the good old men." But in a way she liked it because she admitted that drinking was her one real pleasure. She could stay with us drink for drink. We made her an honorary sergeant in the Nth Field. That seemed to please her a lot.

We were all easy to please. We may not have been *happy,* whatever that was, but we were easy to please. And that's something.

7 THERE WERE only three people in the
whole outfit who really bugged me. I think that
must be close to an all-time record for peace
and goodwill among men. I know it stands as
the record for me.

And each of the three bugged me in a different way.

One was Lieutenant Costello, the battery executive officer.
Now the battery exec is the whip in an outfit, and he has
got to be a hard-nosed guy. He cracks the whip and the Old
Man takes the bows. But my trouble with Costello was personal. He was really down on me, all the time, right from
the first. He didn't trust me a nickel's worth. (I can't say I
blame him for that.) He kept studying me and studying me,
trying to figure ahead and guess when and where I would
foul up next. He was getting himself all coiled up for that
like a rattlesnake. When I made the false move or the dumb
play, he was going to pounce on me. You can feel a thing like
that.

I don't honestly know what the real trouble was. I've got

a theory for what it's worth, though. Lieutenant Costello's parents had come from Italy. I think for some reason he was ashamed of having an Italian name. He really rode herd on all the ones we had working around the *caserma*. He said he *understood* them, they were lazy and worthless and a bunch of crooks. He said if he didn't ride herd on them they would steal everything that wasn't nailed down and never get any work done.

One time he was invited to go over to Italy and visit the little village his folks had originally come from. He didn't want to lose any of his leave time, so he talked somebody down at TRUST headquarters into making it an official duty. He was put on TDY and ordered to go. He took a jeep instead of his own comfortable car and he asked Fishbein to come along as his driver.

"I can't drive worth a damn, Lieutenant," Fishbein told him. "You better get one of the boys from down at the motor pool."

"Come on," the lieutenant told him. "I'll do the driving as soon as we get out of the Territory. I just want some company."

Costello liked Fishbein because he was a college graduate. From Columbia in New York. Costello had got his degree in the Army by correspondence course. He figured he and Fishbein had something in common, being the only brains among all us barbarians. Fishbein *understood* him and what his problems were, but he didn't like him much. Still, he went along for the ride.

Costello went down into Italy to the village with a whole trailerload of junky gifts he picked up at the PX. He was all set to play the bigshot and show off. They let him do that all right, and they were grateful for everything he brought them. And for their part they knocked themselves out being nice to him. They had got flags and bunting somewhere and strung up the streets like for a fair. There were speeches and wine and music and feasts. Fishbein said it was a ball. The only trouble was that the people in the village, all his cousins and relatives, were so damn dirt-poor it made Costello ashamed of playing the bigshot. It made him ashamed of all the trouble they had gone to for him and ashamed, too, that his folks had ever come from such a grubby, crummy little place like that. And finally ashamed of himself for being ashamed of them. Feelings like that spread like a fever. The only trouble is that in the end, for a cure, it's somebody else who has to get hurt.

Fishbein said he cried and carried on all the way home and Fishbein had to do the driving. Costello made him promise not to tell anybody, but even Fishbein had been in the Army long enough to figure out for himself that promises to officers don't count.

Costello got started on me, I think, because he imagined he was some kind of a potential hero and he was pissed off they sent him to TRUST instead of to Korea, where there was still enough shooting going on so he could prove it. He had the wrong ideas about almost everything.

"Riche, how the hell did you ever get the DSC?"

He just up and asked me that, one time, out loud in front of the others. We were down at the motor pool, pulling maintenance on our trucks. He was standing around with his hands behind his back supervising, a dark good-looking little fart with a mean grin on his face. Like maybe he was just kidding. I had just climbed out from under a truck and was trying to brush some of the dirt off of me. That was the kind of a bum Costello was if he didn't like you, the kind to go and take a long look at your records and then bide his time and wait until he could bug you about it in front of everybody.

"Hell, they just *give* them away in Korea, sir. It don't seem like they much cared who they give them to."

"I'm asking you a serious question."

"Oh," I said, "excuse me. I thought you were just farting around."

He kept looking at me and grinning, but waiting for an answer.

"Well then," I said. "I reckon I better come up with some kind of a serious answer. The reason they give me the DSC was for consolation. The Old Man put me in for the Congressional, but I didn't make it."

"What did you *do?*"

"Killed me a bunch of gooks."

"Was it hard? Was it a lot of trouble?"

He must have been crazy, half out of his head that day, to keep going on like that. He kept looking at me with that dirty grin, his hands still behind his back, rocking back and forth slowly on his heels. He didn't have to say exactly what he was thinking. It was written all over his face—*You a hero? You grubby little private? You cheap bum?* He was quietly telling himself that there was no justice in this world, and in the same breath that maybe he was better off, maybe he could thank his lucky stars he wasn't a hero if he had to be like me to be one. His thinking was mixed up bad. I could have eased his mind for him. I could have told him all about heroes, enough to make him forget the whole idea. I could have told him the one thing that freaking medal meant to me was it helped me get away with more than I could have if I didn't have it. I could have told him how all so-called heroes I ever heard of came in all sizes and shapes and descriptions and how some of them got medals and most of them didn't get a damn thing but six feet of dirt. But I wouldn't tell him any of that, because one thing I hate is that kind of wise guy: a phony right down to his bones, where he probably has toothpaste instead of marrow. A phony with a little bit of two-bit power over other people. A man like Costello could spoil almost anything. I made up my mind to grin back and give him the same as he was giving me.

"No, sir, it turned out to be easy. It's as easy to kill a gook as anything else."

"That was another gook you killed on that homicide charge, wasn't it?"

"Lieutenant Costello, I do believe you've slipped around and done some checking up on me."

"I've seen your records, if that's what you mean."

"Maybe you didn't look close enough. Maybe you didn't read the fine print where it says I was acquitted."

"Yeah, you beat that charge anyway. That's one of them you beat."

"Shit, sir, you can't win 'em all."

By that time everybody all around us was just going through the motions of working. They were all listening. I figured as long as we had a fair-sized audience I might as well make the most out of it.

"You're a pretty cocky boy, Riche, aren't you? Pretty smart."

"No, sir, I wouldn't say cocky. I wouldn't say cocky, or smart either. But I wouldn't want to call you a liar."

"You better be careful, soldier."

"That's the word. Careful, that's just what I am. I tell you a man's got to be careful in the new Army. You can't hardly tell the shit from the peanut butter."

A couple of the guys busted out laughing out loud. And Costello didn't like that even a little bit. It woke him right up to where he was and what was going on. He got beef-red in the face and bit down on his lips. And then, even though he hadn't moved, you could almost see him jump back and crawl for cover behind his first lieutenant's silver bar.

"You better walk the chalk line, Riche," he said. "Because the day you don't, the day you step out of line, I'm going to run your bony, no-good ass down to the College on the double and let them give you a cure."

That is Lieutenant Costello, God rest his soul, in a nutshell.

• • •

68

Next there was my roommate, you might say: poor old Sergeant Jethroe. It wasn't a case of hard feelings, it was just that he was crazy. Jethroe had cracked up good. He was far gone. Because he was in the room all the time I had plenty of chances to talk to him. And I talked with him enough, I think, to figure out how he got his push and start on the bumpy, deep-rutted, well-traveled road to Loonyville. I think it had all started for him a long, long time ago in North Africa at the Kasserine Pass, the first time our troops really went into action against the Krauts in World War II.

Now, he had already been shot at by the Frogs during the landing, and he wasn't completely green. I guess the landing was a shock when they didn't expect the Frogs to shoot at them, but it was different. More like a dirty joke than a war. The guys who went in on the landing all had the American flag painted on their steel pots so the French wouldn't make a mistake and shoot them.

"Why they done that I will never know till my dying day," Jethroe used to say. "Them flags was a perfect target."

Some of the Frogs shot at them, some didn't. And it was all over in a few days.

Then later on at Kasserine it was for real. I don't know all the details and they don't matter much. I figure Jethroe got as far as thinking to himself: They're trying to kill me. Those bastards don't even know who I am and they're trying to kill me! . . . And about that time he froze up inside. This is how it goes. Most guys get beyond that idea if they're lucky enough to live through the first few days. If they are lucky enough to stay alive that long, then they're usually able to figure out that there's nothing *personal* about it. Every bullet and shell fragment is postmarked To Whom It May Concern. Even God shrugs His shoulders and you got to take your own chances. The just go down spitting blood right alongside the unjust. Now knowing that may be tough to take too. I mean nobody, not God, not the enemy whoever they may be, or even your own guys, is really interested in *you*. And, of course, all that you are interested in is yourself. It's scary, but once you get used to the idea it's not so bad. You are kind of free in a wild, breathless way. Like an old whore with nothing else left to lose—no cherry, no reputation, no beauty. You're free of responsibility if not worry. You get where one pair of dry socks is the most important thing in the whole universe. Where getting one kind of a C-ration can, say chicken, instead of another, is a victory. And—who knows?—maybe that's the whole truth, in combat or out of it. Maybe one pair of dry socks is the most sense one man all alone can ever make out of any of it.

Well, it was at the point of the first shock that Sergeant Jethroe got stuck on himself like a broken record. Maybe it didn't show. But it was there all the time ever after. He was one of the walking wounded. In every conversation we ever had he always got around to or back to the subject. When he started rambling on about it you could almost feel it like you were there yourself—fear like a dry dead leaf in your mouth; rocks, sand, no cover, too much sun; everything confused, freaked-up, crazy.

"In our battalion we were wearing neckties. *Neckties!* Would you believe it?"

Then with a sad look like a whipped dog: "It's a terrible thing to have to die with a necktie on."

That time was always on his mind and another time too when he really had cracked up. The second time was in the Bulge and naturally everybody was shook. That time the whole Army like to have cracked up. Jethroe was a Chief of Firing Battery then in some sorry outfit. They had been firing missions all night long and just at dawn six big Kraut Tiger tanks came busting out of a treeline and commenced to clobber the whole battery. They didn't have a chance and everybody who could bugged out. Jethroe was there, right in front, leading the pack, running like hell. Pretty soon the battery exec, young and green and fresh from the States, came running up alongside of him, trying to pass. For a minute or so it was kind of like a foot race. They were puffing and blowing and straining to pass each other.

"Goddamn you, Jethroe!" the lieutenant yelled. "What are you doing?"

"Running, sir. Running."

"Jethroe," the lieutenant said, putting on a burst of speed that left old Jethroe eating his dust. "You turn right around and get those tanks out of the area."

Poor old Jethroe—he had a huge respect for officers. He had more respect for officers than anybody else I ever knew. He wanted to believe *they* knew what the score was anyway. He couldn't even imagine that an officer might be wrong or scared or could make a mistake like anybody else.

"That lieutenant must have had *something* in mind. What do you think he wanted me to do? All I had to go up against them tanks was my carbine."

He had cracked up, but they were able to get him shaped up quick and he was back there being shot at in no time. It took him years to crack all the way from the core out. All those years he had been going through the motions.

The thing that finally got him was pretty funny. Jethroe was a very religious man. And he was married to somebody back in the States and tried to live clean overseas. Most evenings he would sit in his room and try to write scrawly letters home to his wife or else read his Bible. But deep down, like a lot of your real Biblethumpers, he was a real heller. It would build up in him and build up on him like a big hot head of steam. Finally he would just have to bust loose and go out on a tear—a rip-roaring, blind-drunk, swaggering, staggering bender. He pulled one of those in Trieste and ended up spending a whole three-day pass with some cheap whore. She took him for a month's pay and left him with a nice dose of VD. By the time he knew he had it he was cold sober, hung over and back on the job. He was too ashamed of himself to go and see the chap-lain and too afraid of what would happen if he went to the

71

medics. Most of all he was afraid that somehow his wife would find out. So he just sweated it out all alone for a while worrying himself sick and wondering what he ought to do. He tried to get some aid from a local quack doctor. That didn't help. In fact, after that treatment it got worse. By the time the medics finally did get ahold of him he had already blown his top out of shame and worry. They could cure the VD all right, and did. But there wasn't a whole lot they could do for his mind. He snapped and fell to pieces and dust inside.

So what? Jethroe was a good guy, a sweet guy without even one ounce of malice or guile in him. Even in his sickness, he didn't wish his harm on anybody else. All he ever did now was to lay around on his sack waiting for them to ship him home to a psycho hospital. He would either play his portable radio or read in his Bible. He loved that Bible and knew it well. He had a quotation from his Bible to apply to everything and everybody. And in his crazy, lunatic way he had every one of us (me and him too) down pat, right on the nailhead if you ever stopped a little while to think about it. Jethroe put me in mind of those old-time prophets. (I used to read the Good Book myself.) He had that madness, that simplemindedness that let God speak through him without old Jethroe having to worry too much about what He meant. The choices that God makes sometimes would astonish you! I remember an old Holy Roller preacher in my hometown who was as worthless a human being as you'd ever want to lay your eyes on. He had two big interests—money and women. And his whole life was just getting caught at it and being run from one town to another. If he hasn't been lynched by now, I guess he's at it yet. He was ignorant and dirty, a coward and a crook, but every time he climbed up in the pulpit to holler he would open his mouth and the Word of God came out like a white dove. Old folks and little children wept and he could almost have made a believer out of *me*. I guess he didn't even know what was happening, and it's no wonder he was restless between the times when the spirit moved him. But that's another story.

Jethroe didn't preach at me or anybody else. But every day he would leave a quotation from the Bible under my pillow for me to read. He would copy it out very carefully and slowly in his childish handwriting on cheap, lined tablet paper. Then he would fold it up small and hide it under my pillow where I was sure to find it. I tell you the truth, it really started to bug me. I'd catch myself wondering what words were waiting for me under my pillow.

One time I came in a little tight from the Hidden Bar and I woke Jethroe up and asked him to try and find a passage that would fit all of us, not just the outfit, not just the Army, but everybody, pigmies and giants, black and white, lame and whole, in the wide world. A big order. I was just drunk enough to want to know.

"Come on, Preacher," I told him. "Anybody can do individuals. Let's see if you know that Book well enough to dig up one that tells the whole story."

Jethroe looked at me, rubbing sleep and whatever crazy dreams he had out of his eyes, surprised. He didn't say anything. He lay back on his pillow for a minute and shut his eyes. I stood there thinking maybe he was just going to ignore me and go on back to sleep. But then he got up and put on the light and got his tablet and his ballpoint pen out of his footlocker. He opened his Bible, flipped through pages, found a passage and copied it down. The only sound in the room was the whispering of his pen and the two of us breathing. He folded the piece of paper and gave it to me. And I still keep it in my wallet to this day for some reason. It was a verse from Isaiah.

Therefore is judgment far from us, and justice shall not overtake us. We looked for light, and behold darkness: brightness, and we have walked in the dark.

Jethroe took his own special quotation out of the Book of

Matthew, the places where Jesus Christ and the disciples suddenly came on some madmen out in the lonesome hills. For old Jethroe it must have been a kind of a prayer.

> So the devils besought him, saying, If thou cast us out, suffer us to go away into the herd of swine.

I never really minded having to share the room with the old-timer. I have shared rooms and cells and sleeping space with worse. And I have been all by myself alone at times when I was mighty poor company for myself. Anyway I didn't hang around the room that much when I was off duty, not enough to let it give me a real crawling dose of the creeps. Even Jethroe wasn't all that special. This world is full of prophets, true ones and false ones and ones that are a little of both. And it's full of the walking wounded. Like one big aid station. I know that much. Still, I'm like the next guy. I don't like to be reminded of it all the time.

The third one in the outfit who bugged me was a no-good guy named Stitch, Corporal Stitch. Old Stitch had been around some and he was partly a member of our bunch. I say "partly" because he was with us only when we were playing blackjack or poker. Stitch was a certain type of hillbilly—a lean, tall, broad-shouldered, hard-looking guy. He had good-looking teeth, thick sandy hair, and eyes as cold as a glass marble. He was a kind of a small-time operator. He had his own car and a girl to shack up with in Opicina. They had a regular apartment. To pay for all of that he had to do business on the black market and to play in all the good card games and crap games we had in the outfit and other outfits too. He had to hustle so hard that I used to wonder if he ever really had any time to enjoy himself. Maybe he got his kicks just from the hustling. I've known people like that. Who knows?

As I say this Stitch character had been around some, not much and not as much as he let on and probably liked to believe he had, but some. And he was a thinker in his own crude way. When I came new in the outfit, first thing Stitch did was to snoop around and get a look at my records. When he saw what had happened to me in Japan and Germany, he figured I must be a real expert, a pro at the black market. With my talent and experience and his information on the local scene, he figured he just might move old Stitch out of the rut of small-time hustling and into the groove of the big. He got to thinking of how it would be if he didn't have to push himself so hard. He got to dreaming how it would be to be a really big operator. It was like he spent too much time in the movies when he was a kid.

He came sniffing around at first trying to see if I would throw in with him. I laughed him off. And that bugged him, pissed him off. He was the kind of a simpleminded character who can't stand to be laughed at. I can understand that, I'm that way myself. But it never did me any good to be so proud. After that whenever we would end up in the same poker game, he'd start in to needle me. Oh, he was a crude one all right. He must have thought if he played the part of the big-time operator around me and at the same time mocked me and knocked me down he could fake me into it. Buddy, he was wrong. I don't get faked that way. I'm not mocked that easy. Why the hell should I be vain about my crimes? Anyway, I've been mocked plenty before and it's no skin off my ass. By that time I was all scar tissue anyhow. Besides, anybody with a brain as big as a fist could see through somebody like Stitch in a minute. Guys like him are a dime a dozen. They're all the same. One of them is as good or bad as the next one. So, even if I did want to work at it again, why would I pick *him?* If I had been thinking about the black market I would have teamed up with somebody else.

This Stitch had a big mouth. He drank too much and he had a quick temper. One time we were playing poker and he pulled his knife on another guy in the outfit. Over a hand of cards. If he would do a think like that he would do whatever popped into his head. You never could tell what he might do if he got good and scared. When he pulled that knife and the blade popped open everybody at the table froze. I figured it was a good time to see who was boss. He was half standing, leaning over the table. I reached up and laid my hand on top of his, the one with the knife, very slow and soft, with no weight on it so he could barely feel the touch. That made him look at me.

"Put it away and sit down," I said as soft as I could like a whisper.

That bugged him. He looked at me and yelled who was I to tell him what to do and so forth and so on. I just kept telling him to sit down. When he had yelled himself out he had turned all his attention on me.

"What are you going to do about it?"

"If you don't sit down," I said in the same old nice-day-isn't-it tone, "I'm going to kill you."

While I was saying that I tightened my grip on his hand quick and forced it down to the table and the knife fell out. Old Stitch chickened. I had him there. I really had killed somebody and gotten away with it and he knew it from my records. He grinned and said he was only kidding. Sat down again and put the knife in his pocket and picked up his cards again.

"I knew you was just kidding," I said. "But I wasn't. I don't kid around."

That was rubbing it in, but anyway he knew who the boss was from then on.

Even so, Stitch wasn't the kind to take no for an answer, ever. He stayed after me like a leech or a horsefly or a puppy dog yapping at my heels. Just having him around bothered me some, but not enough to make me quit playing poker. I just used to grit my teeth like a grin and I tried not to pay him any mind.

There are always people around like that trying to spoil everything. "Little foxes," Jethroe called them, from the Bible. And I guess he was just about right.

PART THREE

Man and Woman

8 POKER WAS my doom and downfall if you want to put it that way. And Stitch, crude bastard that he was, ended up getting all that he wanted and more in the bargain. Whenever I feel like putting the blame on something I can always blame my good luck.

I had a long Saturday, a very long Saturday afternoon in May, payday, where everything seemed to go right. I walked right out of the pay line and got myself in a fast little game. I was just killing time. I couldn't have cared less whether I won or lost. I picked up the first hand and luck kissed me and called me her boy. I could feel it happening. I had been in many a card game before and once in a while I had had a streak of good luck. But only once on a troopship one time had anything like *that* happened to me. I hadn't been playing a half hour before I could feel the same thing coming over me. It must be a kind of craziness. You get taken over by a spirit, like a prophet. You can win with any hand you've got. For once you are among the touched, elected, chosen, blessed.

I don't have any clear memories of the day anymore. I doubt if I had many clear pictures while it was happening. Just smoky hours at one table or another, on the floor playing on a GI blanket, on footlockers, with faces all around me, all serious, worried faces, but none of them with any more to them then or now than the printed faces on a deck of cards. They were sweating faces. And there I was without sweating or worrying (I think I even had my collar buttoned, and my necktie—which we did wear on payday—pulled up tight without ever knowing it or bothering about it), drawing time after time to the good cards and raking in the cold cash in military scrip and *lire*. Before suppertime rolled around I had cleaned out all the serious card-players in the outfit. I emptied Stitch's pockets early, but he kept hanging around me to see how the game went and what would happen to his money. He had gambled enough in his day to be able to tell what was happening.

When everybody started to quit for chow—and because they were broke anyway—Stitch wanted me to go down with him to the Engineers' barracks near Opicina and try my luck there. He said there was always a lot of action there after payday. That's where the big games took place. By now most of the money would be in the hands of a few guys. They would have already done the dirty work for me. I wasn't feeling hungry and I knew I was still hot. So we got in his car and drove down there. I staked him so he could play, and I cleaned those guys at the Engineers' barracks like a string of fish too.

Around midnight it was all over and I had more money than I could use. Every pocket I had was puffed out of shape and bulging with paper money. I had my overseas cap crammed with it, all crisp and nice like the lettuce in an Italian salad. I didn't even have a place to put the loose coins in. Stitch borrowed a gas mask bag from somebody for the coins. Then I started to sweat a little. I knew I would have to come back soon and give the boys another chance at it. And I knew they would get most of it, maybe all and more too. That's the way luck runs. But already I was starting to itch all over with the feeling of having all that money with me. I was bound I was going out and spend some of it before I had to lose it back.

"I know some good places that are still open down in the city," Stitch said. "You let me bring my girl along and I'll drive you around in my car."

"Let's go."

We hopped in his car and drove over to pick up Stitch's shackjob. When we came in the apartment she was still sound asleep. She got up and threw a wrapper around herself and cussed us for making so much noise and waking her up. She stomped around, wild-haired and mad, until she saw all the money we had heaped up on the kitchen table. That took her down like a balloon with a pin stuck in it. She smiled and went soft and sweet like it was a bouquet of flowers or something. When Stitch told her we were going downtown and spend some of it living it up, she didn't make a sound, not a whimper or a groan. She went straight back into the bedroom and started getting herself ready to go.

She was a hard one, that girl. She was a Yugoslav refugee, small and well stacked and pretty enough when she got herself fixed up. But tough as an old corncob. She probably was a good lay, at least I hope so for Stitch's sake, but you can't keep at it *all* the time even if you're Tarzan. Stitch had to live with the girl too. Well, I guess they both had what the other one wanted and that was enough to keep them together. It looked like they deserved each other.

While she was fooling around getting herself dressed and fixed up Stitch and I sat down at the kitchen table and played with the money and passed a bottle of cognac he had back and forth. It was the first drink of anything I had taken all day, believe it or not. Some people can drink and play cards at the same time. Not me. If I get going in a serious game, especially if the cards start to fall good, I won't touch a drop.

For one thing gambling makes me kind of drunk anyway, all sort of breathless and set loose from myself. Then I've got to admit I'm superstitious about it. When my luck is going right with anything, not just cards, I feel like I've got to give myself up to that and nothing else. I owe luck that much. If I'm playing cards, then I concentrate on the cards. Any little thing else might spoil it.

At Stitch's shack I finally let myself go and drank enough so that I started to feel relaxed and good, kind of half sleepy and fine all over, like I had just finished having a woman or something.

Then she was all ready, everything in place, like she was made of metal and had been poured that way in some mold. We took off in the car like a crazy bat, racing down the long twisty downhill road from Opicina to Trieste in one big screechy rush with all the lights of the city blurring and blinking down there far below us. Something got the three of us laughing and we laughed like lunatics all the way down.

We started a round of the late-night clubs, the old clip-and-strip joints. It's a waste of time and energy to tell about them. They're all the same the world over—a hole in the wall, an attic or a cellar, hot and crowded with phonies, not enough light, too much noise and smoke, watered-down drinks, bored girls showing off sagging boobies and dirty navels to a lot of bored people, and some crummy jokes, not especially funny, made up out of the kind of crap people write on walls or in washrooms. And expensive, buddy: you pay right through the ass for that kind of fun. Still, I'd be telling you a flat-out lie if I didn't admit it seemed like some kind of a good time after being cooped up in the rocky hills for so long. I proceeded to get fairly smashed and enjoy myself. And Stitch and his broad seemed to be having themselves a ball. I reckon what with all the hustling he had to do just to keep her housed and fed and clothed the way she wanted to be, he didn't have much time or extra money to take her nightclubbing. And they could relax. It was my money they were spending. That poor jerk, Stitch! I don't see why he didn't pimp for her and let her do a little of the hustling. What a bitch she was. We hadn't been in the first place ten minutes when he had to take off for the latrine, leaving the two of us together at the table, and she looked me right in the eyes and said she liked me, a lucky man like me. Next thing I knew, still smiling sweetly and looking me right in my eyes, she had reached under the table and grabbed ahold of my crotch and was undoing the buttons right down my fly. I told her to keep her freaking hands to herself and let me alone. I told her she was wasting her time on me. That pissed her off plenty and I don't blame her. But I just don't like the idea of being at the beck and call of any woman who's got nerve enough to reach out and grab me by the short hair. I've been down that unhappy road before.

Finally they were closing the joints up and it looked like the end of the evening. But Stitch said he knew of a good place that stayed open until just before dawn. We didn't have to stand reveille on Sunday morning. His girl said it was too expensive and he kicked her under the table, bruising my shins too while he was at it, to remind her that it was my money we were spending and as long as I was picking up the check she better shut up. I thought what the hell, and said Let's go.

The Kit Kat Club, where they took me to spend my money, was a high-class clip joint, kind of like a private club. Mostly American officers and local businessmen were there, though I did notice a couple of ordinary GIs, the ones born with it I guess. You would never see a Limey, even an officer, in a joint like that. Either they didn't have the money or they had too much sense. It was just the way it should have been, soft phony leather seats and booths, dim lights and a rotating reflector on the ceiling that cast fake stars around the room. There was a lot of blue smoke and some pretty fair music for that part of the world. And everything was really expensive.

They had a good skinshow and a whole covey of B-girls to dance with and buy drinks for.

One thing I wasn't thinking about, when we walked in and slipped the headwaiter a big wad to get treated like somebody, was getting mixed up with any women. Especially B-girls. I took that grab in the crotch for a blessing in disguise, a sign and a warning. Women have always been a special weakness of mine and they have pretty near always led me the straightest and shortest route to trouble. All somebody has to do is ask my wife if they ever run into her. The bitch. She could tell a tale or two. Women have run me up and down more thorny paths than a few, and (I'll spare the grubby details) it was a *Fräulein,* a nice warm little puss with blonde hair and a sweet smile, that shoved me off, straight down the path that led to the stockade in Germany.

The thing is, when I have a real big weakness, and I'm lucky enough to know what it is and to be able to name it, I do my level best to avoid taking advantage of it. Lead me not into temptation. If thine eye offend thee etc.

No, that's not quite true. Not the whole truth anyway. Another part of it is that one weakness seems to breed another. I can't afford to have too many things I can't do without.

So, when we first came in the place, with the greasy headwaiter bowing and scraping us to a good table (once he clamped his hairy paw around that wad of *lire* I gave him), and the B-girls came trotting over and buzzing around, I shooed them away. I figured I would be content to sit at the table with Stitch and his girl, to keep on drinking myself silly, to listen to the music, look at the floor show when it came around and just soak it all up. Just let everything happen to me like laying in a warm tub. But Stitch's girl wasn't having much in the way of casual conversation and it didn't take too long before the two of them got tired of just sitting there with me. They wanted to dance and have themselves a good time. I didn't blame them. But when I am spending the money I hate for the people with me to be bored and at the same time I hate sitting alone and being bored all by myself, that's the definition of a drag.

Finally I made up my mind that as long as I could afford it I might as well pay for some professional company. A B-girl is a far cry from a geisha, but it's the same general idea, anyway. I got up and started to walk over to where the girls were sitting around together waiting for someone to come along and ask them to dance and buy them a drink. None of them would have won a beauty contest anywhere, especially at this late hour, but they weren't what you'd call dogs either. Just the usual. Any of them would do and after a couple of more drinks any one of them was going to look good.

Just as I came up to the table where they were sitting and they all looked up and flashed me the big phony smile, one more came in from a back room and sat down. She was a tall one (another weakness of mine) with black hair and skin the color of honey. She had beautiful eyes and a sad, hard, high-boned face. She looked so sad just for that moment that she was sitting down and didn't know that a soul was looking at her. Then when she saw me standing there and looking them over she was able to turn her whole face into one bright smiling mask that would have fooled the best man in the world. If I hadn't already seen her before she saw me first I could have believed the expression in her face. When she turned on the smile and the charm she looked like a devilish creature of joy straight out of a lazy sex dream.

I think it was seeing her both ways like that, true and false, that really grabbed me. Sometimes I am a sucker for the genuine. By the genuine I mean the way people act when nobody is watching and they're not trying to prove anything, not even for that minute at least trying to fool themselves. I remember one time seeing a fat old Mexican whore look at herself naked in the mirror when she didn't know anyone was looking. She looked at herself and then made the sign of the cross and knelt down by the bed and started to pray. I could have married the bag on the spot if my buddies hadn't been with me and started laughing and hollering and spoiled the whole thing.

About now somebody could take out the rule book and start adding up the points against me—luck, money, liquor, a woman equals trouble. True enough. That would add up and come out the right answer if I was simple enough. Trouble is, my big permanent Trouble, I'm not half as simple as I seem or would like to be. I can fool most people most of the time. It's a knack I've got. The thing is, though, like everybody else I spend a lot of that talent and energy fooling and foxing myself. Something happened to me all right when I saw that girl two ways, like in a double exposure. Exactly what it was I'm not sure. I don't have a name for it. Maybe somebody does, but it doesn't worry me a bit. A name helps sometimes. But a lot of the times when you've got a name for something you fool yourself into believing the name is the thing. And just because you don't have a label and a price tag for everything you feel doesn't mean you don't know what's going on. The old-timey preachers are right, anyway, when they claim that like the Bible says the sin begins in the eyes. You look and then you want, before you fall.

It wasn't love I felt then. I had never tried to fool myself with that crap. Funny thing is it wasn't the hots either. Or not purely. Not just the hots. Somebody might wonder about that. A man with a general weakness for women and fresh out of jail with some of the jailhouse color still on him and then being cooped up in a *caserma* up in the rocky hills . . .

I ought to try and explain. I guess I can get a hard on as quick as the next guy. In fact, quicker. And it had been a long, long time. But, as I've said before, my plan, my idea, is not to mix up my pleasures and my vices. One vice at a time, I say. If possible. Start mixing and you get trouble every time. Luck, money, liquor, women—trouble. I knew this. I knew it in my mind. But still, drunk or not, with my mind still clickety-clacketying along, I felt something for her, something close to love and lust at first sight. At sight I knew I wanted her, that one, and I was going to have her too. But in some way more than just sex. Why or what for, I couldn't even have guessed.

I asked her to come over to my table and have a drink with me.

"I'm too expensive," she said. "Very dear."

She spoke good English without any accent or, anyway, she spoke GI English with maybe just the ghost of a Limey accent. She looked me up and down with a cold eye and I suddenly remembered how grubby and out of place we must look in this place even if we did have plenty of money. That made me mad, to be looked over. I hadn't thought of that, what a whole afternoon and half a night of poker playing could do to a decent-looking soldier. Lucky there weren't any MPs around. If there had been they would have picked us up for sure.

"What do you drink that costs so much?"

"Champagne."

"You're liable to get drunk that way," I said. "They can't pour you cold tea and call it champagne."

"But I only like champagne."

That made me madder. All she was really doing was saying no. No, not with you, junior. It's almost as bad and nearly the same thing as having a whore say no to you. The B-girls weren't supposed to get tight even, let alone drunk. She told me she wanted to drink champagne to scare me away. Well, she didn't know just how lucky and rich I was that night. It was clear she took herself pretty seriously, too seriously to want to fool around with a private. And she must have figured at first sight that I had all the markings of a real stupid character. I made up my mind to fool her and make her go through with it.

"All right, champagne it is," I said. "Champagne is what we're drinking."

She made a face and sighed and got up. I took her over to

my table, called a waiter and told him to go get the biggest, most expensive bottle of champagne they had. I told him never mind about the little champagne glasses. Just bring a couple of tall highball glasses. I figured to make her swill the stuff like a pig. And I did that. I doubt that she had ever tasted much of the stuff before, and I kept on pouring it to her. She got tight in a hurry, flushed in the face and talked a lot. But even then, all loose-tongued, she wasn't really telling me anything. She never let herself get all the way out of control. I liked that. I like that in anybody. It made me think of a guy in the stockade in Germany. It was a fairly rough place and you had to tiptoe to keep from being hurt. This guy got tired of it all and walked right up to a bully of a guard and called him a dirty son-of-a-bitch. They got together and beat that guy into jelly. But lying there on the concrete floor, all bloody and racked with pain, he never let go of himself. When they were through with him and standing around and looking down at him like you'd look at a dog you had accidentally run over, he was able to say, "I still think you're a dirty son-of-a-bitch." Now, drunk or sober, triumphant or ashamed, that is exactly what she was telling me. And I had to admire her for it.

We tried dancing awhile, but that caused trouble. She let me know right away she didn't like the way I danced. I told her I knew I wasn't a dancer—I didn't ever get much practice at it for one thing, but I couldn't care less whether she liked it or not. She must have sniffed a weakness because she started to hunt for the source of it, the den. She was right. And it didn't take her too long to find a place to stick in the knife and give the blade a twist.

She started in on my haircut. I kept it cut very short then all the time with a white sidewall all the way around. Like a plucked and dressed chicken ready for the broiler.

"Why do you have your hair so short? I hate a man with short hair."

88

"I just don't like sitting in a barber chair. I go one time and get it over with."

She laughed and then pulled back to arm's length to look me over.

"You are too short, too small," she said. "It embarrasses me."

"It's just your heels are too high. You can't barely stand up on them, let alone dance."

"I never like short men," she said. "It makes me nervous to be with a little man."

She tossed her dark hair, pulled close to me again and laughed in my face. I knew the expression in my face had given me away. She knew she had found a raw, tender scab on me to fiddle with. And I knew it too and hated myself for being so weak that way and for showing it. I haven't admitted up to now just what my size was. I have to admit nobody would ever take me for a giant. In fact even that midget Costello has got me in height by a hair. Sure I'm vain about it. Who wouldn't be? Sure I get along with myself by ignoring it. I can take kidding from the guys. When they see I can take it they leave me alone. But women! I was still weak enough then to resent being kidded by a woman. Everybody understands how a thing like that works. You have to hate yourself for anything weak or silly or shameful somebody else notices about you. And if there happens to be some truth in it, it seems even more unjust and unfair than if they're guessing all wrong about you. Nobody can keep on hating himself and stand it very long without going out of his head. And the good thing is you don't have to. Not if there is somebody else within reach that you can heap some of that hate on. If everybody is up to it, busy doing it, then that makes Life into one big game of tag. The idea is not to be *it*. It's the oldest, simplest and hardest problem. Just like old Adam and Eve must have felt about each other as soon as they swallowed the juice of that apple. This same kind of hate can pass between a man and a man or a man and an animal or even a man and a thing like, say, a rock or a tree or a rifle. But it looks to me to happen easiest and most often between a man and a woman. That's what was really on my mind when I said I didn't believe in love. Because what usually happens is that two people start passing the buck, the burden of what they hate and like and envy and want and need in themselves, back and forth. It's like playing a game of catch with invisible hot coals. When both parties get burned as brown and crisp as bacon, they can always call it love. At least that's the way I looked at it then.

It always hurts me to be insulted and it hurt then. But it hurt me the worst to know that I still could be insulted so easy.

"It's all right," she was saying. "We can keep on dancing if you really want to. I don't mind that much."

"Let's sit down."

"No, if you'd like to dance with me . . ."

"We're going to sit down."

I told the waiter to bring us some more champagne. We kept on drinking and listening to the music and the drunken bullshit Stitch and his girl were talking. I guess it had turned out to be a real spree for Stitch's girl. I asked mine how much she charged, for a quickie and all night and what different things she would do for the money. I didn't ask her in a nice way.

"I'm not a whore!" she said. "No matter what you think."

"Okay, if you aren't a whore, what are you?"

I was pretending to be ignorant just to hurt her feelings. They have the same distinction all over Europe, maybe all over the world these days. B-girls and the regular shackjobs hate to be called whores. They have their own social scale. Wherever there are GIs stationed you can't get any lower on that scale than being a straight out-and-out, professional whore. Myself, I think the plain old whores are the only honest ones. But the girls make these fine distinctions. It's about all the pride they've got left.

She started to cry. I don't think she would have done that or let go of herself even that little bit except that she was drunk off of the champagne. It was mostly tears of stored-up anger, more fury than anything else, but anyhow now it was my turn to give the knife a twist.

"Don't cry," I said. "I believe you if you say so. What would it cost to shack up with you?"

"I have a good job here," she said. "I don't have to do things like that."

Stitch's girlfriend may have been pretty far gone, but she caught that answer and she didn't like it a bit. For a minute the two girls spat at each other in the local Triestine dialect, so fast we couldn't understand a word. Stitch shook his head and grinned at me like a silly goof.

"How much do you make here?" I said.

Now she could grin again. Instead of passing on some more insults I had come to her rescue. A regular Prince Charming. I wasn't so worried about her feelings though. The truth is I just didn't like the idea of Stitch's girl feeling so goddamn superior.

"Too much. Too much money for you or any other soldier to take me away from. It would take too much money to make me come and live with you."

"How much though? What can you make? Maybe at the most thirty or forty thousand *lire* a month, in a good month? Plus whatever you can get from a pickup now and then."

"At least I can pick and choose. I can choose who I go home with and whether I want to or not."

"Even with all that picking and choosing you couldn't make more than double that, say sixty thousand, in a real busy month."

"So I say you never can afford me."

"And so I say you've got a price. You're for sale just like the rest. And you know what? I'm going to buy you."

That idea, the foolishness of it, tickled her no end. She threw up both hands to laugh and knocked her glass right off the table. I looked down at the jagged pieces of broken glass while she laughed.

"Oh shortie, my little shortie, poor little soldier boy! Poor little private. I'm much too dear for you. I cost too much."

"You've been telling me that all along. Let's stop talking about it and you tell me just how much."

She shrugged and pouted and used her fingers to count with.

"First it would have to be a very nice apartment. I wouldn't want to live just anyplace. Then I would have to have nice new clothes and good things to eat and drink and I like to go out different places at night and have a good time. And I would need just as much as I make here for spending. Just to spend when I feel like it. You see I'm very, very expensive."

Stitch's girlfriend started to curse her in Triestine, but she wasn't paying any attention now and neither was I. Stitch must have been scared that I would get mad and not pay his part of the check or something because he grabbed his girl and dragged her out on the floor to dance, leaving the two of us face-to-face, smiling, or you might call it baring our teeth like a couple of dogs over a bone.

"Suppose," I said, "just suppose I was able to come up with all that and maybe more. Would it be worth it to me?"

"Ah! That would be up to you."

"What would you do for me?"

"I can cook good," she said. "I know how to keep a place clean and neat. I can do your GI laundry better than most. And I make love like nobody else in the world."

"Do you cheat? Do you play around?"

She frowned and looked hurt.

"If I am with one man I'm true to him," she said. "I do everything the right way. But there is one thing I do not do. I don't *care*. I never care. Nobody can ever make me care. When it's all finished there aren't any tears or hard words. It is just like another job for me."

• • •

Before they finally closed down the joint and pushed us out into the gray dawn of the street I had myself a kind of an option on the girl. I gave her a hundred dollars in military scrip. For nothing at all. Earnest money, you might call it. Just to sweeten up her disposition and keep her from shacking up with anybody else for a while now that I'd put a new bee in her bonnet. I knew it was more money than she probably ever had in her hands at one time. It was enough to give her the old itch too, to start the old crud and corruption working in her system. I also knew, even though I didn't care one way or the other, that there was some *reason* why she needed money, more than just taking care of herself, keeping a full belly and a roof over her head.

We took her home from the Kit Kat in Stitch's car. At least we drove her as far as we could, as far as the corner of the street she lived on. It was a block at the beginning of a crummy off-limits section of the town, an area of cheap cat houses and so forth, smelling of garbage and piss and the sweat and dirt of a lot of people living too close together. It was a slum section all right and right near it there were some old Roman ruins. Old ruins and the new ones look just alike to me, but they tell me that people used to come from far and near just to look at those old Roman ruins and poke around and take pictures. We stopped at the corner under a street-light to let her off. We sat in the car with the engine idling and watched her walk, drunk enough and very tired, along the cobblestone pavement. She looked sad and silly enough to laugh at, all dressed up in her fancy B-girl clothes, barely able to navigate the stones on her high heels, slump-shouldered with fatigue, out of place in that crummy stinking section of the city. She teetered on out of sight without looking back.

Stitch cleared his throat, hawked, and leaned out of the window to spit.

"You can do a lot better than that, man," he said. "She's not much. What does she think she's got, a mink-lined pussy? If you want a shackjob, if a good shack is what you're looking for . . ."

"She's no good," Stitch's girlfriend said. "I know her. She has a bad reputation. I have lots of friends who can give you a good time."

"What's her name?" I realized that in all that going-on I hadn't even asked the girl her name. Naturally she didn't know mine either.

"Angela," she said. "I don't know her last name. Maybe she doesn't have one."

"Angela? That's the one I want."

"You crazy, man?" Stitch said. "She looks like a bitch to me."

"Bitch she may be. She just may be a bitch, but I'll break her down to size."

"That's nutty," Stitch said. "You can get all the stuff you want for half the price and the trouble."

"Don't you worry about it, buddy. You've been bugging me ever since I came in this outfit about me coming into the black market with you. I know what you want. You want to taste some big money. You want to know the way some real money smells. Okay, all I got to know is, do you have guts enough?"

"Try me and find out."

"All right," I said. "That's just what I'm fixing to do."

He twisted around to shake hands with me, grinning and happy. Then we drove back up the mountain to Opicina in a hurry.

9 WE DIDN'T bother to sack out. We spent that Sunday morning sitting in Stitch's kitchen, drinking coffee and talking about the black market. Stitch's girl went to sleep until around noon. Then she got up and made us some *pasta*. We ate that and drank a bottle of red wine and started to feel a lot better. She sort of hung around, sulky and half-listening to what we were saying, wandering around the little apartment with nothing on but her pants and her bra like I was an old uncle or the family pet or maybe a fairy or something. And the bitch wasn't half bad if you like the type, lean and high-breasted and long-legged like a young mare. But I wasn't about to give her the pleasure of paying her any attention at all. Stitch, the jerk, was proud of her.

In the long run it might have been better if I had given her a tumble. A women like her can nurse a grudge as long as they say an elephant can.

Stitch was eager as a young puppy. But he didn't have too much good news for me. What it turned out was that all he was really doing besides gambling was hustling some cartons of PX cigarettes. Very small operation. No wonder he worked and worried so much! There seemed to be a certain amount of action of different kinds around. But most of it was pretty small-time. Except for a couple of things I didn't want any part of under any circumstances. A master sergeant who was running the main NCO Club had himself a little business producing dirty pictures. He sold them in the Territory and on both sides of the border. He even did his own photography, developing and printing in the empty rooms upstairs at the club. I wasn't interested in anything like that. If there's one thing they really sock you for it's the sex business. Sure, there's easy money in it and there's always a good steady demand everywhere, but the odds are all against you. When they catch you, you have had it. (When they finally caught up with him, he got twenty years in Leavenworth for his trouble. Which is a lot more time than I want to put in anywhere.) Then there was something else just as bad. The whole Territory was lousy with different political parties and groups. And they all wanted weapons. In case of riots. And there were some big riots several times too. There was a regular gang of guys who were in the business of supplying weapons, stolen from the Army or smuggled into the Territory. If there's anything that goes even harder on you than being caught in the sex business, it's selling out the old flag, the lives of your buddies and all that. I'm ready and willing to be crooked now and again to get what I want. But I'm not completely crazy.

Otherwise the place looked like green grass to me. A man hardly knew where to start. It wasn't sewed up tight like Germany or Japan where a new guy on the scene would have to be able to think up some fancy gimmick or maybe even a brand-new kind of market to get his share of the good gravy. Currency deals looked to be in the hands of local gangsters. Well, they could have that too. I didn't want to get mixed up or too deep in anything. Cigarettes would have been all right on a very large scale. There was money in cigarettes. And even the way Stitch was handling it, it could net a man more than sixty thousand *lire* a month. It was almost more trouble than it was worth, though, first having to collect a whole lot of loose cigarette stamps, then having to sweeten up a PX girl or two, then having to haul the stuff all around town and distribute it. I decided to throw in with Stitch in the cigarette business in a modest way and show him how to make the most out of it. But the big and easy and open chance I saw was in drugs and medicines. Nobody was pushing them for some reason. Stitch was even surprised when I asked him about that. He hadn't thought of it. I figured it would take all the poker loot I had left just to get the thing started.

"You better be careful," Stitch said. "Those guys down at Engineers play for keeps. And they want a chance to get their money back."

"Screw those guys. They lost, didn't they?"

"They ain't going to like it."

"Who cares what they like?"

"Man, you'll make yourself a lot of enemies that way."

"You gotta make enemies," I said. "It goes with the job."

Stitch shook his head and looked worried.

"And another thing."

"What's that?" he said.

"It's *we*. It's *us* from now on, old buddy. You have to have the guts for it or I won't even try."

He shrugged.

"Well? Have you got the guts or not?"

"Okay," he said. "You're the boss. Whatever you think."

"You aren't much of a poker player," I told him. "You won't miss out on a thing."

On Monday morning we were training in the field. Of course I had to have an excuse to get down to the hospital and look around. So the first thing I did when we got into the gun position and started to get the howitzer ready was to drop a trail spade on my foot. I hollered and fell down, holding my foot, and everybody came running. Stitch turned white as a ghost and like to have fainted when he saw what had happened and saw me lying there in the grass. I guess it hurt him worse than it hurt me. I almost busted out laughing right then and there. That boy had a lot to learn.

They took me down to the main hospital to get my foot X-rayed and see if it was broken or not. Lucky for me it wasn't. They gave me some therapy in the whirlpool bath and they let me hang around the hospital for a couple of days on crutches, until my foot was good enough for duty with an Ace bandage on it. During that time I found myself a man who would do just fine. Medics are always available anyway. I never met one yet that was worth a damn. What I found was a fairy, a fag. (There are plenty of those in the medics.) This one was a sketch. He had long fingernails almost like a woman and he wore a tiny gold earring in one ear. There was a club of guys who did that in Korea. I don't know what they called themselves, but we called them the Daisy Chain. I waved the wad of money in his face and he got interested in a hurry. I paid him off and he agreed to get what medicines and drugs he could for me.

The plan was that whenever he had a batch he would leave a message for Stitch at this bar near the hospital. Stitch would go to the bar later and meet the medic and pick up the stuff. Then he would take the stuff down to a greasy slob named Pissoni, who owned the Kit Kat Club. That was a nice night-club and I figured that the man who owned it *had* to be a crook. I was right. Pissoni sold a little bit of everything. He would act as a kind of wholesale distributor for us, passing out medicines to the local doctors and any drugs that were narcotics to the local hoods.

I handled it all very careful. I never saw the medic after I set it up. I let Stitch go and see Pissoni and do all the talking after I had rehearsed him over and over. When everything was ready for the first time I watched how it went without being in it. First I went to the bar near the hospital. I had a beer. The medic was there drinking coffee. We passed right next to each other without even looking. Stitch came in after a few minutes and made a phone call. While he was calling the medic paid up and got out. Then Stitch went out and got in his car. There was a little alley less than a block away where the medic would leave the stuff in a laundry bag. Stitch would be right behind him to pick it up. As soon as Stitch strolled out of the bar (we *did* say hello because if there had been a CID man there just by chance he would notice that we were both from the Nth Field), I left in the other direction and took a cab to the Kit Kat. On the way down, alone in the cab, I had the good feeling that comes from something risky going well. But, I'll have to admit, I had another feeling too. I got to thinking about what would happen to those drugs. Somebody needed them—kids, old people, sick people. I would make mine, Pissoni would make his, the doctors would make theirs. And the people who needed them would get drugs, or watered-down drugs, and pay the price for the whole system. I didn't *like* it. Still, that's the way the system works, I told myself. Supply and demand. If it wasn't me it would be somebody else. If it wasn't anybody, well there wouldn't be any drugs at all. Before we got down to the Kit Kat I had myself convinced I was doing a freaking public service. I can rationalize as well as the next guy.

From the first operation the money was very good, better than I had expected, and it was coming in quick. Since nobody had been fooling around with that kind of black market, the hospital was pretty casual, and my medic didn't have any trouble stealing. And the local people were starving for whatever we could give them. At top prices. Naturally everybody was making something out of it too. I guess nobody lost out at all except the American taxpayers who paid for the stuff, and the sick people and addicts in Trieste. They always lose out anyway.

It wasn't quite as big a deal for me as it might have been if

I had cut Stitch and Pissoni out and handled it directly myself. But I wanted Stitch to do the hauling and the dirty work. And Pissoni had the contacts. I was in too big of a hurry to waste a lot of time trying to build up a trade on my own. The truth is, with this system I had plenty of money, more money than I could use or burn, coming in fairly regular. And all of it without having to get my own hands too dirty with anything but the money. That's what you call operating. The thing I had learned from the past was not to get too greedy. Just to take what I thought I wanted. Only two people could really get me nailed to the cross again—Stitch and the medic. The medic was queer as a dodo bird, so I wasn't much worried about him. Fairies think different than other people. They are a different breed. Of course they can't be trusted for one minute with anything that really matters. The only thing that really matters to them is their own skin. But, you've got to remember, they start out on a bad spot, a dirty kind of a boxed-in corner. The way things are set up they have a lot to lose. That gives you one kind of a hold when you have to deal with one. Then, as I said, you can always count on the fact that they want to save their own skins. They will sell out almost anything to save that precious hide. I mean that in a literal way. If this character with the fingernails and the little gold earring ever crossed me in any way his skin was going up on some wall like an animal hide salted and tacked up and stretched out to dry. I made sure that he understood that and knew exactly what all the risks were before we even got started. Of course he liked the easy money, but my own guess is he was in it for the thrill of it as much as anything else.

That left Stitch. Stitch was something else again. He was tough enough and hardworking, but stupid and maybe dangerous. If he ever got to thinking for himself and made the wrong move, he could spoil everything. Well, I would just have to take some chances on him. I calculated that all the

good money coming in for so little effort would be such a
surprise and a change that it would soften him up for a while.
For a while at least Stitch would do everything I told him to
do and the way that I wanted it. I promised myself that before he had time to get really greedy and spoil things I would
wash my hands of it and be shed of the whole grubby business. Then Stitch could go and hang himself if he wanted to.
I couldn't care less.

About now a voice like the old voice of Conscience says:
"Riche, you are no damn good. You are a lowdown crook,
a cheap, vicious little punk!" That's probably the voice of Elwood Goodhart, my old high school principal, with the bald
head and the thick eyeglasses and the rubber hose he loved so
much to lay across me bare.

"You're trash," the voice says.

There is another one, Miss Eversoe, my old civics teacher.
She was going to make something out of me when I was
fourteen. She had read too many books.

I can hear her asking: "How did it really happen, Johnny?
Why did you do a thing like that? What did you ever expect
to get out of it?"

I can take the rubber hose and the insults better than that.
I hate to be asked why. Never ask me why. If I know I won't
keep it a secret. But it's a fair enough question in this case and
deserves some kind of answer. Let's see what I can come up
with.

Let's take it back, Miss Eversoe, and say I came down from
the stockade in Germany way down, beat, crawling on all
fours, slinking along with my tail between my legs like a
whipped dog. No matter what my attitude was or what it
looked like to other people, that's the way it really was. And
I knew it at the time. Then I found myself in a decent outfit
with a decent bunch of guys, a place where I could soldier
and be left alone. The only smart thing for me to do then was
to keep my nose and hands clean and to let well enough
alone. If I could have just cooled it for a sufficient length of

time, I might even have made corporal or sergeant again. I would have gotten one foot anyway out of the grave I had been so busy digging for myself. Then I got that potful of good luck dumped in my lap. I wasn't ready for it. Luck and money and women all mixed up together like a pot of stew. You have a taste and then you've got to get some more. At least I do. You're like a drunk falling off the wagon. You've got yourself squirming on a hook and pulling on a line. In the end it always turns out you are the fish and the fisherman too with his reel.

So it happened this way. I got drunk on the luck. Right on the crest of my foolishness, the bitch hurt my feelings. No, she did more than that. She reminded me in the most simple and direct way what the truth about me was. In her eyes, like a pair of tiny little mirrors, I got a good look at myself. Just like a grinning jackass. Or more like the head of a man with the ears of a jackass. All I wanted to do, I kept telling myself, was to pay her back. To pay the whole wide world back through her. In kind. I was bound I was going to humiliate her. Oh, not just buying her like you might an apple or a tube of toothpaste. Not just getting her to shack up with me. That would be a simple business matter. You can't really hurt or humiliate anybody by buying and selling them. She called it just another job and she was right. Before I was done with her—and I guess I hoped it wouldn't take too much time—I was going to make her *care*. For the first time in her life if she never had cared before. Again if she had. Before I was through I would make her think she loved me.

"Easier said than done," the old voice says.

All I can say is that it's a lot easier than most people would think. I knew it could be done from hard experience. She might be tough all right, but somewhere she would be brittle enough to break and fall down in little pieces. Like an idol to worship and a victim to sacrifice at the same time. Like a shrine and a latrine in the same place. Like the strange gods old King Solomon fell down and worshiped when he just couldn't stand himself or even the thought of God any more. And they say King Solomon was a wise man. Wiser than most before or since. Still, wise or not, he had to go down and chew the bitter grass and howl like all the rest of us.

10 THAT WAS the first Saturday in May, right around the time of the May Day parades and riots, when I won all the money at poker. The next couple of weeks were kind of confused, what with my hurt foot and setting up the business and the whole Territory going off and on alerts because of the riot scares and us having to pull all kinds of extra guard duty and so forth.

Once during that time a very funny thing happened to the outfit. It was our day as the alert company (I guess they didn't expect anything to happen *that* day). We had to hang around the battery area in full parade uniform just waiting. Something got going downtown in one of the big squares and they blew the whistle. We loaded up on the trucks and went down there fast. When we got there thousands of people were milling around, shouting and screaming and carrying on about something. Some of them had knives and clubs and rocks and some of them, I guess, had small arms. When we got off the trucks and formed up and the people saw our red guidon and knew which outfit it was, they changed.

They stopped screaming bloody murder and started yelling and cheering. The cheap whores who hung around the Poker Bar started calling out to us by name. Some of the guys started laughing too and yelling back at them. The riot was over pretty quick. The only real bad trouble the Army had that day was trying to round *us* up again to go back up in the hills to the *caserma*. It must have taken a couple of hours to smoke all our guys out who had jumped off the trucks in all the confusion and made a beeline for the first bar or *trattoria* they could find. A couple of old rummies were dead drunk. Local characters carried them back along with their rifles and all their gear and loaded them onto the trucks.

All that was going on in May, and I was still limping a little on my foot. It wasn't ten days later before I went down to the bar near the hospital to oversee the first milk run of my new business. A month later I wasn't limping anymore, though the foot was still game and I had to favor it a little, and I was all snugly shacked up in a nice little apartment with Angela. The business was doing just fine. And all I had to do now was to sit back on my duff and collect a lion's share of the take just for thinking it up and getting it started in the first place. Once everything was settled it looked like I had it made. A pig in clover. I would put in a day's work at the *caserma,* five to five, can see to can't, then pick up my pass (if I didn't have some kind of extra duty like guard to pull) and cruise on home to my shack. I even bought myself a beat-up, secondhand heap from a guy in the Recon to do my cruising with.

I had found a really good little apartment in Opicina overlooking the city and the bay. It was well furnished with a lot of that phony modern Italian stuff. If you happen to like it. I couldn't care less about furniture. It was sunny and airy. There was a great big bedroom—the main thing—a balcony and a kitchen. We shared a bathroom with the landlord who lived downstairs. And we had a great roof. In the daytime, if

I was ever home, like on a Sunday, we could sit up there and sunbathe. At night we could lay on a blanket and look at the stars or stand up and see way below us the lights of the city winking and blinking.

Angela had never known anything as nice as that apartment before. Except maybe what she might have seen in the movies. And I filled it up with good things for her. A portable radio, a record player with three speeds and a whole stack of the latest records from the main PX. I gave her a good gold watch and a German camera. I bought her clothes. I found out she was crazy about all kinds of plants and flowers, so I filled the whole place with them for her. It got to be like a big garden or some goddamn jungle. I bought her a canary in a pretty cage from a pet shop. I knew that even if she had a high opinion of herself and put a high price on herself, she couldn't ever have had many things of her own. Probably the one decent thing she owned—and I was right about that—was the fancy dress she had worn to work every night at the Kit Kat. When she wanted money I gave it to her.

I don't know why I did all that. I kept telling myself the idea was to soften her up, to break her down. But I wasn't stupid enough to expect that a little taste of luxury would really break her heart or even weaken her willpower. She was too tough for anything like that. And she wasn't stupid, not a little bit. I guess I must have figured that a mild dose of good living would give her a taste for it. The most that would do would be to make her life more complicated than it had been. And that would give me an edge. Oh, when I got good and ready I would pull out the rug from under her and she'd go all in pieces like Humpty Dumpty. Sure.

That's what I was telling myself. But I knew, even as I was busy trying to convince myself of the opposite, that she was as tough or maybe tougher than I was. One of the things that goes along with being tough is the feeling that you can take things or leave them alone. Sure, you ride in style whenever you can. But you walk without bitching if you have to. And

106

to tell some more of the truth, if not the whole truth and nothing but it, it gave me some kind of boot to give her things. I liked to come home loaded with stuff for her. These things were like a strange kind of offering I guess. Offered half in love, half in hate. Half in fear and half in contempt.

Whenever I was with Angela—except in the bed—I was pretty much what you'd call a model character. A little boy scout shacking up. Polite, kind, thoughtful, true, obedient, cheerful, reverent, and so forth. Ready at the wink of an eye or the raising of an eyebrow to give her anything she thought she wanted and to give in to her on everything. In the best American way. When you act that way, you couldn't mix up a foreign girl more. You might just as well pick up a whole fistful of dirt and throw it in her eyes. They don't know how to act with a man who acts like that. It doesn't give the woman anything to get a grip or a purchase on. Well, old Angela was all woman, one hundred freaking percent. So naturally from time to time she was forced to try various old-fashioned tricks to cut me down to size or at least fit me into a shape she could understand from her own experiences. Sometimes she would needle me and try her damnedest to make me mad. Or, shoe on the other foot, she might all of a sudden blow up into a rage over nothing at all. She would get to laughing for no reason. Or there were tears and tears. Or pretended jealousy. Or trying to make *me* jealous. Everybody knows how it goes.

No matter what kind of tricks she tried, no matter what she said or did, I just took it. I was able to keep on acting the same way all the time. A regular choirboy. It was an easy thing to do, I told myself. Because the thing was that none of it was for real. I was just playing the part and I didn't care.

What could she do against all that?

She kept her part of the bargain. She did everything she had said she would. She cooked for me. Wonderful suppers in the evening. Lord, she could cook! Nothing fancy, just *zuppa, pasta, vitello, insalata* and maybe a *dolce,* all good solid plain Guinea food. But wonderfully cooked. I got to where I skipped noon chow at the outfit just to have the right kind of appetite for supper. She did every bit of my laundry, by hand and in a tin washtub, and better than it was ever done before, even in stateside laundries. You would have thought my cruddy undershorts were fine linen handkerchiefs, the kind of care she took with them. That even embarrassed me a little. I don't know why, but it did at first. She kept the apartment neat and clean and spotless. And everything, every single solitary little item, had its right place to be and was supposed to stay there. I used to move something every once in a while just to see if she'd notice. She would never say anything, but when I got home again next time whatever it was would be right back where it belonged. There are only certain types of people who keep things like that. Soldiers, because they have the habit and learn to travel light and make things last. Real professional whores, maybe for the same reason. People who get their lives all screwed up and confused make a big thing out of neatness. They have to keep everything just so, to keep from feeling the whole world's falling apart. Or people like Angela. Somebody like Angela who has never had many things before. More like she was the caretaker than the owner. If you have been beat-up and pushed around enough, not just a little bit and not too much, you're never foolish enough to figure you *own* anything anyway.

Angela joked and laughed and danced with me. We danced to our own records or at one of the places downtown. She taught me a lot about dancing that I had never had a chance to learn. And she was as patient as could be about it. Sometimes we sat around and played cards together or with some other shacked-up couple. Never with Stitch and his girl, though. The two women hated each other. And I wanted to keep Stitch in a strictly business way, no buddy-buddy stuff.

The bed was the real battleground, though. All the rest was just passing the time. It's in bed that a man and a woman really get to know each other and themselves. And win or lose.

In the bed she was about as good as she claimed to be. That surprised me plenty. I always thought even the best and the hottest of them held back something when it was a matter of dollars and cents. Even a wife. In my sad case especially a wife. And you can tell it. A good whore, a real good experienced smooth one, sure of herself, can fool you into thinking while it's happening that maybe she's enjoying herself. At least you can appreciate the skill and the effort. But gradually I have gotten very sensitive and alert to all kinds of phoniness. I've developed a good ear for listening to heartbeats like a doctor's stethoscope. I am always ready to be fooled, on my toes. Strange as it seems, I think Angela really enjoyed every minute of it. And without having to fool herself to do it or slack off on that tight grip of self-control she had. What I mean is that she was able in some way to treat all the different parts of her life and experience like she kept the things in our apartment: each in its right place. She was on top of things and herself. She was able in some way to keep things pure and separate, and she wasn't always troubling herself by mixing up the different parts of herself the way most people have to do. In that way she was able to be good to herself when she had a chance. And without being ashamed.

It's the God's truth. It mixed me up more than a little at first. She was so matter of fact, so casual about it. And still that didn't spoil anything. Most women, if they happen to be casual about going to bed with you, can wilt you like a dying flower. I'd just as soon go to bed with a cold codfish as one of those. Every other good lay I had ever had used to have to fool herself and play the part a little too, to try and fool me, to make it all work right. With most of them you have to pretend something, even if it's just pretending to be in a certain mood. Some women have to be raped every time. Some have to have dirty pictures or jokes or stories to get in the right mood.

Not Angela. The first time I took her to Opicina to see the shack it was in the early evening, a warm summer evening. She took a good look all around, suspicious, just like a GI white-glove inspection. Looked at and under everything. Tried all the light switches and faucets and door handles. Then she sat down on the bed, bounced on it to try the springs and mattress, and said she liked everything fine and thought she would stay. I thought most likely she would want to go back down to her old place and pick up whatever stuff she had there and maybe move into the shack the next day. So I was surprised when she turned back the covers on the bed and made it up. She pulled the blinds to and took off her clothes. She hung up her dress in the wardrobe and folded her underwear neatly on a chair. I didn't know what I was supposed to do while all that was going on or what I was going to do next, so I sat down in a chair and smoked a cigarette, leaning back against the wall and watching her. She acted as if she didn't notice me or had forgotten I was there. When she was all ready she lay down on the bed and smiled at me.

"You paid the rent for the whole month, didn't you?" she said. "Why waste money and time too?"

I thought to myself: *Uh-oh, she's a businesswoman, she's going to turn out to be one of those cold machines, just like a regular mechanical rabbit at the greyhound races.*

I was far wrong about that.

Angela had a wonderful body, edging toward fat and spread here and there. That would come along later. And she wasn't exactly a young girl any more. But just then anyway, for the time being, she was all at the full bloom of ripeness, like an apple on a tree just about to fall, and everything I could have imagined or wanted. She was smooth and round and soft to touch and she had a kind of fine musty animal smell too. Every woman smells different, perfume or no. And when I get thinking about the subject of women, that's the first way I remember them, the good ones, the bad ones, the ordinary ones. Angela knew how to use her good body well and she seemed to like to use it that way. So did I like it, I'm afraid. Maybe too much. I knew I was going to have to watch myself, to be careful not to like it and need her too much.

"Where have you been?" she said, laughing, after the first time. "In jail? In a monastery?"

I said that's exactly where I had been—in jail.

And she seemed to think that was very funny. She lay back on her pillow and laughed at that idea until the tears filled her eyes. And she gave herself to me as many times as I could handle her that night and ever after.

I knew right away where this might lead me. It did, too. It led me to being weak in the knees and trembly at reveille. It led me on to getting myself all worked up and roused as early as three o'clock in the afternoon just knowing that pretty soon I would be on my way home to that stuff. Watching the clock all the time. It led to me getting mad as hell if my name came up on the guard roster or I had to stay around the *caserma* late and pull some kind of extra duty.

Mooney noticed what was happening to me right away. He was a great chief of firing battery and would notice a thing like that in one of his men right away. He noticed and knew all the things he ought to without even asking or having to work at it. Like what foods a man liked and didn't like and how a man acted in different kinds of weather. What a man was afraid of, what he could do and couldn't. When a man might blow his top and when he could keep going, grinning, until he dropped over.

"Riche, what ails you?"

"Nothing, Sergeant. I'm doing fine."

"The hell you are," he said. "I know what's wrong with you. You've been catting around too much."

"So what? It's on my own time."

"You been around the Army long enough to know you

can't cat around and soldier too. Are you trying to be a soldier or a stud?"

"I'm still RA if that's what you mean."

"I don't give a damn what kind of serial number you got. You got to make up your mind, boy, that's all."

"I'm just getting myself a little," I said. "It ain't like a permanent thing. After all, I was six months in the freaking stockade."

"Well, you should've learned you can do without it."

"I can take it or leave it," I said. "But I don't like to do without something unless I have to."

"Well, that's your way," he said. "But you watch yourself. Be careful. Don't foul up."

Mooney, he knew all right and was trying to hang on to me or to get me to hang on to myself before it was too late for anything. He knew I couldn't get a furlough because of all my bad time, but he offered to get me put on TDY to Germany, to go to some artillery school. He could have sent me off there without offering or asking. He didn't work that way. I respected him for it and he knew all that. But soldiering or not, hell or high water, I would never be like Mooney or Ryder or any of the good old guys. I could soldier, but I wasn't a true believer like them. It wasn't enough for me. Mooney was like a priest or a monk in the Army. So was Ryder. Mooney was dedicated to the howitzers and the firing battery. To do it right he couldn't allow himself ever to have to make the choice between one thing and another. He had to be a soldier all the way. And he was right about that. If you are really going to soldier you can't let yourself take women or liquor or anything else too serious. You are fooling yourself if you think you can, with only thirty full days off in a year. You have got to keep your vices on a quickie basis for the rest of your life.

The thing was, though, it was almost too late for me. I had let myself get a good case of the shakes over this woman.

That wasn't what I had had in mind at all. I hadn't planned

on that. What I still thought I was thinking of, the so-called reason for all this, was to shame her in some way. And I must have been thinking that if I shamed her enough it would purge and purify me. I've got to admit I tried to shame her that way too, in the bed. I let myself go and tried everything I could think of to shame her, everything in the book, peeled off the cruddy wallpaper of my brain for dirty pictures, turned loose a whole zoo full of wild crazy thoughts. Anything that popped into my head. Jailhouse daydreams and night thoughts turned into facts of skin and bone, given bodies and brought to life. Like monsters. I remember it in the dark. I remember it with all the lights on and both our shadows huge on the walls and ceiling like fighting animals locked in a death struggle. I remember once seeing myself, my face, in the mirror, frantic and furious, all out of shape and proportion, the way you find your reflection in the funhouse at a carnival. I remember that those summer nights our two bodies were so sweaty and slick and gasping for air, we were like a couple of fresh-caught fish in a creel. It was more like war than love. It was like old Jacob wrestling the angel in the starry dark.

It took me a little while to realize that my mortal combat was with myself. She fooled me there too. She nursed me like a sick man with a fever. She didn't just give in or bear with my monkey whims and notions. And I never could shame her. She was rock and I was just breaking myself over and on her like a wave. Angela would not be soiled that easy.

I even went as far as to talk with her about it. Talk is the final form of shame, the way I look at it. She took that too and I began to get at the truth about her: that, as crazy as I might be or might get, I could never invent anything that she hadn't known before. And the really strange thing was that learning that about her didn't spoil anything for me. I just learned that I couldn't hurt and humiliate her in any way. The only one likely to get hurt was me. Like the lady about to be raped, my slickest move was just to lay back and enjoy it. In a short time all my anger and fury was just gone.

As soon as we got a sort of routine living going it would be like this. Usually I would get home right after five and she would be waiting at the door or sitting on the steps for me. We might drink some beer or some *vino* at home or at a little bar nearby. Or we might go straight to bed, throwing our clothes behind us. Later on we would have a long, lingering supper and drink some cognac with our coffee. At first, for the first few weeks, we used to go out a good deal to the movies or one of the nightclubs. A little later going out only meant going together hand in hand to walk the streets of the city and window-shop. Or maybe to sit and nurse a coffee at one of the sidewalk cafés, or in the Via Settembre, where the tables were in the street and there were lots of green trees and people strolled. Before very long it was mostly staying at home, maybe playing cards for fun or dancing. Sometimes we just lay side by side in the bed and talked and smoked. By the end of July she wasn't even asking me to take her out anymore. The honeymoon, crazy as it was, was over. And we were like a married couple.

I had to get up at four in the morning to get back to the *caserma* in time to sign in, change into fatigues and stand reveille formation. Angela was always up before I was. My razor and shaving soap and lotion and a towel would be laid out for me neatly, waiting. There would be a basin of hot water steaming, and coffee would be ready. I was always slow shaving and I'd have to drink my coffee too hot so it lay in the pit of my stomach like a round hot ball of fire. And then I'd be running down the stairs and outside into the first light of the summer dawn. The last thing I'd see as I drove away in my heap every morning would be Angela leaning from the window, sleepy-eyed, her dark hair all a tangled mess, but still beautiful, to call "*Ciao*" very softly and wave good-by until I turned the corner and was out of sight. Then she would be waiting for me, watching for me out of that window when I turned my car into the little dirt trail of a street that ran past our house and came home.

Already I've used the word "home" several times to describe my shack. In a short time that's what it had become—my home. I remember when it first dawned on me what was happening to me and what had already happened. I was driving fast along the twisty old road out to the *caserma*. It was early morning and a thick dew was on the rocky fields. I passed through a couple of dusty little villages scaring some chickens in one. And suddenly I just knew what had happened to me. In spite of myself. And I didn't mind. I stepped on the gas and whistled to myself.

I left my car in the parking lot and ran all the way to the barracks, signed in at the orderly room, and sprinted up the stairs to my room. I opened the door and came in still whistling, feeling ready to dance. Old Jethroe was already wide awake. He had his clothes on and his boots too and his bed was made up. He lay on top of the made-up bed and stared at the ceiling.

"Jethroe, you crazy old coot!" I yelled at him. "What does it say in that good black Bible of yours about a beautiful woman? What is the best thing you can find for a beautiful woman?"

He sighed, but he took up his Bible. He found his ballpoint pen and his tablet of paper and he wrote me down a verse out of the Song of Solomon.

> I am come into my garden, my sister, my spouse: I have gathered myrrh with my spice; I have eaten honeycomb with my honey; I have drunk my wine with my milk: eat, O friends; drink, yea drink abundantly, O beloved.

I folded that piece of paper and put it in my wallet.
I was elated, excited, inspired. Then, during the long

115

day—and it was a long one because I wanted so much to be home—just as anybody might expect, shame began to set in on me like a high fever. A real fever this time. Real shame. I was ashamed of how it had all started and of what—whatever it was—I had been trying to prove to myself. Then I felt much worse off than before. Sick to death. Sick of shame and sick of myself.

The only thing that seemed right, the only thing that would relieve me, was to try and tell her the whole story. I steeled myself to do that. When five o'clock came around, I didn't wait around for anything. Usually I took a shower before going home, but today I just ran to my room, changed into khakis quickly, signed out at the orderly room, and drove home in a hurry. This was going to be a great big honest moment and who cares how I smelled or if I was dirty?

Slowed down in Opicina. In the square I got cold feet, went chicken. I stopped at a flower wagon and bought an armload of flowers. When I turned into our street and looked up at the window, with my heart like a rock, she wasn't there. I didn't know whether I was happy or sad that I didn't have to wave to her before I had a chance to talk. I parked the car and went up the stairs like an old man, one at a time.

When I opened the door Angela was bent over the stove doing something. She was wearing one of those loose house-dresses the Guinea girls wear. She was barefoot and I found myself staring at her feet.

"Don't look at my feet," she said. "They're so ugly."

She took the flowers from me without a word or a smile and looked for a place to put them.

"You're early," she said. "In five or ten minutes I would have been all ready for you."

"I had to talk to you right away."

"No," she said. "I have to talk to you."

She pushed me toward the mirror where I shaved every morning. There were my razor, the shaving soap, my towel and lotion and a pan of steaming hot water. I looked in the mirror and our heads were together side by side. She nestled soft against me.

"What's this for?"

Then she started to laugh and hugged me. I kept looking in the mirror and she ran her hand across my cheek and chin. It made a scratchy noise.

"I've been wanting to tell you. Your beard scratches my shoulders. I want you to shave when you come home at night."

"All right," I said. "That's all right with me. But if it's been bothering you why didn't you say anything before?"

I saw her eyes start to film with tears. She turned away quickly to the stove and whatever she was cooking there. She picked up a wooden spoon and started to stir before I grabbed her and turned her around.

"Look out!" she said.

Beans from the soup splattered on my nice clean uniform.

"Now look what a mess you've made of yourself," she said.

"Tell me. Answer what I asked you."

"Because until today I never cared. It didn't make any difference whether you scratched my shoulders or not. Now it does."

I kissed her and I shaved. Then she took my hand and we went into the bedroom. Neither of us said a word. We undressed each other with clumsy fingers and climbed into the bed.

"Oh, Johnny, poor little, bad little Johnny Riche," she said. "I have to tell you the truth. I am afraid I'm beginning to love you a little."

11 THEN WE were able to talk. Then it was safe and all right and the right time to talk about it. The thing is that neither one of us had wanted to care. That was about the last thing that either one of us had wanted. She had known all along, whatever I did good or bad with her, that I was just playing the part. Of course as a shackjob she had her part to play too. So she didn't blame me for that and she didn't let it worry her. After all, she said, there were times when it seemed like a pretty good part to play. And then we both knew what we had really known all along. That maybe that's all there is to it between two people—playing your part. That maybe it's all a man can hope for. It would be hard to say if one part was more *true* or *real* than another one. Brave man or coward, wise man or fool, saint or sinner. The thing to do, then, was to act with care, because if you play long enough you may become the part you are playing.

Angela looked through me all right, but she wasn't shocked or hurt or dismayed. She looked into and through me and for some reason she found me good. We looked into each other's eyes and we were suddenly happy with each other and ourselves. If that is being in love, then we were in love. It was the first time anything like that had ever happened to me. I told her. I admitted to her that when it came to that, the mysteries of love, I was a virgin.

She laughed at that notion. It seemed like a funny idea.

Then we were able to have something and share something beyond those few hours we were together. I guess what we really wanted to share and mix together was impossible. We wanted to share our *selves*. Lots of people may believe that's all two people can ever really hope to share or trade, just the few minutes they happen to have together and nothing more. All I can say is I think they are wrong. I think they are wrong, too, the ones who'll tell you that by getting anything else, the past or the future, mixed up with what is happening here and now, you are going to spoil what is happening and end up spoiling everything. I used to think so too. I had learned the hard way to take one thing at a time when it was happening and let it go at that. When I knew that we were in love that seemed to be enough. I couldn't even imagine there could be anything any better than just knowing that much. But I've been wrong before and I was wrong again. There was more, much more to it.

Slowly, like a sick man clearing his throat to spit out his insides, I tried to tell her about myself and my freaked-up life. How I happened to be in the Army in the first place—just a whim, a sudden, tickling, wild hair up the ass that has made all the difference for me. I wouldn't bore anybody else with the silly details, the things she had to put up with from me, me puking up fragments of memories. Just picture a born loser, but a loser with big ideas, who found a home and an asylum among the other losers of the U.S. Army. Without roots or ties, with nothing more than a name, a blood type, and a serial number, and a burning itch and desire to be taller, better, smarter, different from the rest.

I was even able to tell her a little about how it had been for me in Korea, in that summer of '50 before I finally stepped in the way of a mortar shell fragment and managed to get myself thoroughly clobbered and shipped home. I had never talked to anybody about that before. Not any real part of it. I had never wanted to. Not even late at night over beer or whisky with the veterans and old guys you can talk easy with, because you don't have to explain anything. There is a common language that says everything without having to say it, like shorthand. But in that group—and it is still the best group in the world, the ones who have been there and had it and come back—there is so much you take for granted. Fear, dirt, hot and dry, wet and cold, hungry, the death of friends and enemies. The simple things of the trade of soldiering. The truth is I had never put any of it together in my mind because I had never had to. I had never tried to tell a soul, not even myself, about it in words. I had never tried to make any sense out of it.

I had been there stationed in Japan, sitting on my dead ass with the rest of the guys, living it up a little when I could, doing a little elementary work in the black market. Japan. Most people probably think of temples and bells and kimonos, or maybe of the cities with neon signs and nightclubs. I always remember Japan by thinking of a poor farmer I saw one time. We were in the field and I was on guard duty. It was early in the morning. This farmer was out working his little piece of ground. He had to take a crap and he crouched next to some bushes. When he got through he took off at a dead run across the field. As soon as he ran away two other gooks that had been hiding behind the bush popped up. One of them had a shovel. They grabbed the mess he had just made with the shovel and ran over to their field and used it for fertilizer. When he got back with his shovel, it was gone. He looked all around and then started to carry on like a crazy man, screaming and crying. Because it was a real disaster to lose that much fertilizer.

That's living close to the line.

I wasn't living too close to any line like that in those days. The black market was paying me good money and I was shacking up with a cute little gook girl then. We could barely talk to each other. But she had some kind of idea that all white people were savages, long-donged and all sexed-up and ready to go. Like the way a lot of white people think about Negroes. That idea tickled me and I did my best to live up to it. Naturally, she was a worthless slut. She had to be, to shack up with a GI. She cheated on me all the time and stole me blind. That was when I thought I learned all about women.

Then the war broke. Before I knew my ass from third base or what was going on or where Korea was I was already there in that hot (in summer) stinking (all the time) country. And people I had never heard of were shooting at us and trying to kill me. For a long time I didn't have a clue what was going on. Neither did anybody else. It was crazy, like the worst kind of a bad dream, but I was lucky and lived through the first and the worst part of it.

I'll never forget one time being up in an observation post. It was a hell of a good OP, and we could see a lot of country without being seen. (Somebody must have seen us all right, though. Because when we had to pull back and leave, we had to shoot our way back and out.) The only trouble was that we didn't know what was going on, and we couldn't tell one side from the other. Just a whole lot of gooks running around firing at each other and us, without rhyme or reason. The forward observer was a young second lieutenant, fresh from the Fort Sill OCS, younger and greener and fresher than I was, for God's sake. Lieutenant Huff, that was his name. I'll never forget that poor miserable bastard. He hadn't had any sleep for days. He was all tired out and filthy dirty. His eyes were bloodshot and red-rimmed and watery and he had a good start on a scraggly beard. They kept calling us on the radio and asking us to send down fire missions. He kept stalling them and studying the terrain with his field glasses. The radio kept hollering: *Send us a mission. We're laid and ready to fire.* He kept telling me to tell them to wait. Then he cracked. He just crumped out there in front of me. He lowered his field glasses and twisted around to look at me, all white-faced, with tears of anger and fear running down his dirty cheeks.

"Which ones are the enemy?" he yelled. "Jesus Christ, Riche! Which ones are the freaking enemy?"

Gradually I was able to remember a lot of different things to tell her. Not like a connected story that starts someplace and ends another. I didn't and still don't see things that way. I could only do it in bits and pieces. I told her about how at first so many guys just ran. Whole platoons and companies. Threw away their rifles and ran like hell in every which direction. Some of them even ran the wrong way and got themselves killed or maybe stuck in prison camps if they were lucky. And there were a lot of bitter bad feelings when the gooks took to tying our guys up when they caught them and torturing them to death. And some of our guys took to doing the same thing.

How many bigshots turned out to be chickenhearted. All the way up and down from generals to yardbirds. And how many odd ones, all kinds and sizes and shapes, turned out to have some juice inside them and could be as brave as anybody could ever ask a man to be. I tried to explain to her exactly how it feels when you have to see a bunch of your buddies for the first time heels up, and walk over the top of them.

Finally I got around to me, exactly what must have happened to me. In basic training the old sergeants used to say: "Give your soul to God, because your ass is mine." That's the way it was. In certain situations, some very tough spot or corner, you can give your soul to God all right. And then, with that out of the way and all taken care of, you can bear down, concentrate on nothing else but what you are doing. And it's a kind of a clean, crazy joy. If you live through a time like that They sometimes give you a medal for it. But that medal doesn't mean a thing. Because if you really gave your soul to God you can't ever get it back again. Even if you want it back. That's the way I felt. That's the way I feel.

I think she understood part of how I felt about that. Even if she was a Catholic, Angela was a Catholic Italian-style. And that makes a big difference. I think she understood most of what I was trying to tell her.

She started to worry over me some. She wanted to know where I was getting the money, where it was all coming from. I never knew a shackjob yet that really cared about that, as long as the money was coming in. When I told her she begged me to quit the black market. She promised she would stay with me no matter what. Even if we had to sell everything we had and move into some crummy room somewhere in one of the villages. She would work for me if I couldn't make it.

I promised her I would quit as soon as I could.

"I'd die," she said. "I'd want to be dead if they caught you again. I don't want anything to hurt you again."

It wasn't that Angela was worried because what I was up to was *bad* or anything. It was the risk of getting myself caught and in trouble that worried her. Whatever I did was all right with her. And she never bugged me or needled me about it after that one time. She just said what she thought and how she felt and let it go.

That kind of freedom to do what I pleased came mighty damn close to making an honest man out of me.

12

ANGELA opened herself to me completely. Before that we had done nothing. We hadn't been anything. Except maybe a couple of ghosts or shadows holding on to each other for dear life. Now that we were ready and willing to let each other have a past and maybe a future too we were just starting to be really stripped and naked to each other. Naked and solid like statues.

I wasn't jealous of her having a past life without me. Sometimes you have to be jealous of what happened to your woman. Some women use that time like a weapon on you. They dance in and out of their past lives and their memories like stripteasers. Like fan dancers, teasing. Not Angela. We didn't want to hurt each other anymore. We didn't have any reasons to. And we didn't have any weapons left to use on each other.

Angela told me about herself one night in the middle of the summer. We were worn out by love and lay side by side on the bed smoking and talking in whispers. The air was warm and now and then the noises of the streets of Opicina—a motor scooter climbing the hill, the bell of the tram going down to the city, a loud voice and laughter—drifted into the room. A small lamp by the bed was on. It made her skin look golden.

She said she had come back to Trieste about the same time that I arrived. She had been away a long time. About the same time that I must have been sitting in the truck and wondering where they had sent me she was getting off the train, walking through that big ugly barn of a station and coming out onto the square lined with cafés.

. . . I was all alone, she said. There wasn't anybody to come back to for help. I had very little money. I had to find work right away. What kind of work? There wasn't any for someone like me. . . .

"Couldn't you always get a job with the Americans?"

"One time before, I worked as a PX girl, and once as a waitress at the NCO club. But even if I could have gotten my name on the waiting lists, I wasn't allowed to work for the Americans any more."

"Why not?"

"Wait," she said. "We'll get to that part."

She took a cheap room in the crummy off-limits section where the whorehouses were, and she started pounding the streets looking for some kind of, any kind of work.

. . . You might think I could go to one of the houses if worst came to worst. Believe me, there are waiting lists to work there too.

One day I was in a bar having a coffee when I saw an old friend of mine. I hardly recognized her. I thought she was dead or had just disappeared. But she came in with a man, and she had good clothes on and she looked fat and healthy. She saw me too, and it was easy to see how I was doing. I had done some favor for her a long time ago and she remembered that. She said she was working in a nightclub, the Kit Kat, and maybe she could help me get a job there too. . . .

The next morning she went with her friend to meet Pissoni and see about getting a job. A nightclub, as anybody knows, especially in the morning like that, is a sad, ugly-looking place in the middle of the morning with the full daylight coming through open windows and all the stinks and smells of the night before fighting each other to get out in the open air. A phony, expensive joint like that looks worse than ever with all the tables turned over and the chairs stacked up in a corner and the musical instruments quiet.

. . . Two old men were sweeping and mopping the place when we came in. I sat down on a barstool and looked at myself in the mirror like a stranger while my friend went back to see the man and talk him into seeing me. It was very hard to get an appointment to see Pissoni. . . .

I knew him without ever having had one word between us, I was thinking. This Pissoni was making *his,* and his motto was screw everybody else in the world. He was a big freaking deal. He was the kind all over the world that war or any other big trouble always turns up on top, white-bellied and slimy, from under a rock.

. . . I knew about the job already, she said. All you were supposed to do was sit with the customers, dance with them, make some conversation and jokes and make sure they kept drinking. You always order a double cognac or whisky (and they bring you tea in your glass), and you get a percentage of the check. Also when the customer gets drunk you give the waiter a sign and he can serve the customer cheap stuff. It wasn't much money, but the more charming you could be, the better the money was. It was all right, too, to add to your earnings if you wanted to sleep with a customer after hours. They always ask you to sleep with them. But the good thing about working in an expensive club like the Kit Kat was that you didn't *have* to. Unless, of course, it was somebody special, like a friend of Pissoni's or some customer who came often and spent a lot of money. The rest of the time it was up to you, so you didn't have to feel like a real whore. . . .

"Did you do it?"

"Sometimes," she said. "I needed the money. And if he was young and clean-looking and would take me to a good hotel I might go just to sleep in a nice room with clean sheets on the bed and hot water in the bathroom. Sometimes I did it to take a hot bath in a tub."

"I've been dirty like that. I've been so dirty I'd do anything to get a shower or a bath."

. . . This man Pissoni was a big problem. There were plenty of young, good-looking women who wanted to work for him. And he didn't keep a waiting list. Each one had to try to win him over. It was a game he played.

"But," my friend told me, "he's not a bad man, not really. He's ugly as a bullfrog and has a mean, quick temper. But if he decides to like you, he'll be good to you." . . .

I could picture Angela sitting on a barstool in the empty club waiting. She would be shabby and all alone except for the two old bums, breathing deep like porpoises coming up for air, who were cleaning the place up. She would look at herself in the mirror and shrug and wait.

. . . Finally my friend came back. She was messy now, her clothes were messed up and her lipstick was smeared around her mouth. She sat down beside me and winked. She told me to go back to his office and see him.

"He's in a good mood today," she said. "But very active, *sportivo*. Be careful, but be nice. Don't be too proud."

"*Proud?*" I said. "Why should I be proud? What in the name of God do I have to be proud of?"

He did look like a bullfrog. Exactly like a fat bullfrog all dressed up in a striped suit, what you call a Guinea suit, and standing up on his hind legs. I gave him a big smile to keep from laughing out loud in his face because he looked so funny. He stood there with his hands behind his back, like an officer, rocking back and forth on his heels and looking me up and down and all over. He didn't smile.

But (Angela said), don't misunderstand me. It's only the men who worry about their beauty. The truth is that there are only a few, one in thousands, beautiful men. They are nice to look at and maybe to spend one night with. But they're as vain and conceited and silly as young girls. And there are only a very few really *ugly* men. They can make you feel sorry for them, or disgusted and mad at yourself for feeling that way. The rest are all about the same. It makes no difference. . . .

"Come on now," I said. "Don't give me that. Why do some women always prefer a certain type, if that's true?"

"Oh, it's true some women like a tall, thin man and some others a short, thick-bodied, strong one. Some like dark hair and some blond, something about the lips or a certain color and light in the eyes. But the truth is, they are really all about the same when you look at them. Any of them will do just as well as another."

"You don't mean that. What about me?"

"Well," she said, "now that I see you with the eyes of love you are beautiful, but before you were just another man."

Angela had something like the same idea about women. She was sure they were all the same in the dark. A lot of women I've known seem to feel that way. Anybody who's

been with more than one woman knows it isn't true. But as
long as they believe it, it makes them a whole lot easier to get
along with.

. . . Pissoni, bad as he was, wasn't really ugly. He was just misshapen and too fat. Like anybody else, a man or a woman, he
tried to make up for it. Pissoni thought he could live with
himself by pretending to himself and everybody else that he
didn't care. He pretended that he loved himself just the way
he was. He made up for it by having enough money and by
having his whim, his power to give or deny favors to good-
looking young girls who probably wouldn't have given him
their sweat to drink if he was dying of thirst otherwise. That's
the way he saw the world. And all this and knowing it, made
him a mean-hearted old man. He even went so far as to call
attention to the way he looked by the kind of clothes he
wore and the way he stood and walked and talked to people.
He growled when he spoke, all hoarse and bubbling, like the
sound of a fat old frog. It was all done to insult and humiliate
other people. You can see Pissoni is a clown. . . .

Angela had seen right through him to the sad jelly of his soul
at a glance.

. . . "So," he said, "you want to work for me. Do you think
you can work at the Kit Kat?"

He made me pull up my skirt and show my legs and turn
around for him. Then he left me standing there, holding my
skirt up and feeling silly while he went and sat down behind
his desk. He scratched himself and lit a cigarette. I let my skirt
down again and came close to the desk. He let me stand
there. He smoked and blew the smoke in my face and asked
me a lot of questions about myself like a policeman. I kept
smiling and gave him back some of the same thing with jokes
and short answers. After a while he got tired of that. He got
up again and started walking up and down the office. He

studied the photographs of the performers who had been in his club.

"What makes you think you can do the job?" he asked me.

"It's easy work. I can do this kind of work easily."

"You think you're something special? You think you're beautiful?"

"No, but I usually get my way with men."

He laughed at that. He seemed to think that was very funny.

"You've got a way with men, have you? Do you think you can get your way with me?"

"You're a man."

He frowned and looked a little hurt. I saw him steal a look at one of the mirrors in the room.

"That isn't what I meant."

"I think you like me," I said.

"So many pretty girls, younger and prettier than you, come to this office and beg to work for me. I like them. I like them all. Why should I want you?"

"No reason," I told him, "except I can do the job better than the others and make more money for you."

"You think very well of yourself. You have a high opinion of yourself."

"Oh, no. I know myself and my faults better than anyone else can. But I don't fool myself. I believe in telling the truth. If I have a way with men, if men like me, why should I lie about it?"

"Do you think I'm deceiving myself?"

"You're the only one who can answer that, Signore Pissoni. It's not for me to judge."

He grabbed me and twisted me around. He pushed me across the room and made me stand in front of a mirror and look at myself.

"Now," he said, "tell me what you see."

"Nothing."

"Come on, you don't like to lie. Tell the truth."

"I don't see anything. I see myself in a mirror."

"Do you want to know what I see?" His hands were digging into my arms, bruising and hurting me. But I kept the smile on my face and wouldn't give him the pleasure of flinching or fighting back. "I see a plain, ordinary woman, a common girl. She is wearing cheap old clothes. I think she needs a bath. She needs some good food to fatten her up and put the color back in her cheeks. She needs to fix her hair and make up her face. She's getting older and needs to take more care of herself."

"Things like that are simple if you have a little money."

"If you work for me you'll need some nice clothes. You'll have to fix yourself up."

"I know that."

"Do you have any money?"

"No."

"Well, then, where do you expect to get it?"

He turned me loose to light another cigarette and I turned around facing him so I could look in his eyes. "I don't know," I said. "Maybe you'd be able to make me an advance or give me a loan."

Ha! That made him laugh. "You thought that? Where do you think I'd be, if I gave loans and advances to every girl who came here begging for work? If I paid out a hundred *lire* for every sad story I've heard here, I'd be broke. I'd be a beggar. I'd have to go on my hands and knees to somebody else and tell my sad story. And where would I be in the end? I'd be like those two old toothless bums that come here every morning to clean up the club. The same girls would walk past me and spit on me and call me an ugly old man. Believe me, that's the way the world is."

"Maybe," I said. "Maybe I could give you something in return."

"Possibly."

I started to undress myself. I took off my dress and folded it on a chair. Pissoni looked amazed. He was, like you say, all shook up. He didn't know what to do next. He burst out laughing. He laughed so hard that sweat popped out all at once all over his fat face and tears rolled down his cheeks.

"Wait, wait a minute!" he said. "Here."

He opened his desk and gave me money without even counting it.

"You can pay me back later," he said. "After you've worked here a while."

My friend was furious when I told her what had happened. She was even shocked. Nothing like that had ever happened before. It was for sure the wrong thing to do with Pissoni. He took himself very seriously. You were supposed to play the part. It was supposed to be a little like bargaining in the marketplace. You were expected to resist, to cry and plead with him. Then maybe to weaken a little bit. When undressing was done, he was supposed to do it. You were supposed to melt slowly like a piece of ice and let it end in whispers and sighs of satisfaction. My friend was very angry because I had broken the rules. She thought I had probably spoiled a good thing. . . .

"Maybe she was pissed-off because you got the job without the initiation fee."

"I was ready," Angela said. "He could have done it to me on the floor or laying on top of the desk or standing in a corner. I didn't care. I wanted the job. My friend couldn't understand how I got away with it."

How we laughed at that, Angela and I! The picture she made of poor old Pissoni, bug-eyed—shocked, too, probably for the first time in his life. And Angela simply and methodically getting ready to do what had to be done. Without any fooling around about it. No nonsense. Just as she did the first night in our apartment.

"But that's not the best joke of all," I said. "The best part is that the poor, grubby old bastard never will know what he missed. Pissoni missed out on the best piece he would ever have. And why? Because at the last minute he had *scruples!*"

The idea of that nearly killed me. Lord, the whole thing seemed like a comedy. A real comedy.

13 T A K E N altogether and all at once, though, Angela's story wouldn't make anybody laugh much. Not that she didn't try to make it funny where she could, because there were some funny things and she wasn't sorry for herself. Now we were up and more or less dressed and sitting in the kitchen drinking beer. It was late and the night noises had eased off. She told me her story from start to finish, in order and in a simple, matter-of-fact way. Anybody can tell from that, the way she could tell the story without all the loose bits and pieces, that she had a better, tighter grip on herself than I did. So the truth is I could and did learn from her. In her own way she was a veteran of the wars and a hell of a good soldier.

The reason we were in the kitchen was that she had a little collection of cracked and thumbed and yellowing photographs she kept and she wanted me to see them. She spread them out, dealt them out like a hand of cards on the table. Laid end to end like that they told her fortune.

The first one was of her father in a high-collared Austrian

uniform in the First World War. The one they called The War to End Wars. He had a fancy mustache then with waxed points and a big silly smile. He looked more like somebody in a costume than a real soldier. He was a tall, good-looking man. He made it through the war, but he was still young when he died. Angela was just a baby and had no memory of him. All that she had ever known of him was a fading snapshot.

. . . It's a picture, too, of the good times I heard about and never knew. Everybody talked about the time when Trieste was the port city of the old Austrian Empire. There was something comical and fun about those old days, the way they talked about them, something splendid that had been lost. You can still *feel* it if you look at the big stone bank buildings downtown. . . .

Angela was smart enough to know that what she had was a kind of homesickness. And like any other kind of homesickness, it was a longing for something that probably had never been there in the first place. But she was smart enough, too, to know that even if the thing wasn't real, the longing was. And she couldn't help being Triestine, a true Triestine. She was born there. And such longings came with the place.

The next was a snapshot of the three of them that were left in the family after her father died: Angela; her mother, a thin, tired-looking woman in black, looking old, much older than she was, the way years of hard work and troubles make them look; and Angela's brother, Roberto. Roberto was tall and broad-shouldered and handsome. He looked like his father, had the same cocky, silly grin except for the painted mustache, and he was wearing good, well-fitting clothes.

. . . Poor Roberto, she said. He wanted so much. He could never be satisfied. To me and everybody else he was a kind of a hero because he was so good-looking. And he used to be

135

on one of the big Italian professional football teams. He made money playing the sport and his picture was in the newspapers sometimes. I worshiped him and people were nice to me because I was his little sister. But at home, when nobody but us was there to see him, he was moody and sulky. He never went out with girls and my mother wanted him to get married and have a family. He used to go often, though, to one of the whorehouses. Once I came around a corner just in time to see him go inside and I was so ashamed. I cried and cried. When I told him I had seen him go there he laughed at me.

"Angela," he said. "What did you think I was? A priest, a saint?"

Now I know more about life and the world and I have to laugh at how silly I was. I think he was in love with one of the whores in that house. Of course he couldn't marry her, but he loved her.

Then the war came and the Army took him. He was killed in the mountains in Greece. At least that's what we thought had happened. It was late in the war and everything was very confused. We never knew for sure. But some of his friends in the Army thought he was dead. I think so too. I felt he was dead at the time. . . .

There was a photo of Angela when she was sixteen with a bunch of her friends, posing on the beach with the bay behind them. They were all grouped around a motor scooter and she had her arm around a smirking boy who had owned the motor scooter in the picture. She was thinner, more delicate, and very beautiful. Wild-looking too.

. . . If you like me now, she said, you should have known me then. I wasn't so heavy, I was light on my feet and lighthearted. I had a small waist and a nice flat stomach and my breasts were high. I was nice for men to look at and desire. I don't think *I* was very nice, though. I didn't know anything about anything then. I didn't know how to be nice. Not even nice to myself. Oh, I used to *like* myself, to look at myself and admire myself in the mirror. But only as you might look at a pretty picture or a statue or something, because I didn't know what or who I was. I was only sure that I was going to grow up and become a movie star. . . .

This picture had been taken in the early days of the war when everything seemed to be going pretty good. Now she ticked off the people in the picture.

. . . This one is dead, killed in the war. And this one. This one is crippled now. This one, the boy with the motor scooter, is crazy and in the hospital. This girl was working for the Americans the last I knew, but I haven't seen her in a long time. This one here, a lucky girl, born lucky, married a GI and lives in America. . . .

It's true that when she was sixteen Angela was a real beauty. She had bloomed fine and well and early, the way so many Italian girls do. It made her a little sad I think, as I guess any woman would be, to see herself and remember what she had been. But to tell the truth, honestly, in a funny sort of a way it excited me to live with the woman who had been such a beautiful girl. I felt like I had the girl too when I had the woman. And I knew well enough that back in those days she wouldn't have given somebody like me the time of day. I know it's a dirty thought, an ugly idea, pretty much like Pissoni's and maybe for some of the same reasons. But I'd be a damn liar if I didn't admit that knowing what a beauty she had been and seeing a picture of her then didn't give an edge, a kind of spice to my pleasure. In almost the same way, but without love, I once got a boot out of laying a really good-looking woman who had been about as close to just plain ugly as anybody can imagine when she was a girl. That time there was no love, this time there was. I don't know why. It's just that deep feelings, like love or desire, are so mixed up and complicated. Especially in men I think. Sometimes I think men are the complicated ones, living half the time in their heads. It's the women who are simple and cool-headed and reasonable.

. . . Not long after that picture—she was telling me—the Germans moved into the city. There were soldiers everywhere, like you are now. And sailors too. They kept submarines in the cliffs near the beach at Sistiana. I married a German soldier. It wasn't an unusual thing. Lots of girls did. You have to remember they weren't *our* enemies.

She had one picture of him and it was cracked and creased, because she had folded it down so small to hide it once. The Kraut looked blond, square-headed, tall, good-looking and very much at *Achtung* in his uniform. Like old Jethroe always said, you can say what you like about those bastards, but they can really soldier. They just look like soldiers. You have to give them that much.

. . . He was kindhearted and good to me. I loved him. He was the first man I loved. When he took me, he was the first. I was a virgin. It's true, the old story, that the first man is always in your heart, the best and the one you love most. Maybe it has to be that way. We were married. We lived together for a while. I was pregnant. I was very happy then. When the war was over we were going to Germany to live. He was an expert auto mechanic, and after the war he was going to go into business and open a garage with a friend. I was innocent. I knew so little about things. I believed it was all going to stay that way—happiness, the future, all of it.

The end of it came quickly and without warning. Of course we should have known or guessed what was happening. But nobody paid any attention to the news anymore because we knew both sides were lying. And rumors meant

138

nothing. We had heard so many rumors for years. What could you believe anyway? Why believe any of it?

Then one night he came home from his *Kaserne* and told me that most of the Germans were leaving. They had been ordered out of the city. He had his steel helmet on and he was ready to go. I had never seen him like that before, like a real soldier in the newsreels, and it frightened me. I cried. "Please don't cry," he begged me. "It's only for a little while. We'll be back." He had slipped away from the post to tell me good-by and he only had a few minutes. He was sure it would not be for long. It was only a tactical movement. If anything did go wrong he would be in touch with me and we could meet somewhere. He kissed me and was gone.

Behind them came the partisans from Yugoslavia. They came in the city. I had never seen men, soldiers, like that before. They were dirty and ragged and terrible. The few Germans who had been left behind had to fight them. They fought shooting from houses, street by street. The whole city sang with bullets. All of the Germans died because the partisans did not keep promises and it was terrible if they caught a man alive.

Just about the same time the Americans and British came. They came from the other direction, along the coast. We were happy when they came, but for a while they just stayed in their camps and left the whole city to the partisans. They didn't interfere. Then began the Terror. For more than a month it was a bad time for everybody.

Oh, they had *reasons*. They had scores to settle. During the Occupation the Germans had done some terrible things too. Here in Opicina one day they hung men and women, Yugoslavs, from every lamppost on the street in reprisal for something. That is an ugly death and a terrible thing to see. And once when a moviehouse full of German officers and their families was blown up, the Gestapo took many hostages from the city. When the guilty people, the ones who had put the bomb there, didn't surrender, they pushed the hostages into a deep cave. . . .

I knew the cave Angela was talking about. I had seen it. It was a ragged, rocky mouth with rusty barbwire around it, a kind of asshole in the earth. The Krauts had grabbed a lot of people—nobody knew how many, but several hundred for sure—men, women, and even children. They roped them all together. Then they pushed the first ones down the hole and the others were slowly jerked in behind them. They all fell screaming to the bottom of that black hole. It is so deep that nobody has ever been able to recover the bodies. I threw a rock down and I never heard it hit.

. . . Yes, there were plenty of scores to settle. There always are. And if you know anything at all about these things, you know it didn't take long before it was a time of terror for everybody. The partisans were like drunk men. It is so easy to kill when people are helpless. They killed and tortured and tormented as they pleased. Anyone who was denounced as a collaborator was killed without a question. People named others they didn't like. Some people named others hoping to save themselves. Even money and greed were part of it.

In our section there was a barber who saw a good thing. He named all the other barbers in the section and they were all hanged. Then someone denounced him. The men in our section went for a long time without haircuts.

Then, as they were bound to, people got the idea to punish the girls who had been with German soldiers. And the whores too, the ordinary whores. The whores are always punished. I don't know why. Whores are not political.

They came in trucks and dragged us from our houses. They took us in the trucks to a big square. When the trucks came into the square we saw there were great crowds of people there and they were shouting and laughing and gay. It was a mood, a feeling like the *carnivale* before Lent. There was a priest there too, I remember. He was an old man, white-haired and frail. He spoke to the partisans and the people and he begged them to separate the ones who were married in the church from the rest. They laughed at him.

"Shut up, you old fool," they said to him, "or we'll give you the 'treatment' too."

He cried like a woman and they shoved him away.

Then they started dragging us off the trucks. The girls were screaming when they were pulled off the trucks. No one knew what they might do to us. I was so afraid. My heart was beating like a drum and my mouth was dry. My tongue felt like a dead leaf in my mouth.

They took us from the trucks and tore off our clothes. They shaved our heads bald. Then they started to march us in lines through the streets of the city. I think people had seen so much bloodshed and known so much fear, being afraid for themselves every minute, that it was a great relief to them. It was something happening to someone else and they could watch and be safe. Many of them got joy and pleasure out of it as you might expect. It seemed funny to them. It made them happy. Some of the girls were beaten badly and hurt.

I was lucky. You see, I was eight months' pregnant and the baby was almost here. I was terribly afraid at first, not so much for me as the baby. I was afraid they would want to hurt the baby because it was a German baby. I had heard of such things and worse too. But the truth is it helped me some to be afraid for someone else besides myself. Then there was a strange thing. The sight of me walking naked with my stomach all swelled and stretched tight must have made them ashamed. No one touched me and even the girls who happened to be near me weren't hurt.

I started that long walk full of shame and pity for myself. I didn't want anybody to see me like that. And half the people of the city were there. At first I walked along with my head down, trying to pretend to myself that none of this was happening to me. But then a change came, a new feeling.

141

Why do I tell you all this? Because that was the most important day for me. Because I *learned* that day. It came to me that this was the worst thing that would every happen to me. Sure, there might be more pain and humiliation, but that would only be more of the same. Except for death—and there is nothing to be done about that anyway whenever and however it comes—this was the worst. Even if it went on forever, I could stand it. So for me it was a kind of ceremony. I was like a shorn lamb among lambs. I found out that I could get along without shame. There was nothing left to be afraid of or anxious about anymore. Instead of shuffling along with the other lost sheep, I held up my head in pride and looked with clear eyes at the people in the crowd. I looked into their eyes. And I found that by looking in their eyes I could shame them. Maybe it was that shame they felt that saved my baby's life.

My hair was still short and bristly like a soldier's haircut when the baby came. He was a beautiful baby, all pink and blond and fat. I gave him a German name, for his father. I called him Wilhelm. I kept him with me as long as I could, but there was nothing to eat in those days. . . .

There was only one thing somebody in a fix like the one Angela was in could do. You had to give up the baby to the authorities. They found some family that was better off and farmed the baby out. The family got paid something for the care and feeding. And you paid something extra, if you could, to make sure they were happy about it. Someday, if you ever got ahold of enough money and could prove legally that you were able to take care of the child, you could pay off everybody in sight and maybe get your child back again. And if the family was kind and friendly, they might let you visit your child from time to time. By law they didn't have to, and not many did that.

. . . They found a very nice family for Wilhelm (she said). He is well cared for, as well as anyone could expect under the circumstances. He's a fine, strong, growing boy now. They used to let me come and see him. When I first came back to Trieste I went to see him, but he didn't really remember me or know who I was. He called the other woman, the one who looks after him, Mother.

It's better to leave it that way. Better for him, I think. It hurts me, but there isn't anything to be done about it now. . . .

Angela showed me two pictures of the child. One as a little baby looking round and fat and funny like all babies. And one, taken fairly recently, where he had on a little smock with a white collar for school like the Italian kids wear.

That explained why she wanted the extra money. For "spending." She was trying to save up some and would do anything, including shacking up with me, to get it.

. . . After I found a home for Wilhelm I had to find work. I had to get money to support myself and my mother. Mother was sick then, in bed all the time, losing her mind and her memory. But until she died she would be someone to feed and look after. And I even needed a little extra to give the family who were looking after my baby. All the time I waited to hear from my husband. If he was still alive. I thought he must be still alive, I felt it. If he was still alive somewhere I would need money to go to him when the time came.

By this time I was thin and sick myself and my teeth were bad since the baby. But, sick or not, I had to find work.

I was very lucky that time. I found some young British officers who were living in a villa. They needed a maid. I cooked for them and did all the laundry and kept the place clean and neat. They were good to me. . . .

She had a picture of two of them together. One was a tall guy, skinny as a broomstick, who had glasses on about as thick as the windshield on a car. The other one had a great

143

mass of light hair tumbling over his face and looked to be about sixteen years old. He had a big pipe in his mouth. Well, the Limeys will fool you. They can soldier and they don't scare easy. I saw them work in Korea. These two looked all right to me.

. . . They were good to me. I got plenty to eat and took some home. They arranged for an Army doctor to look me over and he gave me some medicine and some pills. I started to feel better. They got a dentist to work on my teeth. They even bought me some clothes and things. They ignored me as a woman and I was glad. I couldn't blame them.

I looked terrible, old and drawn and sad in those days. I wish I had a picture to prove it to you. . . .

I think she would have liked to have seen my reaction to a picture of her then. It was easy enough for me to love her now or even to love her because of the beautiful girl she had been. But what about that? Would I have loved her at her worst?

That's a woman's logic for you. Angela really wanted to know how I would have felt about her if I had known her then. How could I know? How could anybody know about a thing like that? In honesty, I doubt if I would have given her a second look or a minute's thought if she looked one half as bad as she claimed she did. I doubt if we would ever have exchanged a word. But I could say this much: that if she *turned* that way, now—if overnight she became old and ugly—I doubt if it would have made any difference.

I'd be lying, too, if I didn't admit that this too added to my pleasure in her. I liked the idea that she could have changed. That she had been in disguise for a while. Like the ugly step-daughter in all the fairy tales. I don't think I could have loved her if all the truth about her hadn't pleased me one way or another. I call that the right kind of rationalizing.

• • •

. . . With the good food and care my looks started to improve. Then the Limey officers started to notice me. I slept with some of them. Out of loneliness and gratitude. I really liked the Limeys. They all looked so young and they had such beautiful skin and such good hair. Of course they were all troubled about the war too. I was like a mother to them.

Finally they were all ordered home and I had to find myself another job. . . .

She had fought and clawed her way to get work now that she had her strength and health back. She found jobs with the Americans. She worked as a clerk in one of the PXs.

. . . There is where I met Sergeant Culver from Tank Company. . . .

She had a picture of him too. He was a long, tall hillbilly from Tennessee or North Carolina or some place like that, and he was good-looking—but he looked about as friendly and trustworthy as a rattlesnake. Oh, I knew his type! They made plenty of soldiers from that mold. I looked at old Culver when I heard about him. And I told myself that one fine day I was bound to run into him, because the world is small. I'd like that.

. . . He was going to marry me and take me back to the States, he told me. Of course, I couldn't marry him until I found out what had happened to my husband. But he was persistent and he told me he could wait. I believed him and we lived together.

I didn't know much about the Americans in those days. They all seemed to be so frank and honest and simple compared to the European men. They treated a woman with more respect. It took me a while. It was later before I learned how that kind of respect could drain the lifeblood out of a woman.

145

Culver was never one way for long. Sometimes he was very tender. Sometimes he treated me like a goddess. If he had come to me on his hands and knees to lick my feet, I wouldn't have been surprised. Other times he would be moody and mean or drunk. Sometimes he treated me like a mongrel bitch. He would fight with me. He would beat me black and blue and chase me around with a knife, threatening to kill me. He would insult me and humiliate me every way he could think of. Then, the next moment or the next day, he would change. He would come home with armloads of presents from the PX. He would be so sweet it would break my heart.

I learned all about Americans from Sergeant Culver. He was like my university. So, you see, I was all ready for you. . . .

That hurt, but there was a lot of truth in it. I shared a lot of things with Culver. Maybe that's what made me hate him so much. Sure, Culver was going to marry her someday. Maybe he even kidded himself and thought he was. Who knows?

. . . One morning he left the apartment as usual, said so long honey-doll, I'll see you for supper. When he didn't come home that night, I didn't worry. Probably he had guard or some other duty. After the next night, though, I started to worry. I went to the gate of the *caserma* and waited all morning until a soldier I knew came out.

"Where's Culver?" I said.

"Don't you know?"

"I wouldn't be here waiting if I knew. Tell me where he is. Has anything happened to him?"

"Don't that beat all," the soldier told me. "That Culver is one slick operator all right. You sure you don't know."

"Tell me please."

"Old Culver's gone, doll. He's out on the high seas. He shipped out day before yesterday."

He wrote to me as soon as he arrived in America and he sent me a money order for twenty-five dollars. He said he would be coming back for me or else he would send me the money to come to him soon. But then I didn't hear from him for a long time. When a letter did come it said he was out of the Army and that he was broke. He wanted me to send him some money. It was a crazy, angry letter and I tore it up. He cursed me and called me a dirty whore. He said he was sorry for all the money he had wasted on me. He said he thought that I should pay him back some of it anyway. That I owed it to him. . . .

Later still, and this was a strange how-do-you-do for Angela, she got a long letter from Culver's mother. She had saved that letter, and she showed it to me. Somehow Culver's mother had found out that her son had been shacking up with Angela. Mostly she blamed Angela, though she said she partly blamed her son. The only sense or reason I could make out of the letter by reading between the lines was that old Culver, true to form, must have been trying to con some money out of his mother by telling her he had to have it to send to Angela. Maybe he told his mother that Angela was trying to blackmail him or something. She sure must have been a simpleminded old woman to believe a line like that. Especially from Culver. Even if he was her blue-eyed, darling boy. For me it was like reading a letter from Mars or somewhere. I don't know where the old woman had been living all this time. Not in this world. Not in the one the rest of us have to live in. Some kind of a cloudland she had dreamed up to live in.

> My son, Willie, was a nice, clean, religious boy before he went in the Army [the letter said]. He didn't drink or smoke and he very seldom went out with the girls. I just do not know for the life of me what has happened to him but he certainly has changed. Nowadays

147

he drinks and smokes all the time and hangs around the honky-tonks and carries on and gets into fights. He cannot seem to keep one job for long. He always seems to be in one kind of trouble or another. I don't know I'm sure, I cannot imagine, what it is you did to him. Don't think I blame it all on you. I know very well what a nice attractive young man my boy is and he would make anybody a fine husband. And I think I can understand how lonesome it was for you foreign girls with so many of your own kind of men dead and gone, far from home. But don't you ever forget it was lonesome here for us too. I do blame you for bringing the Poison of the World into my son's life. If you ever really loved him, how could you do it? I ask myself and ask myself and I just don't know. Sometimes I only wish I knew what the whole truth was.

I don't know what the whole truth was myself about old Willie Culver. The *plain* truth was, among other things, that when he left Angela without a warning or a good-by and with only a few thousand *lire* in the house for groceries, she was already pregnant for the second time.

. . . My mother had died before I met Culver. I was all alone. I had the baby in the charity hospital. The little girl was born blind, and I was very sick and had to stay in the hospital a long time. . . .

It turned out that Culver, that "nice, clean, religious boy," had left her something after all. He had picked up a not so nice and not so clean dose of VD somewhere and passed it on to her and the baby. A souvenir.

. . . Of course I had to give up that baby, too. I go to see her as often as I can, sometimes one day a week these days. The strange thing is that she is just the opposite from Wilhelm. She has never even seen me, but she remembers me perfectly. . . .

All this probably sounds like a long, corny tale of woe to some people. If it does, believe me, those people are either dumber or luckier than they will ever know. They are people like Culver's mother, living in cloudland. Jethroe may have been crazy, but he was right when he took his mottoes mostly from the Old Testament. These are the times of Jeremiah and Isaiah and Job. Sure there are plenty of people safe at home in some safe town where when the night comes on they can say "Let there be light," and flip a switch. And there, by God and Thomas Edison, it is! And all the shadows pull back out of sight. In those safe towns people go off to work in the morning and you can count on it that they'll be home for supper. On a Sunday all the nice, clean, religious people can gather together in church and sing hymns and pray God to spare a little more time for them and their problems. They may not want to hear about the way things are out there in the wide world. Let God worry about all the falling sparrows. That's His business.

All I can say is that Angela's story was true and typical. I wasn't moved to tears or anger. I had already heard almost exactly the same tale in Japan and Korea and Germany. It is a very common story these days. But to me it couldn't be such a common story because I loved her. What happened to her was like what happened to me. It was the same almost as if it *had* happened to me. I could itch with her scabs and scars. I could sweat for the times she had been hot and shiver for her when she had been cold. I could wish that all of it had happened to me instead of to her, to spare her. I longed for her so much, I almost wanted to *be* her. I wanted to know her. In the Bible's sense of the word. Meaning, translated, to know her skin and bones, every inch and hair, every minute past and present, body and soul. And I wasn't jealous of her other lovers. And the truth is she had even loved *Culver* a little bit and could still speak well of him. I didn't envy them. I wasn't jealous of them. And I don't think she was ever jealous of me either.

. . . After all that, she was telling me, when they finally said I was cured and they let me out of the hospital, I got work wherever I could find it. It was hard to find work because I couldn't work for the Americans anymore or the Allied Military Government because of my VD record. And I had to be very careful because the Vice Squad was watching me. If I went with any soldiers I could be put in jail. Still, I got along some way and I even saved some money. I was still hoping that my husband wasn't dead. I had no reason to think he was still alive, but I had a feeling. Perhaps he was living in East Germany and couldn't write to me.

Then, almost two years ago, a letter came from him. It was not in his handwriting. It was sent by someone else for him. . . .

She showed me the letter. It was on some hotel stationery. I don't read much German, but it was simple and clear enough. He said he was alive and all right, but he could never send for her now. And she must not try to find him or come to him. He said he had been a prisoner of the Russians for a long time after the war and that was why he hadn't been able to get any word to her. He said she must think of herself as free to marry again. All that had been a long time ago in another world . . . and so on. He didn't mention or ask about the child. Maybe he had forgotten about that or maybe he just assumed the baby was dead.

. . . In my joy I wasn't worried or upset. I still knew the names of some of his family. I knew where they had been living before the war. I was sure that I would be able to find him. Maybe he was sick after being a prisoner for so long. Or maybe he had been badly hurt. He might need me to help look after him. I knew I had to find him again.

I scraped up all the money I could and I started out for Germany. I was completely ignorant. I didn't really have any idea where Germany was or how big it was. I had spent my whole life in Trieste. I had never even been as far as Venice in those days. But I got my papers together somehow and bought a railroad ticket and went looking for him.

It's a long story, too long to tell, and most of it doesn't matter. The things that happened to me don't matter because they didn't matter to me. There was only one thing I wanted—to find him. Whenever my money was gone—and that happened often—I had to stop and earn enough to begin again. I had to do everything you can think of to get money. I was a maid. I was a waitress. I even danced and sang for a while in a nightclub because I know English and the words to the American songs. When I had to I was a whore. I even stole. None of that mattered. It was as if none of it was really happening to me, not the me that was searching like a detective to find my husband. My body was just a means to get there. It could suffer a little to get me there.

My long search ended in Austria. I heard that my husband was living on a farm there in the American Zone near Linz. The people who told me warned me to give up, begged me not to go there. They said I would be sorry if I did. But they couldn't stop me.

I remember exactly how it was. I got to Linz on the train. After that I had to walk. It was a gray, bitter cold day. The snow was deep and piled high on both sides of the country roads I walked on. There was the coldest wind I've ever known. It came blowing in from the mountains in the East. Nobody else was out walking that day. I walked along for miles all alone.

I came to the farmhouse and they let me in. I saw him at last, though I hardly recognized him. He had changed so much. He was pale and thin and had a face like an old man.

151

He was huddled near the stove in a chair and I saw that he had lost a leg. There was a tall, stout, plain woman there. She let me in the house. She was sullen and suspicious. She said that Wilhelm was her husband. He nodded, but he didn't make a sign that he recognized me. There were two other men in the room—her brothers. It was a poor farm, and they looked worn and bitter. It must have made them that way to have to work to support him too.

"My husband and I were in Russia together," she said. "He would have died if it hadn't been for me. I nursed him and kept him alive."

I could see that all the joy she had in life came from taking care of her one-legged husband. There are women like that. Without a crippled husband she would have been an old maid. With a cat or a dog. Kind to animals. I didn't know whether he had ever spoken to her about me. I think maybe he had, because everyone was so stiff and suspicious.

But as soon as I came in and saw the whole thing at once I made up my mind not to say anything. What else could I do? How could I ever get Wilhelm back to Trieste? How could I take care of him? I almost laughed. In all that time it had never even occurred to me that he might have *married* again. I had been a fool.

With him looking right at me and not showing anything at all in his face and eyes, I explained to them that I had made a mistake. I was looking for someone else. I said I was sorry, and they gave me some coffee and I left.

I wish I had a snapshot of that grim family, she said laughing. Yes, I can laugh about it now because it was a joke on me. I left them all grouped around that stove. None of them smiled. They had hard lives too. I started back along the roads I had taken. It was turning dark now and a cold icy rain was falling. The wind smelled different than anything I had known before. It smelled of great lonely spaces and I thought it must come all the way from Russia. I wanted to cry but I didn't have any tears left. . . .

• • •

Somehow Angela got to Salzburg, where the main American camp was. It was just a few days before payday. She held on until payday.

. . . On payday I fixed myself up as nice as I could and went hunting. I found a young boy, a child, fresh from the States on his first pass. It was funny and sad because he had never been with a woman before and he was nervous and frightened. I got him to buy me some dinner. Then I let him take me to a cheap hotel. He was so worried and anxious. It took all the courage he had to go to bed with me, and it was all over before it even began. The poor boy hardly had a chance to know what had happened to him. I felt sorry for him, but he seemed happy enough. He fell asleep like a child, hugging me with both arms. When I was sure that he was sound asleep, I slipped out of his grip and put the pillow where I had been. I took the money out of his wallet and tiptoed out of the room and started home for Trieste. . . .

Well, the kid would have a whole month's time on his hands until the next payday to consider the facts of life. By the middle of the month he wouldn't be able to scrape up enough money to buy a tube of toothpaste with. He wouldn't even be able to buy a postage stamp to send a letter to his mother. He would have to sweat out the chance of having picked up a dose of VD. He would be cussing himself for being a damned stupid fool. And he'd be so ashamed of being rolled on his first pass he wouldn't dare to tell a soul. But he'd live through it. By the end of the month and next payday he would have figured out how to live with himself and his foolishness. He'd be all ready to go on pass again with the swing and swagger of a worldly-wise veteran who knew all the answers and couldn't be fooled by anything. The education of a young draftee, you might call it.

153

The way I looked at it, hearing Angela tell the story, was the poor boy was lucky and would never know it. He couldn't have gone out hunting and picked a finer woman to be rolled by. He couldn't have lost his cherry more honorably. Or for a better cause.

When she finished talking it was turning gray and the roosters in Opicina were crowing. The night had gone and we didn't even know it. She fixed coffee and I shaved. And then it was time for me to go to work.

What did all or any of all this add up to? Nothing that would make the rivers run backward or stars fall down and stones bleed. Only that two people, a couple of the vast tribe of losers, found out that they could share themselves. They could take their separate selves and their pasts and mingle them together. That they could speak to each other about these things in words without having to tell lies. Anything shared and exchanged that way becomes less of a burden to bear. If I couldn't hate myself in her eyes, why should I hate myself at all? Both of us, each in a different way, had had all the big jokes played on us. And we could still laugh. We were able to love. We didn't have to feel sorry for ourselves or anybody else.

Somebody might say that this kind of knowledge and experience might spoil things. Concern, tenderness for somebody else's wounds and scars, and even privacy have ruined many a good thing. Real feeling is for the dark, somebody might say. There are plenty of good reasons to flick off the lights when you make love. People can stand only so much of the truth. All that may be so. I can't argue or defend myself. All I can say is that for us anyway, we lived a little while in full daylight. And nothing was spoiled then. When we were together it was like we were dancing. We were in step and in tune with everything under the sun.

Which is, I guess, a fancy way to talk about anything that was so good and simple. Better to say it was good and simple. Better to say that once we were able to shuck off our disguises and costumes as simply as shucking off our clothes we had lost a heavy weight. We felt lighthearted and able to rejoice.

PART FOUR

Old Man

14

AS ANYONE with half a brain could tell, I was getting myself into a fix. All these things, these adventures and discoveries, I've been talking about happened to me at home. My new home. Before that the only kind of a home I ever had was the Army. Now it was not anymore. It was just the place where I put in my day's work. It was just a job.

I didn't start to notice this change right away. And even when I did notice it I pretended that it didn't mean anything and wouldn't have any consequences. When you know something, work or a way of life, well enough, it's easy to go through all the right motions without sweating or straining. And for a while you can fool everybody including yourself.

Sure, I hadn't been able to fool Mooney. And I respected his judgment and understood his way of looking at things, but I didn't think he was right. I figured I could split my life right up the middle and get away with it as well or better than the next guy. Most of the guys who hung around the

Hidden Bar didn't pay it much mind. People come and go, drop in and out, without having to make excuses. If they thought anything about it at all, they probably just figured I was off on some kind of a kick and would be back in the fold as soon as it was played out. I tried to play it very cool about the black market. Never flashed money around or talked about it. Never bought much at our own PX. I'd go elsewhere and get one thing at one place. You have to be careful, because news about a thing like that can get around in a hurry.

The only one to put two and two together and guess what was really going on was Singletree. He waited until he had a chance to talk to me alone to say anything about it. Even then he didn't pry and ask questions. He just told me what he knew. Which was the same thing as showing me where I had left tracks and traces behind me. A help.

"That Stitch is a worthless guy," he told me. "You have to watch him. You have to watch out for him."

"I know it, but I've got my eyes on him."

"Well, if you get yourself in a spot and there's anything I can do, just let me know."

I mentioned before how I used to catch myself getting mad every time my name came up on the guard roster or I had to pull extra hours in the gun park or the motor pool to finish some job that had to be done. I didn't worry about that, though. Not enough to try and find out what it was really a sign of. What was really happening, I can see now, was I was gradually losing the one thing you have got to have if you're going to be any kind of a soldier at all—the old shrug, the old that's-the-way-the-ball-bounces attitude. My strength and protection, my cover and concealment before, had been that I didn't have anything left to lose. That was all the power I had. Like Samson's head of hair. Well, now I was getting myself in a position where I could be hurt again. I was getting as vulnerable as any man can be.

• • •

Lieutenant Costello know something was going on. He should have noticed something. After all, he had been studying me and bugging me ever since I joined the outfit.

"You look kind of tired, Riche," he'd say. "What's the matter with you? What have you been doing to yourself?"

If I happened to screw up some way, make a mistake on the gun say, he wouldn't come running up and give me the benefit of a real reaming-out. That would have been all right. That's something I understood and I could take that any time. In one ear and out the other. But instead of chewing me out he would just cluck his tongue and shake his head like he was deeply and personally disappointed.

If he ever had anything to say to me, he'd call me aside to do it.

"You know better than that, Riche," he'd say.

Or it might be the little things of sloppy soldiering that caught his eye. He knew damn well from the first time he ever saw me that I could soldier with the best of them. Now sometimes he would be able to catch me with something like a pocket button undone. He'd come up close to me and flip the unbuttoned flap with his finger.

"Getting careless, getting sloppy," he'd say. "Better watch it."

Always quiet and calm, always as if in some strange sort of a way he had some kind of respect for me. But I could feel the kind of respect it was. Like a hunter's respect for the animal he's after. It slowly started to get to me and bug me when it was clear that all he was doing was cat-and-mouse stuff. Everything he did seemed to be telling me without words: *Riche, I've got my eyes on you all the time. You're starting to get soft, to slack off and get careless. Watch it. Watch out, boy, you better stay right on your toes.*

It went along like that for quite a while before we came to the right time and the right place to lay out our cards in words.

That happened one day in the mess hall. The mess

sergeant, Sergeant Loller, had taken a liking to me and sometimes during the afternoon if I had a break I'd go over there
and have a cup of coffee and shoot the breeze with him. This
particular afternoon I went into the kitchen and poured myself a cup of coffee. Loller wasn't around anywhere, and if
there's one crowd I don't like to spend time with it's the
cooks. So I went into the empty mess hall to drink it. It
turned out there was somebody else there having himself a
coffee break—Lieutenant Costello. He looked up from stir-
ring his coffee when I came walking in and he jerked his head
at me for me to come and sit down with him. I sat down and
we sipped our coffee and talked all around the subject as
pretty as you please. We talked about the late summer
weather, about how things were going in the outfit, about
the training schedule and whether or not we'd be going up
to Germany for maneuvers in the fall. But all the time we
were talking about this and that—and I even went and got us
both a second cup of coffee—I could feel it coming on and
building up like the change in the smell of the wind when a
rainstorm is going to blow in.

"Riche, whatever happened to you? When you first came
in the outfit, I figured you had pretty well shaped up. I
thought you'd keep right on bucking until you could make
sergeant again. You looked like you were bound and determined to be a chief of section."

"I don't know what you're talking about, Lieutenant."

"Sure you do. You just don't give a damn anymore, do
you?"

"I wouldn't say that."

"*I* would. I'd say now you never did give a damn and you
never will."

"Maybe you're right, sir. Maybe I was just born to be a
bum."

"That may be true," he said. "But let me tell you, I don't
have any place for lazy bums in my firing battery. I haven't
got any use for bums."

He was still very soft-voiced and still grinning at me, all sweetness and light, not showing an ounce of anger to go along with the meaning of the words. I made up my mind to play the same part. I kept the tone of my voice and expression on my face friendly.

"You might be wrong, sir. It's *possible*."

"I doubt it."

"Tell you what," I said. "If you've got any real complaints, any legitimate ones, let's hear them. Or, I'll tell you, better yet, let's you and me go have a talk with the Old Man about it."

"We will," he said. "We'll be doing just that one of these fine days."

He reached in his back pocket and pulled out a little notebook. He riffled the pages to show me, like a gambler shuffling a deck of cards, then stuck it back in his pocket.

"I keep a notebook," he said. "A man just about has got to keep a notebook in the Army nowadays. In this little book I've got several pages devoted to the problem of Private Riche."

"It must be very interesting. I'd like to read it sometime," I said. "Maybe I'll start keeping one too. In self-defense. That would be pretty good, wouldn't it, sir? Instead of arguing or talking to each other we could both whip out our notebooks and write."

Well, that was sassy enough. He finally got bugged at that and changed his tone. His face flushed red and he stood up to go.

"I know you're up to something. I have a pretty good idea what it is. When I know for sure—and I'll know, all right— I'm not going to be satisfied with anything less than a good long session at the College for you. I'd a whole lot rather it was Leavenworth, but the College will do. You may not know it, but you've already bought yourself a one-way ticket there."

He was standing over me, leaning his weight on his arms,

bent across the table close to my face. He looked like the thing that would have made him feel a whole lot better fast was to clear his throat and spit in my eyes.

"Lieutenant Costello, how come you keep bugging me all the time? What do you have against me? What did I ever do to you?"

"You don't know, do you?"

"Sir, I don't have a clue."

"It's guys like you that are ruining the Army," he said. "It's all you slimy, no-good, worthless, slick operators, like a bunch of snakes, that are ruining everything. So you got sent to Korea and got yourself shot. So they gave you a Purple Heart and the DSC. Does that make you a special, privileged character in this world or something? Do you think the Army owes you something? Let me tell you, the Army doesn't owe people like you a damn thing."

So that was it. The bastard loved the Army, and guys like me were spoiling it for him. Well, I could understand that. Under other circumstances, say if I was in *his* shoes . . . But, goddamn it, I wasn't in them and he had no right to ask that of me.

"Lieutenant, may I ask you one question? That's all, just one question."

"What's that?"

"Why are you pissed-off they sent you here instead of Korea?"

"Just what do you mean by that?"

"You know exactly what I mean."

I got up quickly and turned my back on him and started walking out of the mess hall.

"Just a minute there, soldier," he yelled after me. "Where do you think you're going?"

I didn't stop. I didn't even slow down.

"I wouldn't know about you, sir. But *I've* still got some work to do."

• • •

Jethroe couldn't seem to get himself shipped out of the Command. Every time he came up for shipment and was all set, something or other would go wrong with his orders. One time they even had him to pack his duffel bag and go stand in front of the barracks waiting for a jeep to come from the motor pool and take him down to a troopship in the harbor. At the last minute, with the jeep in sight and coming, Fishbein came tearing out of the orderly room waving his arms and yelling to wait. Something was wrong again and he would have to wait until the next shipment.

Poor old Sergeant Jethroe looked so sad and helpless and confused, standing there and trying to take it all in. Fishbein was so ashamed (even if it wasn't any fault of his) that he picked up Jethroe's duffel bag and carried it back upstairs for him and even unpacked it and made up the bed.

Jethroe still had his portable radio and his Bible to keep him company. He still left quotations from the Good Book under my pillow for me every day. He lay up there in that room and vegetated. I got the feeling that he was slowly freezing up. Like an old worn-out, rusty piece of machinery. By the time they got him to a psycho hospital, if they ever did, he would probably be too far gone to be cured.

Stitch started to worry me too. I started to get the feeling he was turning salty on me. I didn't want to keep mixed up in this hustling of drugs and medicines forever. I wanted to get out. Just a little while longer. Just long enough to stash away a little more so I could make it through the winter with Angela without having to move or sell our stuff. After that maybe I could make ends meet the rest of the time by handling a few cartons of cigarettes and playing a little payday poker. The thing I had to worry about was if Stitch got out of control too soon and spoiled everything.

For one thing, Stitch was starting to act like he was scared of his own shadow. He kept coming to me with stories about how some car was always following him around. And once he said some characters had come around the neighborhood where his shack was asking questions about him and his girl. Well, that might mean something or it might not. If it was really the CID or the local VG cops, they probably would have made their play now . . . If they had one to make. They would move fast as soon as they knew anything at all. I didn't think they knew anything yet. I told Stitch that, and I told him not to worry about it. What I didn't tell him was— if there was anything at all to his story—it looked to me like a situation where some local gangsters might be fishing around. They might be fixing to move in and try and get a good thing away from us. Somebody like Pissoni might be behind it, or have put them up to it anyway. Naturally it would be a bonehead play. How could they get at the stuff except through the Army and us? Still, they might be able to put the bite on us and cut our profit in little pieces. I could tell it was getting high time to wash my hands of the whole thing.

"What are you worrying about?" I said. "What are you afraid of?"

I was surprised when his lips trembled and he blinked his eyes.

"Jail," he said. "I don't want to go to jail."

"Aw, it's not so bad. You can get used to it like anything else."

"Riche, I'm not as rugged as I used to be. I don't like hard living any more."

"You can get rugged again. They break you in fast."

"Don't kid about it. I ain't joking. I'm telling you the honest-to-God truth. I don't think I could stand it anymore."

"You got a gun?"

"Yeah," he said. "I keep one under the seat of the car."

"Then you don't have to let anybody take you. If you're so anxious to keep out of jail, don't let them take you."

"Jesus, though. I don't want to get myself *killed* to stay out of jail."

"Don't then," I said. "Anyway you've always got the gun in case you need it."

For some reason I'll never know that idea seemed to cheer him up and make him feel a lot better.

Stitch was yellow all right. But not in the usual way. Not the way most people might think. He was trigger-happy yellow, the way I figured. He would be the kind of guy who would shoot prisoners in combat when he didn't have to. (I didn't have to ask him to guess that he probably had, too.) You would never want to stick him out on your perimeter defense with a machine gun. He would be blasting away at shadows all night long and nobody would get any sleep. If you were in the Infantry with Stitch, you would never want to be on a reconnaissance patrol with him, where you're not supposed to shoot unless you have to. But yellow and trigger-happy or not, he wouldn't be afraid to kill. His kind can kill easy. They don't want to *get* killed, but they aren't afraid of doing some killing themselves.

What I was really interested in was something else. I had asked him that just to find out if he had a gun. That was going to change my plans for me now. I would have to get hold of one too. For several reasons. Sooner or later, Stitch might get it in his head to come after me. It wouldn't take a whole lot, not if he got good and worried and scared, for Stitch to start thinking that I was the cause of all his troubles. People get funny ideas when they're worried and scared. Still, I didn't take this too seriously in Stitch's case. It takes more brains than he had to fool yourself that way. Then there was always the outside chance that he might get himself in a game of tag with the local gangsters. In that case, I would want to have a gun around too. Just for bluff, if nothing else.

What were the real reasons? What I mean is, why did I decide I needed a gun? It turned out to be important, and looking back on it now I can make more sense out of it than I could then. I guess that deep down I was worried. I was starting to get good and scared, too. I was afraid of losing what I had. Even if I had come by it by accident. I don't mean things. I mean Angela and our life together. The gun was a sign of weakness, then. And having a gun stood for the idea that I would rather die than have to lose Angela. Whether or not I ever intended to use it is something else again. Probably I didn't. I just don't know. So I guess what I really wanted it for was as a kind of lucky piece, like a saint's medal or a rabbit's foot. Even a pistol can mean something like that sometimes. In Korea I had seen some guys who would have done anything, even to killing their best buddies, to get one. Somebody even wrote a book about it. Anyhow I knew I wanted one.

That took some doing. Because a pistol is hard to come by in the Army. *Especially* in the Army. You just can't steal one from the Army and expect to get away with it for long. You could buy one in Trieste, an Italian pistol, but you would have to go through a whole lot of routine and paper work if you wanted to get it there. In my case that would be begging for trouble. All I needed was to get myself investigated. It would be possible to buy one illegally, but I would have to pay through the nose for a piece of junk. I might as well get one made out of pure gold. I had to find the right place to steal one.

I went and asked Angus Singletree about it.

"Where can I get me a gun?"

"What kind of a gun?"

Anybody else in the world would have said: "What do you need a gun for?"

"A pistol."

"Has your boy gone and got himself one?"

"Yeah."

"Christ," he said. "What do you know about that? I guess you better get one."

Angus told me how. They kept all the personally owned weapons in the arms room. First thing to do would be to find out what they had down there and who owned what. You wouldn't want to steal one that belonged to the Old Man, for example. Next thing was to buddy up to the armorer and see if I could get the run of the arms room.

This I did. I volunteered or else got myself put on all the weapons-cleaning details. There was always plenty of machine guns, thirties and fifties, to be cleaned up and taken care of, and then there were the rocket launchers, the spare rifles and carbines and grease guns and the officers' side arms. One thing I know is weapons. I got down there and worked hard and well all the time. Never goofed off and showed a great interest and respect for weapons. I always talked sweet to the college-boy corporal. I never let on to him that I knew more about weapons than he would ever learn. I let him tell me about them. And I acted like I liked it.

In no time at all I had me a pistol, a neat little Italian Beretta. He went out of the arms room for just a few minutes—"Mind the store for me, will you, Johnny?"—and, buddy, it was all mine. It used to be Jethroe's. Well, poor bastard, he would never use it. He wouldn't need it, where he was headed.

When I took it home with me—that's where I planned to keep it, right next to the bed in the dresser drawer—Angela found it. I had brought her some presents from the PX and a bunch of flowers too, a lot of stuff, so I could sneak it in the house. I thought I had gotten away with it. But later we were playing around and wrestling on the bed and she happened to open the drawer. She must have thought it was just a toy or something. She grabbed it and rolled over on top of me and pointed it right between my eyes.

"Boom! Bang, bang!" she said laughing. "Cowboy, you're dead."

I'm telling you I was sweating bricks for a second or two there. I wasn't even breathing. Very slowly I reached up and moved the pistol away and took it from her.

"Jesus Christ, woman. That gun is loaded."

I don't know what I must have looked like, what kind of crazy expression was all over my big, bare face, but she got the message and jumped back like it was red hot. I put it back in the drawer. And then we had a talk about pistols.

She told me a story about some friend of hers who had been a dancer in one of the nightclubs a few years before. This girl got mixed up with some American officer. He got her knocked up and then he was going to leave her. The girl shot him in bed with his own pistol. Then she was going to kill herself. She didn't do such a good job of it. All she ended up doing was blowing away the top of her head and half of her face. She didn't die. They managed to save her, and even now she was alive somewhere in the Territory in a hospital, out of her mind but living on, like some kind of an ugly vegetable.

I remember now that I showed Angela exactly where somebody ought to point a gun if they wanted to be good and dead. I used my index finger and my thumb, like a kid playing.

When I tried to explain to her why I had gotten the pistol, it turned out to be hard to explain. I couldn't. Angela didn't care and wasn't worried. As long as I wanted to have it, it was all right with her. I left it in the drawer and forgot about it.

15

IF WE HADN'T been out in the field for ten days on some kind of half-assed maneuvers . . . If my name hadn't come up on the guard roster the first night back in the *caserma* . . . I keep going over it and telling myself *if* this and *if* that. Things might have been a whole lot different. It's one of the ways I have to keep on kidding myself.

The point is I was away from Angela at the time when she needed me.

It had turned fall already. A cold, dry wind was blowing in hard and steady from Yugoslavia. The little trees up where we were looked like picked chickens. Old stewing hens. Nothing but rocks, dust, dead trees, and that cold wind. The cuckoo's season was long gone. Downtown they had already closed up all the sidewalk cafés for the season, until the next spring. The Via Settembre was wide and empty. Wind in the streets stirred up little clouds of dust and chased trash and dead leaves along the sidewalks and gutters. It was changing

171

into a gray bitter time when everyone would huddle close to stoves at home.

As soon as we got back to the *caserma* from the maneuvers, they posted the guard list and my name was on it. I tried to call Angela and let her know. That took some doing. I had to shave and shower and put on a clean uniform and stand Guard Mount first. The nearest phone to our apartment was in the bar about a block away. I always had to argue with the guy who owned the bar in my miserable Italian and promise him something from the PX to get him to send a message for her to call me at the *caserma*. That took a lot of time too. By the time she called, the first time, I was already on guard walking my post. So I had to start in again as soon as I was re- lieved. We were finally able to get on the phone at the same time after midnight.

"What's the matter with you?" I said. "What's the trouble? What's wrong?"

She told me she was pregnant.

I knew she had missed her period. But I didn't worry about that too much. It happens. And if I let myself get all worried about a thing like that every time it happened, I would have been dead and buried from just worry long be- fore I ever got to Trieste. But this time, while I was away on the maneuvers, she had gone to see a doctor and it was pretty definite. There wasn't a whole lot I could say to her on the phone. You never can say much on the phone anyway. And there I was in the orderly room with the CQ and a whole lot of other guys hanging around, playing cards and waiting to use the phone themselves. It was a kind of one-sided conver- sation. She begged me to slip away and come on home and at least be with her a few minutes and talk. I couldn't, be- cause Lieutenant Costello was officer of the day. Going AWOL from guard duty, that was all he'd need on me to ship me the whole way to Leavenworth. And I couldn't explain that on the damn phone. Not in front of people. Not with Costello himself sitting at a desk right in the orderly room.

She didn't understand how one time I would break a law or a rule and another time I wouldn't. I asked her please to wait until I could get home the next night. That's the best I could do at the time. She hung up on me. I can't say I blamed her. But it didn't help anything.

When I finally did get home the next evening everything was thoroughly freaked up. The apartment was a complete mess. She had been drinking *vino* all day long I guess. Anyway she had gotten sick off of it and puked all over the bedroom floor. I got good and mad. I knew it was dumb to let myself get mad about a thing like that. And it wasn't helping things, either. But, anyway, I got mad as hell and stomped around the place yelling at her for a few minutes. Somehow or other I was able to see how silly I was and I stopped carrying on and got busy and cleaned the whole place up. Then I helped her wash and I fixed some strong coffee. When she got the coffee down I made her take the real cure—cognac. She shook herself out of it and we could talk.

Angela knew I was still legally married in the States. I had never hidden that from her. Even if I could get a divorce the first thing in the morning (and it was a sure thing that my wife, the bitch, wouldn't divorce me if the next day was scheduled on the calendar to be Judgment Day), I still wouldn't be able to get married to Angela. It was hard enough, in fact damn near impossible, for a GI to marry one of the local girls. (No wonder there are so many little GI bastards all over the world.) But with Angela's official record—a marriage to the Kraut soldier that was still legal here, anyway; her two children, one of them a bastard; and her VD record—it was out of the question. I figured I might be able to support my own baby all right, so she wouldn't have to give it up like the other two, but we both knew that sooner or later I would get shipped back home to the States. She would be right back where she started, on her own again except for one more mouth she couldn't feed.

The thing to do, the simple thing, the thing most of the

173

local girls had to depend on, was an abortion. It was the obvious thing to do, the only move that made any sense. But Angela would have none of that. She wouldn't have anything to do with the idea. She said it was the same thing as murder.

"You don't understand," she said. "I love you. I want to have your baby."

"But you can't. Don't you see that?"

"I want to."

"That's crazy."

I kept arguing with her and telling her that the only thing to do was to get an abortion. This slowly led us into a real knockdown and dragout. We said a lot of angry bitter things to each other. She cursed me for being like every other no-good American GI. She said I was just like Culver all over again. And I slapped her silly for that.

We said and did a lot of things we shouldn't have. She cried and carried on, screamed at me. I got so mad at her that I walked out and left her. I drove downtown and got drunk.

I got back after midnight and found she had locked me out. I had to climb up and go through a window and I was so drunk I slipped and almost fell and broke my fool neck. But I wasn't mad at her anymore. I wanted to hold her in my arms and say how sorry I was. She pretended she was asleep. I knew she was just pretending, but I didn't blame her. She mumbled something and turned away to the wall with her ass toward me. She hugged her pillow. That was the only time Angela ever pulled a trick like that on me. I went to sleep with all my clothes on, feeling bad.

If I had only had a chance to talk to her in the morning . . . One more big *if.*

The trouble was I overslept. If I missed the reveille formation I would wind up being restricted to the *caserma* for a week or ten days. That would only make things worse. As it was, I barely had time to jump out of the bed and run for the car and drive out to the *caserma* about eighty miles an hour. I didn't have time to change into fatigues and I had to stand formation in my OD uniform. Sergeant Ryder didn't like that a damn bit. He always figured if *he* could get himself into fatigues, then anybody else could. But he just gave me a hard look. He didn't report me or anything.

That day was supposed to be payday. My own personal payday. Stitch was supposed to meet me in my car in the parking lot during noon chowtime and divide up the money. I was feeling so sick and shaky with a hangover I couldn't eat anything anyway. I drank some coffee in the mess hall and then went straight on out to my car. He was already there waiting on me.

"How did we make out?"

Stitch shrugged. "Pissoni wouldn't buy. He says he's got himself a new source."

"What did you do with the stuff?"

"It's at my shack."

"Jesus Christ, Stitch, how dumb can you get?"

"I couldn't think of anything else to do with it. What else could I do? What would *you* do with it?"

My brain wasn't working too well. I had a headache and that's all I could seem to think about.

"You know what I think?" I said finally. "Pissoni doesn't have any other source. He's bluffing. He couldn't have another source. He just wants a bigger cut."

"He said his new source was a whole lot cheaper."

"What did you do?"

"What could I do?" Stitch said. "Nothing. He told me he wasn't buying and I left. That's all."

"Too bad."

"Well, what was I going to do—shoot him or something?"

"Forget it. Don't worry about it," I said. "A thing like this happens sometimes."

"What are we gonna do now? We got to do something."

"There's a couple of things we can do. One is, we can wait."

"*Wait?* Listen, man, I can't just keep all that stuff laying around my shack while we *wait.*"

"You just cool it and listen to me," I said. "I'm trying to think about this out loud. We can either wait a while and sweat him down until he comes back begging for it . . ."

"Why would he do that?"

"Quit asking so many dumb questions."

"You're the one that got me into this," Stitch said.

"If you keep your fat mouth shut, I'll get you out too."

That made him mad and he went for his knife. It was that snake instinct of his. When he reached for it I grabbed him by the throat before he could even get his hand out of his pocket and I banged his head against the rolled-up window hard.

"Turn loose of that knife."

He took a good look at my face and guessed I wasn't fooling. He relaxed and went limp and showed me his empty hand. Then I let go of him and smiled and went right on talking like the whole thing had been a slight interruption.

"We got something else we can do," I said. "We can always go down and see him. Lay our cards on the table. Sweat him out. Right away, this evening."

That was the kind of idea that would appeal to Stitch. When in doubt, *do* something, anything. His whole way of life and philosophy in a nutshell. Well, that's the way I would play it, then. Anyway I couldn't wait around until Pissoni decided to do business again. That might take a month or so. With Angela pregnant I would need the money right away.

"Do you think it'll work?"

"Sure it will," I said. "He's a fat, yellow slob."

"When do you want to go?"

"We'll go early, right after supper. Say seven-thirty or eight. We'll scare the shit out of him and he'll change his mind."

That was that. The first sergeant's whistle was already blowing for the afternoon formation. We had to run to make it.

• • •

I will never know what would have happened if we had gone through with it like we planned. Judging by what did happen, I'd probably be dead and wouldn't be around to tell the story. Maybe that wouldn't be such a bad thing. I don't know what might have happened. All I do know is what happened to Stitch and me separately.

I got through that afternoon some way or another. At five o'clock I was through and I went over to the little branch PX at our *caserma* and picked up about twenty cartons of cigarettes. It was easy to do if you could get the coupons. There were always plenty of guys willing to sell theirs. Getting the coupons wasn't such a big thing. In a command the size of TRUST a guy could hustle a couple of hundred cartons a week if he really worked at it. I figured as long as I was planning to go downtown on business anyway that evening I might just as well make a few extra bucks. I would see if I could make Pissoni buy the cigarettes. And at a good price too. I stuffed the cigarettes in my laundry bag underneath some dirty clothes and headed for the parking lot.

I was just opening the trunk of my car when out from behind of another car popped Lieutenant Costello and a guy in civilian clothes. The other one in the civvies was a CID man if I ever saw one. They said hold it. I grinned at them and looked surprised.

"What have you got in that bag, Riche?"

"What do people usually put in a laundry bag—peanuts?"

"Dump it out."

"Right here on the ground?"

"You heard me."

"Is that a direct order?"

"It's an order."

Lieutenant Costello's face lit up like a lantern when all those cartons of cigarettes came tumbling out on the ground. Twenty lousy cartons of cigarettes! I would probably draw sixty days at the College for it. If they could make it stick.

"Okay," the CID man said. "What's your story?"

177

"Thing is, I'm nervous," I said. "I'm a chain smoker. I smoke all the time. Sometimes I get two or three cigarettes going at the same time."

"You're under arrest."

"You are confined strictly to quarters until further notice," Lieutenant Costello said.

"You mean my *room?*"

"That is correct."

"Is it all right to walk across the hall to the latrine or do I piss in the wastebasket?"

"That's all, Riche. Check in with the first sergeant and then report to your room."

I shrugged and turned away and started strolling over to the barracks.

"Riche!"

"What?"

"What—"

He was fit to be tied. He couldn't say "What *what?*" like he started to without sounding pretty silly. He stopped himself just in time and glared at me red-faced.

"You want me?"

"You forgot something, soldier."

Again: "What?"

He was doing his best to control himself. I'll give him that much. I was pushing him pretty far in front of the CID man.

"You forgot to salute."

"Oh," I said, giving him a big stupid grin. "I didn't forget. I just *didn't,* that's all."

He was choking as I turned my back on him and headed for the orderly room.

Sergeant Ryder listened to what had happened—I just told it to him straight, why try and lie to somebody like him?— without even changing expression. I think Ryder would have had the same look on his face if somebody had come running in and said a man from Mars was running amuck in the motor pool. Nothing surprised him anymore.

"Okay, you've gone and done it now," he said. "You've messed up my morning report."

"Relax, Sarge. I'm not in jail yet."

"You will be, soon enough."

"Well, I'll try and soldier my way out quick, so you won't have to fool with it too long."

"Hell, once you get down there you might just as well stay. It's just as much trouble to pick you up again on the morning report when you get out."

"I always try and oblige."

"The Old Man ain't going to like it."

"How come? It's no skin off his ass."

"It seems like every time we get a real good gunner in the battery, they jail him. The Old Man thinks it's some kind of a plot or something."

So there we were, Jethroe and me, two old scarecrows, two old crooks, just laying on our bunks and staring at the cracks in the ceiling. One thing good about sharing a room with Jethroe: at least I didn't have to explain to him what I was doing there. Truth is, we hadn't had a word between us in a long time. No hard feelings, just nothing to say. No communication except for the notes under my pillow. He was sweating out another shipment home. Any day now, they said. A couple of chronic losers, Jethroe and me.

Poor Angela! By morning they would know about her. And in the morning the CID would probably go and search the apartment. They wouldn't find any cigarettes or anything. Except maybe that stolen pistol. And she might even be able to keep them from finding that. They would find the signs of good, expensive living, way beyond my salary, and that would be evidence against me. They would ask her a whole lot of questions. And naturally they wouldn't tell her anything. She would assume the worst and worry herself sick before I could get some word to her. I hoped she was feeling better. I hoped a chance would come along so I could get word to her. I hoped she wouldn't have to be called as a witness for the court-martial.

I lay there sweating it out—oh, they finally had me by the balls all right!—when Stitch came ducking in.

"Where can we talk?"

"Right here," I said. "What's wrong with here?"

He jerked his head at old Jethroe. Jethroe hadn't even paid any attention when Stitch came in the room.

"He don't know what's going on," I said. "Or if he does, he don't care."

"What are we going to do now?"

"Nothing I guess. There isn't anything to do."

"Look, man, I gotta do something about all that stuff."

"Throw it away. Drive over to that big cave near Opicina tonight and dump it in. They'll never find it."

He smiled at me and shook his head. It dawned on me that old Stitch was pretty loose. He was feeling pretty good. With me out of action, that made him the top dog. He liked that fine. All he wanted out of life was to be a bigshot. Or, anyway, to be able to think he was a bigshot. The poor ignorant bastard!

"Don't worry," he was telling me. "Don't you worry about a thing, Johnny. I'll go down and see Pissoni tonight. I'll get the money from him and I'll keep everything going along. Don't you worry, you'll get a fair share."

"I don't want a share. I want out as of right now."

"Suit yourself."

"You know what? If I was you, Stitch, I'd get rid of that stuff quick and then forget the whole thing."

"You don't think I can handle it all by myself, do you?"

"It don't matter what I think," I said. "Your slickest move is to forget the whole thing. Let well enough alone. Things are liable to get hot around here."

"You just don't think I can do it."

"Okay then. I don't."

"Things are hot for you. Not for me."

180

"Have it your own way, buddy. Go ahead and kid your-self along if you want to."

"Don't worry about me," he said. "I'll take care of everything."

"Sure you will."

I was going to ask him to get word to Angela. To tell her I wasn't in any bad trouble yet, I would be in touch soon, not to get all worried and so forth. But I gave up on that idea. Stitch would only make things worse.

He winked at me and left the room. On tiptoe, for God's sake! I kept staring at the ceiling until night came on and the whole room was dark. And I fell asleep.

16

NEXT THING I knew somebody was shaking me very gently to wake me up. I sat up straight and looked at my watch first thing out of habit. Past three o'clock. Then I saw who it was. Fishbein was leaning over my bed. He put his finger to his lips to signal hush. For some reason it made me remember the hospital. He looked like a nurse standing over my bed. It made me feel better about things and I smiled in the dark.

"Get up and come in the latrine," he whispered.

I got up and went across the hall. We sat down on a couple of crappers side by side. He gave me a cigarette and a light.

"I got bad news for you," he said. "It's terrible. I never thought anything like this would happen to him."

"Who?"

"Stitch."

"What did he do? What happened to him?"

"He was downtown. He killed somebody."

"Did they catch him?"

"No," Fishbein said. "You wouldn't exactly say they *caught* him. After he shot this man he got away. But he got himself cornered up on a roof. He wouldn't give up. He tried to shoot it out with some VG cops and they killed him. They said he hit two of the cops and one of them may die. Would you believe it?"

"All except one thing. I don't know how he ever hit the two policemen. I wouldn't have bet that slob could hit the broad side of a barn with a pistol."

"It *was* a pistol," he said. "How did you know?"

"Everybody knows Stitch had a pistol."

"Are you mixed up in it?"

Fishbein seemed worried about me. It was almost funny, a nice clean college boy like that worrying about me. Except having somebody you think you hardly know really worry about you is more than a joke.

"Not so as you'd notice," I said. "Not so anybody can tie me in—I think."

"Well, anyway, I thought you'd probably want to know."

"Thanks."

For a while we sat there and smoked and didn't say anything. I could tell Fishbein had something else on his mind though.

"I hope you don't mind," he said finally.

"Mind what?"

"When I picked up my pass this evening I went and told your girlfriend where you were and what had happened. So she wouldn't worry too much."

"Why did you do that?" I said. "I mean, I thank you for it. But why?"

He shrugged. "Somebody had to."

Fishbein was just a soft round guy, and working behind a desk as the battery clerk hadn't helped his shape any. He looked like he was a butterball, soft all the way through. But a man can fool you like that. I knew he was good and tough and you could count on him. You could go anywhere with a guy like that.

"She's a good-looking woman," Fishbein said.

"How did she take it?"

"All right," he said. "She was worried, but I don't think she scares too easy."

I knew I wasn't going to be able to get back to sleep right away. So I thought I might talk awhile, as long as he was willing.

"What you going to do when you get out?"

"I don't know," he said. "I guess I'll go back to school. Maybe law school or something."

"This must be hell for you, being in the Army. A real waste of time."

"No," he said. "That's what you might think. I mean, sure I hated it at first. And I still don't *like* it. It's not for me. But I wouldn't trade the experience."

"Sure," I said. "But what can you do with it? Write a book."

He laughed. "Maybe. I just might do that."

"Shit, they've written them all already."

All of us read all the books about the service. They were in cheap paperbacks and they sold them in the PXs. A paperback just exactly fits the back pocket of a pair of fatigue pants or field pants. You can button the pocket and it doesn't make too much of a bulge. I've read a lot of books that way. You spend so much time waiting around you might as well read as sit on your thumbs. Reading is as good a way to kill time as any. I've read a whole lot of them—*Naked and the Dead, Caine Mutiny, Walk in the Sun*—oh, a lot. Far and away the best of the bunch for my money was *From Here to Eternity*. It was the truest. Up to a point. I told Fishbein I didn't see how he could improve on that. I mean that pretty well said it about Army life. Funny thing, when I said that Fishbein's eyes lit up. I had got to him. Now we were talking about something he really liked and cared about. You never know what somebody will care about.

"Sure," he said. "That was a pretty good book. But that was quite a while ago."

"Things haven't changed that much. Soldiering is about the same."

"Well, maybe so," Fishbein said. "But there's one big difference. All those characters in the old prewar, peacetime Army were different in one way. None of them had been in a war. Almost all of you guys have been shot at. Some of you, like Ryder and Mooney and Loller, say, have been in *two* wars. That makes a hell of a difference."

"Okay, maybe we've all got more miles on our shoes."

"That's not all," Fishbein went on. "You guys have even read the books . . ."

"Even me."

"So now a new book would be about how you really are, how you old-timers think and act. How it is to be shot at and then come back and soldier in peacetime. Only this time it's not really peace at all. You've got to be ready to be shot at again maybe tomorrow morning. You're all pros."

"Take a good look at Jethroe. There's a pro. When you write your book put him in it."

All of a sudden Fishbein started laughing.

"What's so funny about that?"

"Not that," he said. "I don't know. It's just crazy as hell. I mean here we are, you and I, sitting on a couple of crappers and having a *literary* argument at three o'clock in the morning. You're under arrest and a buddy of yours just got killed. I mean, who would ever believe it?"

"Put it in your book and find out."

First thing in the morning they told me to get dressed in a Class A Uniform. I had to go downtown to CID headquarters. Sometime during the night they had picked up Stitch's girl and she told them everything she knew. Which couldn't be much. I wasn't too worried. They didn't really have anything to connect me with Stitch except her word. Anything she might have heard from Stitch would be hearsay evidence. And I hadn't even seen the girl since that weekend in May.

I got myself all slicked up and sharp and they took me down to CID in a jeep with an armed guard—one of our own guys, for God's sake. When we got there, on the way in, I saw a whole bunch of medics from the main hospital sitting on a bench waiting to be questioned. My boy was right in there among them waiting his turn. I noticed he had gotten rid of the gold earring and was busy clipping his nails while he waited. He looked up and saw me and his face didn't show a thing at first. I had just time as I passed by to give him one good look. *If you say one word about me, I'll crucify you. I'll castrate you,* my look said. Or I hoped it did. I was pretty sure he wouldn't talk. Even if they got him. It's a funny thing about fairies, but, like I said, they are tuned in on a different wavelength and frequency. They hear different music. I think that look scared him a whole lot more than the idea of going to jail. Anyway, a fairy could be a lot worse off than in jail. He could get all the action he wanted there.

They bombed away at me and my story all morning. I don't blame them. With my record and on paper I looked like their man. It was the biggest case they had had in a long time and they put a couple of pretty good interrogating officers on me. But I could tell, even with all Stitch's girl had told them, they were bluffing. I kept answering their questions and denying everything. I kept on smiling and shaking my head.

"Let me ask *you* a question, sir."

"All right."

"If I'm half as slick as you think, if I'm the big-time operator you make out, how come I got busted with twenty measly cartons of cigarettes?"

One of them started to laugh, but the other one let him know it wasn't funny.

"Alibi," the serious one said. "You had yourself covered and let the other guy take the fall."

"Is anybody going to believe that? This ain't the movies, sir."

"We know you were in this," the other one said. "We know it."

"Well, sir, when you think you can prove it in a court-room, you let me know."

"Tell you the truth," the serious one said, "we really don't give a damn. Your buddy is dead and we'll salt you away on this other charge."

"Don't that make it nice?"

They were plenty pissed, but finally they just had to let me go.

I was feeling bad, but it still didn't look like all my luck had run out on me. I mean, if I hadn't been caught with the crummy cigarettes, I'd probably be laying in the morgue with Stitch. Providential you might say. Even if it was cold comfort.

It was only when I got in the jeep, and we started up into the hills to the *caserma* . . . Stitch's girl had flipped and gone out of her head when she saw me coming out of the CID smiling. She tried to claw my eyes out. "You killed him! You killed my man!" she screamed . . . leaving the city and climbing up into the rocks and the dry bare country, only then did I really let it dawn on me that Stitch was dead. Poor boy. I could close my eyes and pretty well picture how it had gone. Stitch coming barging in on Pissoni all clumsy and tough. Probably waving that pistol around like a cowboy in the movies. Pissoni may have been a joke of a man, but he fooled me. A smooth one too. Otherwise, and there was the answer plain as day, how did he get where he was in the first place? I could see how he would keep talking fast to Stitch, saying anything, promising anything, while he slowly edged himself over behind his desk and even slower worked a drawer quietly open so that when the time came he could make a fast pass for his pistol. When he went for it and came up with it Stitch had to fire, more out of nerves and instinct than anything else. Then had to stand there while the smoke cleared, shocked, confused. Pissoni laying there on his back like a large dead bullfrog. What next? Run, run, run! Naturally he ran. Out the back and down the street. Probably with the pistol in his hands. Chased! Went up, climbing and crawling, to the rooftops. They came after him, taking it slow and careful, boxing him in. Up there ducking among the chimney pots something had come over him. Something I should've guessed he had, but didn't, a plain simple animal thing maybe. The cornered rat. Rat in a trap. They holler at him in bad English or maybe only in Italian to give up. And then he fights for it against the VG cops with their London bobby hats and their M-2 fully automatic carbines. Drops two of them before they clobber him and cut him down.

Some people might call it brave. I don't know what the name for it should be. I know I probably would have come out with my hands up. And I know he had saved my skin by getting himself killed up there, instead of caught. So there was some truth in the way his bitch of a girlfriend felt about it. If it hadn't been for me, Stitch wouldn't have ended up dead on that rooftop. I felt bad about it, sure, and even a little bit sad about the guy. But *sorry* for him? I'd be a liar if I said I was. I wouldn't kid myself about feeling guilty. I had enough on my own head without taking on the sins of somebody like Stitch.

17

IT WAS ONLY a few days later when I had to go for my own court-martial. It was held in the *caserma* of the First Battalion near Opicina. It was like an old-fashioned fort with its high walls and the huge green parade ground where parades for the whole command were held. I was surprised that it rolled around so soon. When They want to They can work fast. I guess They wanted to get me safely in Trust College as soon as possible.

I put on the best-looking uniform I had. Fishbein, that crazy kid, had gone to all the trouble of locating every ribbon my records said I was entitled to wear. (That's the one time you really need them—at a court-martial.) He put them on my blouse for me in the correct order according to the book. To tell you the truth I had never seen them all before and all lined up like that. When he got finished I put on my blouse and looked in the mirror. And I was pretty pleased with myself.

"Christ, kid," I said. "I look like a freaking hero, don't I? Maybe someday they'll make a statue of me and put it in a park. So the pigeons can come and shit on it. Serve me right."

Fishbein tried to laugh, but I could tell he was worried. Isn't that a funny thing—how he got himself so worried over me?

"It's a snap, a breeze," I told him. "I'll be back with the outfit in less than a month. I'll tell you all about it so you can put it in a book."

He shook his head. "Not with this outfit," he said.

"What do you mean? Where else would I go?"

"The rumor is—and I think it's right—they're going to bust up the Nth Field right away. We always have given the command a bad name. All this business with Stitch is the last straw."

"Where will everybody go?"

"Mostly to Austria, I hear. But I don't know."

"Does anybody know about this?"

"Nobody except the orderly room. Don't tell anybody."

"Don't worry. I won't."

That news set me back. It meant when I came out there wouldn't be any outfit to come back to. Maybe Fishbein was wrong, but probably not. The clerk would know before anybody else. And he wasn't the kind to pass along scuttlebutt. It was probably a sure thing. Unless I could work a deal and get assigned to one of the Infantry battalions, I'd get shipped out when my time was up. Poor Angela! What was she going to do when the news was out and the outfit busted up? Well, I would fight like hell to beat the charge. And anyway they wouldn't give me much time. Maybe I'd even be out before she really knew.

I was wrong. Oh, I was way wrong. Lieutenant Costello had primed them to throw the book at me. My lawyer turned out to be a slob, a young green second lieutenant from Quartermaster. A sock counter! He meant well, I guess, but he never really figured out what was going on. He didn't know his ass from third base. Besides he couldn't help feeling that I probably deserved whatever it was they were going to give me. He had never run into anybody like me before in his whole life. Except maybe in a book. He acted like he was afraid I might suddenly bite him or something. He let them get away with holy murder. For one thing they had Stitch's girl to testify. Now a thing like that wouldn't hold up in any court. Even a court-martial. What she had to say only prejudiced the court against me and didn't have a thing to do with what I was being tried for—twenty cartons of cigarettes in a laundry bag. The best I could hope for is that somebody would notice that error when the verdict and the sentence came up for review.

They even called Angela as a witness. I could have cried when they called her name and she came in. She was great, though, and did all she could to help me. At first I couldn't figure out what she was up to. She came walking in the court all raggedy and stringy-haired and dirty-looking. She acted stupid and scared, and they had to keep repeating the questions. For a minute or so I was really mad.

. . . What's she trying to do? I was thinking . . . Trying to prove what a cheap freaking guy I am?

Which, it slowly dawned on me, was just exactly what she was up to. From the testimony of the CID it was clear that they didn't find a thing of value in the apartment. No signs or evidence of high and fancy living in my shack. So what she must have done, I guessed, was hidden everything. Probably right downstairs in the landlord's apartment. And sitting there in the court she certainly didn't look to be the girlfriend of any big-time operator, any wheel on the local black market scene.

When I saw the job she was doing to fool them, I had a hard time to keep from laughing out loud.

I also had a few character witnesses in my favor. Mooney got up on the stand and said I was a helluva good gunner. Ryder got up there and glared around at the court, like who

191

the hell did they think they were, and told them I never gave him any trouble and always performed my duties. Singletree got up and said I was a real gentleman and a scholar. That didn't help a bit—not with *his* record. But I appreciated the sentiment. (Which is what Angus would have said if I had testified for him.)

Costello got up with his notebook and presented in evidence another side of my character. To hear him tell it I was a first-class prick with ears.

All in all, things could have been a lot worse. My service record was read out. That wouldn't help me much now in the court, because all the bad things more than canceled out the good. But in review that Distinguished Service Cross was going to jump right off the page and fly around the room. It would bring tears to some old corny colonel's eyes.

What it boiled down to was twenty cartons of cigarettes that I just couldn't get around. And my official reputation, so to speak. My record as a petty crook and a troublemaker. I guess they must have decided I was nearly incorrigible. Not *quite,* because if they had wanted to they could have kicked me out of the service while they were at it, with a Dishonorable or a Bad Conduct Discharge. When I stood up for the sentence, the major who was senior officer gave me a long speech about that, and about how they were giving me one more chance. I figured maybe I was home free. I stood there stiff as a broomstick, looking like a model soldier. Then he gave the sentence. It was the maximum possible sentence in the College—six months! I was stunned. I stood there sucking wind. I could have fainted on the spot. Of course it was bound to be reduced when it finally went before a review board. They always end up reducing my sentences. But for a minute there I was even too shook to think of that. I just kept standing there blinking and gasping like a fish out of water until two MPs came up and took my arms and hustled me out of the room.

In the narrow hallway outside the courtroom we passed

right by Angela. She stood there leaning against the wall with the tears streaming down her face.

"Don't you worry, baby," I called out. "Everything's going to be all right."

"Good-by, Johnny," she said. "*Addio.*"

And that was all. Then we were outside again moving quick along the gravel walk that ran beside the parade ground, into the parking lot, and climbing in a jeep.

"Take it easy, buddy. Just take it easy," one of the MPs said. "You can soldier out of the College in ninety days if you're lucky."

When you are sent to a disciplinary barracks you have to take along more than your razor and your toothbrush. You have to take along all your uniforms and personal equipment. You go down there to soldier. That takes a little time to pack up and it serves to add to the routine after sentence. (Who would ever jinx himself by having everything ready even before he was sentenced?) People don't often remember that part. It seldom gets in books and movies. The guy gets sentenced, and usually the next time you see him he's already in his prison uniform and being led to a cell and locked in by a guard. Well, I don't blame the people who put it down that way. It's the big moment, all right, the dramatic one, when they clang the door and it's you and nobody else who's locked in.

They miss a whole lot of the truth, though, by all that they skip over. The truth is, like everything else in this life, there is a whole lot of paper work that goes with it before they shut the door on you. You have to nearly drown in papers first. Later on you can put yourself to sleep at night just by trying to remember and count up all the different pages with your signature or initials on them, all with your name printed backwards for convenience and efficiency, and usually, too, some kind of number that's a whole lot more important than your signature or your initials or your name printed, last name first. I'll tell the world, a man nowadays can almost get writer's cramp just getting himself locked up in a jail.

When it's a stockade you're bound for, not a DB, it's plenty bad enough. First you go through all the ceremony and the drama of getting yourself sentenced. Then they take you back to your outfit and hang around while you strip your blankets and bedding off your bed. (You will have signed for that on one form.) You have to tote all that stuff along with all your unit equipment (another printed and signed form) to the supply room. You turn it in and get your name scratched off the original forms. Since all you need in the stockade is your fatigues, you have to put everything you own in a duffel bag or a footlocker and put a padlock on it. You sign and get a receipt for it. You pick up your toilet kit and you are ready to go. Once you get over to the stockade you start in on a whole series of paper work again. Sign for your bedding. Turn in all your valuables. Get a receipt for them. Etc.

Going to a disciplinary barracks just about doubles the whole routine.

Meanwhile, don't ever forget that all during this time there are people all around you. You don't have a chance to be alone with yourself for a minute and catch your breath. The guys in your outfit don't know what to say or do. If they are buddies, they may be sorry at the time. But if they've got any sense at all they will have forgotten your name inside of a couple of days. A man has got to look out for himself. Maybe a good guy who's been around some will give you a smoke while you're packing your stuff. Somebody else will slip up and whisper to you who's good and who's bad at the stockade, what you better watch out for there.

When you finally get back it's the same thing all over again in reverse. Sign forms. Get receipts. Draw stuff from the supply room . . . Sign your name a few more times. At last you get back to your room or your space in the barracks and you start in unpacking a lot of wrinkled uniforms that won't fit you anymore.

Somebody looks up from a funny book or a skin magazine and notices you are there.

"Hey, Riche, where you been? I ain't seen you around lately."

"Who me? On vacation," you say. "I took me a rest cure."

The long and the short of it is that all during the long ride—first downtown to the provost marshal's, then back from the city to the *caserma*—I was feeling sorry for myself. Of all things! I had forgotten about everything in the world. I was just playing with my memories of this kind of a day. Getting myself ready for it. As if that ever helped anything.

When we got to the outfit it wasn't as bad as I thought, though. Sergeant Ryder met us at the front door. He told the two MPs to wait in the orderly room. Said *he* would be responsible for me while I was in the building. Didn't want them tracking the place up.

I went straight on up to my room to get started. It really *was* a good outfit—nobody had to tell you what to do to get ready to go to jail. There sat old Jethroe on the bare bedsprings with his mattress all folded up and his duffel bag packed. He was waiting for somebody to come and take him down to the troopship. He had his overcoat on and his hat on and his Bible in his big hands. He looked at me with a long sad face. He looked old enough to be my grandfather that afternoon. Maybe he was really going to make it this time. Maybe he was finally going home. All of a sudden I loved the crazy, beat-up old bastard. I could have kissed him. I really cared what happened to him. I hoped he would live forever. Long live Jethroe!

"Jethroe, old buddy, let me trade places with you. You take my place and I'll take yours."

He stared at me a minute, puzzled, then laughed. I think he knew exactly what was going on and understood what I was feeling perfectly. But his laugh was gone like a ghost in the first light of the morning. He pointed at my pillow.

There was a note underneath it for me. I took it, read it over, memorized it, crumpled it up and threw it in the wastebasket. It was about the gloomiest one yet. He took it out of the Book of Job. Whether it was meant for me or him or both of us together or everybody at once I didn't know. I would have to think about it for a while. I thanked him for it and he nodded. Then I got down to my business of getting ready.

By the time I got back from my first trip down to the supply room Sergeant Jethroe was gone for good.

When I left it wasn't too bad. Ryder had got the whole bunch together in the orderly room to say so-long to me before he handed me back to the MPs. It was kind of like a party. The whole crowd from the Hidden Bar. Zwicker, dirty as a pig because he was right in the middle of cleaning out the greasetrap in the mess hall, Longman, Mullins, Cool Breeze Clayton, Mooney, Singletree, Fishbein, Pat the dog. The only one missing was the Snake.

"I'd trade all you guys in if the Snake was coming with me."

"Man, she would stand that freaking College on its ear."

"Maybe they'll teach you to play the harmonica down there."

"Maybe you'll learn how to be a private detective, like Cool Breeze."

"Don't play poker. You might get in trouble."

"Zwicker," I said. "When in the hell are you going to get some teeth?"

"I don't need them. My girlfriend says I'm pretty enough as it is."

Everybody was laughing, even me, when I walked outside. I left them arguing with each other about whether or not Zwicker had a new girl. And if he did, where would he put the new tattoo.

"You took long enough," one of the MPs grumbled.

"I'm not in a hurry," I said. "I've got nothing but time on my hands."

At the main gate of the College, just as the MPs were handing me over to the regular guards (more paper-signing and handing over receipts, for *me* this time), Lieutenant Costello came driving up fast in a jeep. I knew some officer from our outfit would have to be there to get a receipt for the unit equipment I had brought with me. I guess he was happy to volunteer. I should have figured he would be the one.

"I just want to see them lock the gate behind you," he said.

The slob was wearing a holster and a .45 pistol on his hip like a combat man. He probably would have worn a steel pot too if he could have. Big day for him. Too bad the bastard would never be a hero. I wished he was a statue and I was a pigeon. I watched the pistol on his hip, slap-slapping on his thigh as he walked toward us.

The pistol! That damn pistol! In the midst of all the bull-shit and routine and thinking about myself and feeling sorry for myself I had managed to forget all about the pistol Angela still had. All at once I knew what it was that had really been worrying me all day long.

"Listen, Lieutenant," I said, trying to keep calm, trying to keep a calm, even voice. "Would you do me one favor? Would you please do me one favor?"

"I'll do anything you want, Riche," he said, "about six months from now."

"Please, sir," I said a little louder. "I mean it. It's really important. I got a confession to make."

He grinned at me and shook his head.

"Okay," he said. "When you get out you come tell me all about it. Maybe we can arrange to send you right back."

That's what did it. I let go and blew up all the way. It had been building. It had been coming on. Looking at him grinning, rocking back and forth on his heels. His hands behind his back. That .45 on his hip triggered me. I just went for him. They grabbed me as he backed and jumped out of the way. I fought them all and cussed him. I hollered I would kill

197

him if I ever got out. I kept kicking and screaming and trying to fight back, even after they got me down and got my arms pinned behind me. The only thing they could do was get a straitjacket and drag me off to solitary confinement, hauling dead weight, to start my sentence.

Once they got me in the cell and the door slammed to behind me it was over and done with. I knew I was done.

18

THEY BROUGHT me out of the hole blinking for light, blind as a mole. Two of them took me by the arms and marched me over to one of the barracks. They told me to take a shower and shave. Then they told me to put on my OD uniform and bring along my overcoat. It had turned cold, they said. I unpacked the wrinkled stuff from my duffel bag and started getting dressed. I didn't say anything and I didn't ask any questions. I kept my mouth shut and did what they said. They were watching me close. They weren't going to tell me what was going on and I wasn't about to ask.

When I was all dressed and ready to go two more guards came in. They were all just kids. But they looked scared and serious in their helmet liners. You would have thought I was some kind of dangerous character. With the four of them all around me we started marching across the drill field toward the main gate. The wind was still blowing and it was cold. The wind came over the field in sudden gusts and stirred up whirls of dust. These dust whirls spun around a few times like

199

a dance of crazy men, then vanished. Way across the field the students were marching, screaming their fool lungs out counting cadence. At this distance it almost sounded good.

I knew. I really knew all the time without asking. But I didn't know. I had to hear it. With four of them assigned just to get me from the barracks to the main gate, they must have figured for sure I was going to blow my top again or do something crazy. Well, they didn't know me at all yet. They would later on. They would remember me, too. Right now I wasn't going to give anybody the pleasure of doing what they expected and maybe even wanted me to do. I may be a lot of different things. Some of them pretty worthless and disgusting. But, by God, I am a man. Not a machine. You don't push a button and make me go.

I stopped dead in my tracks. They almost fell all over each other trying to stop too.

"Where are we going?"

"Never mind," one of them said. "Keep moving."

"You might just as well tell me," I said. "I'm not fixing to move until you do."

One of them behind me started to prod me in the back with his short-handled broomstick. Another one held him back.

"Tell him if he wants to know so bad."

"Go ahead and hit me with your goddamn sticks. You may beat me down to my knees, but I'm not going anywhere until I know what's coming off."

"Tell him."

"All right," the one behind me said. He must have been the ranking one. I hadn't even bothered to notice who had stripes. "The woman you were shacking up with is dead. You've got to go over to the morgue and identify the body."

That was when all four of them braced themselves. Ready for me to go off. I think they were ready for anything. Except what I did next.

"Let's go then," I said.

I stepped off toward the main gate so fast they had to hop, skip and jump to keep up with me. At the gate they shook me down, then handed me over to two MPs and a very young MP lieutenant. He looked more like an Eagle Scout than an Army officer. He was a nice-looking young college kid fresh out of OCS or maybe the ROTC. He looked embarrassed. And a little worried too. It was probably the biggest, most serious thing he had done in his life so far.

We started for a jeep.

"Do you think we ought to put handcuffs on him?" the lieutenant asked in a low voice. Maybe he thought I couldn't hear good. More likely he thought if he spoke polite enough and soft enough I couldn't take it personally.

"You don't have to do that, sir," I said. "I ain't going nowhere. If I even looked like I'm going to run, these two boys of yours would shoot me down like a dog."

"You damn right," one of them said. "Get your ass in that jeep."

The young lieutenant sat in front with the driver. The other one, the one that had spoken up, sat in back with me. He had a busted nose and bloodshot eyes and looked about as pretty in the face as a ring-tailed monkey. He suited me fine. I could tell he was a good enough guy. He watched me close for a minute or so. Then when he had me sized up, he pulled the visor of his garrison cap down over his eyes and slouched and dozed.

We had to drive clear across the city to the morgue. I sucked in all the sights and sounds and smells of it. I tried to cram all of it, everything in my head, so that later on, alone in the Hole again or at night in my sack in the barracks I could close my eyes and play it all back again in bright bits and pieces like a kind of a private movie.

"You must be damn glad to get out of that place," the MP said to me.

"It ain't bad after you get used to it," I said. "But it's always good to be outside."

201

We got there and parked and went inside the ugly building. The routine was simple. We went in a whitewashed room with a lot of bare light bulbs burning from the ceiling. There were several VG policemen around. We had to wait while two Italians with white smocks on went back to get the body.

"What happened to her?"

"Don't you know?" the lieutenant said.

"Killed herself," my MP said. "Shot herself with a pistol."

After a short while they came back wheeling her body in. The table had rubber tires on its wheels and it didn't make a sound when it moved. They lifted the sheet over her for me to have a look.

Angela lay there stiff and stark. If I hadn't known and loved every inch of that body from the tips of her toenails to the roots of her hair I would never have known her. She had done a complete and thorough job on her face and head with that Beretta. She had done it right.

One of the VG policemen asked the MP lieutenant to ask me about the pistol. Just for the record. They had it there with them, with a label tied to the trigger guard. I held it up and took a good look at it.

"I'm sorry," I said. "I never saw this pistol before."

One of these days the VGs would get around to tracing it. They would trace it back to Sergeant Jethroe. He would be gone. The outfit would probably be busted up. Even if they could do it, it wouldn't be worth the trouble of trying to tie me in. Sometimes I wonder what they finally ended up doing with it. Most likely one of the cops kept it for himself, because it was a nice little pistol. Somewhere, though, there would be on file a piece of paper that proved that it was the property of Sergeant Jethroe. No matter who had it or owned it now.

We were all through. Then the MP lieutenant did a strange thing. It was the one thing I hadn't expected. He told me that he and the two MPs would wait outside the door for me. They were giving me a chance. Like taking a last private look at somebody in the family. A semiprivate look anyway. The two Guineas in the white smocks stayed.

I looked down at her and let my heart crack and break to pieces. I could picture how it would break. Like a smashed phonograph record. End of the music for me. I hadn't known there was that much left of me that was brittle enough to break. They can always find one more thing. One more part. Break every freaking bone in your body and you think you're done. You're not. Before you are finished you have to go the whole way. Be shredded up into fine dust and scattered to nothing in the wind. Then maybe, finally, you are free of it.

She was free of it. Angela was. All that was left on that table with wheels and soft rubber tires was a large chilled slab of meat like a side of beef. But, Lord! How that sweet flesh had lived once. How well she had been able to live in it. Myrrh and spice, honey with the honeycomb, wine and milk. I blessed her then with all the cracked music of my cracked heart. I blessed her and silently begged her Roman Catholic God to pardon her for killing herself. It's easy to do for a God. If you are God you can pardon any or all of it with no more than a wave of the hand. Me? I wasn't asking Him for any favors. We'll come to that by and by.

"*Finito?*"

"*Sì, sì, grazie. Finito.*"

They tossed the sheet back over her and started to wheel her quietly back to wherever they keep them. The thing is the sheet didn't quite do the job. It didn't quite cover her feet. Her toes stuck out from under. I could have kissed them. I want God to remember it in my favor one day, on the Judgment Day, that I laughed out loud then and both of the Guineas whirled around and glared at me with hate in their eyes. I laughed only because her toes were funny and unbeautiful and she had always been shy and ashamed of them. And I loved them more than all the parts of myself put together. I swear to God it was an honest laugh. And the best prayer I could leave her with.

They wheeled her out and shut a door behind them. I was all by myself for a minute.

Then a curious thing that somebody might not care to believe happened to me. I remembered the last note from the Bible that Jethroe had left under my pillow. It came back to me, word for word, just as if a moving finger had painted it in black or bloody red up there on those bare whitewashed walls, written in that crude, silly, childish hand of Jethroe's.

I have said to corruption, Thou art my father: to the worm, Thou art my mother, and my sister.

I said these words over to myself a couple of times. The words left a nice dry taste on my tongue. One day soon I would slowly and carefully chip those words into the wall of my cell, called the Hole. Maybe they would stay there for a long time. And somebody would find it someday and wonder what it meant. The way people do now about the things the old Roman soldiers wrote or chipped on walls. People still come and copy them down.

I came out of the door to where they were waiting for me. The lieutenant looked pale and strange now. Like a man very sick or scared or both. I guess he was putting himself in my shoes and it hurt him.

"Are you all right?" he said.

"Sure, I feel just fine."

"Is there anything I can do for you?"

Just like a freaking chaplain.

"Yeah, one thing," I said. "If you can spare me a cigarette, I'd be grateful. I sure would like to smoke one before I have to go back."

That surprised him some, but he gave me a cigarette anyway and held a light for me. I took a long deep puff and grinned at the three of them.

"Man, you don't know," I said pleasantly. "You never

know how good one tastes until you've had to do without them for a while."

The nice young college boy, my MP Eagle Scout, looked shocked and angry. Now he was hurting worse than before. First he had put himself in my shoes so he could feel sorry for me. That was all right. But when I wouldn't play the part and be worthy of his pity, he was pissed-off. I wasn't going to let the guy have a nickel's worth of cheap, phony feelings. Let him live and learn like the rest of us. Let him earn his own lumps.

"You lived with that woman," he said. "She was pregnant with your child. Is a goddamn cigarette the only thing you can think of?"

"I'll tell you what, sir. After you've seen one or two of them, you've seen them all."

"Seen what?"

"Corpses," I said. "Stiffs."

He turned away quick so he wouldn't even have to look at me. He looked like he was fixing to puke on the floor. I think it would have made him happy to spit on me. Let him live a long time. Let him live to tell his grandchildren all about it around the fireplace.

We climbed in the jeep and started the trip back. I was smoking that cigarette fast. Thinking that with the traffic the way it was maybe I would have time for another one before we got back to the main gate again. I figured I could bum one off the MP in the back, old broken-nose. He was a good guy and I knew he was a smoker too. I had noticed the dark nicotine stains on his fingers.

I was thinking that as long as I could keep on smoking and concentrating on nothing else but the pleasure of it, I wouldn't have to cry in front of them. Even if I did, though, even if I let go and couldn't help myself, the wind blowing in my face would dry my tears so fast no one would ever notice it.

The
Old Army Game

Stories

FALSTAFF: *Though I could 'scape shot-free at London, I fear the shot here . . . Here's no vanity! I am as hot as molten lead, and as heavy too. God keep lead out of me. I need no more weight than mine own bowels. I have led my ragamuffins where they are peppered. There's not three of my hundred and fifty left alive, and they are for the town's end, to beg during life. But who comes here?*
—Shakespeare, *Henry the Fourth,* Part I
Act V, Scene III

"Madame, the Battle of Waterloo was won by the worst set of blackguards ever assembled in one spot on this earth."
—Attributed to the Duke of Wellington

Author's Note

Here is a selection from the Army stories I have written over the years. Of course, in a bloody and remorseless century like ours there are always some wars going on somewhere, in and out of sight, in the quietest of lives and stories. There has not been peace on earth for one day that anyone can remember. It is hard to imagine that there will be peace on earth, even briefly, in the lifetimes of anybody alive here and now.

One part of my life, real and imaginary, as I said at the outset, has been spent soldiering. These, then, are some of the short stories, of various kinds, coming more or less directly out of that experience.

I have arranged them in chronological sequence according to the time they were written, the chronology of their publication. Some people from *Which Ones Are the Enemy?* reappear, pop up like bad pennies. Old Stitch, for instance.

Two military stories—"Tanks" and "Whistling in the Dark"—have been left out of this selection because they appeared recently in *Whistling in the Dark* (1992) and are easily accessible there. Two others—"Crowfoot" and "Heroes"—have not previously appeared in any collection of mine.

—G.G.
1994

How the Last War Ended

(A Cartoon)

T H E Captain lay face down in a ditch by the road, the stagnant water, strangely warm for such a bitter day, soaking through his fatigues. It crawled along his stomach and bathed his loins. His head, hidden from the sky by the dark bowl of his helmet, was just above the water, his lips close enough to kiss the disturbed scum. He lay there while all the noise was above and elsewhere, not in the least afraid, feeling almost sleepy. He was thinking of himself as a bullfrog sprawled in the mud at the edge of a hyacinth-choked lake, but this image dissolved and he began to have an erotic daydream. It was absurd, the things that came into his mind while the war was going on all around him. It was absurd, too, for the war to *be* going on. They had signed the armistice yesterday and it was all over, on paper at least.

He was neither astonished nor afraid when he raised his head into the silence and saw the mud-gorged boots at the edge of the ditch, the pants ripped at the knees, the heavy belt, the downslant of the bayonetted rifle at the hips, and, gradually, the whole shape of the enemy soldier like an isosceles triangle converging on a small troubled face, dirt-stained, half-bearded under the flat shadow of the steel helmet. It was like being a little child again and looking up at the angular and inscrutable shapes of the adult world. He laughed out loud and splashed water with his feet and hands.

"I'm taking a bath," the Captain said in the soldier's language.

The soldier looked at him and laughed. The rifle drooped.

"I'm taking a bath," he repeated.

"You look like a sow in the sty," the soldier said. "Come on out. You're dirtying your uniform."

"Come on," the soldier said, good-naturedly enough, "come out of the water."

The Captain got up slowly and climbed out of the ditch. He stood beside the soldier and without speaking they both looked at the road. The truck had turned over on its side, the front wheel still spinning like a roulette wheel running down. The Captain's driver was a limp shape beneath the shadow of the turning wheel. He'd been trying to load his carbine but the clip had dropped when he was hit and some of the penny-colored shells had rolled on the road. The other two bodies were behind the truck, one in a dark splash of blood, rolled sideways as if asleep, clutching his rifle to him like a toy. The other one was spread-eagled alongside the far ditch. He had no weapon and his helmet had come loose and fallen on the road. He had been keeping toilet paper in his helmet so it would stay dry and now it was festooned extravagantly on the road. It looked as if a huge wave, an ocean breaker had crashed over them, scattering them in its flashing roll, and dashing them up drowned. All around the cropless fields were bare and the sky was pale and smudged like a dirty sheet. The air was still sweet with the smell of gunpowder.

"It is curious how awkwardly they died," the Captain said.

The soldier grunted and then without paying any attention to the Captain he sauntered across the road to the body of the spread-eagled soldier. He had seen the glint of a wristwatch. The Captain squatted by the road and policed up the carbine shells and put them in his pocket. Then he looked carefully at the fields. Three-quarters of a mile away maybe was the farmhouse, a poor dung-colored block of stone with a couple of wind-picked, stunted trees nearby and behind that the gray haze of woods. He saw a crow, laborious, ungainly, leathery, fly out of the woods and light on a limb of one of the trees near the farmhouse. He was concerned about that. He decided to ask the soldier if he would mind shooting the crow and he turned to look for him. He was coming back across the road, grinning, looking sheepish.

"Broken," the soldier exclaimed.

"It's no wonder," the Captain said, looking at the shattered watch.

They walked over the muddy field to the farmhouse, taking their time, smoking. The soldier had slung his rifle on his shoulder and tipped back his helmet jauntily. He kept talking about how good the Captain's cigarette tasted to him. When they got up close the Captain could see the machine gun, but nobody was around it. It sat in a little hole, idle and captivating on its slim tripod, surrounded by a wealth of spent cartridges. Another soldier came around the side of the house eating something out of a can with his fingers while he walked. He walked right by them without paying them any attention. The first soldier pushed the door of the house open and the Captain walked in behind him.

"Sir," he said, "here is one of them." He walked out the door again.

Getting used to the dark room, the Captain saw a man lying on the floor, blanketed, rubbing his eyes. The man leaned on his elbows with the blanket still wrapped around his legs and looked at the Captain.

"You're all wet," the officer said. "How did you get so wet?"

The Captain remembered that he was still wearing his

pistol. He pulled it out of his holster and offered it, grip first, to the officer.

"I suppose you'll have to take this."

The officer stood up slowly and stretched. He didn't have his pants or shoes on.

"I see you're not wearing the regulation socks," the Captain observed.

The officer fumbled in a corner of the room until he found a candle and lit it so he could look at the pistol.

"An inferior weapon," he said. "Definitely an inferior weapon."

He seemed to be very cold. His thin legs were goose-pimpled and his hands were shaking. He threw the pistol across the room. It landed on the edge of a table and fell off on the floor. It could easily have gone off. Quite suddenly the Captain was angry.

"This is fantastic," he yelled. "The war is over. Don't you understand? They stopped it last night."

"Really?"

"Of course. Why would I lie to you? You should be *my* prisoner. You are all my prisoners."

The officer shrugged and went back to the corner where he began to fumble on his hands and knees for something else. The Captain went to the door. It had started to rain. Three or four of the soldiers were sitting in the mud near the machine gun playing cards.

"Put up those cards," the Captain shouted. "Put them away. You're supposed to be on duty."

They looked up, stared at him for a moment, and resumed their game without a word. Angry, the Captain strode towards them, but when he saw the soldier who had captured him, he took off his wristwatch and gave it to him.

"It's all right," he said. "You can have mine."

When he got back inside the farmhouse, he found the officer squatting on the floor trying to get the cork out of a wine bottle with a bayonet. The Captain stood over him watching with concern until the officer gave up and pushed the cork down into the bottle.

"One never has time enough for all the amenities," the officer explained.

"It's quite all right," the Captain said. "I am not a connoisseur."

They sat down on the cold stone floor facing each other and passed the bottle back and forth politely while they talked.

"I know what it's like to be defeated," the Captain said.

"So?"

"I would like to tell you a story about wine, if you don't mind."

"Please," the officer said, "by all means, go ahead."

"My great-grandfather was a very important man. He had a large house, many acres and several hundred slaves. But you mustn't think he was provincial. On the contrary, even though he was living way out in the country, he was a cultured, I might even say cosmopolitan man. He could read books in Greek and Latin and he played the violin."

"Is that so?"

"Please, I'm getting to the point of the story."

"Excuse me. Go ahead."

"I'm trying to tell you about the defeat and the part about the wine."

"Go ahead, please."

"Among his other accomplishments, my great-grandfather was a connoisseur. He had a wonderful wine cellar and they bought wine from all over Europe for it. Now, it happened that he was away during the war and his wife was alone with the children and the slaves."

"Naturally," the officer said, nodding.

"And, you see, Sherman's Army came through that part of Georgia. They were terrible. They lived off the land and the truth is that wherever they went they burnt and raped and looted. Well, they hadn't arrived yet at my great-

215

grandfather's house. And one day my great-grandmother was in her room knitting socks for my great-grandfather when Lewis, that was the house servant's name, came in the room.

" 'Ma'am,' he said, 'I hear there's a troop of cavalry in the neighborhood.'

" 'Whose cavalry, Lewis?'

"That was just like my great-grandmother. She knew very well that there wasn't a troop of Confederate cavalry any nearer than Atlanta, but she wouldn't be made to appear irrational even in defeat."

"A remarkable woman," the officer said.

"Lewis didn't even sigh or appear exasperated. 'Shermer's cavalry, ma'am,' he said. He had form, too. He wouldn't even pronounce the name right. 'In that case,' she said, 'we ought to do something. What shall we do?' 'I'm in favor of destroying the stock of wine before they get their hands on it.' 'I think you are quite right,' she said. 'It wouldn't do to have a troop of drunken soldiers in the yard.'

"So now I ask you to imagine it. Late afternoon, the light and heat only just beginning to fade. The lady sitting upstairs in her quiet room. Outside they are busy. The slaves bringing up out of the dark, cool cellar all those wonderful bottles and barrels while other slaves are digging a shallow trench. When the digging is finished Lewis gives the order and one after another the bottles are broken and the barrels staved in. The wine flows in the ditch. Every last bottle cracked into the trench, the red and the white mixing together indiscriminately, almost golden in the light, I imagine, a shining river of wine.

"Then, suddenly, into the yard, kicking up dust, scattering the lazy chickens in a blizzard of feathers and squawks, the cavalry troop arrives. They're wild men, dusty, bearded, thirsty. In a moment they've leapt off their horses and, lying flat on their bellies like pigs in the mud, they are lapping the wine with their tongues, cupping it with their hands, splashing it on each other and all the while laughing outrageously, deliriously!"

The Captain finished and they sat for a moment in the quiet room hearing only the faint whisk-broom sound of rain on the roof.

"What a pity," the officer finally said.

He got his blanket and wrapped it around his legs. The night was coming and it was getting colder.

"You and I know about these things," the officer said, "the utter absurdity of defeat."

"And the triumph," the Captain exclaimed. "Don't you see the triumph, the splendid indifference. There is always the marvelous shrug of the surviving."

"No," the officer said emphatically, "only the perversity of the defeated."

He rolled over and wrapped the blanket more tightly around him. He groped for something to use as a pillow.

"Use my helmet," the Captain offered.

"So what does it mean?" the officer said.

"Nothing. It doesn't mean anything," the Captain said. "Does it have to mean something?"

The officer smiled, closed his eyes gently and dozed. The Captain again felt anger coming on him. He stood up and walked up and down the room briskly.

"There was a crow," he said. "There was a crow that lighted in one of your trees. I would like you to have that crow shot."

There was no answer, not the least stir of life.

"I insist that you have that crow destroyed," the Captain shouted. "I order you to do it!"

But by this time the officer was already sound asleep and there was no one in the room to notice the Captain whether he wept or not.

What's the Purpose of the Bayonet?

1. Hooray for the Old Nth Field

W E W E R E the bums of the Army. There was no other unit like ours. We were the losers, the scum, flotsam and jetsam, the scrubs, the dregs, the lees, black sheep, Falstaffs, n'er-do-well uncles, and country cousins. Our outfit was formed up overseas, ostensibly composed of men from the regimental infantry companies who had an artillery MOS. What really happened in this case is as follows. They sent a letter down to all the infantry company commanders, letting them know about the new outfit and asking them if they had any men to spare who happened to have an artillery MOS. The company commander, sitting behind his polished and dusted, almost virginal desk, would puzzle out the letter and, as its contents dawned on him, a great big grin would light up his face and he'd holler for the first sergeant and the company clerk. It's amazing how all the misfits, deadbeats, eightballs, VD cases, alcoholics, and walleyed, knock-kneed, slewfooted stockade-bait suddenly turned out to be trained artillerymen. Then an officer was flown over from the States to take charge of this pirate crew.

218

Picture him the first time he realized what had happened. He's the man who sat down on the Whoopee Cushion. He's the Original who was sent out in search of a left-handed monkeywrench and a bucket of polka-dot paint. He's scheduled to be nailed to the cross in the company of thieves and tramps.

We were lucky. The CO they sent us was a bum himself. Somebody in the Pentagon had a nice sense of decorum. He was potbellied and middle-aged. All his contemporaries were bird colonels or one-star generals. He was still a captain. He chewed on an enormous two-bit stogie all day long and most of the time he forgot all about having it in his mouth. He didn't even take it out of his mouth when he saluted. No matter how clean his uniform was when he put it on, in fifteen minutes he looked like he'd slept in it on the ground. He had been through some hellish times in the War and he had come out the same man who went in. He was one of those men who valued the accident of living so highly they will never betray themselves for anything. Least of all ambition. He didn't seem to be the slightest bit sorry for being exactly what he was, and he didn't seem to be gnawed by the furtive wish to be anything or anybody else.

The first time the battery fell out for his inspection we looked like the early American cartoons of the Continental Militia.

"I'll be a son-of-a-bitch," were his first words to the assembled troops. The rest of his speech was short and to the point. "F—— you guys!" he said. "You are without a doubt the crummiest collection of decayed humankind I ever laid eyes on, so help me God. We deserve each other. If you want to be soldiers, try it. See if I care. First Sergeant, take charge of this so-called battery. I'm going to get drunk." The entire battery cheered him. We threw our helmet liners in the air. He just shrugged his shoulders and walked off the parade ground, slumped over, chewing on his cigar stub, feeling maybe the way Francis Drake and Henry Morgan sometimes used to feel.

It was the best outfit I was ever with in every way. You might not think so, but I'll tell you why. We were inside-out men. All our vices were apparent. Our virtues were disguised. Talk all you want about your *camaraderie,* your *esprit de corps.* We had something better than that. We clung together hand in hand like men overboard. We found out that with sleight of hand we could soldier when we wanted to or if we had to. We found out that when we felt like it we could outmarch the infantry, outrun the airborne, and outdrive the armored. Most of the time we were worthless, a crown of thorns to the commanding general, a severe drain on the taxpayer. Between inspections the billets we lived in were a pigsty. Off duty we drank and fought and whored. We always had beer and vino cooling in the breechrings of our howitzers. Combat ready. Rust and dust were our constant companions, shooed out of sight only on very special occasions.

Needless to say the Army was ashamed to have us around. They stuck us up near the Yugoslav border in what used to be the Free Territory of Trieste, miles from anywhere, in a village called Padricano. Look it up in an atlas sometime. See if you can find it. We were supposed to guard the border. Before we came up there it had been pretty tense, but we soon discovered that the Yugoslav soldiers—called Jugs— were almost as notorious tramps as we were. We used to drink together and the border almost vanished. One time the lady who used to be the ambassadress to Italy came up and inspected us. They were so afraid they notified us a month ahead of time. After she left the CO called for the battery clerk, who was a college boy. "Say, son," he said, "who in the hell *was* that Clara Bell Lou we fell out for?"

Once a week they'd let a truckload of us go down to the city of Trieste to get civilized for an evening. We played hide and seek with the MPs all over town. Even though we didn't get down there often, we knew every whore in the city by her first name, which was a lot more than the Vice Squad was ever able to accomplish. Once, during the riots, this paid off. They alerted the Nth Field and made us put on the full combat costume—steel helmets, field packs, gas masks, fixed bayonets, the works. We were taken down in trucks to the main square in Trieste. Thousands of people were milling around, shouting and screaming about something. Some of them had clubs and knives and rocks, and some of them, I guess, had small arms. When we dismounted and formed up and they saw our guidon and saw what outfit we were, they started laughing and cheering. The whores were calling out to us by name. So we started laughing and yelling back to them. The whole riot was over in minutes. The only real trouble the Army had was rounding us up again to go back to Padricano. It took a couple of hours to smoke out all our guys who had headed for the first bar or trattoria they could find. A couple of them were dead drunk, and the local people carried them and all their gear and loaded them gently on the waiting trucks.

Eventually the Army just gave up on us. They broke up the outfit and sent us far and wide. They sent me up to Linz, Austria. The Army thought we were barbarians and maybe we were, but if you ever have to die with combat boots on, you could do worse than to do it with the Nth Field. Save me, good Lord, from companies and battalions of well-adjusted, dead-serious, clean-cut, boy-scout post-office-recruiting-poster soldiers. Deliver me from mine enemies, West Point officers with spit-shined boots and a tent pole jammed up their rectums, and their immortal souls all wrapped up cutely like a birthday present containing at its secret heart something about as insipid as a shelled peanut. Save me from good people, on a piece of graph paper, percentagewise. Give me the bottom of the barrel, men who still have themselves to laugh at and something real to cry about, who, having nothing to lose and being victims of the absurd dignity of the human condition, can live with bravado at least, and, if they have to die, can die with grace like a wounded animal.

2. Guts

People take up boxing for a variety of reasons, none of them very sound. Show me a fighter, amateur or pro, and I'll show you a man who's got some impelling obsession, hidden maybe, that makes him want to destroy and be destroyed. I suppose with the pros, they get over it with experience. They reach a point where they don't care much anymore; the original motivations have been lost, disguised, or maybe even satisfied. By that time there isn't much else they can do and it's just another dirty business.

The obvious reason I boxed in the Army was to get out of work. If you made the team you got to sleep through reveille and you didn't have to march or stand any inspections. Officers didn't harass you. You just went down to the Post Gym twice a day and worked out. The true reason why I took up boxing, way back in public school, is more complex. The easiest way to explain it without going into much detail is my size. I'm a natural welterweight. All the lacerations of flesh and spirit that go along with being small are partially compensated for by being given the opportunity to face another small man and try to heap some of the stinking weight of your own anguish on him.

Joe was just about my size. He had fought some professionally around Philadelphia. He started fighting in self-defense at the state prison where if a little man couldn't fight he was as good as gone. He was really good, he had class. He could make the light bag dance to any rhythm he set his fists to. He had a hundred different ways to skip rope. He could bob and weave like a machine when he was shadow-boxing and when he hit the heavy bag it seemed to groan under his punches. He used to take it easy on me when we sparred and I learned a lot from Joe. I wasn't trying to be any competition for him. I just wanted to stay on the team as a substitute.

Often I'd go on pass with Joe. He had a shack—he was living off post with what you'd probably call a whore, a big blonde about twice his size named, believe it or not, Hilda. He paid the rent, bought the groceries and some clothes for her, and now and then he'd bring her a present from the PX. In return she had to do his laundry, cook dinner for him, and make love like an eager rabbit. It wasn't a bad deal for some of those girls because jobs were scarce and a lot of them might have been hungry otherwise. And it was a definite cut higher on the local social scale than being a regular prostitute. There were two big dangers: pregnancy and rotation. Sooner or later every soldier had to rotate home to the States. Once their man was gone they either had to find another one or become prostitutes. Pregnancy was something else. Either they took their chances with quack abortionists or they had a baby. The whole place was full of little GI bastards. Some of the girls had two or three.

Hilda and Joe seemed to have a happy shack. She always cooked up schnitzels with fried eggs on top, served with potatoes and Austrian beer. We weren't training so hard that we wouldn't drink beer. Not for three three-minute rounds.

"Hilda is the girl I used to think about in jail," Joe would say. "I didn't see a woman, not even a picture of one, for two years. I used to close my eyes and picture a big blonde, one with boobies the size of Florida grapefruit and a big soft ass as wide as an ax handle. I had to come all the way to Austria with the U.S. Army to find one along those lines."

Hilda used to laugh at that and she didn't seem to mind much when he compared her with his wife back home.

"Now you take my wife in Philly," he'd say. "Hilda is a pig alongside of her, a slob. My wife is a real beauty. She even won a bathing-beauty contest when she was in high school. She could be in the movies if she wanted to I guess."

"Who do you love?" Hilda would say. "Tell him which one you love."

"That's easy. You, you big barrel of lard."

"Tell him which one is good in the bed."

"Well, hell now, Hilda, that ain't fair. Give the girl a chance. You've had a whole lot more experience."

I really admired Joe. I took everything he said for gospel and I studied his fighting movements and copied all the ones that I could. Some of the other guys on the team said he was a fake. Wait and see, they said. We know his kind. Notice he don't like to muss his hair. He's a liar. He never was no kind of a fighter. He might of been in jail, but even that don't seem likely. I didn't pay any attention to them. I figured they were just jealous. I noticed none of them wanted to get in the ring with him.

Finally, the night of our first match came around. The gym was packed with people—troops, officers and their wives, and civilian employees. It's surprising to me how so many nice people and nice girls would come to see a thing like that. The same people would be sick at their stomachs if they saw a dogfight. To tell you the truth I can't think of anything uglier than a couple of men beating each other bloody under the bright lights for the amusement of a lot of people.

It was almost time for his bout when Joe came up to me.

"I'm sick," he said. "I can't fight tonight." He was supposed to fight a sergeant from Salzburg, a little guy with heavy muscles like a weight lifter who looked like he could really hit.

"The hell you're sick, Joe," somebody said. "You're chicken."

"I'm sick," he kept saying. "I'm too sick to go in there."

"Okay, Joe," I said. "I'll fight him for you."

"Don't be a knucklehead," somebody told me. "Let him fight his own match."

"Go ahead if you want to," Joe said. "I couldn't care less."

I just had time to slip on my trunks and get the gloves on

before the fight. I went in there and jabbed him and kept moving. He turned out to be one of those big hitters who have to get both feet set flat before they can punch. So I just kept moving around him and sticking the jab in his face. After the first round he got mad and started to run at me like a bull. All I had to do for two rounds was to keep my left hand out and he'd run right into it. He was dazing himself. The madder he got, the less chance he had to get set and tag me, and that's how come he lost the fight. We were both glad when it was over, him because it had been so frustrating and me because my luck would have run out in another round or so. As soon as it was over I ran back to tell Joe what had happened. He was sitting in the dressing room, crying.

"Joe," I said. "Joe, I won!"

"Think you're pretty good, don't you?"

"No," I said, "I was lucky."

"Listen," he said, "you'll never understand this, but tonight I just lost my heart for it. I was sitting here and it dawned on me that there wasn't no reason, none at all, to go in there and get beat around anymore. It made me sick."

"I can see how you'd feel."

"No you can't," he said. "You'll figure just like the rest of those guys that I was nothing but a big liar."

"No, I won't," I said. "I'm just glad I could win the fight."

"You rat," he said. "How do you think that makes me feel, you bastard?"

He put on his cap and left. The next day he quit the team and went back with his regular outfit. I heard he even quit Hilda. I felt bad about it, but what could I do?

3. The Art of Courtly Love

You can fool yourself quicker in a dozen ways than it takes to tell about it. Then, if you discover the irony of your self-deception, you are liable to turn right around and cast your guilt on somebody else. That truism, I suppose, explains how

225

it was with Inge and me. Inge lived in an apartment just across a little field from an off-limits *Gasthaus* where a few of us used to go in the evenings or on Saturday afternoon and drink beer. One Saturday I looked through the window and saw her hanging out her washing. She was a small woman, curiously dainty and precise in her movements, with a pretty, troubled face. It was almost like watching a dance seeing her hanging out her washing in a brisk wind. For no good reason I said to myself I must have that woman. I'm not going to rest until I have that woman. I asked around about her and found out that she was a DP, a refugee from the old German part of Czechoslovakia. Nobody knew much about her except that she had shacked up with an officer for a while and that he had rotated to the States a year or so ago.

It took some doing. At first she didn't want to have anything to do with me.

"I don't like you," she said. "I don't even like your type. Little nervous men make me sick."

All right, I said to myself, we'll see. We'll see about that. I almost crawled for it. I tried everything I could think of. I kept coming around, bringing her food and gifts from the PX, spending my money like a drunk. One night I brought my portable record player and records and a bottle of wine. Once she heard the music playing I was home free.

"I hate you," she said. "All this time I have been living with so little, but you keep bringing things and now I start to want again. I want to eat good food and I want to wear good clothes again. I want to start to live good again."

That suited me fine. At the time it seemed like a big victory. I moved in and set up a shack. I felt like a rooster in the henyard. This is pretty hard to explain because it was easy enough to find a girl to shack with around Linz, but this had been a real quest. Inge did everything she was supposed to. She cooked and did my laundry and made love, but I could tell that she didn't like it at all. The truth is her barely concealed distaste added to my sense of pleasure. She used to be so ashamed she kept all the shades pulled down when I was in the apartment. She liked to make love in the dark, but I used to trick her by suddenly snapping on the bedside lamp to astonish her in the light.

Inge had been married in Czechoslovakia, but her husband had been killed in the War and she didn't know where her children were. She was at least ten years older than I was. The American officer had been very good to her, she said, and he had promised to marry her. After he went to the States she never heard from him again. Still, she kept a leather-framed picture of him on her bureau, overseeing everything, a lean, good-looking, smiling man. She had a vague notion that someday, any day, the postman was going to bring her a letter from him telling her to pack her things and come to the States. We used to play a game with his picture. When she undressed to go to bed, she used to turn his face to the wall, but as soon as she wasn't looking, I would turn him around again.

Inge kept the apartment neat and trim—everything had its exact place. If you moved a bottle of perfume an inch on the bureau from where she had put it, she sensed right away that something in the room was out of order. She had some cheap jewelry and some knickknacks that she cared for like a saint's relics. She was very fastidious about her clothes and she used to bathe every day even though this meant a lot of trouble. The only thing to bathe in was a big washtub and she had to bring the water by the bucketload from a pump in the yard. On the other hand I used to go for days without taking a shower out at camp just to infuriate her. She stood this and a hundred small humiliations as well or better than anyone could be expected to under the circumstances.

Oh, I was as happy and thoughtless as an apple on a tree until another girl told me that Inge had an Austrian boyfriend and that whenever I was on guard or had some other night duty he came and stayed in my apartment. I could hardly believe that, but I decided I had to find out. I told her I was going to be on guard one night. After dark I came off post and sneaked up close to the apartment. The shades were up and I looked in the window. She was all dressed up in the best clothes I had bought her, dancing with a young Austrian. They danced and she was laughing as I'd never seen her do before, and all the time my portable record player was playing my records. I went over to the *Gasthaus* and watched from the window. I sat up all night, fuming and tormented, and at dawn I saw him leave, blowing a kiss to her. As soon as he was out of sight, I ran across the field to the apartment and opened the door. She sat up in the bed, clutching the sheet over her breasts.

"What are you doing here?" she said. "What are you going to do?"

"You bitch," I said, starting to take off my belt. "I'm going to beat the living hell out of you."

"Please don't," she said. "Please, please don't touch me. I never said I loved you. You've been good to me but I never said I loved you."

"So what about the Kraut?"

"I love him," she said. "That boy doesn't have any money, but I love him. You've got to understand."

"Okay," I said. "You go ahead and love who you want to. I won't lay a finger on you. I've got a better idea. I'm going to tear this place apart."

"Don't!" she said. "Don't do that."

"I'm gong to tear this place to pieces and if you say anything about it to anyone I'll turn your name in to the CID as a whore."

That frightened her because if she was even arrested under suspicion of being a prostitute she was done for. As a DP she could never hold a job or be legally married in Austria, and certainly with that on her record she would never get to the States. I was in a terrible rage, more at myself than anything else, I guess. She sat in the bed sobbing hopelessly while I broke everything to pieces. I even smashed my own records and the player. I took her clothes out of the bureau drawers and off the hangers and ripped them into shreds and ribbons. I tore that smiling photograph in half.

"You had no right," she said.

I slammed the door and ran to catch the bus back to camp. At first I felt almost good about it, but after a day or two I began to realize how much I had fooled myself and what a terrible thing I had done. I went to the PX and bought a lot of things to take to her, but when I got to the apartment the landlady told me that Inge had run away and left no address. I paid her the rent we owed and went back to camp. I don't know where she went or could have gone. Salzburg probably, where there are a lot of troops. I never heard from her or found any trace of her again.

4. What's the Purpose of the Bayonet?

I always used to hate pulling stockade duty. They had some regular personnel up there, but the actual guarding was detailed to individual units. When your name came up on the list you had to move up there and guard the prisoners. This meant hours in the towers around the barbwire compound or else being a chaser. I hated being a chaser. You had to pick up a little group of prisoners at the gate in the morning and take them to whatever job they were supposed to do. You weren't allowed to smoke or talk to the prisoners. You were just there to shoot them if they tried to run away or refused to obey an order. You had to be spic-and-span and pass inspection every morning. It was almost as bad as being a prisoner yourself. Not quite.

This time I was assigned to a different job—the cage. In the center of the compound they had a building they had converted into a kind of stronghold for very serious cases—men who were being sent back to the States for long terms. They had double doors with armed guards outside, and inside they had two rows of cages with bars all the way around.

It was kind of like a zoo. They kept the men in the individual cages like wild beasts. They were afraid they would try to kill themselves rather than go back to the States and do time in Leavenworth. They wouldn't let them shave. Some of them grew long beards waiting for shipment. They wouldn't give them silverware with the chow. They had to eat it off the tray with their fingers. They were like savages. There weren't any windows but the room was always brightly lit. You could easily forget whether it was night or day. You couldn't hear a sound from the outside world. I had four hours on and eight hours off, sitting alone in the middle of the room at a big desk. I had a telephone and they called me every half hour to find out how everything was. If anything happened I was supposed to shoot the prisoners with a .45 pistol.

There were four men in the cages while I was there, two long-term AWOLs, a lifer who had killed his shack job while he was drunk, and a rapist. They said the rapist was going to hang when they got him back to the States. He seemed crazy as hell. He was filthy and obscene and he probably was guilty. He had been accused of raping a young Austrian girl and they threw the book at him. They gave him a big public trial and invited the local population to come and see the show. They had buses to pick them up, free lunch, and earphones for the trial so they could follow by interpreter what was going on. A real goodwill gesture.

This particular guy used to worry me more than all the rest. They had their moods, but all in all they seemed resigned. He didn't seem to know what was going on. I don't think he had the faintest notion he was going to hang. He used to talk to me all the time about what he was going to do when he got home. He received mail once in a while, but the people writing him didn't have any idea he was even in trouble. He either talked about home or else he paced up and down his cage silently and you could tell there was a big blowoff coming. After a while he'd start hollering at the top of his voice, crazy things. I remember he used to yell questions and answers like the ones from basic training, the one they yelled at you in bayonet drill. "What's the purpose of the bayonet?" they'd yell. And everybody was supposed to answer back, "Kill! Kill! Kill!" He'd carry on like that. The rest of the prisoners put up with it most of the time, but sometimes it got on their nerves and then a couple of the regular stockade people had to come in and hold him while the doctor gave him a shot that knocked him out cold.

The officer in charge at the stockade was a recent graduate of West Point and he was plenty mad to have a dirty little job like that. He used to come in the cage and take it out on the prisoners. He never touched them, he just teased and harassed them, hoping that one of them would give him an excuse to get tough. Helpless men like that seem to bring out the worst in some people. One day he was standing in front of the cage of one of the AWOLs, telling him terrible stories about Leavenworth and how rough they were going to treat him there for the next ten years. The guy finally got tired of just listening and walked over to the bars. He cleared his throat and spat in the lieutenant's face. The lieutenant didn't flinch or move a muscle, I'll say that for him. He just took a handkerchief out of his pocket and wiped his face clean.

"That's going to cost you," he said.

He was right. A day or so later they came in and shaved and cleaned the guy, put a uniform on him, and took him away to be court-martialed.

"It was worth it," he told me when they brought him back. "It was worth a little more time just to get a shave and a bath and a clean uniform on. I'll spit again if he gives me half a chance."

The lieutenant must have been satisfied. He never bothered that particular prisoner again, except in little ways like taking chow off of his tray. Finally some MPs from Livorno showed up to take the prisoners to the ship.

"So long, old sport," the rapist told me. "I'll see you on Times Square."

"In a pig's eye you will," the MP guarding him said. "You're going to hang, buddy."

That was the last that I saw of any of them. I was put back outside as a chaser and I was glad to be back in the fresh air and in the open view of the world again. The first day one of my prisoners, a seventeen-year-old kid who was pulling sixty days for some minor infraction, started to act up. He asked me what I was going to do if he tried to run away.

"I'm going to kill you if you try and run, fatface," I told him. "Because if I don't kill you, they'll throw you in the cage and in a week you'll wish you were dead."

He shut up and went to work.

5. Torment

There are always things going on out of sight. Creatures move in disguise and there's a vigorous invisible life everywhere. You have to poke around or have an accident to discover it. Trip over a decayed log or just roll it upside down and you'll find a swarm of white wormy life, or death if you want to call it that, lively death; and I know no matter how content your eyes are with the green sweetness and your nose with the winey odor of the woods, you'll turn away almost sick at your stomach. On the other hand, in innocence, in ignorance, you may be fascinated by the idea of corruption, just as leaning over a fence and watching a great-bellied sow wallow in the dungy mud you may have wished to be a lot less than human. Knowledge is always something else. If somebody rubs your face in the filth you may yearn for even two-legged dignity.

When I was a boy we had an old leather-bound set of books purporting to be the history of the world and even before I could read I used to rifle those pages for the illustrations of great events. Before I ever went to school I had an idea about the Pyramids and the Fall of Rome and the Storming of the Bastille. As a matter of fact that first experience of history, flipping pages and looking for pictures, ruined me for any of the conventional ways of looking at history. Your first impressions, like your first wounds, are deepest. So I've always had a kind of haphazard view of time. What difference does it make whether you begin or end with the Fall of Rome?

There's one picture I remember quite well from another period of my childhood. It was a favorite of mine during the nervous time of early puberty when a woman is only a sign or signal of desire and might as well be two-dimensional. Next to the rather vapid girls in underwear available in the Sears Roebuck catalogue the best pornographic material I had access to in those days was in *The History of the World*. There was one especially titillating picture—"The Inquisition in Session." It showed a full-blown woman as naked as God made her, hiding her face. A huge executioner with a black mask on had just ripped away the last shreds of her clothes. In the background there was a raised bench with ecclesiastical dignitaries, bored or leering, and in one corner there were instruments of torture, whips, and irons heating red-hot on a fire. It was a perfect field day for undeveloped sexuality. An innocent's paradise.

The reality of torment is somewhat less appealing. I used to pull Courtesy Patrol downtown in Linz. We had an office in the main police station and whenever we were off duty we used to gather around the stove in that room. It seems to me it was always cold in Austria. The police station was a big gloomy building, cold and high-ceilinged, poorly lighted. In the rooms around us the local police carried on their daily jobs with a muted efficiency. You could hear their heavy boots sometimes in the hall and there was always the faint insect noise of a distant typewriter, but most of the time the place seemed as quiet and decorous as a tomb. We had a feeling of awe for those cops. They were all big, handsome men and they never seemed to relax from a dignified, unsmiling position of attention. Their high boots gleamed and their uniforms were immaculate. Next to them we felt like a bunch of civilians in costume.

Every once in a while the authorities would decide to crack down on prostitution in the town. Sometime around midnight they'd wheel out the trucks and be gone, and in an hour or so they'd start bringing in the night's catch. Then there was some excitement in the halls. The whores would be shepherded in, old ones and young ones, fat ones and skinny ones, in all stages of dress and undress, expensive ones as shiny and clean as a model in an advertisement, cheap ones with black ruined teeth and an itchy look. They all seemed dazed or numb. They were taken down our hall and through a door at the end. After that crowds of cops went down there, too, and pretty soon you could hear military band music being played on some kind of loudspeaker. Once I got curious about what was going on. I asked the interpreter they had assigned to our office about it. He just grinned and shrugged.

"See for yourself," he said. He was an easygoing guy who was happy just to sit around the office and smoke our cigarettes.

I went down the hall and opened the door into the blaring military band music. It was a hell of a sight. They had all the whores stripped and the cops were running among them beating them with rubber truncheons. It was like a picture out of Dante's *Inferno*. The women were all crying and screaming and begging and praying. The cops were running around in circles like crazy sheepdogs. They'd beat at random and then spontaneously single out an individual and beat her down to the floor, the truncheons blurring with fury and speed. Some of the cops had their shirts off. They had wild faces like men hopped up on dope. One man sat on a table where the record player was, changing records, smoking and just watching. When the whores were like this, naked, scared, and in pain, they all looked alike, just poor flesh and bones suffering. But the worst thing was the blood. Nobody ever talks about the blood of beatings. Their faces were swollen and bleeding from broken noses, cheeks and jaws, split lips. Their bodies were bleeding from dark bruises and cuts. The floor was slick with blood like the back of a butcher shop. They were slipping and falling in it, cops and whores alike.

I shut the door and went back to the office.

"So?" the interpreter said. "Now you have seen our floor show."

I felt so numb I didn't want to say anything.

"Why?" I said finally. "Why do they do it?"

He shrugged. "There is no severe penalty for prostitution," he said. "They try to scare them."

"Does it work?"

"No," he said. "It's the same ones all the time. They can't afford to be anything else."

"What's the sense of it then?"

"Maybe some of them leave town," he said. "Who knows?"

I went to the window and looked out at the soft, foggy winter's night and the old sleeping city. All those people sleeping safe and sound for the time being, having dreams, rooting among the wreckage of their absurd, forlorn desires. Down the street the Beautiful Blue Danube flowing. On the other side of the bridge, the Russian Zone, the lonely Russky guard stamping his boots, blowing on his hands, thinking about the big lost spaces back home. And me sick. I was sick thinking about the fine avenues and boulevards of this world where you walk with your head up, strut if you want to like a god, and meanwhile all the time there's an invisible world breeding and thriving. In back rooms, in hidden corners, behind blank smiles, all over the world people are suffering and making other people suffer. The things God has to see because He cannot shut His eyes! It's almost too much to think about. It's enough to turn your stomach against the whole inhuman race.

Don't Take No for an Answer

O M E N ! " Stitch said. "Haven't you guys got anything to talk about?"
"What else?" somebody said. "Name something else."

"You want me to tell you a war story?"

Everybody laughed. It was a Saturday afternoon, the last long Saturday before payday, and a bunch of us were sitting around the orderly room playing cards. For nothing. Who's got money the week before payday? Stitch was CQ. He had to stay there over Saturday to answer the phone and put out the lights. You can bet he would have signed the pass book and been gone, money or no money, if he hadn't pulled CQ.

"This is no joke, Stitch. How come you pulling duty on Saturday?"

"First Sergeant dumped on me," Stitch said. "He figures to shoot me out of the saddle and spend the weekend in my shack."

"What are you going to do if you catch that slob lying in your bed with your *Fräulein* when you get home tomorrow?"

Stitch spun around in the swivel chair he was sitting in

next to the phone. He just looked at the guy who'd said that and the whole room got quiet. All of a sudden his big hand shot into his pocket and in one motion came out again with a little click and there was the glint of a switchblade in the light. It was funny. The instant the blade flashed in the light Stitch grinned and leaned back easy in the chair, laughing to himself.

"Why, I'll kill him," Stitch said. "I'll cut that bastard in four pieces."

Everybody relaxed and the card game got going again. You never could tell about Stitch. Know what I mean?

"What about the *Fräulein?*"

"Who, Irma?"

"Who else?"

"What about her?"

"What would you do to her?"

"You guys don't know nothing," Stitch said. "Just nothing. Irma's worthless. She ain't good for nothing—except bedroom push-ups. But she's so good at that, I wouldn't have the heart to hurt her. I'd just whip her fanny good and she'd love it."

"Tell us a war story, Stitch."

"Listen," he said, "I'm trying to read this magazine."

"Tell us about Paris."

Stitch had just come back from furlough, ten days in Paris. He could always tell a good story if you hit him in the right mood. The thing about Stitch was he was moody. He seemed okay at the time, though.

"What about Frenchwomen, Stitch?"

"I couldn't tell you," he said. "I seen some but I never even talked to one."

"Go on. Don't give me that. You went all the way to Paris and you never even talked to a woman?"

"Maybe he didn't have to talk to one."

—You guys make me sick, Stitch said. You don't know nothing. I went to Paris and had nothing but one good time, believe me. But not with no French girls. If I was to do things that way, like you suckers, I'd end up broke with nothing to show for it. Now if you guys want to learn the facts of life— you got to plan, you got to figure your chances, you got to play the part. Once you see what you want to get, don't hesitate, don't wait, it's yours. Don't take no for an answer.

—Now this woman was American. She was plain, oh my God she was plain as Missus Murphy's pig. I meet her on a sightseeing bus. First thing I do when I hit town is get rid of this uniform, put on my civvies, grab my camera, and hop a sightseeing bus.

"I reckon you wanted to see all the sights."

—Didn't I? So I get me a seat in the back of the bus and I just wait. I'm sizing them up. I'm looking for one that's alone and not too sharp. Know what I mean? A woman that's sharp has got a notion about the value of her body. A sharp woman wears a price tag on her panties. What I'm looking for is one that not only ain't sharp, she's got to know it too.

"Are you kidding?"

—Don't interrupt. Stick around and learn something.

—So, sure as the world, last one on the bus, there's this pig. She's alone—that's good. She's kind of shy, keeps looking around for somebody to give her ticket to and then she kind of sneaks up the aisle—excuse me for living—looking for a seat all by herself or at least by some nice old lady. I just sit back and light a cigarette. I say to myself, little lady, give your soul to God, because your ass is mine.

"What does she look like? Is she awful?"

—Awful. She's thirty or thirty-five if she's a day, dressed like she was fifty. Got a spread, some gray hair and a stupid hat.

"False teeth?"

—How the hell do I know, yet. I only just seen her get on the bus.

—I wait till we get off the bus in front of a church to take pictures.

—I wonder, I say, if you'd mind posing for a picture in front of the church.

—Why, she says, surprised, all shook up, I don't know . . .

—I only want to show how big it is, I say. I want to send a picture to my mama and I want her to see how big the church is with somebody standing in front of it.

—All right, she says. I'll be glad to.

—Thanks a lot.

—So she stands there like a GI sack of spuds in front of this church and I fiddle with the gadgets on my camera. —Just a minute, I say, I've got to get it in focus. I leave her stand there a minute or two. I can see she's trying to smooth the wrinkles out of her skirt and fix her hair so the gray won't show. Then I say, quick, how about a big smile? Boy! she gives me the pearly whites. You'd think she was a movie star.

—Would you like me to take a picture of you? she says.

—Oh no, I say. It's just a waste of film.

—Come on, she says. Stand over there. Wait. You'll have to show me how to work it.

—I come around behind her and show her how the camera works. I don't touch nothing but the camera but I can see her hands shaking. Come on, smile a little bit, she says. So I give her a smile and we climb back on the bus.

—Would you mind, I say, if I sat with you? It's so good to talk to an American.

—Yes, she says, it's nice to talk to somebody from home.

—We sit down together.

—What am I going to tell my mama about the picture? I say.

—Who will I say the pretty girl is? —She just blushes and clams up.

—I'm Pete Brown, I say.

—Oh, she says, oh. I'm Ellen Cook.

—From then on it's life-story time. I want her to feel easy with me so I tell mine first. This Pete Brown he's in the paratroops, a jumper. He's had an awful sad life. I tell her I like it all right overseas but I miss the old hometown and my poor old mama too.

"Get off it, Stitch. You couldn't say that with a straight face."

—Couldn't I? Now this Ellen, she's a schoolteacher from Kansas. She teaches the third grade. —Do you like it? —Oh yes, she says, only it does get trying sometimes. —Married? —And honest to God she blushes, like a kid. —No, she says, not yet. —Me either. Well, Ellen, you're wise. No use being hasty in a serious step like that. Are you traveling alone? —She nods. —I had a girlfriend, she's the gym teacher at the school where I teach, who was planning to come with me. But at the last minute she got this job as lifeguard at the country club. —That's too bad, I say. It's always more fun to travel with a friend. —Yes. —And safer too. —She blushes again. —Now's the time, Stitch, you start moving in. —I wonder, I say, if you'd mind seeing me again while you're here. I've got ten days furlough and I don't know a living soul. We could have fun seeing things together. You could tell me all about everything. I don't have much education. If you wouldn't mind, I mean. —I wouldn't mind, she says. Really, I wouldn't mind at all. —Just like the movies.

Stitch lit a cigarette and blew a couple of smoke rings.

"So what happens?"

—Cool it. Take your time. Rush things and you ruin them.

—Okay. I take it slow. For two whole days I never lay a hand on her. We go everywhere. We see all the buildings and museums and pictures. We sit in the parks and in the sidewalk cafés. The second night we go walking by the river. It's a real nice night for that kind of thing. I just feed her the questions and she talks. She talks so much about herself you'd think she never had a chance to talk to anybody in her whole life. She tells me about being a kid in Kansas, about going to school and Sunday school and all about her Daddy. He's a big

Bible-thumping son-of-a-bitch, straight as a shotgun six days of a week and drunk as a lord on Saturday night. Raises hell around the house. Runs around buck nekked hollering "I am the Emperor of the Island" or some crap like that. Gives Ellen and her mama a bad time. Well, the old slob killed himself in a car wreck. She loved him but she hated him too. She knows she shouldn't hate him at all, but she can't help hating the awful things he used to do when he was drunk.

"Sounds like your old man, Stitch."

"Stitch never had no daddy. He was born in a cathouse."

—This ain't my life story.

—I understand, Ellen, I say. I know just what you mean.

—I believe you do, she says. I believe you do understand. I can talk to you. I can tell you about things.

—I hope so, I say. I hope you feel easy with me. And I give her hand a little pat.

"Her hand?"

—One thing at a time. One thing at a time.

—Why did you come to Paris?

—I wanted to, she says.

—You must have some reason.

—Well, she says, yes. Not exactly reasons. I just have feelings. You'll laugh at me.

—No, I say. I'm just a big, dumb guy without much education but I'll never laugh at you.

—I believe you, she says. You see, Paris was always in the back of my mind since I was a little girl. It was everything in one word to someone who never saw anything in the world except in her geography book. I loved geography. And Paris was elegance and splendor and beauty, all in a kind of music in my mind. There wasn't anything, except space, but that was big in my town, nothing cool and gray like the pictures of Paris.

—Then there was the wickedness, too, she says.

—Wickedness?

241

—You know what I mean. I mean ever since I was a kid I had heard things about the American Legionnaires in our town. I used to see them when they had a parade. I'd see them snicker and pinch the grown girls. I've seen them laughing at jokes I couldn't hear and looking at pictures with their hands cupped around them.

—That was Paris too?

—You've got to try to understand. These things were just feelings, they weren't ideas.

—I understand how it was.

—And then there is another thing. I don't know if I should tell you this. You wouldn't mind if I tell you this? You won't misunderstand?

—You can tell me anything, Ellen.

"Stitch, I believe you could sweet-talk the devil."

"He'll get a chance in hell."

—You guys got it all wrong. I'm not bad. I just play the part. You got to play the part.

—Well, she says, there was this boy. I loved him. I was crazy about him. Of course he never knew it because I was too shy and he was a class ahead of me in high school and it was silly. But he was very different from the others. He was gentle and different. He was beautiful, I thought. I loved him so much I wanted to be him. I wanted to be inside his body. This is awful to say, but in those days I used to stay awake in the dark in my room to watch him undress. He lived next door. Wasn't that scandalous?

—No, I say. Not if you loved him.

"Do you think she was telling the truth?"

—I figure she made up the last part, but what the hell, she talked like she believed it. Stitch, I say to myself, just keep your buttons on. You've got it made.

—Well, she says. The war came along and he was killed in it, just before the liberation of Paris. I was in college then and I cried and cried thinking about that beautiful boy dead.

—And that's the other reason you're here.

—Yes, she says, if you put it that way.

—I'm glad you're here. I say. I'm glad.

—Why? she says.

—If you weren't here, how would I know you?

—But you don't know me.

—Yes I do, I feel I do.

"What were you feeling, Stitch?"

—Quit interrupting.

—You don't really know me, she says. You don't know me at all. And she starts to cry.

—Maybe I don't, I say. Maybe not. But I want to. And I give her a nice quiet Hollywood kiss.

"For Christ's sake, Stitch, is that all?"

—Slow down, soldier. I have to look at the river and the buildings and the lights.

—This is the music you used to think about, I say.

—Yes, she says, it's so beautiful.

—You want to see the wickedness too?

—All right, she says. I guess it would be all right with you along.

—So I take her to this clip joint in Pig Alley. Cheap champagne, nekked women, and dirty jokes. She acts shocked. —I don't see how they can walk around like that with no clothes on in front of men. —They get used to it, I say. It don't bother them. —I could never get used to it, she says. I'd be so embarrassed. —Yes you could, I say. You've got a nice figure. Nothing to be ashamed of. —Then I concentrate on getting her drunk which is no big problem. When she's drunk out of her mind, I take her to a cheap hotel. She don't say nothing until we get in the room.

—Where are we?

—Take off your clothes.

—No, she says, no.

—Okay, I say, I'll do it for you.

—She fights me like a bitch, scratching and biting, but she don't holler. She don't make a sound. She just fights.

243

—All right, I say, when I get her stripped down. You see. You got a nice body.

—Don't touch me.

—You look better than any of them girls.

—No, she says, no, I'm ugly and old and flabby and nobody loves me.

—I love you.

"Tell her, Stitch!"

—I love you.

—No you don't, she says.

—Yes I do, I keep saying. And all this time I'm playing the old tune on her just like you play a guitar.

—I'm a virgin, she says. Please, I'm a virgin.

—Yeah? I say. Well, so am I.

"So what happens?"

—What do you think, soldier?

"Was it any good?"

—It's always good. I just close my eyes and she's a movie star. When she finally turned loose of herself she's like a rabbit. Crazy! She was carrying on so I thought they was going to throw us out of the hotel. You see, nobody was ever good to her before I guess. Nobody ever treated her like she was somebody.

—The next morning, first thing, before she has a chance to start feeling sorry for herself, I ask her to marry me. I tell her I love her and I want it to be proper and all. I tell her that just as soon as my furlough is over I'm going back and get the chaplain's permission and we'll get married.

"Did she fall for that?"

—Didn't she? It's all like a dream come true, she says. And she runs out and buys a whole lot of clothes. I got to admit they made an improvement. You keep telling a pig she's wonderful and they start believing it. Hell, I almost believed it. By the end of the time I almost started to like the bitch.

"That's too much for the heart."

—I even started to feel bad about spending all her money.

244

She even bought me a suit of clothes. I felt kind of bad, not real bad.

"Stitch, you're just too softhearted."

—Yeah. She even come down to the station to see me off on the train.

—Don't leave me, Pete, she says.

—I'll be back in two or three days.

"Maybe she's pregnant."

—Maybe.

"What would Irma say if she found out what you was doing on your furlough?"

—You guys! That's the first thing I done when I got back, was to tell Irma.

"What did she do?"

—She cried for the poor woman. Irma's always sorry for the women. She said I was terrible. She said I ought to be killed and she hated me. She said she was going to find that girl and make me marry her. She said everything. Then we hopped in the sack and she was all over me like a tiger.

"That don't make any sense, Stitch. That's crazy. It don't make a damn bit of sense."

"The trouble with you," Stitch said, "is you don't know nothing about women. If you don't know nothing about the subject, the best thing is to shut up."

Stitch looked so damn mean for a minute nobody moved. One guy held a card in midair. Everything was frozen like a photograph. Then Stitch started laughing and cleaning his fingernails with his switchblade.

"You poor simple bastards," he said, and he kept on laughing.

He was crazy that way. As long as he was happy, we decided to go ahead and play cards.

The Old Army Game

EVERYBODY has got a story about the Bad Sergeant in basic training. Sit down some evening with your buddies, and you'll find that's one subject everybody can deal out like a hand of cards. And that's not a bad image for it, because those stories, told or written or even finally mounted in memory, acquire a bright conventional two-dimensional character. All the people in them are face cards. Which seems to me as good a way as any to introduce Sergeant First Class Elwood Quince.

Lean and hard-faced, a face all angles like a one-eyed jack. Perfectly turned out, everything tailored skintight, glossy, spit-shined, and glowing. Field cap, almost white from washing and wear and care, two fingers over the nose. Casts a flat gray semicircular shadow that way. Calls attention to the mouth. The thin tight lips. Open, you'd expect to see even rows of fine white teeth; instead you'd see them yellow and no good and all awry and gaping like a worn-out picket fence. And when he did smile, it was all phony, like a jackass chewing briars. Back to the field cap. Calls attention to the mouth

246

and hides the eyes in shadow like a mask. The eyes—with the cap off and resting on a desk and his large restless hands patting his straw-blond hair, long and rich on top, but sidewalled so that with cap or helmet on he looks as shaved clean as a chicken ready for the oven, the eyes are peculiarly light and cloudy at the same time, like a clear spring that somebody has stirred up the mud in the bottom of with a stick. Can you see him yet? But he's standing still. Let's breathe upon him and let him walk because Quince's walk is important. He has two of them. The official walk when he's marching troops, in formation, etc. The former is conventional, ramrod, but natural. Well-trained soldier. The latter is really quite special. Light-footed, easy, insinuative, cat- and woman-like. Creepy. He seemed like a ghost to us. You always look over your shoulder before you speak because chances are he's right there behind you and everywhere at once.

Talk? Oh my, yes, he can talk. Arkansas mountain accent. Part Southern and part Western and a little bit nasal and whiny and hard on the *r*'s. Picturesque. Rural similes abound. Some extended to epic proportion. For example, to Sachs, our fat boy from New York: "Sachs when I see you draggin' your lardass around the battery area, you put me in mind of a old woreout sow in a hogpen with a measley little scrawny litter of piglets sniffin' and chasin' around behind her and that old sow is just so tired and fat and goddamn lazy she can't even roll over and let 'em suck." Also frequently scatological. Here is a dialogue. Sergeant Quince and Me. In open ranks. Inspection. He right in front of Me. I'm looking straight into the shadow his cap casts.

Quince: Do you know how low you are, boy?

Me (*Learning to play by ear*): Pretty low, Sergeant.

Quince: Pretty low? No, I mean just how low?

Me: I don't know, Sergeant.

Quince: Well, then, since you're so ignorant, I'll tell you. You're lower than whale shit. And you know where that is, don't you?

Me: Yes, Sergeant.

Quince: On the bottom of the ocean.

(*Quince passes on to the next victim.*)

The tone of voice? Always soft. Never raises his voice except in giving commands. Otherwise speaks just above a whisper. You often have to strain to hear him.

When we arrived at Camp Chaffee, Arkansas (the Army's mansion pitched in the seat of excrement now that Camp Polk, Louisiana, and Camp Blanding, Florida, are closed up tight as a drum, left to hobos, rats, bugs, weeds, etc.) we were assigned to take basic training in Sergeant Quince's outfit. I call it his outfit because the battery commander had some kind of a harelip and was shy as a unicorn, stayed in his office all day. The First Sergeant had V-shaped wound stripes from the First World War, I swear, and didn't care about anything but getting a morning report without any erasures and also the little flower garden he had all around the orderly room shack that he tended and watered with a cute watering can just like Little Bo Peep's. Nevertheless Sergeant Cobb started out as at least a presence. Austere and lonely and unapproachable, but thought of and believed to be an ultimate tribunal where wrongs might be righted, a kind of tired old god we might turn to one day in despair of any justice or salvation from Quince, come to him as broken children, and he'd sigh and forgive us. Believed until there came a test one day. Sergeant Quince marched the whole battery, one hundred and sixty-odd men in four heavy-booted platoons, right across one side of Cobb's garden. By the time the First Platoon had passed by Cobb was out of the office, hatless, necktie askew and loose like a long tongue, eyes burning. (Ah ha! thought we of Sergeant Quince, the original "young man so spic-and-span," something unpleasant will sure hit the fan now.) But it didn't. Cobb stood there looking and then wilted. He watched his tended stalks and blossoms go down under the irresistible marching feet of Progress, Mutability, Change, and Decay. And he never said a word. He slumped and shook his fist, a helpless old man. Meanwhile Quince ignored him, counted a crisp cadence for the marching troops and grinned just like a jackass chewing briars. And our hearts sank like stones to see how the mighty had fallen.

So, though he was merely the Field First, it was Quince's outfit to make or break. His little brotherhood of lesser cadre revolved like eager breathless planets around him. From our first formation, we in rumpled new ill-fitting fatigues and rough new boots, he sartorial with, glinting in the sun, the polished brass of the whistle he loved so well.

"Gentlemen," he said. "You all are about to begin the life of a soldier. My name is Sergeant Quince. Your name is Shit."

War going on in Korea, etc. We would learn how to soldier and how not to get our private parts shot off by gooks whether we liked it or not. We would "rue the day" (his actual words) we ever saw his face or this godforsaken battery area. We would learn to hate him. We wouldn't have dreamed we were able to hate anybody as much as we were going to hate him. Etc., etc., etc.

"Let's be clear about one thing," he said, looking down from the barracks steps into our upraised, motley, melting-pot faces. "I hate niggers. They're black bastards to me, but I'll just call them niggers for short around here, during duty hours." (A Negro standing next to me winced as if he'd been kicked in the stomach.) "If anybody don't like it, let him go and see the IG. I also hate Jews, wops, spics, micks, cotton pickers, Georgia crackers, Catholics, and protestants. I hate all of you, damn your eyes."

I believe he meant it.

At this point, according to the conventions of the Tale of the Bad Sergeant, written or told, the story usually takes a turn, a *peripeteia* of a modest sort. You're supposed to be given a hint of his problems before moving on. So let's do it. I have no objection. But I reserve the right to call it giving the devil his due.

We were a crazy mixed-up bunch. Farm boys, black and white, from the Deep South. Street boys from the jungle of the big cities. College boys. Accidents: a thirty-five-year-old lawyer who got drafted by mistake, a cripple who was used for some weeks to fire up the boilers and keep the boiler room clean before his medical discharge finally came through. Two fat sullen American Indians . . . Mexican wetbacks . . . I remember one of these had a fine handlebar mustache. Quince walked up to him and plucked it. "Only two kinds of people can wear a mustache around here and get away with it," he said, "movie stars and cocksuckers. And I don't recall seeing your ugly face in any picture show. Shave it off, Pedro!"

So there we were. I'll give Quince this much credit. He wasn't the least bit interested in "molding us into a fighting team." His reach didn't exceed his grasp that much. He was merely involved in getting us through a cycle of basic training. We hated each other, fought each other singly and in groups in the barracks and in the privacy of the boiler rooms (with that poor cripple who was responsible for the care and maintenance thereof cowering in a corner behind the boiler, but armed with a poker lest he too became involved). We stole from each other, ratted on each other, goofed off on each other ("soldiering on the job" this is sometimes called in Real Life with good reason), and thus made every bit of work about twice as hard and twice as long as it had to be. And, if anything, this situation pleased Quince. He perched on his mobile Olympus and chewed briars while we played root-hog and grab-ass in the dust and mud below.

Strict? My Lord yes. I would say so. No passes at all during the whole cycle. GI Parties every night until our fatigues fell to shreds from splashed Clorox and the rough wood floors were as smooth and white as a stone by the shore. Polished the nailheads nightly too with matchsticks wrapped in cotton, dipped in Brasso. Long night hikes with full field pack. GI haircuts (marched to the so-called barber) once a week.

Bald as convicts we were. Police Call was always an agony of duck waddling "assholes and elbows" on our hands and knees like penitents. How he loved Police Call! How he loved Mail Call! Gave out all the letters himself. That is, threw them into the packed hopeful faces and let us fight and scramble for them in the dark. Opened mail and packages when he pleased. Withheld mail for days at a time as a whim. Didn't make soldiers out of us, but tractable brutes. Brutalized, cowed, we marched to and fro like the zombies in mental hospitals that they haven't got time to bother with, so they pump them full of tranquilizers. And when we passed by, eyes front, in perfect step, he was complimented by any high-ranking officers that witnessed our coming and going.

Let me say this for Quince. I know another sergeant who tried exactly the same thing and failed. He was of the same mold as Quince, but somehow subtly defective. In the end he had to fall his troops out of the barracks with a drawn .45. Not Quince. His lips touched to the brass whistle, even before he breathed into it, was quite enough to make us shiver.

A sadist too. Individually. Poor white, soft, round, hairy Sachs suffered indignities he couldn't have dreamed of in his worst nightmares. Once or twice was nearly drowned in a dirty toilet bowl. Sachs with the other fat and soft boys, "Quince's Fat Man's Squad," had regularly to participate in "weenie races." What's a weenie race? I think Quince invented it. The fat boys kneel down at the starting line, pants and drawers down. Quince produces a package of frankfurters, wrapped in cellophane. One each frankfurter is firmly inserted into each rectum. All in place? Everybody ready? Quince blows the whistle and away they crawl, sometimes a hundred yards going and coming. Last man back has to eat all the frankfurters on the spot. Tears and pleading move Quince not a whit. Nor puking nor anything else.

One time Quince lost his head about one barracks which had someway failed to live up to his expectations. He and his attendant cadre went raging through that barracks, tearing up beds, knocking over wall lockers, and destroying everything "personal!" they could get their hands on: cameras, portable radios, fountain pens, books, letters, photographs, etc.

How did these various things happen? you're bound to ask. Didn't anybody go to the Inspector General, the Chaplain, write a Congressman or Mother? Not to my knowledge. Anyone could have, it's true, but all were very young and in mortal fear of the man. Who would be the first to go? No one went. And—*mirabilis*—nobody cracked up. If anything we got tougher and tougher every day. Gave our souls to God.

Or maybe—entirely justified in your contempt, "Don't give me no sad tales of woe"—you'll just say, "So what— what do you want me to do, punch your TS Card?" That would be to misunderstand. Agreed that in a century like ours these things are small doings, negligible discomforts. It would be sheer sentimentality to claim otherwise. And I'm not cockeyed enough to think that such events could arouse Pity and Terror. Nothing of Great Men Falling from High Place in our time. A battle royal in the anthill maybe. No, the simple facts, arranged and related, my hand of cards, will never do that. But they are nevertheless not insignificant. "Why?" you say. "Why bother?" Excuse me, but Maxim Gorky said it once and better than I can, and so I quote:

Why do I relate these abominations? So that you may know, kind sirs, that all is not past and done with! You have a liking for grim fantasies; you are delighted by horrible stories well told; the grotesquely terrible excites you pleasantly. But I know of genuine horrors, and I have the undeniable right to excite you unpleasantly by telling you about them, in order that you may remember how we live, and under what circumstances. A low and unclean life it is, ours, and that is the truth.

I am a lover of humanity and I have no desire to make any one miserable, but one must not be sentimental, nor

252

hide the grim truth with the motley words of beautiful lies. Let us face life as it is! All that is good and human in our hearts needs renewing.

Thus we survived, endured, lived through it, and finally the cycle came to an end, a screeching halt. Last day on the range (rocket launchers) we fired $25,000 worth of ammunition into the side of a hill as fast as we could, so that the range officer could get back to camp early. If he didn't use the ammo all up, he'd be issued proportionately less for the following day. We were glad to assist him in his dilemma. We fired it away with joy and abandon. What explosions! What flashes of flame and clouds of smoke! It's a wonder we didn't kill each other.

That night we sat in the barracks packing our duffel bags. A fine cold rain was falling outside. And we were quiet inside, lonesome survivors, because somehow you never quite imagined something like that coming to an end. It was a calm, respectable, barracks-room scene. You could have photographed it and mailed the picture home to the family.

Up the steps, weary-footed, his cap soaking wet and his raincoat beaded with raindrops and dripping, came the old First Sergeant—Cobb. He asked us to gather around, and he talked to us quietly. There had been a personal tragedy in the family of Sergeant Quince. (*That bastard had a family?*) His wife had been in a terrible automobile accident and was dying. (*A wife yet?*) He wanted to go home before she died. He had to arrange for somebody to look after the children. (*Children?*) The trouble was that this time of the month Sergeant Quince didn't have the money, even for train fare one way. He was broke.

"Why don't he go to the Red Cross?" somebody said.

Sergeant Cobb shrugged. "He ain't got time, I guess," he said. "I know he ain't a kindhearted man, boys. And you don't have to do this. It's strictly voluntary. But give a little something. He's human and he needs your help. Give from your heart."

He took a helmet liner off of the top of somebody's wall locker and held it in his hand like a collection plate in church. Somebody hawked and spat on the floor. I didn't think anybody would give anything. We just stood there and stared at Sergeant Cobb until Sachs pushed through to the front.

"Here's my contribution," he said. And he dropped a dime into the helmet liner.

Everybody started to laugh, and even the thick-headed ones caught on. Each of us put a dime in the pot. Ten cents for Sergeant Quince in his hour of need. Sergeant Cobb emptied the liner, put the dimes in his raincoat pocket, placed the liner back on top of the wall locker, and started to leave. At the front door he turned around, shook his head, and giggled.

"Don't that beat all?" he said. "They done exactly the same thing in the other barracks too."

Half an hour later we had the exquisite pleasure of looking out of the windows and seeing Sergeant Quince in his Class-A uniform with his double row of World War II ribbons stand in the rain in the middle of the battery area and get soaking wet. He cussed and cussed us and threw those dimes high, wide, and handsome and away. He wished us all damnation, death, and hell.

And this is where it ought to end. It would be a swell place to end, with the picture of Quince *furioso* throwing fountains of dimes in the air. Enraged and possessed and frustrated. Yes, Quince in insane rage, hurling our proffered dimes in the air, wild and black-faced with frustration and tribulation, would be a fine fade-out in the best modern manner. But not so. Not so soon did he fade out of my life. Nor, I guess, did I expect him to.

Sachs and I went on to Leadership School. What happened to the rest of them I wouldn't know and couldn't care less.

But Sachs and myself took our duffel bags and waited in front of the orderly room. The harelipped Captain came out and painfully wished us well. We climbed over the tailgate of a deuce-and-a-half and rode to the other side of camp where they try to make you into an NCO in three months flat or else turn you into jelly.

"Why are you going?" Sachs asked me. As if I understood at the outset why he was doing it. I had hardly even spoken to Sachs before that.

"Because that son-of-a-bitch Quince is trash," I said. "I don't like to be pushed around by trash."

Sachs grinned. "You Southerners," he said. "You Southerners and all your pride and all your internal squabbles!"

I won't bore you with the sordid details of that next place except to say that they made us and we made it. It worked. Sachs shed thirty pounds, went at every bit of it with fury and determination and emerged as the top man in the class. Believe it or not. Many a husky specimen fell among the thorns and withered out of school, but Sachs thrived, grew, bloomed. I was in the top ten myself, and both of us made sergeant out of it. We soldiered night and day like madmen. We learned all the tricks of the trade. When we were finished we were sharp. Bandbox soldiers. The metamorphosis was complete. Still, it's only fair to point out that we kept laughing about it. Sachs called it being in disguise and referred to his uniform as a costume. He called us both "the masqueraders." I called myself "the invisible white man."

One anecdote only of that time I'll insert. The Anecdote of the Word. It helps to explain the kind of game we were playing. One week early in the course I was doing badly and it looked like maybe I would wash out. I'd get good marks and only a few gigs one day, poor marks and many the next. The TAC/NCO wrote on my weekly report that he thought I was "a good man," but that I had been "vacillating." He was a college boy himself and used that word.

Well, shortly thereafter the company commander called us both into his inner sanctum. We got shaped up in a big hurry and reported. His office was a room as bare as a monk's cell except for one huge sign on the wall that read THIS TOO SHALL PASS. He, the Captain, was a huge hulk of a man, a former All-American tackle from some place or other, a bull neck, a bulging chest behind the desk, and all jaw, lantern and/or granite with the Mussolini thrust to it. He was dead serious. We were quivering arrows at attention in front of him.

"I have this here report before me," he said. "You say here that this soldier has been *vacillating*. What do you mean?"

The TAC gulped and patiently tried to explain what he had meant by means of the image of the pendulum of a grandfather's clock swinging back and forth. The Captain heard him out, nodded.

"Clerk!" he roared.

The company clerk came tearing into the room like somebody trying to steal second. Saluted. Quivered too!

"Get me a dictionary."

We waited in breathless anticipation. The clerk soon returned with the dictionary. Captain opened it to the *v*'s and followed his index finger, thick and blunt-ended as a chisel, down the line of words. Looked at the word a while and the definition. It was a pocket dictionary and defined as follows:

VAC-IL-LATE, *v.i.,* -LATED, -LATING. 1. Waver, stagger 2. fluctuate 3. Be irresolute or hesitant.

"Nothing about pendulums," he noted. "Damn good word, though. Good word."

He wrote it down on a pad in capitals and underlined it several times. That was that. We were dismissed.

Now from within that orderly room issued forth each week reams of mimeographed material for the benefit of all students. Ever after that incident the Captain cautioned that those who wished to complete the course successfully *must not vacillate!* This got to be a standing joke in that mirthless place.

"If I catch any of you guys *vacillating* in the company area," the TAC used to tell us, "you've had it."

Sachs and I made it through, were transformed from anarchists to impeccable sergeanthood. We didn't end up going to Korea to be shot at either, but instead were sent to Europe to join a very sharp outfit where we would be able to maintain the high standards we had so recently acquired. Which we did for the rest of our service time. Sachs was so good he even made sergeant first class without time in grade.

More than a year later we were in Germany for maneuvers. It was the middle of summer and we were living in tents. In the evenings we used to go to a huge circus tent of a beer hall and get drunk. It was there on one hot night that we met Quince again. He was sitting all alone at a table with a big crowd of empty 3.2 beer cans around him. He was a corporal now, two stripes down, and by the patch on his shoulder we knew he was in a mucked-up outfit, a whole division of stumblebums with a well-known cretin commanding. He looked it too. His uniform was dirty. His shirt was open all the way down the front, revealing a filthy, sweat-soaked T-shirt. Of course it's hard to look sharp if you're living in the field in the middle of the summer. But Sachs and I took pride in our ability to look as sharp in the field as in garrison. It took some doing, but we could do it.

"Let's buy the bastard a beer," Sachs said.

Quince seemed glad to see us as if we were dear, old, long-lost friends. Once we had introduced ourselves, that is. He didn't recognize us at first. He marveled at our transformation and good luck. We couldn't help marveling at his transformation too. ("This is the worst outfit I was ever with," he admitted. "The battery commander has got it in for me.") He bought us a round and we bought more.

257

Late, just before they shut the place down and threw everybody out, Quince went maudlin on us.

"I can't explain it, but it makes me feel bad to see you guys like this," he said. "I hated you guys, I'll admit that. Long before the dimes. But I didn't know you hated me so much."

"What do you mean by that?"

"To hunt me down after all this time and shame me. Soldiering is my life. It's just a couple of years for you guys. And here you are with all this rank looking like old soldiers. Sergeants! Goddamn, it isn't fair."

"Do you know what the Army is, Quince?"

"What? What's that?"

"I'll tell you what the Army is to me," Sachs said. "It's just a game, a stupid, brutal, pointless, simpleminded game. And you know what, Corporal Quince? I beat the game. I won. I'm a better soldier now than you ever were or ever will be and it doesn't mean a thing to me."

Quince turned his head away from us.

"You hadn't ought to have said that," he said. "You can't take everything away from a guy. You got to leave a guy something."

We left him to cry in his beer until they tossed him out, and walked back under the stars to our tents, singing the whole way. We sat in our sleeping bags and had a smoke before we flaked out.

"You were great," I told Sachs. "That was worth waiting for."

But Sachs was a moody kind of a guy. He didn't see it that way.

"You can't beat them down," he said. "No matter what you do. They always win out in the end. Sure I got in my licks. But he won anyway. *He made me do it.* So in the end he still beat me."

"You worry too much."

"That's just the way I am," he said bitterly.

"You don't feel *sorry* for him, do you?"

"Hell, no," he said. "You don't get it. The trouble is I still hate him. I hate him worse than ever."

And he stubbed out his cigarette and turned over and went to sleep without another word, leaving me to ponder on that for a while.

Unmapped Country

THE Captain pulled his car off the road and got out and opened up a map. He spread it out on the hood, smoothing down the creases, and studied it. He was only a few hours away from a city and only a few minutes away from the highway, but the map showed nothing at all. The narrow dirt road he had been driving on dwindled away ahead. He had to make the choice of continuing to follow it or taking what was not much more than a rutted kind of trail that forked off to the left into the woods. He decided that he favored the dirt trail because it had to go somewhere. The road from here on looked like it might come to an end soon.

He folded the map and got back in the car, smiling. It was hard not to be smiling on a day like this, an April day in the Tennessee mountains. The air was fresh and sweet and warm, the sky was bright and clear. The leaves were newly green and he had seen dogwood blooming, wild puffs of white among the trees. With everything suddenly new, renewed, it was hard not to smile, not to feel good. It was hard to think of death. The Captain's impulse was to loosen his necktie and

260

loll back his head and sing to the whole wide world. But he resisted that temptation. He drove along carefully, both hands gripping the wheel, silent and alone.

The Captain braked suddenly and the car skidded to a stop in the ruts. Deep mud ahead. And just beyond the patch of mud a choked mountain stream, water swirling in white mustaches around rocks. More mud on the other side. If he went ahead he would probably be up to the axle in the mud or else drowned out in the stream. He twisted around and backed up slowly until he found a piece of hard ground for the car. Then he got out, locking the car, and walked, glad that he was in uniform with his trousers bloused in his jump boots. Of course the high shine of the boots would get messed up with mud and dirt, but it was better than getting his whole uniform dirty. He skirted the edge of the mud the best he could and then crossed the stream, stepping from rock to rock, finding his way with care. The ruts began again beyond the fresh mud on the other side.

The path wandered close to the stream for a while in a dense cool shade. He could see in clumps, close to the earth, the leaves of wild strawberry plants, promising later on the small, pink fruit, the kind that set the teeth on edge just to taste them, they are so sweet. Then the path left the shade and went uphill, twisted away up a hill and dropped off again into a pie-shaped section of low ground. He was sweating by the time he reached the top and waited a minute to catch his breath. The ground ahead was cleared ground, stony, but cleared for farming. Across it in a shade of trees there was a ramshackle unpainted shack.

He was about halfway across the field, cutting diagonally toward the shack, when he saw the dogs coming at him. Two lean, mangy hounds, pale as twin gusts of smoke, coming swift and low to the ground and barking at him. He stopped still. A man, a tall man in overalls with an ax in his hands, came around from the back of the house and shouted. The dogs held up as if he had yanked them on a leash. He shouted at them again and they slunk back, obedient, to the edge of the porch, still snarling. Then behind the man with the ax the Captain could see children, two girls, barefoot and raggedy and shy, and a boy about twelve or fourteen, who was leaning his weight against a large stick. Looking closely, the Captain saw that the boy was propped up on a homemade crutch. The three children continued to stare at him until a woman appeared and, seeming to gather them into the folds of her full, long skirt, shooed them back out of sight like a mother hen.

The tall man in overalls had not moved. He stood next to the shack, holding the ax in huge, slack hands. The edge of the blade caught the light and glinted.

"Hello," the Captain said.

There was no answer. The man might have nodded. There was what might have been a briefest tip of his head.

"I'm looking for somebody. Wonder if you can help me."

Still no answer. The man seemed to tighten his grip on the ax handle. He stared at the Captain, suspicious and hostile, but with a kind of ease and pride too.

It must be his land, the Captain thought. *He must have cleared it stump by stump, rock by rock with his own hands—*

"I'm trying to locate a Mr. Cartwright that lives around here somewhere. Edward T. Cartwright."

"Are you the law?"

"No, sir, I'm not a policeman."

"How come you're wearing that uniform?"

"I'm a soldier," the Captain said. "I'm in the Army."

"What army would that be?"

The Captain would have laughed out loud except for the expression on the tall man's face—still suspicious, still hostile, but now also simply curious—that stopped even the beginnings of laughter in the Captain's throat.

"The United States Army," the Captain said.

"Why didn't you say so?" the man said. "Come on over here where I don't have to yell at you."

262

He mumbled something at the dogs and together they slid off the porch like two streams of poured water and crawled under it. He waited for the Captain to approach.

"I haven't done anything wrong," the man said. "Nothing against the law as I know of. But a man can't be too careful—"

"No, sir. I understand how it is."

"I don't want anybody to have the idea, especially the government, they can come tramping across my land just any damn time they feel like it, without I give an invitation first."

The tall farmer was a powerfully built man. His wide heavy shoulders were stooped as if under the strain of a yoke of heavy weight and his hands were gnarled and misshapen. His hair was cut short and shot with streaks of gray. The Captain could not have guessed his age.

"I'm sorry to trouble you—" the Captain began.

"You say you're looking for Ed Cartwright?"

"That's right."

"Are you a friend of his?"

"No, I just want to see him about something."

"Do you know him? You know what he looks like?"

"If you can just tell me where I can find—"

"What do you want to see him about?"

The Captain started to speak and then checked himself. Never mind whose business it was. The farmer was making it his, and he might just as well play his part in the ritual interrogation or he would have to go all the way back to the place he had come from with nothing accomplished.

"It's about his son."

"Eddie? The boy's dead."

"I know," the Captain said. "That's what I came to see him about."

"Did you know Eddie in the Army?"

The Captain nodded.

"What was he to you?"

"I was his commanding officer."

263

"I'm Ed Cartwright," the tall man said. "Let's go around front and sit on the stoop. It ain't no use standing up to talk if you don't have to."

The farmer set his ax against the wall and together they walked around to the front of the shack and sat down on the low first step. The Captain offered him a cigarette and he accepted it, pinching the end so he could grip it with his lips like a roll-your-own. He struck a kitchen match against the rough board and held a light for the Captain.

"He must not have been such a much of a soldier," Cartwright said, "to get hisself killed so quick."

"It was an accident," the Captain said. "It could have happened to anybody."

"Tell me about it."

"Don't you know? Didn't they give you the details?"

"Surely," Cartwright said. "They notified me and they give me the details. And then they even sent a sergeant with a box and a flag. I just want to hear you tell it, that's all."

A day on the Grenade Range. A cold raw grassless place under a low gray winter sky. The Captain stood on the range tower with the young Range Officer, stamping his feet against the cold. His lunch lay heavy in his stomach and the long afternoon was ahead of him. The Captain was a combat officer by experience and inclination, condemned for the time being to the boredom and frustration of training new recruits. You get them in their civilian clothes, wrinkled and dirty from a bus or train ride, shaggy-headed with their duck-tails, sideburns, and pompadours, and so forth. You make them shave their faces and shine their boots. And you have a few weeks during which to try to turn them into something like a soldier. They come and go. You don't even have time to learn how most of the list of names you command corresponds with the faces in front of you before they are gone and you are starting all over again—

Below and at a little distance from the range tower six pits had been dug into the hard clay. Each with a sergeant instructor. Six at a time the men of the Captain's company come double-timing forward from a place to the rear and take places in the pits. The Range Officer calls off commands and instructions with his hoarse bullhorn. And left to right in steady sequence the recruits are to throw two live hand grenades over the top of the sandbags and duck while a slight explosion rocks the startled earth. They are young and new to the hand grenade. Some of them are scared. Their palms sweat—

There is a sudden shout from one of the pits. The instructor is shouting something. The Captain looks and finds the Sergeant is locked in a furious embrace with a soldier, wrestling. The soldier has frozen from fear with the pin pulled and the grenade in his fist. Over the Captain's shoulder the Range Officer is yelling something into the bullhorn, something which is lost in a blur of static. Now the Captain is moving, swinging over the side of the tower and quickly down the ladder and so he does not see the grenade fall free, losing its handle, and roll into the pit. He does not see the recruit standing there still and stiff as a bronze statue or the Sergeant swooping, grabbing for the loose grenade. The Captain drops heavily to the ground and is already running forward hard toward the pits when the blast knocks him flat. Dazed, he staggers to his feet and runs on.

The accident has killed instantly a veteran sergeant and the recruit—Cartwright, Edward T., Jr., Private E-1.

The farmer listened to the story quietly smoking. When the Captain had finished, he put out his cigarette.

"I told him. Don't anybody say I never told him. I said, son, you were born to be a dirt farmer. They won't be able to make you into no kind of a soldier. They can't make a soldier out of you. You're liable to get yourself killed or something. But that boy, he was nothing if he wasn't stubborn and willful—"

"He was only seventeen," the Captain said.

"Sixteen," Cartwright said. "He wasn't but sixteen. He was a big boy and he lied about his age."

The Captain looked at the man sitting next to him. He looked older than the Captain's father, a handsome, healthy, and successful lawyer who could still shoot the country-club golf course and break ninety. It startled the Captain to think that this man, worn by work and hard times, was probably nearer to his own age.

"Was he any good of a soldier?"

The Captain was tempted to lie. In his own defense as much as anything else. After all, the training cycle had hardly begun when the accident happened. He had known the name, one among many on a variety of lists that passed across his desk and on papers that had to have his signature. There had not been a photograph. He had looked at that name, even written it out carefully on paper, trying to rake his mind for any recollection of the face that went with it. He had looked at the faces of his whole company drawn up in formation trying to see if by *absence* he could recall the missing face. In combat men under his command had been killed, but he had known them. He felt an acute sense of failure. He should have known the boy. At the same time he could not repress a sense of outrage, anger that this guilt had been imposed on him by a stranger, a soldier he could not have known even by sight because of the hectic, inevitable confusion of the first weeks of training.

"It's hard to say in such a short time whether a man can make a good soldier or not," the Captain said. "He didn't get in any trouble while I had him. The men in his platoon liked him. He had some friends."

"He was a likable one all right. He always had friends. The only thing that surprises me is he stayed out of trouble. He was never what you would call a good boy. He had a kind of wild, restless streak in his nature. He never learned how to keep still."

"A lot of boys that age are restless."

"What? What's that?"

The farmer stared at him.

"What I mean is it's not such an unusual thing. Most boys that age are pretty much alike."

"I know what I'm talking about," the farmer said. "Don't you just sit here on my front steps and act like you knew more about him than I did. I'm his daddy!"

"I'm sorry. I didn't mean that. I was only—"

"A good boy! Would you call that 'a good boy' to go running off and join the Army and leave me here all alone with the wife and the girls and the other boy to look after? All of it falling on my shoulders. I need that boy bad this spring. I ain't hardly going to be able to raise a decent crop without him. What did he expect me to do?"

"You don't mean it that way."

It was a soft voice, the woman's voice. The Captain turned and saw her standing there on the porch behind him. He stood up.

"I do too!"

The farmer stood up, too, abruptly, and stamped away out into the bare, grassless yard, keeping his back to them.

"He was a damn fool to do like that," the farmer said. "To run off in the Army and get hisself killed."

"He don't mean a word of it," the woman said. "He is just hurting bad and he's got to try and hide it."

The farmer whirled and came back toward the porch, fury in his face.

"What I want to know is what's he doing here?" he said. "Can't they just leave us alone now? They done sent telegrams and letters and a sergeant with the box and the flag. Seems like it would all be over and done with. What's he trying to do, coming way out here all dressed up in his soldier suit?"

"He's doing the right thing, the Christian thing," the woman said. "It's what you would have to do if it was his boy that got killed."

"The whole thing is," the farmer said softly, "it was my boy that got killed."

Then he was gone. He passed by them and around the side of the shack and out of sight. In a moment they heard the ringing sound of the ax.

"Chopping wood," the woman said. "He'll chop awhile and work up a sweat and then be all right."

"I'm sorry to have upset you people," the Captain said.

"We haven't got any reason to be mad with anybody," she said. "Not even with the boy. He done what he thought was the right thing to do. I thank you for coming to see us."

She offered the Captain her hand.

"I wish we could ask you to stay for supper or something," she said. "Maybe some other time."

"Thanks just the same," the Captain said. "I have to try and get back to the post this evening."

"That's a pretty long trip."

"I've got my car down there on the other side of the stream," the Captain said.

"How about some coffee? I could heat up a pot of coffee."

"No thanks," he said. "I'll tell you what, though. I'd be grateful for some water."

"Help yourself," she said and pointed to the well.

She turned back into the shack. The Captain walked to the well and hauled up a bucket of water. He took a tin dipper off a nail and filled it. The water was sweet and cool and his mouth felt very dry. His tongue felt heavy. He stopped drinking. The sound of the ax ringing against wood had stopped. He looked up and saw the farmer coming toward him. He stiffened.

"She was right," the farmer said. "You done the right thing to come and see us. There's nothing to say, but you done right to come here and meet me face-to-face like a man."

The two men shook hands. When the Captain had finished drinking the farmer took the dipper. He sloshed water around in it, splashed it on the ground, then dipped himself a drink. He sipped it and spoke to the Captain over the shiny edge of the dipper.

"That boy," he said. "I sure am going to miss him. He had a wild streak all right. No use pretending he didn't. But, you know, he had a light heart and a light heart is a rare thing in this world. He could make you laugh with his tricks and jokes and all. We used to go hunting sometimes. He used to be good with a gun. I don't see why he was afraid of a hand grenade. I don't see why—"

Quite suddenly the dipper slipped out of his fingers and fell with a splash. He seemed to sag on his feet. The Captain put his arm around his shoulders and held him while the farmer leaned against him and wept.

It was over in a moment. He blew his nose and drank some more water. He hung the dipper back in its place.

"I'm sorry to bust out like that," the farmer said. "It's a shame to have to watch a grown man crying."

"It's not the first time I've seen a man cry," the Captain said.

"Pray God you don't end up crying yourself."

The Captain walked back to his car. He went slowly, taking his time. He loosened his necktie and opened his collar button. Near the stream he heard a rustling. It was the other boy. He grinned at the Captain. He was a very thin boy with a pale, pinched face, a face that was used to some dull steady pain. But except for that sense of pain, like a shadow cast on the face, and except for the game leg and the crutch, he was the image of his father.

"What's that thing?" the boy said, pointing to the shiny little parachute badge the Captain wore above his breast pocket.

"It's my jump badge," the Captain said. "It means I'm a paratrooper."

"So was my brother. He was a paratrooper in the Army."

"Is that right?"

"That's how come he joined up. So he could jump out of an airplane. He told me so."

Jesus! the Captain thought. *If he froze with a live grenade in his hand what the hell would have happened with him all hooked up and standing at the door of a moving airplane?*

"A lot of them join up so they can be paratroopers," the Captain said.

"Did you know my brother?"

"A little."

"I wonder how come they didn't send his badge home along with the rest of the stuff? I went through all the stuff they sent us and there wasn't a badge like that."

"Maybe they made a mistake," the Captain lied. "Sometimes they make a mistake like that."

"Maybe they lost it."

"Here, you take this one." The Captain unpinned the parachute badge and handed it to him.

"Can I keep it?"

"Sure," he said. "It's yours."

He stood there for a moment watching the boy hobble away on the path, using his crutch well, moving along quick, holding the small badge carefully in the cupped palm of his free hand, looking at it. Then he turned back to the path.

For some reason he remembered something that had happened to him quite a while ago. He was a young recruit himself then. The training company was about to move out on their first twenty-mile hike with full field equipment. He remembered standing in ranks with the gray dawn just beginning to come over the camp, hearing a radio playing in the lighted mess hall, thinking about the sun that would be coming on soon. It was going to be a scorcher. The steel helmet felt heavy on his head and the pack was already cutting into his shoulders. His feet in his boots felt small and detached. Small-boned and separate from the rest of him. Then on the orderly room steps the First Sergeant was standing in front of them looking them over. Hard, tough, with the face of a clean-shaven prophet. An articulate man who pronounced the message the Captain now lived by.

"All right," the Sergeant said. "When I tell you to, you

going to pick up your feet and move out smartly. I don't want to catch nobody worrying about when we going to get there. You ain't got nothing to worry about. All you got to do is keep picking 'em up and putting 'em down."

Texarkana Was a Crazy Town

HEN I went back to the barracks for the last time to pick up my stuff, there was Mooney waiting on me.

"Well," he said. "You feel any better now?"

I didn't answer. I kept busy stuffing things in my duffel bag. I didn't want any trouble with Mooney. I knew how he felt, like I was running out on him.

"How does it feel to be a civilian?"

"How would I know?" I said. "I ain't even been off the post yet."

"You're making a mistake," he said. "You'll be sorry."

"Maybe."

"Maybe nothing!" Mooney said. "Listen here, boy. You've got it made here. You don't know it. You just don't know how it is. You don't know anything else but the Army. It's going to be tough out there for a guy like you, believe me."

"Listen, Mooney," I kidded him, "you came in the Army during the Depression. They had bread lines and all that then.

272

People selling pencils on the street corners. Things are different now."

Mooney grinned. "I may look old," he said, "but I'm not that old."

"You look old to me."

"You don't know anything," he said. "What's the matter?"

"We've been all through this before."

"Never mind about before. I want to know."

"I just don't like being pushed around," I said. "And that's all there is to it."

"Who's been pushing you around? You tell me who's been giving you a hard time."

"Nobody," I said. "It's just the idea of the thing. I'm sick of it."

"Jesus Christ!" Mooney said. "That beats all."

Mooney was about the best friend I ever had. I knew him ever since I was seventeen and joined the Army. We had been in the same outfit all along. In the beginning Mooney was my Chief of Section on the howitzer. He made a soldier out of me. Now I was a Chief of Section and he was the Chief of Firing Battery. He could have been First Sergeant if he had wanted to. He turned it down because he wanted to be with the guns. Mooney was what you'd have to call a dedicated man with those guns. He really cared. That's why he just couldn't understand why I was leaving.

"What are you going to do?" he asked.

"I don't know."

"Maybe you can make use of your service experience and repair the old cannons in front of American Legion halls."

"Yeah, sure," I said. "And maybe they'll let me fire a salute on the Fourth of July."

"It's too bad you never learned how to play a bugle," Mooney said. "You could double up and play taps."

"I can always teach dismounted drill to the Boy Scouts. Or maybe I'll open a real high-class professional shoeshine parlor."

"You're crazy."

"I'd rather be crazy than chronic," I said. "You're chronic, Mooney. Nothing but an old chrome-plated chronic."

"Don't go," he said suddenly. "Change your mind."

I was all through packing and I was ready to leave. I didn't want to hang around talking to Mooney all day long. We had been through it all so many times before.

"It's too late," I said. "They already give me my mustering-out pay and my permanent grade of PFC—poor freaking civilian."

"What's everything coming to?" Mooney said. "What am I supposed to do for soldiers?"

"Hell, just grab ahold of a couple of those new kids and give them the sales talk. Maybe you'll convert some of them. If you signed up enough of them they might even make you Recruiting NCO and you could get yourself a bonus."

"You got ninety days," he said. "You got ninety days to change your mind. Just remember that."

"Okay," I said. "Just give me ninety days. So long, Mooney."

I stuck out my hand to shake hands with him.

"Don't give me that shit," he said. And he turned his back on me and walked away.

I didn't blame him. I guess I would have been mad, too, if I was Mooney. I knew how he felt, but that didn't help me a whole lot. He was my friend, a good one, and about the best soldier I ever saw. He was a great guy and you took him for himself. You just forgot all about Mooney being a nigger.

I didn't go home. What was the sense in that? I joined the Army in the first place to get away from that. They never would miss me. They've got a houseful anyway. Somebody told me jobs were easy to come by in Houston, Texas, so I went on down there and got a job driving a truck for an ice company. Now you might think in this modern day and age

there wouldn't be a whole lot for an iceman to do. I mean
with refrigerators and freezers and all. So did I. I was wrong.
There was plenty for me to do all day, and there were plenty
of people right there in a great big city who had an old-
fashioned icebox.

That job lasted three days. The first day on the job the boss
took me aside and told me what was what. There was one
special case I had to worry about.

"There's a woman at this address, a real good-looking
woman," he said, showing me the number on the delivery
roster.

"Yeah?"

"Now, when you go in the house, this woman will be in
the living room taking a sunbath under a sunlamp, buck
naked with the door wide open to the kitchen."

"That's all right with me," I said. "I don't mind if she
don't."

"Now you listen to me, sonny boy," he said. "You take
the ice in and you put it in the top of the icebox. You don't
look left and you don't look right. You don't stop and talk,
even if she talks to you. All you do is put the ice in the icebox and get out. If you look, if you stop and talk, she's going
to call up the company just as soon as you leave and I'll have
to fire you."

"She must be a pretty good customer."

"Yeah," he said. "She's regular."

"Why don't she get herself a refrigerator?" I said. "That
woman must be crazy."

"Don't talk like that," he said. "She's my wife."

I think that woman was crazy. She didn't need an icebox
even if her husband did run an ice company. They had a nice
house with air conditioning and everything. The kitchen was
full of all kinds of machines and appliances. And, to top it all,
she had this great big funny old icebox. Well, I put up with it
for two days, sneaking in and out of the kitchen like a dog. I
couldn't see her, but I could hear the portable radio playing

and see the glare of the heat lamp out of the corner of my eye and I could feel the heat of it. And I could tell she was just waiting to see what I was going to do.

The third day she tried to trip me up. I got inside and was just putting the ice in the icebox.

"Honey," she called out. "Would you kindly open a can of beer for me and put it by the sink so I can come get it when you leave?"

"Sure," I said.

It was a hot summer day in Houston, really hot and so humid the air seemed to stick to you. I was tired and I wouldn't have minded a beer myself.

"Don't you drink any of it."

"Don't you worry, lady," I said. "When I want to drink a beer, I'll buy it myself."

"You're kind of sassy," she said. "What's your name, honey?"

I came right up to the living room door and leaned against the doorframe and just looked at her. She was laying on her stomach facing me, so she couldn't very well move to cover herself up. I'd say she was a pretty nice-looking woman, a little on the heavy side, but a nice, very nice ass.

"Puddin' Tane, you bitch," I said. I figured I was as good as fired anyway.

"That's no way to talk to a lady," she said.

I lit myself a cigarette and looked around.

"I don't see no lady."

"You got a nerve," she said. "I'm going to phone my husband."

"You know what I'd do if I was your husband?"

"No," she said. "What would you do?"

"I'd whip your ass good and throw you out in the street where you belong."

I walked over and smacked her fanny so hard I left a print on it, all five fingers included, and then I walked right out of the house with her hollering rape and murder and everything

276

else. I drove straight back to the company and gave the boss the keys to his truck.

"I'm sorry," he said. "But don't say I didn't give you fair warning."

"Mister, you can have this job."

"I'm sorry," he said. "I can't help it. It's just the way things are."

"The hell you can't!" I said. "You ought to knock some sense into that woman. And if she won't shape up, get rid of her."

"I can't help it," he said. "I'm sorry but that's just the way it is."

"Okay," I said. "Have it your own way."

At the end I almost felt sorry for him. He was just an old guy with a young wife. You know how it goes.

A few days later an oil exploration company hired me to drive a pickup truck for some of their crews. I was really hoping they would send me to South America or Arabia or some place, but they sent me up to Texarkana instead. Texarkana was a crazy town. I don't know how it is now and I couldn't care less, but it was a crazy place then. The state line between Arkansas and Texas ran right up the middle of the street and they said you could break the law on one side and then run across to the other and thumb your nose at the cops if you felt like it. One state, I forget which, was partially dry. You could buy only beer there. If you went across to the other side you could get beer and whiskey and pretty nearly anything else you wanted. Naturally it was heavenly country for bootleggers. On a still calm day you could see the smoke rising up from a half a dozen stills out in the pinewoods. The law wouldn't do anything about it, or, anyway, I guess they couldn't.

About the same time I showed up there was another kind of crime that had everybody worried and worked up. Somebody took to killing off couples parked out in the woods. Whoever it was would sneak up on them in the dark, kill the man, rape the woman, and then kill her too. Then he would carve up the bodies with a butcher knife. All the newspapers were full of it. They called him the Phantom Killer and everybody in the area was supposed to be on the lookout to catch him. All this was in the middle of summer when everybody is edgy anyway. Life goes on the same everywhere, with or without no Phantom Killer, but I don't mind telling you it made the town a nervous, kind of suspicious place to be in.

All that part didn't bother me one way or the other at first, though. I was too busy on the job and getting used to the people I was working with to worry about what kind of a place I was living in. The whole crew lived together in a boardinghouse. We would be up long before daylight and out on the road, driving miles to wherever we had to work that day. I had to drive a pickup for Pete, the surveyor, and all his gear. We would drive way out in the woods or swamps somewhere and then run a survey for elevation and distance, setting up known locations, stations where the gravity-meter crew could come along later and take readings. The driving on those back roads was pretty bad, but I was used to rough driving. The only tough time I had was getting along with Pete. Right from the first day. Part of it was my own fault, I'll admit. He reminded me of my old man. Pete was a little scrawny guy like that and all puffed up with himself like a banty rooster. I guess he figured everybody was against him to start with, so he might as well give everybody else a bad time before they had a chance to do it to him. He went out of his way to let you know right away he thought you were dirt. The first time I ever drove for him he started in on me.

"What did you do before you came to work for us?" he asked me.

"I was in the Army."

"Yeah? I thought so."

I didn't say anything. Plenty of people have plenty of good reasons for not liking the Army. I even have a few good ones myself. When he saw I wasn't about to take his bait, he kept after me.

"Well," he said, "don't try any of your Army tricks around here or you won't last too long."

"Yeah?"

"I know how it is. I was in the Army. The idea is to get out of as much work as you can and let somebody else do it. That's right, isn't it?"

"I wouldn't know."

"Come on now," he said. "You know what I'm talking about."

"I hope you do," I said. "I don't."

"Just don't try any tricks on me."

Like I've said, one of my big troubles is I don't like to get pushed around by anybody. And another one is a quick temper sometimes. I pulled the truck off the road and stopped.

"What are you doing?"

"I'm playing my first trick on you," I said.

"I wasn't joking," he said.

"Now listen, you," I said. "I don't want any trouble with you. Let's get everything straight right now. You tell me what to do on this job and I'll do it. Just as good or better than the next guy. But let's just leave the bullshit out of it. They don't pay me to listen to you."

"You talk pretty big for a kid," he said.

"Try me," I said. "I'd just as soon whip your ass as any-body else's. Just try me and find out."

He shut up and we drove on. Later he asked me what rank I had in the Army and I told him sergeant. He said, "I might have known," or something like that. I let it pass. I let him get away with that. He was like my old man. He had to say the last word even if it killed him.

After that Pete didn't give me any trouble for a while. And I didn't bother him. Which is more than the rest of the guys on the crew. They didn't like him either and they always had some practical joke to pull on him. They made him pretty miserable I guess. The hell with it. I just worked with him and let him alone.

We always worked until pretty near dark and then we would drive hell for leather back to town. After we got back and cleaned up and had some supper, we would either go over to the café across the street and drink beer or else hang around the filling station.

The filling station was run by this one-arm guy that used to be in the Army away back. He had been a mule-pack soldier in the days when they still had mules and I liked to go over there and sit around and talk with him about how it had been in the old days. We could talk the same kind of language and I got to where I really liked to hang around there in the evening. Except for one thing. He had this nigger they called Peanuts working for him. Peanuts was tall and skinny and kind of funny-looking with great big loose hands and feet about half a block long. He wasn't very smart, but he was a good-natured simple guy and I got to where I couldn't stand the way they picked on him. Everybody played jokes on Peanuts. They would send him all over town on crazy errands like getting a bucket of polka-dot paint or taking the slack out of the state line. He never caught on. Once or twice somebody gave him a bottle of cheap whiskey and got him drunk. He would stagger around the station singing and hollering and slobbering and carrying on until he just passed out cold. Whiskey put him out of his head. There would be a crowd of the guys to see this happen. They thought it was pretty funny, like seeing a pig drunk. In a way I guess it was funny too. Except a man is not a pig. So I made up my mind. I would rather sit in the café and drink beer by myself than to put up with a thing like that.

"What's the matter?" Pete asked me. "You don't hang around with the rest of the guys anymore."

"I'd rather drink beer."

"That Delma is a nice piece."

"Who?"

"Delma," he said, "the waitress."

"Which one is she?"

"Don't try and fool me," Pete said. "I know what you're up to."

"Well, you know a lot more than I do then."

To tell you the truth Pete put an idea in my head. I hadn't thought about it before, but there was this good-looking waitress working over at the café. And I was lonesome and horny as a jackrabbit and I figured that getting tied up with a woman wouldn't be such a bad thing. I never had a whole lot to do with women before I went in the Army. The only women I really knew anything about were gooks. I like them fine, especially the Japanese, but they sure are different from American women.

Delma was a pretty good-looking girl, short and stacked with dark hair and a good smile. Of course they all look good when you want one bad enough. It didn't take long for me to get to know her a little. When business was slack she would come over and sit in the booth with me. She talked a lot and joked. She was full of laughs about everything. She seemed all right.

One night, after I had been around Texarkana for a few weeks, she asked me if I wanted to go out with her.

"Sure," I said. "The only trouble is I don't have a car."

"We can use mine," she said. "I don't feel like working tonight. I feel like going out and having a good time."

She went back to the ladies' room and changed out of her white uniform and into a dress. She looked good in a dress. I never had seen her except in her uniform and so she looked like a different person. She had that clean, kind of shiny look American girls have when they're all dressed up to go some-where. Like a picture out of a magazine. We got in her car and drove out in the country to some honky-tonk where they had a band.

"I don't dance much," I told her. "I never had much time to learn."

"That's all right," she said. "I'll show you how."

We tried dancing awhile, but it didn't work too well. So we sat down at a table and just drank and listened to the music. That Delma could really drink. I had a hard time keeping up with her.

"This is a pretty rough place," she told me. "A lot of really rough guys come here."

"Is that so?"

"You see that big man?" She pointed at a great big guy standing at the bar. "He is one of the toughest men in this whole part of the country. A big bootlegger."

"What did he do to get so tough?"

"They say he's killed two or three men."

I started to laugh. I don't know why. I just couldn't help it. I was drunk and it struck me funny to hear somebody talk like that, like he was some kind of a hero or something.

"What's so funny?"

"I don't know."

"Something must be funny."

"Is that what you have to do to get a name around here— kill somebody?"

"You better not let him catch you laughing at him."

For some reason that made me mad.

"I don't give a damn who catches me laughing," I said. "I'll laugh whenever I damnwell please and take my chances. Listen, I've seen bigger, tougher guys than him break down and pray to Jesus. I've seen plenty of great big tough guys that was as yellow and soft as a stick of butter. It don't take no guts to kill a man. I've seen the yellowest chicken-hearted bastards in the world that would shoot prisoners. I've seen some terrible things. So don't come telling me about no big bad country bootlegger."

While I was sounding off like that she reached across the table and grabbed my hands and squeezed hard. She kept staring at me.

"Finish your drink," she said. "And let's go somewhere."

We went out in the parking lot and got in the car and necked awhile. She was all hot and bothered and breathing hard.

"Let's go somewhere," she said.

"Where do you want to go?" I said. "Out in the woods?"

"No," she said. "Not out there, I'm scared."

"What of?"

"I'm just nervous since all that Phantom Killer stuff has been in the papers."

"All right, you name it."

We drove even farther out the highway to a cheap motel. After I paid the man we went in the cabin and sat down on the bed.

"I've got to have a drink," she said. "Go ask the man for a pint of whiskey. He sells it and don't let him tell you he doesn't."

When I came back to the cabin with the whiskey all the lights were out.

"Hey," I said. "I can't see anything."

"Hurry up and get your clothes off," she said. "I'm so hot I can't stand it."

I climbed in the bed and we drank out of the bottle. You would never believe the first thing she said to me.

"Have you ever killed anybody?" she whispered. "Tell me about it."

I told her I didn't know. In the artillery you don't see what you are shooting at most of the time. They telephone or radio back when they have got a target for you to shoot at and then you just keep on shooting until they tell you to quit.

"I don't mean like that," she said. "I mean up close with a knife or something."

The only thing I could figure was she was drunk and had all that Phantom Killer stuff on her mind. I could tell she wanted me to say yes. I don't know why. I guess she wanted to feel bad, dirty maybe. She wanted to pretend she was in bed with some terrible man. Maybe she wanted to pretend that the Phantom Killer was raping her or something. I was drunk enough myself so I didn't care. So I told her yes I had killed a whole lot of gooks with my knife. I made up a couple of long-winded phony stories and that seemed to excite her. I'll say this for Delma, she was all right in bed even if she did carry on, laughing and crying the whole time until I was afraid the man would throw us out.

Later on, in the early hours of the morning, she got up real quiet and started to get dressed. I sat up in bed.

"What are you doing?"

"Let's go," she said. "It's time to go home."

It was still dark. I snapped the lamp beside the bed and it didn't go on. I tried the bulb and it was tight. I gave the cord a pull and it was free. She must have yanked the plug out while I was out buying the whiskey when we first came in.

"How come you unplugged the light?"

"What do you mean?"

"What's the matter with you?"

"I don't want you to see me," she said.

"I saw you when we came in," I said. "I know who you are."

"Not like this," she said. "You didn't see me like this."

Then she started crying. I thought the hell with it. Just the hell with it all. And I got up and found my clothes and got dressed in the dark. Before we went out the door she took hold of me.

"Aren't you forgetting something?"

"What?"

"It's going to cost you twenty dollars."

"I'll be damn," I said. "I didn't know you were a whore."

"I'm not!" she said. "I'm not a whore. But I've got my kid to think about."

"Your kid? I didn't even know you were married."

"Now you know," she said. "And it costs twenty bucks to spend the night with me."

"That's a pretty high price."

Even if I felt bad about being fooled, I went ahead and gave her the money. What was the use of arguing? It was my own fault.

We drove back to town without saying a word. I turned on the radio and picked up some hillbilly music. We finally got to the boardinghouse and I pulled over to let her take the wheel. I got out and started to walk away. She called to me.

"Listen," she said, "you're not mad, are you?"

"Mad? Why should I be mad?"

"I just want to be sure," she said. "I don't want you to be mad at me."

"What difference does it make?"

"I just wanted to know," she said. "Will I see you again?"

"I don't know," I said. "How would I know?"

"Suit yourself," she said and she drove off.

I just about had time to put on my boots and work clothes before we left for work. I didn't even have time to shave. Pete was already waiting for me when I walked in the house.

"Where the hell have you been?"

"Go on out and wait in the truck," I told him. "I'll be ready in five minutes."

The others left without us. We drove out on the highway alone for an hour or so. Pete just curled up in a corner of the cab and went to sleep. I had a hard time staying awake myself, driving along the long straight road in the first light of the morning. The tires were humming. I nodded and rubbed my eyes and drove on. After a while I turned off onto a back road that led into swamp country where we had been working before. I drove as far as we had worked yesterday. Then I nudged Pete and woke him up.

"Where are the other guys?" I said.

"Where are we?"

He looked around a minute, blinking his eyes.

"Goddamn!" he said. "You went to the wrong place."

"I thought we were supposed to finish the line we were running."

285

"Yeah? You thought! Well, it's been changed."

"You could have told me."

"Drive on up the road and see if there's a place we can turn around. I think I remember a shack down the road a piece."

I started up the truck again and drove on.

"Well," Pete said, "while you were out catting around with Delma last night, you missed all the fun."

"What fun?"

"Peanuts," he said. "They beat the living hell out of him."

"Jesus Christ! What did they do that for?"

"They got him drunk last evening, see? Usually when he's drunk he's just funny. But this time he was kind of mean, mean drunk. Some of the boys egged him on and he was just drunk enough to swing at them. They gave that black son-of-a-bitch a real going-over. Hell, they had to take him to the hospital when they got through."

"Jesus Christ!"

"You should've been there."

"I can't believe anybody would do anything like that."

I was thinking what a crazy terrible thing it was for some grown men to beat up a poor feeble-minded nigger like that. I was sleepy and hungry and hung over and it was all mixed up in my mind with all that had happened to me last night. Thinking about that married woman, Delma, and how she had to get herself all worked up by pretending she was in bed with some kind of a killer. She couldn't have believed it, but she needed to pretend that she did. Just like those men in town at the station had to pretend that Peanuts had done something to them and then beat him up to feel better. I felt so sick about everything in the whole world I wanted to die. I just wanted to fall over dead.

"Hey!" Pete yelled. "Turn in here."

There was a shack all right, just a patch of bare ground with the swamp all around it. It was all falling to pieces, but there were chickens running around the yard and a nigger without a shirt on was sitting on the front stoop picking at a guitar.

"The hell with it," Pete said. "He had it coming."

"Who?"

"Peanuts. They shouldn't let anybody that stupid run around loose."

"For what?" I said. "For what does anybody have things like that coming to him? Answer me that."

"I said the hell with it. Turn the truck around and let's go."

"I'm asking you."

"And I'm telling you to shut up and turn this truck around."

"All right," I said, turning off the engine and putting the keys in my pocket. "It was bound to come to this sooner or later."

"What are you going to do?"

"I'm fixing to beat the shit out of you."

I'll have to say he put up a pretty good fight for a little guy. He was tough. We fought all around the truck and all over the yard, rolling on the ground, kicking and punching each other. I was so tired and sleepy I felt like I was dreaming, but I kept after him and I finally got him down so he couldn't get up. He just lay there panting, all bloody on the ground, and I started kicking him.

"You going to kill me?"

He looked bad lying there. He was too weak to move. In my blood and my muscles and my bones I never wanted to kill anybody so much. I wanted to tear him into pieces and stamp them in the dust. But I couldn't do it. When he asked me was I going to kill him, all of a sudden I knew what I was doing. I knew what had happened to me and I knew I wasn't a damn bit better than those guys that beat up Peanuts or Delma or Pete or anybody else. I was so sick of myself I felt like I was going to puke.

"I don't know," I told him. "I ought to."

I went up where I saw a well and hauled a bucket of water and splashed it all over me. The nigger sat there and stared

287

at me with the guitar hanging loose in his hands. I wonder what he thought was going on.

After that I splashed Pete with water, too, and I put the keys in the truck.

"Drive me back to town," he said.

"Drive yourself," I said. "I'm walking."

I was lucky to get back in my old outfit with my old job. I came into the Battery area on a Sunday afternoon. The barracks was empty except for a few guys on the first floor, broke maybe or without a pass, playing cards on one of the bunks. They were sitting around, smoking, concentrating on the game. When I walked in and went on through they just looked up and looked back down to the game. They were new since I left. They didn't know me and I didn't know them.

I climbed the stairs and went into Mooney's room. He wasn't there but the room had his touch on everything in it. It was bare and clean and neat. The clothes in his wall locker were hanging evenly. The boots under his bed, side by side, were shined up nice, not all spit-shined like some young soldier's, just a nice shine. I made up the empty bunk. I made it up real tight without a wrinkle, so tight you could bounce a quarter off of it if you wanted to. Then I threw all my stuff in the corner and just flopped down in the middle of my bunk. I felt like I was floating on top of water. I lit myself a cigarette and looked at the ceiling.

After a while I heard Mooney climbing up the stairs. He always came up real slow and careful like an old man. Once you heard him walking up stairs you would never mistake it for somebody else. He opened the door and came in.

"How many times do I have to tell you not to smoke in bed," he said. "It's against regulations."

"Don't tell me," I said. "I've heard it all before."

"You think you know it all," he said. "Let me tell you, you got a lot of things to learn."

"Oh yeah? I've been around. I've been outside. I've seen a few things since the last time I seen you."

"Did you learn anything?" he said. "That's what I want to know."

"Not much."

"Nothing?"

"There's one thing, just one thing I've got to find out from you."

He waited for me to ask it.

"Mooney," I said, "how come you're so black?"

Mooney looked at me hard for a minute. Then he leaned back, rocked on his heels. The whole room rattled with his laughter and it was good to hear.

"Sunburn," he said. "Son, I got the most awful, the most permanent case of sunburn you ever saw."

Wounded Soldier

(Cartoon Strip)

WHEN the time came at last and they removed the wealth of bandages from his head and face, all with the greatest of care as if they were unwinding a precious mummy, the Doctor—he of the waxed, theatrical, upswept mustache and the wet sad eyes of a beagle hound—turned away. Orderlies and aides coughed, looked at floor and ceiling, busied themselves with other tasks. Only the Head Nurse, a fury stiff with starch and smelling of strong soap, looked, pink-cheeked and pale white as fresh flour, over the Veteran's shoulders. She stared back at him, un-flinching and expressionless, from the swimming light of the mirror.

No question. It was a terrible wound.

—I am so sorry, the Doctor said. It's the best we can do for you.

But the Veteran barely heard his words. The Veteran looked deeply into the mirror and stared at the stranger who was now to be himself with an inward wincing that was nearer to the sudden gnawing of love at first sight than of self-pity. It was like being born again. He had, after all, not seen himself since the blinding, burning instant when he was wounded. Ever since then he had been a mystery to himself. How many times he had stared into the mirror through the neat little slits left for his eyes and seen only a snowy skull of gauze and bandages! He imagined himself as a statue waiting to be unveiled. And now he regretted that there was no real audience for the occasion except for the Doctor, who would not look, and the Head Nurse—she for whom no truth could be veiled anyway and hence for whom there could never be any system or subtle aesthetic of exposure or disclosure by any clever series of gradual deceptions. She carried the heavy burden of one who was familiar with every imaginable kind of wound and deformity.

—You're lucky to be alive, she said. Really lucky.

—I don't know what you will want to do with yourself, the Doctor said. Of course, you understand that you are welcome to remain here.

—That might be the best thing for any number of good reasons, the Head Nurse said. Then to the Doctor: —Ordinarily cases like this one elect to remain in the hospital.

—Are there others? the Veteran asked.

—Well . . . the Head Nurse admitted, there are none quite like you.

—I should hope not, the Veteran said, suddenly laughing at himself in the mirror. Under the circumstances it's only fair that I should be able to feel unique.

—I am so sorry, the Doctor said.

Over the Veteran's shoulder in the mirror the Head Nurse smiled back at him.

That same afternoon a High-ranking Officer came to call on him. The Officer kept his eyes fixed on the glossy shine of his boots. After mumbled amenities he explained to the Veteran that while the law certainly allowed him to be a free man, free to come and go as he might choose, he ought to give consideration to the idea that his patriotic duty had not ended with the misfortune of his being stricken in combat. There were, the Officer explained, certain abstract obligations which clearly transcended those written down as statute law and explicitly demanded by the State.

—There are duties, he continued, waxing briefly poetic, which like certain of the cardinal virtues, are deeply disguised. Some of these are truly sublime. Some are rare and splendid like the aroma of a dying arrangement of flowers or the persistent haunting of half-remembered melodies.

The Veteran, who knew something about the music of groans and howls, and something about odors, including, quite recently, the stink of festering and healing, was not to be deceived by this sleight of hand.

—Get to the point, he said.

The High-ranking Officer was flustered, for he was not often addressed by anyone in this fashion. He stammered, spluttered as he offered the Veteran a bonus to his regular pension, a large sum of money, should he freely choose to remain here in the hospital. After all, his care and maintenance would be excellent and he would be free of many commonplace anxieties. Moreover, he need never feel that his situation was anything like being a prisoner. The basic truth about any prisoner is—is it not?—that he is to be deliberately deprived, insofar as possible, of all the usual objects of desire. The large bonus would enable the veteran to live well, even lavishly in the hospital if he wanted to.

—Why?

Patiently the Officer pointed out that his appearance in public, in the city or the country, would probably serve to arouse the anguish of the civilian population. So many among the military personnel had been killed or wounded in this most recent war. Wasn't it better for everyone concerned, especially the dependents, the friends and relatives of these unfortunate men, that they be permitted to keep their innocent delusions of swirling battle flags and dimly echoing bugle calls, rather than being forced to confront in fact and flesh the elemental brute ugliness of modern warfare? As an old soldier, or as one old soldier to another, surely the Veteran must and would acknowledge the validity of this argument.

The Veteran nodded and replied that he guessed the Officer also hadn't overlooked the effect his appearance might have on the young men of the nation. Most likely a considerable cooling of patriotic ardor. Probably a noticeable, indeed a measurable, decline in the number of enlistments.

—Just imagine for a moment, the Veteran said, what it would be like if I went out there and stood right next to the recruiting poster at the post office. Sort of like a "before and after" advertisement.

At this point the Officer stiffened, scolded, and threatened. He ended by reminding the Veteran that no man, save the One, had ever been perfect and blameless. He suggested to him that, under the strictest scrutiny, his service record would no doubt reveal some error or other, perhaps some offence committed while he was a soldier on active duty which would still render him liable to a court-martial prosecution.

Safe for the time being with his terrible wound, the Veteran laughed out loud and told the Officer that nothing they could do or think of doing to him could ever equal this. That he might as well waste his time trying to frighten a dead man or violate a corpse.

Then the Officer pleaded with the Veteran. He explained that his professional career as a leader of men might be ruined if he failed in the fairly simple assignment of convincing one ordinary common soldier to do as he was told to.

The Veteran, pitying this display of naked weakness, said that he would think about it seriously. With that much accomplished, the Officer brightened and recovered his official demeanor.

—I imagine it would have been so much more convenient for everyone if I had simply been killed, wouldn't it? the Veteran asked as the Officer was leaving.

293

Still bowed, still unable to look at him directly, the Officer shrugged his epauleted shoulders and closed the door very quietly behind him.

Nevertheless the Veteran had made up his mind to leave the sanctuary of the hospital. Despite his wound and appearance he was in excellent health, young still and full of energy. And the tiptoeing routine of this place was ineffably depressing. Yet even though he had decided to leave, even though he was certain he was going soon, he lingered, he delayed, he hesitated. Days went by quietly and calmly, and in the evening when she was off duty, the Head Nurse often came to his room to talk to him about things. Often they played cards. A curious and easy intimacy developed. It seemed almost as if they were husband and wife. On one occasion he spoke to her candidly about this.

—You better be careful, he said. I'm not sexless.

—No, I guess not, she said. But I am.

She told him that she thought his plan of going out into the world again was dangerous and foolish.

—Go ahead. Try it and you'll be back here in no time at all, beating on the door with bloody knuckles and begging us to be readmitted, to get back in. You are too young and inexperienced to understand anything about people. Human beings are the foulest things in all creation. They will smell your blood and go mad like sharks. They will kill you if they can. They can't allow you to be out there among them. They will tear you limb from limb. They will strip the meat off your bones and trample your bones to dust. They will turn you into dust and a fine powder and scatter you to the four winds!

—I can see you have been deeply wounded, too, the Veteran said.

At that the Head Nurse laughed out loud. Her whole white mountainous body shook with laughter.

• • •

294

When the Veteran left the hospital he wore a mask. He wanted to find a job and wearing the mask seemed to him to be an act of discretion which would be appreciated. But this, as he soon discovered, was not the case at all. A mask is somehow intolerable. A mask becomes an unbearable challenge. When he became aware of this, when he had considered it, only the greatest exercise of self-discipline checked within him the impulse to gratify their curiosity. It would have been so easy. He could so easily have peeled off his protective mask and thereby given to the ignorant and innocent a new creature for their bad dreams.

One day he came upon a small traveling circus and applied for a job with them.

—What can you do? the Manager asked.

This Manager was a man so bowed down by the weight of weariness and boredom that he seemed at first glance to be a hunchback. He had lived so long and so closely with the oddly gifted and with natural freaks that his lips were pursed as if to spit in contempt at everything under the sun.

—I can be a clown, the Veteran said.

—I have enough clowns, the Manager said. Frankly, I am sick to death of clowns.

—I'll be different from any other clown you have ever seen, the Veteran said.

And then and there he took off his mask.

—Well, this is highly original, the Manager said, studying the crude configuration of the wound with a careful, pitiless interest. This has some definite possibilities.

—I suppose the real question is, will the people laugh?

—Without a doubt. Believe me. Remember this—a man is just as apt to giggle when he is introduced to his executioner as he is to melt into a mess of piss and fear. The real and true talent, the exquisite thing, is of course to be able to raise tears to the throat and to the rims of the eyes, and then suddenly to convert those tears into laughter.

—I could play "The Wounded Soldier."

—Well, we'll try it, the Manager said. I think it's worth a try. And so that same night he first appeared in his new role. He entered with all the other clowns. The other clowns were conventional. They wore masks and elaborate makeup, sported baggy trousers and long, upturned shoes. They smoked exploding cigars. They flashed red electric noses on and off. They gamboled like a blithe flock of stray lambs, unshepherded. The Veteran, however, merely entered with them and then walked slowly around the ring. He wore a battered tin helmet and a uniform a generation out of date with its old-fashioned, badly wrapped puttees and a high, choker collar. He carried a broken stub of a rifle, hanging in two pieces like an open shotgun. A touch of genius, the Manager had attached a large clump of barbed wire to the seat of his pants.

The Veteran was seriously worried that people would not laugh at him and that he wouldn't be able to keep his job. Slowly, apprehensively he strolled around the enormous circle and turned his wound toward them. He could see nothing at all outside of the zone of light surrounding him. But it was not long before he heard a great gasp from the outer darkness, a shocked intaking of breath so palpable that it was like a sudden breeze. And then he heard the single, high-pitched, hysterical giggle of a woman. And next came all that indrawn air returning, rich and warm. The whole crowd laughed at once. The crowd laughed loudly and the tent seemed to swell like a full sail from their laughter. He could see the circus bandsmen puffing like bullfrogs as they played their instruments and could see the sweat-stained leader waving his baton in a quick, strict, martial time. But he could not hear the least sound of their music. It was engulfed, drowned out, swallowed up by the raging storm of laughter.

Soon afterwards the Veteran signed a contract with the circus. His name was placed prominently on all the advertising posters and materials together with such luminaries as the

Highwire Walker, the Trapeze Artists, the Lion Tamer, and the Bareback Riders. He worked only at night. For he soon discovered that by daylight he could see his audience, and they knew that and either refused to laugh or were unable to do so under the circumstances. He concluded that only when they were in the relative safety of the dark would they give themselves over to the impulse of laughter.

His fellow clowns, far from being envious of him, treated him with the greatest respect and admiration. And before much time had passed, he had received the highest compliment from a colleague in that vocation. A clown in a rival circus attempted an imitation of his art. But this clown was not well received. In fact, he was pelted with peanuts and hot dogs, with vegetables and fruit and rotten eggs and bottles. He was jeered at and catcalled out of the ring. Because no amount of clever makeup could rival or compete with the Veteran's unfortunate appearance.

Once a beautiful young woman came to the trailer where he lived and prepared for his performance. She told him that she loved him.

—I have seen every single performance since the first night, she said. I want to be with you always.

The Veteran was not unmoved by her beauty and her naïveté. Besides, he had been alone for quite a long time.

—I'm afraid you don't realize what you are saying, he told her.

—If you won't let me be your mistress, I am going to kill myself, she said.

—That would be a pity.

She told him that more than anything else she wanted to have a child by him.

—If we have a child, then I'll have to marry you.

—Do you think, she asked, that our child would look like you?

—I don't believe that is scientifically possible, he said.

Later when she bore his child, it was a fine healthy baby,

297

handsome and glowing. And then, as inexplicably as she had first come to him, the young woman left him.

After a few successful seasons, the Veteran began to lose some of his ability to arouse laughter from the public. By that time almost all of them had seen him at least once already, and the shock had numbed their responses. Perhaps some of them had begun to pity him.

The Manager was concerned about his future.

—Maybe you should take a rest, go into a temporary retirement, he said. People forget everything very quickly nowadays. You could come back to clowning in no time.

—But what would I ever do with myself?

The Manager shrugged.

—You could live comfortably on your savings and your pension, he said. Don't you have any hobbies or outside interests?

—But I really like it here, the Veteran said. Couldn't I wear a disguise and be one of the regular clowns?

—It would take much too long to learn the tricks of the trade, the Manager said. Besides which your real clowns are truly in hiding. Their whole skill lies in the concealment of anguish. And your talent is all a matter of revelation.

It was not long after this conversation that the Veteran received a letter from the Doctor.

—Your case has haunted me and troubled me, night and day, the Doctor wrote. I have been studying the problem incessantly. And now I think I may be able to do something for you. I make no promises, but I think I can help you. Could you return to the hospital for a thorough examination?

While he waited for the results of all the tests, the Veteran lived in his old room. It was clean and bright and quiet as before. Daily the Head Nurse put a bouquet of fresh flowers in a vase by his bed.

—You may be making a big mistake, she told him. You have lived too long with your wound. Even if the Doctor is

successful—and he may be, for he is extremely skillful—
you'll never be happy with yourself again.

—Do you know? he began. I was very happy being a
clown. For the first and only time in my life all that I had to
do was to be myself. But, of course, like everything else, it
couldn't last for long.

—You can always come back here. You can stay just as
you are now.

—Would you be happy, he asked her, if I came back to the
hospital for good just as I am now?

—Oh yes, she said. I believe I would be very happy.

Nevertheless the Veteran submitted to the Doctor's treatment. Once again he became a creature to be wheeled into
the glaring of harsh lights, to be surrounded and hovered
over by intense masked figures. Once again he was swathed
in white bandages and had to suffer through a long time of
healing, waiting for the day when he would see himself
again. Once again the momentous day arrived, and he stood
staring into a mirror as they unwound his bandages.

This time, when the ceremony was completed, he looked
into the eyes of a handsome stranger.

—You cannot possibly imagine, the Doctor said, what this
moment means to me.

The Head Nurse turned away and could not speak to him.

When he was finally ready to leave the hospital, the Veteran
found the High-ranking Officer waiting for him. A gleaming
staff car was parked at the curb, and the Veteran noticed by
his insignia that the Officer had been promoted.

—We all hope, the Officer said, that you will seriously
consider returning to active duty. We need experienced men
more than ever now.

—That's a very kind offer, the Veteran said. And I'll certainly consider it in all seriousness.

Crowfoot

S TICK with me baby and you'll be farting
through silk.
God, that takes me back. A long way back.
Remember who used to say that all the time?
Somebody. Some guy in the old outfit.
Sure. But who?
How should I know?
Guess.
Stitch! It sounds like something he would say.
No. Not him. Not Bledsoe either. Or Saucier or old
Zwicker.
Singletree?
Not a bad guess.
Okay, I give up.
It was Crowfoot.
Crowfoot!
Crazy ass fucken Indian.
Jesus, I forgot all about old Crowfoot! How did that
happen?
Lucky you.

300

Whatever became of him anyway?
What do you care?
I'm just asking.
What difference does it make?
Don't be such an asshole.
Asshole. Who're you calling asshole?
You brought him up in the first place.
Yeah.
Right? Am I right?
Yeah.
Well, I don't give a shit but maybe you do.
What's that supposed to mean?
Look. Do you know what happened to him or not?
Oh, I know. I know all right.
So?
So what?
So let's hear it.

You could blame it on Benny if you wanted to. Remember those big white Italian tablets? I don't know about the rest of the company, but the guys in my squad were pretty much hooked on those things by the time we shipped out of Trieste. I made a connection with a medic on the troopship and I had a whole shitpot of them. There were a number of us on that kick and I had charge of the pills. I gave them to my buddies. And we sold some to guys we thought we could trust. We were back in the States, land of the Big PX, and we needed all the money we could get ahold of if we were going to go out every night and have ourselves a good time.
Well.
So one night there we were, all bathed and shaved and dressed and shined and stoked up on Benny, lined up outside the orderly room to pick up our passes, when the shitbird first sergeant of the transient company we were assigned to told us he had pulled all our passes. Seems like there was some kind of a weapons cleaning detail at Battalion. I was still a sergeant

then and he put me in charge. We went back to the barracks and put on our fatigues.

I will pause here to remark that I should have known better, should have known something weird was going on when nobody bitched or complained or anything. Even with Benny up to my eyeballs I should have known better. Nobody seemed to care. In fact we all just laughed when he told us. Maybe *he* should have noticed something, too. It must have puzzled him. But it didn't make him suspicious.

Anyway, we formed up and they loaded us all into a deuce-and-a-half and drove us a way across the camp somewhere. We ended up in the basement of some cinder block building under the supervision of some dumb fucken Pfc. fresh out of basic training. The guy didn't know the first thing about weapons.

A whole big huge basement room full of weapons and ammo.

It was kind of strange. All the way over we had been hollering and singing and laughing it up in the back of the truck. Then we come tumbling downstairs into that basement like a stampede of Shetland ponies, really loud and noisy. But once we entered the locked cage where all those weapons were, everybody got real quiet. I never saw so many weapons all in one place. Stacks and racks of them, all gleaming and beautiful. Our stuff, man. Infantry stuff. And none of us had even touched one since we shipped out of Trieste.

You got to picture how it was, coming in out of the dark and then down in that big basement cage full of shiny new weapons.

By daylight it was all routine there. Busy work. Paper work. All these yawning and unhurried chores filled up our days while we waited to get out or reassigned. By dark we were poor stumble-bums drinking and whoring and fighting each other and anybody else in the way. Greedy to recover and make up for lost time.

And we were tired out and all jazzed up on Benny.

So there was this great hush, this sense of awe when we came into that basement with all its odors of oil and bore cleaner, of wood and leather. The feel and weight and heft of familiar gear. All of it—who knows?—maybe to be known for the last time ever.

It was like the hush and awe of pirates when the treasure chest is finally cracked open and all the gold and silver and jewels are sparkling in the sunlight.

If it had been anyone at all except a brand-new Pfc., he would have known something. Would have guessed a bad ending when a dozen or so men cut out all the laughter and horseplay at once, as if by command, and set to work at the rough wooden tables field-stripping, cleaning and reassembling weapons. It was almost in complete silence except for the noise of metal on metal and some soft whispering. It was swift and efficient.

But this kid, he noticed nothing. He put his feet up on the desk and was looking at a magazine.

It took us maybe a couple of hours to get the job done.

Since I was in charge of the detail, I didn't have to clean weapons, too. But I worked as hard or harder than the others. Who knows why? Maybe I do know why, at least here and now I do; but I would rather not try to remember that part. Not just yet.

I picked up the very last weapon, a BAR. Remember the BAR? God almighty, what a wonderful weapon! Heavy, though and kind of clumsy to carry. But, Lord, you could shoot that sucker if you knew how. I wonder how they get on without it nowadays . . . ?

I took that BAR, hard to clean anyway, and this one was all dirty and fouled from neglect. The others, finishing up one by one and putting their rifles and carbines and grease guns and pistols back in the racks and in neat rows where they belonged, all of them clean and shiny, inside and out, and lightly oiled, the other guys gathered in a kind of a loose, silent huddle around the table where I was still working. It

303

felt good, wonderful, to be there doing it right, the way it's supposed to be, with all of them watching me. The Benny was pumping and I was feeling good, feeling fine. I took that BAR down as far as I could. As far as I knew how. No. Farther than that even. I took her down beyond where they let you, beyond where the field manual has names for things. I even took the trigger housing and assembly all apart until all I was holding was springs and screws and little teeny parts I had never seen or heard of before. Then I cleaned it like it had never been cleaned before. Or since then, I imagine. I cleaned it and oiled all the parts and then reassembled the weapon. Taking my time about it. But without any wasted motion either. Just steady and methodical. Finished the whole thing at last and for the first time looked up at the others, the guys all around the edges of the table and the limits of the light from the overhead lamp.

They were quiet and all watching. Waiting for me to say something.

"And that, gentlemen," I said, "is all she wrote."

And I slammed the weapon back into its place in the rack.

"Wahoo!" somebody yelled. "Whee doggie!"

And then all of a sudden they were all of them laughing and yelling like crazy at the top of their voices.

I think now that if that Pfc. had maybe yelled or done anything else except what he did, that's where it would have ended. But what he did, see?—he blew a whistle. A polished brass whistle on a lanyard. A terrible screeching thing. We had already stopped yelling before he quit blowing on that whistle. And we were all looking at him. He looked arrogant and insolent and so damn foolish with his cheeks all puffed out and swollen and his lips pursed on that whistle. And the noise and screeching trailed off until there was nothing left of it but spit and air. He kept the whistle tightly in his lips and his eyes bugged out as if he had surprised himself.

It seemed like he deserved a bigger surprise than that.

So I reached and snatched the BAR from the rack. And then moved over to where they had the boxes of ammo.

"Hey, what are you fixing to do, Sergeant?"

He said it, letting the whistle fall away with the first movement of his lips.

"Watch me, sonny boy," I said. "You just watch me."

By the time I had that BAR loaded the others had grabbed weapons and were armed and loaded, too. And everybody commenced to yelling and carrying on again. The kid turned white and turned away to run up the stairs.

"Wait a minute, sonny!" I yelled after him. "Wait a minute! You forgot . . ."

And he was already gone and the rest of them were standing there waiting for me to finish. To say or do something.

"You forgot to turn off the lights," I said.

So I did it for him with my wonderful BAR, shooting out every light in the long room with a series of short fast bursts.

Then we ran up the dark stairs and outside to finish the job. To shoot out all the lights in the whole world . . .

By dawn, reveille, they had us all in tow and in handcuffs. All but one. We sat around, slowly coming down from the high, in the Stockade Compound waiting for him to be brought in. Nobody said anything. Too tired to care. Next we heard boots and voices and some excitement. Then an MP officer wearing, of all things, a steel helmet, came in.

"Which one of you is the sergeant?"

"I am, sir."

"You stand up when you address me, goddamn it!"

We were all sitting on the floor.

"I got on handcuffs," I said. "I don't know how to get up. I never had handcuffs on before."

"Somebody help him up."

Two MPs boosted me. And then he turned and walked out and they shoved me along behind him. We went outside, moving pretty fast, past the gate and the gate guards. And they lifted me into a jeep. We took off across camp.

Went way the hell somewhere and drove among warehouses and loading docks. There were trucks and jeeps parked all around at odd angles. Some still had their headlights on. I heard someone talking into a radio, that old familiar hushed singsong, as we drove past.

On foot now. Stepping careful over railroad tracks and ties. Moving among the warehouses. There were MPs and GIs (probably off the guard roster, I guessed) bent over and crouched down, armed, and taking cover. Up ahead an officer in a trenchcoat—a brave one or a fool, one or the other—was standing straight up, walking very slowly toward the last building in the line. He was standing in the open holding onto a bullhorn.

"All right," he said, in the hoarse static voice of the bullhorn. "Let's make it easy for yourself. Let's make it easy on everybody. Put down your weapon and stand up with your hands in the air."

Here came a burst. From a BAR. A little line of bullets flicked along the ground in the general direction of the officer's feet. Making him dance back in a very undignified manner. Then he turned and ran for it. Ran back to where we were partially hidden and sheltered by the corner of a building. When the officer came around the corner, panting and big-eyed and sweating, he slipped and fell down on his knees. And I busted out laughing and one of the MP bastards hit me a lick in the ribs with his stick.

"Here's the sergeant, sir," the MP officer said.

"Do you know that lunatic?"

"Crowfoot?" I said. "Yes, sir. He's in my rifle squad."

"Is he an Indian?"

"About half of one I think, sir."

"Jesus Christ," the MP officer said. "A drunk Indian."

"He ain't drunk," I said. "If he was drunk, you and him both would be dead by now."

"We don't want to have to hurt him, Sergeant."

"We don't want anybody to get hurt if we can help it."

Well, now. That was good to hear. What it meant was old Crowfoot hadn't shot anybody yet.

"He is in your squad?"

"That's right, sir."

"Do you think you can get him to come down?"

"Maybe so."

"Listen here, Sergeant. Any way this thing goes, you aren't going to be a sergeant for very much longer. But it can be just a whole lot easier for you and him both if you can talk him into coming down from there."

"It's a risk," the MP officer said.

"No shit, sir," I said.

"He could shoot you, too."

"He is just liable to do that," I said. Then: "Somebody give me a smoke."

An MP gave me a cigarette and held a light for me. Then he helped me smoke it because I still didn't have the full use of my hands.

"How about it?"

"Okay," I said. "I think I'll give it a try. Only one thing . . ."

"What's that?"

"If I can get him to stand up, don't nobody shoot at him. Understand. Nobody shoots at him. Not a round."

"You don't have to worry about that."

"Well, I am worried or I wouldn't be asking you."

"Nobody shoots," the MP officer said.

"How about these fucken handcuffs?"

"Leave them on."

"Suit yourself."

So I went around the edge of the building and toward the other one. Walking quickly across the open space, my eyes on the roof line. I was walking too quickly for him to see and be sure who it was. And I knew he would pretty soon take a bead on me and have me in his sights. The second I saw the light glint and wink in his barrel up there, just a puff of light, I stopped dead in my tracks.

"Crowfoot!" I yelled. "Don't shoot. It's me."

A second wink of light as he lowered the barrel again.

"Are you drunk?"

"Hell no," he said. "You got something to drink?"

"They say you are drunk. I say you are not."

"You're right, Sergeant. I am stone cold sober. But I feel crazy as hell."

"That's what I told them. You're just a crazy fucken Indian."

"Hey! We shot the shit out of all those lights, didn't we? *Didn't we?*"

"I'm really not drunk, Sarge. I swear."

"You wouldn't shit an old buddy, would you?"

"Only if I was drunk I might."

After that I just stood there awhile. Waiting. Looking up. It wasn't quite right yet. The morning sun was coming on stronger. Blinding on the tin roof of the warehouse. I could sense all of them behind me, tense and nervous. I don't know why, maybe it was just the last of the Benny wearing off, but I felt really old and tired. I never felt so old and tired before or since. I stood there looking up and all of a sudden almost wishing he had shot me right out in the open before he recognized who it was.

"Getting hot up there?"

"You better believe it."

"Why don't you come on down?"

"Aw shit, Sarge."

"Hey, man, I mean it. All you've got to do is put down your weapon and then stand up with your hands up."

"They're fixing to kill me."

"All they want is for you to quit."

"Let me think about it."

I think now that the whole trouble was that he made up

his mind and then stood up too quick. Suddenly, all in one jerky motion, there he was standing up in plain view high on the roof with both hands up. There was the loud noise as his weapon dropped on the tin roof at the same time, simultaneous with the movement of his body. Sun, that rising sun, behind him now, turning him into a tall silhouette.

(And I was thinking: *Like a pop-up target! He just popped up like a target!*)

Even as that figure jerked into view, loomed against the sun, even before it was fully formed, it spun in a crazy circle and collapsed again out of sight. All this happening at once. Awkward and yet smooth, all part of the same action and movement. Like he was dancing. Clang of the weapon on the roof merging and blending with the single report of a fired rifle. Which could well and might even have been the same weapon he dropped going off.

But wasn't.

And I without even thinking was running toward the building, clumsy in my handcuffs. It was like we were linked by a wire or chain. And his fall had jerked me forward. I was staggering to keep from falling. I could hear shouting behind me and the bullhorn blaring commands. But they might as well have been in the Unknown Tongue. Staggering forward, then pitching, falling face-down in the gravel, stunned, pinwheels of light and raising my head up from where I was lying prone and feeling blood, small as sweatstreams, running down my face. From the cutting gravel . . .

"Shoot, Crowfoot! Shoot me! Shoot me!"

Seeing then again that glinting wink, that puff of light on the barrel I had seen before. Myself prone as a pilgrim, helpless, bleeding, and (God knows why) begging him to shoot me.

Then hearing him. Hoarse and hurt: "I can't see! I can't fucken see!"

Another wink of the light as he let the weapon go then, *clankety clank,* as the thing rolled away free down the roof to fall. And as it fell lowering my face to the gravel. Eating dirt. Ignoring all the shouting and footsteps around me. Just feeling nothing, limp as a fresh corpse, in the arms that took me up, raised and lifted me, carried me away from there.

That's it?

That's what?

I mean, is that all of it?

You asked me the last time I seen him and I told you.

You never saw him again after that?

Not even to look at. I was back in the stockade when they buried him.

Didn't they ship him home?

Nobody must have claimed him. They buried him right on the post.

He was dead before they even charged him with anything.

Yeah. They blew taps and everything the way I heard it.

Crazy fucken Indian!

One fucken shot and he was dead before he even hit the roof good.

Wait a minute! You said he spoke to you.

Did I?

Fucken-A. You said that.

Well, he didn't. Couldn't. One shot right between the eyes, they told me.

Lucky shot. Just lucky.

Maybe. Hell of a shot, though, luck or not.

Hell of a way to go.

I wouldn't say so. Neat. Quick. I can think of worse ways.

Oh yes, sweet Jesus, I know. I know. I know it now . . .

Heroes

*T*H E *Browning Automatic Rifle, model of 1918,
is an air-cooled, gas-operated, magazine-fed shoulder weapon . . .*

2.

Smell my fingers.
What?
Smell my fingers. Try and guess what I've been doing.
Fuck you, man. You smell your own fucken fingers.
Wait a minute. Hey, I'm not kidding around. I'm serious.
So am I. If you want somebody to sniff your stinking
fingers, you better go find somebody else.
Don't be chicken. Come on.
Forget it.
It's nothing like that.
Like what?
What you think. I dare you.
You dare me what.
I double-dog dare you that you can't smell my fingers and
guess what it is. Guess what I've been doing.

311

Okay. Tell you what. Make me a bet and I'll do it. I got a good nose. Very sensitive.

Ugly. What you got is a big fat very ugly nose.

I didn't say good-looking. I just said good.

All right. I got ten dollars says you can't smell my fingers and guess what I was doing before I came here.

You got yourself a bet. Gimme.

So?

Gun oil. And bore cleaner. That's what. You owe me ten bucks. How did you think I could miss that? How the hell could I ever forget it? You been cleaning guns. Pay me up.

No problem. Double or nothing you can't guess what I was thinking about. Who am I thinking about right now?

No way. No bet.

Go on. Take a chance.

You just tell me.

Hero.

What?

I am thinking about Floogie the hero. Flat Foot Floogie . . .

He was a hero all right. You can't take that away from him.

I'm not taking anything away from him. Or anybody else.

You can't even if you wanted to. They gave him his medal and that's that.

Posthumously.

So what? That's the way it's supposed to be. The big medals go to dead guys. Mostly.

Yeah. And they can have them, too.

You can say that again.

Neverthefuckenless, whenever I clean weapons I always get to thinking about the BAR. And that starts me thinking about ole Floogie. I remember him every time. Know what I mean?

• • •

3.

Sequence and Method of Field Stripping
Steps in stripping will be taken in the following sequence:
   a. *Cock the piece.*
   b. *Remove gas cylinder tube retaining pin.*
   c. *Remove gas cylinder tube and forearm (let mechanism forward easily).*
   d. *Remove trigger guard retaining pin.*
   e. *Remove trigger guard.*
   f. *Remove recoil spring guide and recoil spring.*
   g. *Push hammer pin through hammer pin hole in receiver.*
   h. *Remove operating handle.*
   i. *Remove hammer pin.*
   j. *Remove hammer.*
   k. *Remove slide.*
   l. *Bolt guide pushed out.*
   m. *Remove bolt, bolt lock, and bolt link.*
   n. *Remove bolt link pin and bolt link.*
   o. *Remove firing pin.*
   p. *Remove extractor and spring.*

4.

In those old days, not all that long ago in our lives, the ones who were there and lived to think about it and to tell about it, back when the BAR was still a basic infantry weapon, one to a rifle squad, as I recall, well, in those days the BAR was viewed as a kind of a punishment. Was assigned to some fuckup or loser or eightball. And if, by some weird chance, there wasn't any one such in the squad—and that's hard to believe or imagine, but I guess it could happen—then, of course, the privilege of the BAR went to the smallest and weakest man in the squad. Because the BAR was genuinely heavy, see? Big and heavy and hard to carry and a perfect bitch to keep clean. And then there was all that ammo for it that you had to carry. I am telling you it was no fun to be a BAR man. As long as there was somebody in the squad with a BAR, you could feel better off than somebody else.

It wasn't hard to feel a lot better than Floogie, most of the time. Big tall skinny guy with white-blond hair. Looked like some kind of an albino. An albino wino. I mean goofy looking. Clumsy as a bear cub. Couldn't do much of anything right. Couldn't make his bed right or lace up his boots right. Couldn't keep in step. Every step he took he bobbed his head like an old chicken. Always in some kind of trouble. Got his squad and the whole platoon in trouble.

If you think Floogie was hopeless, you should have seen his brother.

I didn't know he had one.

Not in our outfit. He might have been. But somebody with some pull or maybe a dynamite sense of humor got him assigned to special duty as the driver for a major general at Fort Campbell.

So?

The thing is the brother was exactly like Floogie. A total basket case.

I wouldn't let Floogie behind the wheel of anything. I wouldn't let Floogie have charge of a wheelbarrow.

This brother of his couldn't drive for shit. And he proved it on the first day on the job. He run the general's jeep off the road and into a deep ditch and put himself and the general directly into the hospital. In traction and all wrapped up in bandages. I went to see the guy and there he was, all trussed up, and laughing his ass off because they were fixing to put him out of the Army as soon as he could get up out of the bed.

Probably on a lifetime disability pension, too.

Hey, it was line of duty, right? He was entitled.

The dumb brother goes home with a limp and a couple of little scars and a lifetime pension.

Floogie and the rest of us get our sad asses shipped off to Korea.

Quit complaining. I'm not the chaplain.

The whole thing is, once an eightball always an eightball. Floogie was exactly the same, a total and complete fuckup from beginning to end, all up and down the Korean peninsula. Now he wasn't chicken. You have to give him that. He was too dumb to be really scared. Mostly he had his mind on ways to get out of work and to stay off duty details. You can't blame him for that. The first time you had to put together some kind of a shit detail, the first person you would think of was Floogie. If he hadn't gotten very smart about making himself scarce, he would have met himself coming and going from dirty details. But he was always there. Where can you go hide in the middle of a rifle squad in a rifle platoon of a rifle company in the stinking big middle of stinking Korea with all kinds of dinks and slopes coming at you from all directions, day and night? And, besides, he was toting the BAR and all that ammo. He couldn't get very far if he had to.

Nevertheless he got very good at becoming and being invisible. Come some dirty detail and you couldn't find old Floogie anywhere. And another thing. He was lucky. Pure lucky. We lost guys all of the time. Mortars and mines. Firefights. People got their asses shot off all around. But not a nick on Floogie. What's funny is that if he had lived he wouldn't have even gotten the Purple Heart. The other guys thought he was a freak. But Floogie, he was like immune or something. He started believing it himself. The unit would be under fire, heavy fire. Every swinging dick would be trying to figure out a way to shrink and to climb completely inside of his steel helmet. And Floogie would get up, stand straight up and just stroll along in full view to find a better firing position. Then he would set up his BAR and start shooting. After a while he got pretty good with that BAR. It didn't come natural to him but you do something enough times and you start getting good at it.

5.

General Data
Weight of rifle, 15 pounds 8 ounces.
Weight of magazine, empty, 7 ounces.
Weight of magazine, filled, 1 pound, 7 ounces.
Length of barrel, 24 inches.
Over-all length, 47 inches.
Sights graduated to 1600 yards.
Caliber bore, 0.30 inch.
Gas port from muzzle, 6 inches.
Rate of uninterrupted automatic fire (cyclic rate), 600 shots per minute.
Chamber pressure, 47,000 to 50,000 pounds per square inch.
Muzzle velocity, about 2680 feet per second.
Habitual type of fire, semi-automatic.
Head space limits, 1.937 inches to 1.943 inches.
Length of recoil spring, 15.5 inches.

6.

I missed out on all that. I was already out of there, in Japan, in the hospital.

I almost forgot about all your troubles.

I'm pretty easy to forget about.

Hey, it was better that way. A lot of people came and went, you know.

Tell me about it.

We were falling back as fast as we could. Running half the time. The gooks were right behind us. Nobody could kill enough of them. They just kept coming. We killed them and then more came.

One evening just about dusk, we got orders to relieve some outfit on a hilltop not too far off the main road. We were to go up and relieve them and to hold onto that hill unless and until we heard otherwise.

It could have been worse. Those guys had already dug their holes and were in them. We could switch off easy and quick and quiet, fix things up our own way a little and then settle in. A few little shit details to take care of. But mostly just settling into the new position for the night. With any kind of luck at all maybe a good night's sleep for a change.

Very late, it must have been past midnight, the word was passed to pack up very quietly and get ready to pull out of there. No noise. The gooks were pretty close out there somewhere to the front. And we were going to try and fool them and pull out. Pitch dark and no noise at all. We had to leave quite a lot of our stuff behind. We came down the hill very slowly and got to the road and then headed back south. Hiking. Breathing hard and sweating in the stinking dark.

Hadn't gone very far before we started to hear bugles and shouts and then all kinds of hostile fire coming in on the position we had just pulled out of. They were pumping all kinds of stuff in there. The sky was lit up with explosions and tracers. Wasting all of it. Getting themselves all psyched up for an assault. And we were long gone.

Some of the guys couldn't help laughing in the dark. Dumb fucken gooks.

Then they blew the bugles again and we knew they were starting their assault.

Surprise! Surprise! Ain't nobody home.

But then there came clear across the dark the absolutely positively unmistakable sound of a BAR firing on full automatic.

"Floogie!" the Sergeant—remember old Zyder?—said. "We left Floogie."

"We couldn't have. No. Where's Floogie? Anybody seen Floogie?"

Somebody was firing and firing, sometimes on full automatic but mostly on semi. And the sound of the firing was moving around like he was moving around the position.

317

More bugles and then some quiet. The gooks seem to have pulled back a little from the hill. They pumped up a couple of flares.

Then we halted in the dark by the sides of the road. And the CO—that would be Captain Freer—came trolling up the road looking for Sergeant Zyder. "What the fuck is going on?" the CO said. "Who's firing that BAR?" "Floogie," Zyder said. "And from the sound of it he's giving the gooks fits up there."

Long pause. Deep breathing.

"Oh, shit," the CO finally said. "What do we do now?" Zyder said: "Hey, let me take a few guys, a detail. And we'll go back and get him." The CO thought about it for a minute. You can give him that much. "No way," he finally said. "No way at all. I am not going to lose anybody else. He was probably asleep somewhere and the gooks woke him up." "Probably," Zyder said. "And now he's up there holding onto the hill all by himself." "Only he may not know that yet," somebody else said. "Floogie probably thinks we're all still there with him." "He'll figure it out soon enough."

"Let me just take a few guys back up there."

"No way," the CO said. "We've got to keep moving."

Column started up again heading down the road on both sides.

Bugles again and then a whole lot of firing.

Old Floogie was really cooking with that BAR. I don't know where he found the ammo for it, but he did. And then we were beyond where we could hear it good anymore, although when we looked back, we could still see light and flare and a lot of floating tracers . . .

So Floogie, the dumb fart, sneaked off when we first occupied the position and fell asleep and never got the word when the outfit pulled out of there.

That's about the size of it.

All of a sudden there's nothing but bugles blowing and all kinds of incoming shit and pretty soon Chinamen everywhere. And Floogie says, what the fuck, I might as well be a hero.

I don't think so. I think he woke up and didn't know at first that we were gone. He just did what he's here for. Probably didn't notice anything much—he would be scared shitless anyway—until the gooks fell back to regroup. Then I can picture Floogie crawling around the position in the dark. Feeling for his buddies and not finding anybody. And then there would be the flares and the bugles again and the yelling gooks.

He could have run right then. A lot of guys would have hauled ass.

Floogie would be deeply pissed off. He would think we left him behind on purpose. That's the way he was.

Yeah. Like paranoid, right?

Something like that. Anyway. He would be up there talking to himself and shooting at gooks until they finally got him.

So what finally happened, see?, was the next morning, early, first light, they sent us back to that position. And we didn't have to take it back or anything. The gooks had pulled back during the night to the high ground north of our hill and they were dug in there. We went back to the position. And I'm here to tell you there were dead Chinamen everywhere you looked. We spent a couple of days just digging a hole big enough and deep enough to hold them all. God only knows how many he got before they got him.

How?

How what?

How did they get Floogie?

Grenade. At least that's what it looked like. He was sure enough very dead no matter what. Still had hold of his BAR, though.

I heard they put him in for a Congressional.

Fat chance.

Well, it was worth a try. And he got a medal anyway. Can you believe it?

You know, when I got back to the States, I went to see his folks—his mama. His old man was dead. She looked exactly like ole Floogie, you know? It didn't look as bad on a woman. The brother was there, limping around. And they took me down to a park where there was a monument with all the dead guys' names on it. Floogie's name was there. It was weird to see his name on a stone.

I would rather be almost anything but a dead hero.

Even if you was Floogie?

Even that. Maybe especially that.

7.

. . . *The rifle is fed from a magazine having a capacity of twenty cartridges. The rifle can be fired effectively from all positions prescribed in TR 150-30. It is capable of being fired at the rate of 150 rounds per minute. The rate of fire, however, which gives the best results in the normal case is 40 to 60 shots per minute, semi-automatic . . .*

from War Department Training Regulations No. 320-25 (March 25, 1925).

About the Author

Hoyns Professor of Creative Writing at the University of Virginia, GEORGE GARRETT is the author of six novels, six collections of short fiction, seven books of poetry, two plays, and numerous pieces of literary criticism. Best known for his Elizabethan trilogy of historical novels, *Death of the Fox, The Succession,* and *Entered from the Sun,* Garrett has been the recipient of a PEN/Malamud Award; Guggenheim, Ford, and National Endowment for the Arts fellowships; and an Award in Literature from the American Academy of Arts and Letters, along with many other professional and personal honors over the four decades of his literary and teaching career. With his wife, Susan, Garrett resides in Charlottesville, Virginia.